Stealing

Mercury

An Arena Dogs Novel

Charlee Allden

DEDICATION

For you—the reader. You're what it's all about.

Charlee Allden

ACKNOWLEDGMENTS

This book has been made better through the encouragement and generosity of author friends, wonderful readers and my loving family. I thank them all whole-heartedly.
Any deficiencies are entirely my own.

PROLOUGE

RomaRex Arena, Roma
Earth Alliance Beta Sector
2210.140

Mercury clenched his fists. The blood on his hands had started to dry, making his skin feel tight and brittle. He stood in the center of the arena, shoulder to shoulder with Lo. He breathed through his mouth to avoid the stench of the frenzied crowds, but the taste coated his throat and turned his stomach.

The patrons wouldn't want to see any hint of softness, so he kept his face carefully blank. He fought the urge to drop to his knees alongside his three other pack brothers where they lay, chests heaving for air, their life's blood soaking into the dirt.

The crowds were on their feet.

In the cheap seats, boots stomped rhythmically on the metal stadium decks—an unnatural boom-boom-boom echoing to the city dome over their heads. On the other side of the dusty field the crowd had long ago abandoned their plush cushioned seats to bounce and weave for a better view. In the luxury boxes the patrons leaned forward, some pressing pale, skeletal hands against the transparent security barrier.

Voices swelled in a mix of cheers and boos as the Game Master stepped onto the platform that jutted out six meters above the arena floor. The crowds would try to influence his decision.

Life or death for the losers.

Mercury ignored the chants and watched as the crimson robed man extended an arm, fingers clenched tight, thumb pointed to the side. The outcome had been promised—make a good show and his pack brothers would live.

Three on two, brother against brother.

They'd made a good show.

Maybe too good.

He wanted the verdict declared, the match finished, so the three in the dirt could be tended before they bled out. Bled out from injuries he and Lo had inflicted.

The Game Master's thumb dipped suddenly down.

Death.

Mercury's lungs seized. Shock tightened around his chest like a ruthless leather cinch. Animal rage pulsed dizzyingly through his oxygen-deprived brain. Beside him Lo howled.

Mercury glanced down to Carn, lying at his feet. His pack brother. His friend. Eyes glassy, Carn met his gaze with acceptance. Carn knew Mercury's pain. Knew he'd look after Carn's mate. Knew he had no choice.

Fuck that.

Air rushed back into his lungs. His chest expanded. His muscles twitched and jumped. Had the owners forgotten the power of the bodies their genetic engineering had created?

The crowds had picked up the verdict. They chanted it like a heartbeat. "Death. Death. Death."

Yes. He would give them death.

He flicked a glance to Lo, coated in the blood of their brothers. Lo's eyes glowed with rage. His body quivered with aggression.

Mercury sucked in air then loosed three short barks. He flicked his gaze to the patrons' box, then to a point below the Game Master's platform, and back to Lo. His pack brother nodded, leapt over their fallen, then sprinted to the point Mercury had indicated.

Adrenaline flooded through Mercury's bloodstream. His animal nature strained against the reigns of his control. The muscles of his thighs burned as he surged over Carn's prone body and pumped arms and legs to build momentum. In his peripheral vision he saw the guards run forward and aim weapons, but he trusted his speed.

His muscles were on fire as he planted one foot in Lo's cupped hands. He sprang into the air, muscles working with the momentum of Lo's throw, and flew. His body stretched and twisted. Pain snapped from knee to groin as something tore. His fingers closed around the Game Master's ankle and he ripped the man off his perch, tossing him to the arena floor as he flung his own body onto the platform. The Master's scream choked off suddenly, but Mercury focused on his target.

The patrons' box and the Owner inside.

The Game Master was his puppet. The startled face behind the polycarbonate wall was to blame for this latest betrayal. Mercury raced up the platform then launched into the air, arms and legs extending to clear the impossible distance.

His body slammed hard into the transparent barrier. A wave of black flashed through his vision, but he managed to tighten his grip around the corner and dig the toes of his flex-boots into the ledge. He struck the glassy surface with all of his strength. Beneath his fist, it splintered but didn't shatter. He pulled back for another blow.

The surface gave under the force of his fist. A man stepped into the path of his reach, putting himself in front of the Owner. Mercury twisted his fist in the man's garment and jerked him through the shattered barrier and out of his way. He reached—

Tentacles of pain crackled along his spine—the familiar agony of a shock whip. He fell back, muscles no longer in his control. His back smacked against the platform. Lightning zinged along his nerves again. His body bowed tight.

The lightning faded, slowly, leaving him unable to move.

He'd failed.

The blue of the city dome overhead mocked him. *You surrendered to rage. You've only made things worse for your brothers. You've condemned them with your arrogance.*

The mocking voice was right. Their blood was already on his hands.

CHAPTER ONE

Roma Spaceport, Roma
Earth Alliance Beta Sector
2210.145

Samantha adjusted the pack on her shoulder as she waited in the shuttle for the hatch to open. The familiar hiss and pop as it gave way only wound her nerves tighter.

"Good luck, Sam!" The pilot's voice over the intercom reminded her that she'd chosen to leave relative safety behind in favor of a shortcut that was both risky and profitable. This one job would triple what she'd made in the last year.

Wishing the pilot a smooth journey, she hopped out and strode through the docking tunnel. The gate closed behind her, eliminating any possibility of retreat.

Sevti Allandson waited inside the hangar, looking very corporate in his slim-fitting, gray uniform. The man beside him was a surprise. Samantha recognized Grande Owens, principal partner of The Roma Company. The silver haired man with a crooked nose and ruddy cheeks had been on every news feed she'd scanned since Sevti messaged her with the job offer. Behind them the hangar stretched out, cavernous and nearly empty. The *Dove*, a stellar class courier ship, stood at the far end, cargo doors open for loading.

Sevti clasped her hand in two of his. "Good to see you again."

She forced a smile that would have come naturally if anxiety wasn't eating a hole in her gut. "Been too long, Port Chief."

He nodded and released her. "Back at Midway Station, right? I remember you were always fending off that skinny letch. What was his name?"

Samantha had never been any good at deception. She wanted to beg him not to drag out the chatter that had to be for Owens' benefit. "That was Knock. Dad hired him in the end. Turned out to be a good communications man." And a total failure as a friend.

Sevti must have heard her silent pleading to hurry things along or maybe he'd seen her nerves fraying. Whichever, she was grateful when he got back to business. He introduced her to Mr. Owens with no sign of duplicity or guilt in his easy smile. Only eight hours earlier he'd calmly explained how he needed her to help him steal from the man.

No, he didn't actually want her help with the deed. He just wanted her to let the stealing happen. To let the cargo go without a fight when Sevti's friends boarded the ship she was being hired to pilot.

Simple.

No one would expect a pilot flying alone to be able to fend off a band of determined thieves. Sevti would see to it she got paid for her trouble and she'd finally have enough to put down a deposit on her own ship. What could go wrong? Her stomach tightened again. Apparently, *it* wasn't convinced.

Owens studied her as if he could read her guilty conscience in her face. "Allandson speaks highly of you, Ms. Devlin. He's explained the job?"

She nodded. "Said you had a problem with your flight crew and needed a last-minute replacement."

"Every flight officer in my employ is in medical with the Diztigo virus and this shipment can't wait. Lucky for us you were traveling on the *Reliable Liner*."

"Luckier for me, sir, but I hope your crews will be all right." She couldn't stop the flick of her gaze to Sevti. Her father's old friend was taking a huge risk and she didn't understand why. He couldn't need the funds. Roma Port was a dream post. Roma might only be a stage one terraformed rock, but The Roma Company owned it outright. The city with its cluster of habitation domes had been built to be a playground to the wealthy. The port sprawled along the edge of the primary dome like a happy parasite, swollen with the bounty offered up by its host.

"The flight crews will recover," said Owens. "But we'd like you to get underway as soon as possible. We don't want you to…" He grimaced. "To catch what seems to be going around."

The hesitation in his voice told her clearly that he knew his crews had been intentionally infected with the debilitating virus and he wasn't going to tell her. Wasn't going to tell her he suspected someone was out to stop this shipment. He might be putting her life in jeopardy and he wasn't even going to warn her. It eased her conscious just a little.

"I do have one question before we finalize your contract." Owens pressed his lips together as he looked her up and down in her plain brown trousers and pullover top. She'd have liked to dress up for the meeting, but she hadn't needed dress clothes since she signed on to the *Reliable* as a tool slinger. She'd at least gotten the engine grease out from under her fingernails. "We verified your credentials," he said. "Why were you working as a mechanic when you have your pilot's certification?"

Her face heated as she met his gaze levelly. "Most corporate lines prefer to hire pilots with academy training." He had to know she'd been an indie pilot with no corporate backing, no academy connections. He couldn't know the rest. Her father had bullied the best hacker in the business to forge her birth records. "I got my training on the job. Mostly, I piloted my father's freighter until last year."

"You left his ship for a job with Reliable?"

"My father is dead." No need to mention the rest of his crew had left her behind, stranded her on a backwater planet.

"Ah." He punctuated the singular sound with a quick lift and dip of his chin.

She could feel more questions coming, but she couldn't let him get to the questions she couldn't answer. "I took the same tests as the academy grads and I have more flight hours than any academy pilot my age."

"Samantha's logged hours on dozens of ships, Mr. Owens." Sevti patted the man's shoulder, smile gone impossibly wide. "I can assure you I've seen her pilot ships similar to your stellar-class courier."

It had been part of upgrading her license to avoid paying local port pilots to maneuver their ship in and out of the Class Two ports. She'd logged the hours through her father's connections…and not one of them had lifted a finger to help her after his death. Not until Sevti.

Samantha held Owens' gaze. "Your ship will be safe with me." She carefully avoided any mention of the cargo. *That*, she would not be keeping safe. But her assurance seemed to satisfy Grande Owens.

He threw his chin and chest out like a bird strutting to impress. "Roma isn't corporate. We're a privately held company and most of us started out without the proverbial silver spoon, so your background is no concern here. I'll leave Mr. Allandson to show you to the ship. I—"

At first Samantha's mind couldn't process the sound that drowned out his voice. Her brain told her it had to be an animal howling, but as the sound swelled into something haunting and mournful she knew it wasn't an animal at all.

Her confusion must've shown on her face because Grande Owens laughed. "That's our Dogs."

"Dogs?" Her voice came out weak and horrified, because she knew, knew in her bones, they weren't talking about the kind of dogs that ran around on four legs.

Another howl echoed in the hollow space of the hangar. At the far end, a loading crew in red Roma jumpsuits maneuvered three large cages across the dull gray floor plating and into position alongside the courier ship. The hangar lighting glinted off the crude metal prisons that looked more like low-tech jail cells than animal containment crates.

Arena Dogs.

That's what the news vids had called them. But her scan of the news feeds hadn't prepared her. They hadn't actually included vid of the gladiators known as the fighting Dogs of the RomaRex Arena.

She couldn't see them well from across the hangar, but she could clearly see they were men. Men locked in cages and shipped as freight.

A new ache started in her chest. They were men and they were her cargo. Living, breathing, cargo. Bronze chests left bare, dark hair past their shoulders, heads thrown back, the thick columns of their throats working to make those haunting howls.

"They're out of sorts today. Their handler says they're melancholy over being separated from their mate, but I'm not convinced." Owens spoke from near her shoulder. He'd shifted to stand at her side, looking over the hangar like a feudal lord surveying his land.

"Their mate?"

He chuckled again, a sound she was coming to despise. "They have this odd practice of sharing their females. They have quite a complex social structure. We weren't expecting it from this mix of DNA, but..."

Samantha didn't follow any of what came after *sharing their females*. That thought stopped her overwhelmed brain. Her head wanted her to be appalled, and she *was* appalled that he talked about them as if they were nothing more than animals, or a science experiment, but her reaction to what he was saying could be more aptly described as...fascination. Fascination and guilt. While she stood there captivated by the raw emotion in their howls, they were imprisoned and suffering.

Her stomach churned and she knew she was in over her head. She wanted to ask why Roma was calling the men Dogs. Why they'd put them in cages. Why the men with her weren't freaked out by the howling that was scraping *her* insides raw.

By the time her brain re-engaged, Owens had gone and Sevti was leading her toward the cages.

The weight of his hand on the center of her back urged her forward. "I'm sorry I wasn't able to prepare you more. Even scrambled messages are risky."

"*Messages* are risky," she hissed. "What part of this *isn't* risky?" She knew her outrage at the whole situation was bleeding into her voice and they needed to keep quiet, but she'd heard the change in his tone. His earlier calm had been icing over a sticky, stressed center.

"They're slaves, Samantha. We're helping them get to freedom."

"I know the Alliance denies citizenship to the non-earth races, but slavery?" She managed to lower her voice. They were still walking toward the hellish looking cages. The loading crew had temporarily disappeared through a door marked *Crew Only*, but the workers in their crimson uniforms could return at any moment.

"They're genetically engineered fighters. You've heard of the Arena Games?" He didn't wait for her to answer, just continued on in a rush of words. "Roma wanted gladiators, only better. Stronger. Faster. More lethal. They force them to fight. To slaughter each other. They're considered property of The Roma Company."

"How is that—"

"They claim they're a result of a genetic manufacturing system, property. And they used enough animal and non-human alien DNA to get the Council of Earth Allied Planets to declare them non-human…animals."

Samantha didn't exactly have one hundred percent human DNA herself. She shuddered at the idea of being deemed non-human just because her grandmother had been Cerrillian. It was bad enough to know she'd lose her pilot's license if anyone learned what her father had done—but *slavery*. She fought the urge to tug at her sleeves, to make sure the distinctive bands of color along her arms stayed covered. She was a mixed-breed on the wrong side of the Alliance-Gollerra border. Why had she thought this risk worth taking? "Why haven't I heard of this? I thought the gladiators were—"

"It's not like Roma is going to advertise it. But we're a long way from the core, Sam, and most people here don't give a damn."

"But—"

"We don't have a lot of time and I have to tell you."

If he was going to tell her he'd lost his mind, she could only agree.

Sevti kept his pace, but dabbed at the fine sheen of perspiration across his forehead with the arm of his uniform jacket. "Owens is suspicious."

She wanted to shout *of course he's suspicious, you infected fifteen of his people with a virus* but she managed to keep her mouth shut and listened.

"He's sending two of his men with you to accompany the Dogs."

She stopped, body jerking to a halt that ripped her out of Sevti's hold. Her boots were suddenly lead, fused to the floor plating. "What am I supposed to do with passengers?" What was she supposed to do with genetically engineered fighters in her cargo-hold? Her heart pounded out a fast tattoo in her chest and her legs had turned rubbery.

"They're not just passengers." He wrapped his hand around her forearm and squeezed as if he thought the gesture was needed to convey the seriousness of the situation. "They're two of his goons, handlers from the arena. These men are hot-tempered and arrogant, used to dishing out abuse with impunity. Steer clear of them as much as possible and stay out of the way when the resistance team boards. Keep your head down and you'll be fine."

She couldn't imagine anything less fine. She was well aware of the seriousness of the danger she'd landed in. Samantha looked over to the nearest cage and the man inside. The tips of his pointed ears peeked up through a shoulder-length fall of dark hair. They twitched, but his attention focused in the direction the workers had gone. The prisoner's broad shoulders and wrists were marred by silver ropes of scar tissue that made her ache to look at them.

He might be a victim, but that didn't mean he was an angel. They fight to the death and *share their females*, she reminded herself. But if they cared so little for life and for their mate, why would they infuse their howls with such grief?

When she started forward again, urged on by Sevti's insistent tugs, the Arena Dog jerked around to press against his cage directly in front of them. He gripped the unrelenting bars tight enough to make his knuckles whiten and the muscles in his arms bunch. Thunder clouds and lightning flashed at her from the depths of his silver-gray eyes.

Her mouth turned into a desert and tiny bumps rose across her skin. A steady low growl rumbled up from somewhere in the man's chest. His facial features weren't dog-like, but they weren't wholly human either. His face was all sharp angles and wide, flat nose.

The rest of him seemed more human, if overly large. He hunched over, too tall for the cage that could have held her with more than a dozen centimeters to spare. Bruises in a rainbow of hues mottled his ribs and chest. Knee length black pants hugged him tightly and rode low across his hips. A pair of black, ankle high flex-boots completed the outfit.

Sevti leaned close putting his lips near her ear. "You can't tell them."

"What?"

"The Dogs. They don't know what we have planned and you can't tell them."

It occurred to her that maybe Sevti hadn't gone crazy. Maybe she was the one who'd lost touch with reality.

Sevti tightened his grip on her arm. "The Dogs have led simple lives. They're naïve. They don't understand lies and deception. They might give it away. We can't put the resistance at risk. You have to keep them in the dark until our team makes it to you."

Samantha pulled her arm free of his grasp. "Okay. I get it."

But she didn't. Not really. The Arena Dog was clearly used to violence. How could Sevti call him naïve?

Gaze locked on the lethal looking man behind the bars, Samantha strode straight toward him—the Arena Dog with the stormy eyes. Behind her Sevti called out, "Don't get so close. They're dangerous, Samantha."

Slowing, she closed the last meter more cautiously as Sevti's voice faded out of her awareness. The world drew down to the bubble of stillness where she stood face to face with a man in a cage.

"Hello." The word whispered across her lips.

The man's ears twitched and his features softened for an instant. His nose flared and his head tilted as he studied her. In a flash of movement too quick to follow, his hand shot out and he grabbed her wrist. She gasped, but managed not to struggle or panic.

At least on the outside.

Inside her heart raced like an over wound crank. He gripped her firmly and pulled her forward, crushing her breasts against the bars and threading her hand through one of the gaps.

The heat of his palm branded her skin. She couldn't look away from the flashes in his eyes, flashes she couldn't interpret. Something about those eyes called to her. They held intelligence and maybe even a fascination as powerful as hers.

She flexed her fingers, accidentally brushing the sharply defined muscles of his abdomen. They jumped beneath her touch but he held steady, as implacable as a glacier, as volatile as a sun. This close, she could see the sadness behind the thunder and lightning of his eyes.

He lifted her hand and pressed the tender inside of her wrist to his nose. The touch sent a tingle along her nerves. The warmth of his breath on her skin was beyond intimate.

Giving in to instinct, she leaned in and breathed him in. The ordinary citrus tang of a commercial cleanser common throughout the sector surprised her. Beneath that a hint of something wild and utterly masculine teased her senses.

The scrape of boot heels behind her startled them both and his attention flicked to something over her shoulder. He released her then snarled and threw himself at the bars.

Samantha jumped and stumbled back. Her surroundings snapped back into focus and she realized Sevti had been calling her name. He pulled her away from the cage as a brutish hulk of a man barged past her. The man jabbed a stun-stick into the cage. The stun-bolt crackled as the Arena Dog's body jerked. Was this why they used such a ridiculously designed cell? All the easier to torment the men inside?

A chorus of howls went up from the other Arena Dogs. The steely-eyed man who'd held her wrist so tenderly crouched in the corner of his cage, tossed back his head and howled.

Loud, terrifying, heartbreaking.

"Shit-for-brains pilot." The new arrival, dressed in work trousers the color of rotting leaves and a simple shirt, towered over her. Tufts of short brown hair stood up in clumps atop his head making him look as if he'd received a shock from his own weapon.

"You didn't have to hurt him." She ground it out through clenched teeth.

He scowled. "You're cracked. These Dogs are trained to fight to the death. Trained to make it gory for the arena fans." His face had colored up in angry red splotches. "They'd as soon eat you as hump you." He shook his head. "Shit for brains."

A second man stalked into view. "Funny how the brainless always choose that insult."

The idiot looming over her stepped aside. "She should be thanking me, Drake." He gripped his belt, adjusting it on his hips. "That Dog had a grip on her."

"And you played the hero, giving you the right to berate the lady. Is that it, Resler?"

"Yeah. I mean no. I mean..." The man shifted his feet. His jawed tightened, a muscle twitched as he locked his jaw, biting off whatever he would have said and making it clear that the other man held the authority.

Sevti spoke up, filling the void. "Gentlemen. Let me introduce you to Samantha Devlin." He introduced Ivor Resler and Jansan Drake, the two men Owens had chosen to accompany her. Just great.

"Mr. Resler is one of the guards in the arena and Mr. Drake is a trainer." Sevti's smile slipped as he continued. "The title is whip-master, I believe."

Drake was lean with close cropped hair and a narrow chin strap beard. He dressed shoulder to ankle in soft, black synth—comfortable and practical without looking it. Bracers circled his wrists and a coiled whip made of brown leather hung from his belt, providing the only contrast.

"Let's not stand on titles. My apologies, Sam." He extended a hand. "For my rude colleague and for any trouble our Dogs were causing."

She gripped his hand firmly, noting the roughness of calluses that lent credibility to the whip he wore like an accessory. The oil he used to care for the leather tinged the air and wrinkled her nose.

Drake looked her up and down, subtly. Not rude but not indifferent either. The personal scrutiny bit at her like a sand burr against her skin.

"We should get out of the loading crew's way." His eyes narrowed and something cruel glinted in the soft brown depths. "These three Dogs have caused my boss a good deal of trouble. He wants them gone as soon as we can get them loaded."

"Of course," Samantha said. She offered Sevti a restrained farewell then watched him stride away. She hadn't felt so adrift since she'd been left on a nowhere planet, staring at the empty platform where her father's ship should have been waiting.

"You're lucky, Sam."

Drake's comment pulled her attention back to him and the men caged behind him. "Am I?"

"You picked the right Dog to be careless around." Seemingly unaware of the verbal slap he'd delivered, he strode over to the cage, wrapped his hands around the top bar and leaned forward. "This is Mercury."

The man inside tensed, his gaze locking onto a slender green code-key dangling from Drake's neck. It was clearly a taunt. The code-key might unlock the cages and, if Mercury were willing to try for it, the cord around Drake's neck could serve as an improvised garrote. Resler moved around behind the cage, stun-stick ready and eager to inflict pain.

"Mercury is actually the least bloodthirsty of this lot," Drake continued. "He's the thinker. The others look to him. His leadership made their group one of the most successful in the arena." An undercurrent of bitterness laced his words.

Samantha pressed her hands flat against her thighs, resisting the urge to tighten them into fists. "You call them dogs, but you credit him with leadership?"

He straightened, tucked the cord beneath his shirt and met her gaze baldly. "I trained them. I know what they are and what they're capable of and I know my job. I'll stick to my job and you'd better stick to yours. Do that and I'm sure we'll all get along."

With a flash of teeth, Drake's expression shifted. His whole body softened from hard-ass to swagger. "I sense you're feeling sorry for them and that's dangerous, Sam. Mercury and his pack were champions of the arena until they decided to incite a pointless insurrection. Last week they made it over the arena barriers, got into the crowds and attacked a group of our high profile patrons." Drake strode toward the next cage, motioning her to follow. "This is Diablo and over there..." He pointed at the third cage where a brawnier male with shoulders as wide as a shuttle and sad eyes howled softly. "That's Carnage."

Samantha licked her dry lips. From behind the bars, Diablo studied her with night black eyes. Red embers flecked the black, making it easy to see how he'd come by his name. Like Mercury, he was leanly muscled with dark hair and pointed ears, but his jaw was more pronounced and prominent canines pressed against narrow lips.

A large hand landed in the middle of her back with a firm shove. One minute she was standing there and the next she went flying forward. Drake's fist in the back of her pack stopped her short of tumbling into the cage. A hand full of claws swiped at her so close the brush of air whispered against her cheeks. Samantha jumped back, colliding with Drake. She gulped air past the constricted muscles of her throat, heart racing. The howls of the other two caged men turned into low growls that vibrated through her body.

"A month ago," said Drake, voice ice cold, "he clawed up another patron, a woman."

The man in the cage snarled, jerking on the bars with mindless determination. As her heart rate steadied, Samantha couldn't look away. There was rage in him to be sure, but there was something more in those eyes, in the mindless way he struggled against the bars that caged him. The man they'd named Diablo radiated pain with every movement, every breath.

What had they done to these men?

Samantha spun on her heel, breaking free of Drake's grip. "You shoved me!"

He grinned. "I also held you back."

Samantha swung. Her fist connected with Drake's jaw with a satisfying smack. His head snapped back. A stifled laugh told her Resler had enjoyed her punch more than she had. The moment the explosion of rage receded she regretted it. He'd likely make her pay for punching him, but oh did he deserve it.

Drake stroked his jaw and frowned as if her efforts had yielded no more than a tap. "I thought you should understand what you're dealing with here. Why Mr. Owens wants them gone. Today." He spit blood onto the hangar floor.

Samantha watched him thumb the remaining blood from his lip. She had to swallow to dampen her throat before she could speak. "Have your men start loading." She turned and took a step toward the ship's crew entry. "I'll be clearing us for launch."

"Sam!" Drake's shout stopped her before she made it halfway across the hangar. "I'm looking forward to getting to know you better. I love a challenge."

Samantha should have hit him harder. "You want a challenge, I'll be sure to give you one."

Confusion churned as Mercury watched the female walk away. She moved differently from the females of his kind—sensual but not intentionally seductive, full of energy but not aggressive enough to survive the arena. His hands could easily span her narrow waist, too small, too breakable to be a fighter, but he'd never be able to resist running his hands down her hips and around to her toned, muscular ass.

Pushing away the unwanted thoughts, he threw his head back and howled. He needed to reassure the others. His pack brothers were hurting.

The whip-master's taunting had Lo in an unthinking rage and Carn, still weak from their last battle in the arena, was mad with worry for his mate. He'd gone wild when his cage was loaded into the ground transport and he'd only just recovered from the tranquilizer the handlers had used on him.

They needed to be alert to watch and listen for anything that might give them an edge. There had to be a way to get Carn back to his mate. The mate Mercury had promised to protect with his life. They all had to restrain the instincts telling them to fight. Drake was looking for a reason to kill them all and Mercury couldn't allow that. He sucked in air and threw his head back in another howl, willing his brothers to join him.

When he heard the change in their baying, from raw to purposeful, he allowed his thoughts to drift back to the female. He shouldn't have reacted to her nearness. Shouldn't have allowed her to become a distraction.

He'd wanted to find out how her skin would feel beneath his touch. He'd wanted to taste her soft lips. He'd wanted to free her gold-brown hair and bury his nose against the pale skin behind her ear, to drag in her feminine scent.

It had been her scent he'd noticed first. Irresistible. Like honey. She smelled...right.

He could no longer see her, but her scent lingered, mixed with the vile stench of the whip-master. She worked with the whip-master. He'd let himself be distracted by a female in league with his hated enemy.

He'd failed his brothers too often. Lost control of his rage in the arena. Acted on instinct without thought, like an animal. He'd gathered his brothers together one by one. Jupiter and Seneca were dead but Lo and Carn still lived. Lo, the first of his brothers. They'd been raised in the same nursery. Learned to take a lashing together at the hands of the whip-masters that had begun sorting them by aptitude at the age of four. Carn had joined them later. He'd been an oversized and uncooperative monster headed for a short life in the cage matches until he'd learned to fight as part of their team, their family.

Mercury tugged at the unbending strength of the bars as he watched the red-suited workers load Carn's cage into the ship. His belly twisted with the realization that they weren't going to be removed from the cages until after they left Roma, probably not until their journey was over. How long would Carn's mate be left defenseless in the clutches of the monsters that ruled the arena? For now all they could do was stay alive. Stay strong. Ready to act when the cages were finally opened. He had to believe it wouldn't be too late. Too late to save what was left of his family.

CHAPTER TWO

The Dove
Earth Alliance Beta Sector
2210.146

"You can't be serious." Samantha spun around to face Drake. He and Resler sat at the table tucked into a corner of the crew commons room. Twenty-four hours into the journey and they already looked comfortable and relaxed, while she was still suffering from the nerves chewing a hole through the lining of her stomach.

Drake had again dressed in all black, wearing the synth and leather like a macabre uniform. The precise cut of the thin beard that defined his jaw provided a stark contrast to Resler's unkempt appearance. The man must not own a comb. A deck of silver and white lambda cards stretched across the shiny black expanse of the tabletop like an asteroid field. Their half-eaten meals had been shoved aside to make way for the game.

"Very serious," said Drake. "No food for the Dogs, Sam. None." He met her glare with a calm that beat against Samantha's outrage like water on baked coolie-clay. One good tap and she'd explode like a shower of pottery shards. "Come, sit." He waved her forward with a flick of his wrist then scooped up the cards and shuffled them. "We'll deal you in."

"Hey," Resler grumbled, "I was winning."

"Don't be an ass." Drake tapped the cards on the table.

Samantha rolled her shoulders and waited for their bickering to die down. Stars she was tired. It had been twenty grueling hours of flight prep, getting up to speed on the peculiarities of the *Dove* and getting them all safely into skipspace—that wonderful state that bent the laws of ordinary physics and made faster than light travel possible.

She'd spent the last four hours walking the ship, doing systems checks, and she needed sleep before she had to be back at the pilot's station to prep for the first skip-point. At each skip-point the ship had to drop back to normal space for the skip-field generator's cool-down period before jumping again. The *Dove* was top of the line. She could probably recalculate to a 48 hour interval between skip-points. Unfortunately, she had to stick to the standard 36, if she wanted to end up at the rendezvous coordinates on schedule to meet Sevti's people.

The ship was in tip-top shape, but she couldn't boast the same. She needed to find a bed and climb in, but first she needed fuel. And she refused to fill her own belly until the Arena Dogs had been fed. Their cages had built-in waste and water units, but no rations. She couldn't let Drake's decree stand.

Patience gone, she filled her lungs, ready to shout for their attention. "The Arena Dogs, Mr. Drake. I won't let them go hungry."

He flipped the triangular cards through his hands again. "It's not your concern, Sam."

She pinched the bridge of her nose and willed away the building headache. "As pilot, the wellbeing of everyone on board is my responsibility."

Drake set the cards down in a tidy stack. "They aren't passengers." He twisted in his seat to face her more fully. "They're property. And *my* responsibility, not yours. But, if it will ease your mind, there's nothing to worry about. The Dogs were engineered for endurance and efficiency. They can easily survive without food for the three week journey."

That stopped her for a half a minute. He said it so casually and looked at her like he thought it made everything all right. "It might be true, but it's also cruel. The ship is fully stocked. There's no reason to let them suffer."

Resler smirked then reached over and snagged a chunk of tuber from his plate. "You should tell her."

Drake shot the man a glare to rival the chill of space.

"Tell me what?" She considered that look and what it might mean. If there was something, anything, she could use to break through his resolve she'd jump at it and worry about the consequences later. Fisting her hands on her hips, she stepped close enough to tower over the seated men. "I get it. You're afraid."

All expression slipped off Drake's face. "Afraid? Of you?"

"Not me. The Arena Dogs."

"Ha!" Drake slid off of the seat then stood, forcing her to look up to hold his gaze.

Samantha resisted the urge to step back.

He leaned in, crowding her even more. "They're afraid of me, not the other way around."

She'd been bullied by bigger men. "You'd have to get close to the cages to feed them. I think you're afraid they'd make a grab for you."

He shook his head and smiled. "Did you really think I'd be that easy to provoke?"

She shrugged, impressed that he saw through her ploy. She'd have to be careful not to underestimate him again, but that didn't mean she was ready to give up. "Prove it then. Feed them."

The smile tightened, giving him the pinched look of a man wearing a belt synched one notch too far. "I've worked with them—no bars between us—for years. If I wanted to feed them, I would."

Samantha nodded. "Sure. But I bet you had a bunch of guards there to back you up."

He stepped forward and her muscles tensed in reaction, but he brushed past. The pop of a storage bin opening drew her around as he dug into one of the built-in containers that lined the wall.

He pulled out a protein ration bar and tossed it to her. "If you want to bet, I've got a better wager."

The packaging crackled as her hand tightened. Jaw clenched, she waited for him to continue.

"You get the Dogs to take a ration bar from your hand and I'll let them keep it."

She shivered as the memory of the swipe one of them had taken at her flashed her back to that terror, but the memory of the man's pain was just as clear. And the thought of the one they called

Mercury, of his breath against her wrist, created a wave of heat that chased away her fear and left her edgy and breathless.

She held the bar up. "I get one of them to take this...and they all get fed...daily."

Drake dug back in the bin for two more ration bars then nodded. "They each get one bar a day."

"Deal."

"Not so fast." Drake shoved the bin closed. "You're asking for a lot. I think we have to make this more challenging and I want something out of the bargain."

Samantha huffed her disgust, wondering if he had any intention of dealing fairly. He struck her as a man who'd have no twinge of conscious over dealing from the bottom of the deck. He might keep adding on conditions until there was no way for her to succeed. "Risking my life isn't enough?"

"Now, Sam. We aren't going to let our pilot die. The worst you'll get is a few scratches. Maybe a broken bone."

Resler got up and shoved his empty tray into the disposal. "She's right. They could snap her neck."

"If they did," said Drake, "that certainly wouldn't benefit *me*."

So they were back to that—what was in it for him. "What do you want?"

"Just your company at meals, daily. Seems fair." His smile was friendly and open as if he wasn't bargaining over whether three men would go hungry.

Samantha bit her lip to contain her own less charitable smile.

Drake raised his eyebrows.

"Do you realize," she said, "that you just put eating a meal with you on par with risking death?"

He scowled, twisting his lips in a cruel mockery of his earlier expression. "Let's add a time limit. Say, five minutes."

She sighed. If this was the only alternative to letting them go without food, what choice did she have? "All right. I'll do it."

Resler chuckled as he headed for the door. "This should be good. I'll get the stun-sticks."

Stars, she hadn't meant to give them any excuse to hurt their prisoners. "That won't be—"

"We won't use them," said Drake. "Unless it's the only way to get you out of there." He nodded to Resler. "Meet us in the cargo-hold." He waved a hand at the door. "After you, Sam."

He was uncharacteristically quiet on the short walk through the pale blue corridors. She knew the color was supposed to be relaxing. A lot of ships used it. Maybe it helped the normal crew get along better on the long journeys, but it did nothing for the coil of tension constricting her chest. Samantha entered the code, gave the door a solid push, and led Drake into the hold.

Cargo crates stamped with the red Roma logo and locked in place with gravity clamps lined the wall to the left. To her right, nothing stood between them and the bare metal of the loading doors and the hatch leading to the emergency cargo-drop. In front of them, the three cages formed a barbaric row about five meters away. Mercury and Carnage were lying quietly, but their eyes tracked her. In the center cage, Diablo paced in small, three step laps. As Resler came in behind them and handed Drake a stun-stick, the Arena Dog stopped and faced them, hands wrapping around the bars. The other two didn't even stir.

How had she forgotten how beautiful they were? She didn't realize she was staring until Diablo's low growl drew her gaze to his eyes. Red fire flashed in the depths.

He spoke in a voice full of teeth. "Come to taunt us?"

The question startled her. Not the question so much as his speaking at all. They'd been so silent, not even talking to each other.

"No." She looked to Drake who nodded.

"Five minutes," he said.

She stepped forward and held out the protein bar where they could all see. "I brought ration bars." She smiled, but she knew her nerves showed in the tightness of her lips.

Diablo was directly in front of her. His whole body had gone on high alert the moment she'd stepped forward. His eyes stalked her, his body twitched in readiness, drawing her attention to his sleek muscles. She wanted to stroke a hand across his skin to ease his hurts, but the memory of his claws swiping at her face kept her from walking toward him. Instead she kept well out of his reach and headed for Mercury—the man who'd touched her with sensual promise.

He lay still on his side like a sculpture, all defined muscle and the sharp relief of golden skin stretched tight over cheek bones, ribs, hips. He looked relaxed at first glance, but his muscles were taut and his storm cloud eyes followed her, alert.

She kneeled in front of his cage and held out the ration bar.

He didn't move.

She huffed out a breath. "I need you to take it."

His eyelids lowered and opened in a slow-motion blink. His gaze shifted past her to the men at the door, stun-sticks in hand.

Samantha lowered her voice. "They aren't going to hurt you. Please. Take it."

His nose flared and his eyes traced her face as gently as the soft press of lips. For one pregnant moment she thought he'd reach for it, but instead he rolled over, turning his back. The thick, white scars marring the muscular expanse lashed at her determination. Why did she think a man who'd been treated so cruelly could trust her offer?

"Three and a half minutes, Sam." Drake's voice made her jump.

She pushed to her feet and made a fast, wide, arc around Diablo to get to the one they called Carnage. Stars, he was big. Even lying down. She didn't think she wanted to see him standing up close. She quickly dropped down, just out of his reach and held out the bar.

"Please," she said. "If one of you take it, you'll all be allowed to eat."

He rolled up to a kneeling position facing her. A silver scar cut across his jaw, an old wound. Four parallel cuts, newly healing, wrapped around his ribs and dark shadows rimmed his black eyes. "If you want to help us…" His voice was low, barely more than a whisper. "Get us off this ship."

The pain-filled request gutted her. The rendezvous with Sevti's friends couldn't come soon enough. She wanted to offer reassurance, hope, but the presence of the men at the door kept her silent.

"Two minutes, Sam."

Drake's reminder was a weight settling across her shoulders. Why had she thought it would be easy? Stars. She'd never been a quitter. The ration bar's wrapper crinkled as she nervously tapped it against her thigh.

Carnage's ears flicked and his gaze tracked to the source of the noise.

A flare of hope had her fumbling the package. Her fingers found the pull tab and the wrapper fell away. She broke off a corner and popped it in her mouth then held out the rest of the bar. She chewed then swallowed, dismissing the pain of working the still too large chunks of dry protein mixture down her throat. "See? Nothing wrong with it."

Diablo growled. "Leave him alone, human."

His earlier accusation echoed in her thoughts. He'd accused her of being there to taunt them and she'd effectively done just that.

"Not going to try me, little female?"

She looked up to find him looming in the corner of his cage, teeth bared, eyes flashing. Samantha pushed to her feet. With all his rage it would be easy to convince herself the pain she thought she'd seen had been a mirage. That this man might have lost all his humanity.

Diablo's lips pulled back further, trembling with a growl so low it rumbled across her skin and made her shiver. She could see it in the expanding muscles of his chest. His hands flexed, scraping claws along the metal bars. The sound drew her shoulders tighter. The tension in the room crackled like electricity building up to a strike.

Suddenly, it was harder to breathe—as if everyone in the room had taken in a deep breath all at once, stealing the oxygen.

He could kill her. *They could snap her neck.* Resler's voice echoed in her head.

She stepped forward, still well out of reach. She couldn't have more than thirty seconds left.

A sharp bark sounded from Mercury's cage and Diablo answered back.

Distantly aware that Mercury had sprung to his feet and started a steady growl, Samantha stepped forward again.

And again.

She felt the prick of Diablo's claws on her arm before she saw him move. The icy chill of panic washed over her—the fire of his hand on her forearm seemed the only warm place left on her body. He'd had to stretch to reach her and for a frozen moment she registered the muscles of his shoulder and arm sharply defined as they pulled taut. She registered the cacophony of growls and shouts that swelled to fill the room. She registered the soft whisper of fabric tearing and the tug on her wrist as he tried to pull her closer.

Samantha jerked hard against his grip. Her ass hit the floor and she crab-walked backward, scrambling out of his reach. Hands reached from behind, grabbing her beneath her arms and pulling her up and away, wrenching her tight muscles in a stab of pain. She sucked in air as her feet found the floor.

She shot out an arm to bar Resler from reaching Diablo with his stun-stick. "No!"

"But—"

"No," she said again.

"Time's up, Sam." Drake's words came low and mean near her ear.

She cradled her arm against her chest, hiding the skin bared by the ripped fabric. "I know."

Drake's hands squeezed her shoulders. "I hope I've made my point."

His point? She knew he wanted this to prove to her that his prisoners, his slaves, were nothing more than animals. Dangerous. Deadly.

She studied the caged men. They were all on their feet now. Agitated, breathing heavy, waiting. She still struggled to breathe past a tight throat and a tugging sensation in her diaphragm. But it wasn't from fear.

Yes, they were dangerous. Yes, she knew they could be deadly. But if they were nothing more than animals, why was the arm cradled to her chest uninjured? No blood, no pain, no scratches.

And, because she'd failed—for Diablo, Carnage and Mercury—there would be no food.

CHAPTER THREE

The Dove
Earth Alliance Beta Sector
2210.149

Four days into the trip and Samantha was exhausted. Exhausted and lonely. The exhaustion was no surprise. The *Dove* was intended to have a four person crew. Most of the systems were automated, but systems checks and navigation updates ate up her days. Dinners with Drake and Resler taxed her better nature and did nothing to make her feel any less lonely.

The loneliness was the biggest surprise. She'd told herself she'd become self-sufficient. That she needed no one. Stars, how she'd lied.

Samantha pulled her legs up onto the seat and rested her chin on her knees as she stared at the blackness of space. It filled up the exterior monitor and threatened to spill into the small pilot's station. The work area to her left was completely dark, the empty seat turned with its back to her. A small monitor to her right provided the only light, a soft glow as her calculations for the next skip-point crunched by in a scrolling fountain of numbers.

The metal wall that curved up from the monitors to curve over her head was bare. On her father's ship the walls had been covered with paintings she'd made as a teenager, her first year traveling with him. She couldn't help but wonder if Shred had left them or had the walls been scoured back to the metal. Back on the Reliable, she'd been too busy crawling around the enormous ship's systems to dwell on the betrayal of her father's crew—men she'd lived and worked with for years. And then there were the more complicated emotions twisted up with her father's death.

She tapped the monitor, switching to a view of the cargo-hold. Like every other time she'd checked on them, the strangely beautiful men were all lying on the floors of their cages. Not sleeping, but quiet and calm. They were probably conserving energy. She sighed. These so called "dogs" had been better passengers than the jerks currently drinking their way through a container of whiskey in the crew commons room.

Samantha zoomed the view on Mercury's cage. It had been bad enough to know they were going hungry while she ate her fill, but now she was facing the prospect of watching them starve for three damn weeks.

The rendezvous ship should have been waiting at the last skip-point. Ten hours ago. If they didn't show at the next one, chances were they weren't coming. And she'd have to make a decision. One that could cost her any hope of holding any job in Alliance territory, let alone the chance to pilot her own freighter.

On the small monitor, Mercury scrambled to his feet. Samantha tapped the screen, returning it to the wide view of the hold. All three men were up and agitated.

Her feet dropped to the floor like the clumsy legs of a marionette and her spine straightened. She was leaning toward the screen when the back of Resler's head came into view. She pushed back, unable to think of any good reason why a drunken Resler would be in the hold in the middle of the night.

As he moved further into the room, more of him came into view. He held a stun-stick in one hand. She bolted for the nearest hatch and the corridor beyond. Samantha sprinted down toward the cargo-hold. Her heartbeat echoed the heavy thunk of her boots on the decking.

A tiny voice in her head warned that getting between Resler and his prisoners would be dangerous. Would make things harder for her if the rendezvous ship never appeared and she did have to make the hard choice. But all of that was later. Right now she couldn't let him hurt them.

Sliding to a stop at the cargo-hold hatch, she jabbed the code into the entry pad then twisted the handle and shoved. The moment the seal broke, she heard the shouts and snarls and agonized yelps. She shoved open the door. Resler stood at the end of the line of large cages on the far side of the hold.

He shoved a stun-stick into the nearest cage. "That's right," he taunted as Mercury's body twisted and bowed. "Can't get away now, you bastard. You need to learn to keep your damn mouth shut when I'm talking."

In the next cage Diablo snarled and snapped.

"Hey!" Samantha yelled, but Resler seemed too engrossed in his torture to notice. Bile rose in the back of her throat as another bolt jerked Mercury's body. His muscles locked in response to the shock, making him helpless to avoid the next attack.

"Hey," she yelled again as she sprinted across the hold. She closed the last few yards and gave Resler a solid shove. His heavy bulk landed hard against the metal floor, pulling her down with him. He expelled a whoosh of breath as Samantha landed on his ribs.

She fisted the heavy cloth of his shirt and shook him. "What in the hell do you think you're doing?"

Despite the adrenaline giving her an extra boost of strength, she expected him to throw her off, but his hands came up and he latched onto her arms. He leaned up, shoving his face inches from her nose. "You want a piece of me, bitch? I'll give you what I was saving for Carnage's whore."

Spittle and rank air struck her face as solidly as a blow. She jerked away instinctively, but his grip on one arm tightened to bruising force while he released her other arm and took a swing at her.

Pain bloomed in her cheek as her head reeled. She leaned in close not wanting to give him a chance to put any more power behind his next punch.

His body jerked beneath her and he was pulled toward the cage. "Fuck!" His eyes widened like the boggle-fish of Celas5.

Taking advantage of the moment, Samantha rolled, jerking free. On hands and knees, she panted. She had to catch her breath. By the time she scrambled to her feet, Resler was thrashing madly.

He wrapped a hand around her ankle, trying to pull himself away from the cage in a belly crawl. "Get him off! Get him off." Red faced, he screamed.

Samantha's gaze shot to Mercury. Reaching out of the cage, he gripped one of Resler's legs. Resler kicked his free leg back toward the bars, but he couldn't connect with Mercury and his kicks weren't well-planned enough to get any momentum pushing off the cage. He was doing more thrashing than anything. Mercury jerked Resler back and used the bars to wrench his leg. The sickening snap of bone blurred with the sound of Resler's high pitched squeal and, suddenly, her ankle was free. Over the din she heard the slap of feet running toward the hold. She hadn't bothered to close the door and the noise must have carried through the corridor to Drake. This was only going to get worse.

"Wait!" She leapt toward the bars and fell to her knees to get down to where Resler and Mercury were locked in violence. "Mercury, stop."

His eyes snapped up to her and his lip curled in a snarl.

Her heart pounded in her chest. He could easily release Resler and rip out her throat. Taking a chance, she stretched out a shaking hand and laid it over his.

His hand jerked, but he kept his grip on the still squirming Resler.

"Drake is coming," she said. "Please, you have to stop."

Gaze still locked on her, his grip eased but he didn't release Resler completely. He breathed hard, nostrils flaring, body still taut and ready to fight.

Samantha spoke softly, "Resler, be still."

"Fuck that. Get him off!"

"Shit." Drake's muttered curse echoed weakly from the hatch. Samantha kept her eyes on Mercury but spoke to Drake. "Come get your man, Mr. Drake. And," she said, deliberate and even, "don't bring any weapons over here or make any threatening moves."

The cargo hold had gone eerily quiet with only the sound of the men panting from exertion and Drake's boots as he strode across the floor then came to a stop at Resler's head.

Samantha slipped her fingers under Mercury's wrist and slid them along the heated skin, stroking gently over the large artery. His nostrils flared in response. For an instant they were back in that moment when she'd first laid eyes on him. When he'd pressed his nose against the same spot on her wrist. It had been a moment of trust. She'd trusted him, now it was his turn. "Please," she said. "Let go."

His hand eased away and Drake pulled Resler free. She knew Mercury could change his mind and grab her at any moment, but she refused to show her fear.

She glanced over her shoulder as Drake hauled Resler up, arm over his shoulder, and to his feet. "Take him to the med-bay. I'll be there in a minute."

Drake looked grim as his attention darted from her to Mercury and back. "I'm not leaving you in here alone."

Slowly she edged back away from Mercury's cage then stopped. "I'll be fine."

He huffed. "Don't be long."

"I won't."

She watched until they disappeared through the hatch then she scooted forward and wrapped her hands around the bars of Mercury's cage. She looked for signs of injury. There were plenty of scars, but nothing that looked new. "Do you need medical attention?"

He stared back, chest rising and falling on deep labored breaths. She wanted him to trust her more than made sense. He had no reason to trust her and every reason to be angry at the world. She didn't expect stopping Resler's attack to change that.

"One look and I should've known you'd be trouble." She bent her head on a sigh. She noticed the stun-stick had fallen, or more likely been pulled, into the cage. It lay a few inches inside.

Still on her knees, Samantha met Mercury's gaze and edged her hand between the bars. Staring back at her, he seemed unaware of her reaching for the stun-stick, but the moment she touched it his hand manacled her wrist. She waited, heart in her throat, for him to break her arm or hurt her, but he knelt there motionless.

Samantha swallowed, pushing her sand-dry tongue against the roof of her mouth. "You know they won't let you keep it. Keeping it will just give them an excuse to hurt you again."

His grip flexed, but he made no move to let her go.

"*I'm* not going to hurt you. Stars," she cursed. "That's the last thing I'd want to do. There may be nothing I can do about you being in these cages, but I'll try to keep you safe as long as you're on board."

Mercury's grip eased and Samantha slowly pulled the weapon between the bars.

"I know Resler is scum, but try to avoid drawing his attention, okay?"

Mercury said nothing. Big surprise.

"You probably didn't do anything this time, did you? Why would you?"

She'd accepted that Mercury wasn't going to speak. She'd been talking more to herself than to him, but it was Diablo who finally answered.

"He did it to draw Resler off Carn." His voice made her think of the rumble of an approaching sand storm. "He's still weak from our last fight in the arena."

She hadn't bothered to check the others. Stupid. Carnage lay limp on the floor of his cage. She rushed over and reached in to check his pulse.

Diablo snarled and growled. "Don't. Touch. Him." He'd followed her as she moved past his cage to reach Carnage. His command turned into a steady snarl, but he didn't make a grab for her.

Samantha held his gaze. "I'm not going to hurt him."

Carefully she pressed her fingers to Carnage's neck. His pulse was steady under her fingers. She remembered Resler saying something about Carnage's whore. He must have been taunting him about their mate. Did these men really share one woman? He'd said *Carnage's* whore not theirs. Maybe Owens had it wrong. "I think he's just out. If he seizes or doesn't come around soon, call me. Okay?"

Diablo quieted. He tipped his head and his ears flicked. The very un-human gesture made her pulse race more than his growls.

She struggled to her feet, legs feeling rubbery and started for the door.

"How?"

Samantha spun around. Mercury was on his feet, watching her with those stormy eyes. The one word had sounded dragged past his lips.

His gaze flicked toward Carnage and back. "How do we call you?"

Her cheeks felt tight, a smile barely contained. He might be stubborn but the other two men meant more to him than his pride. "Just say, *emergency response.*"

"Emergency acknowledged." The ship's computer spoke in cold metallic syllables.

"Cancel emergency response." She went back to his cage and picked up the stun-stick she'd forgotten in her concern for

Carnage. "When the ship responds like that you can talk to it the same as you would talk to a person. It'll understand and respond. Within limits. Got it?"

Instead of answering he pushed his hand forward. He pressed his palm high on her chest, warm fingers spreading against her bare flesh. Her shirt had torn at some point. She knew the skin there would have flushed golden during the fight, but it should have returned to normal.

Mercury's thumb traced her skin, leaving a trail of heat. "The color changed when you were angry," he grumbled softly.

Samantha grit her teeth and counted in her head until her breathing slowed. Maybe Resler and Drake hadn't noticed. A lot had been happening. She brushed his hand away and smoothed the fabric back into place. "I'd explain, but I don't have time to give you a Cirrillian biology lesson."

Mercury released her, only to palm her cheek. "You were injured protecting me."

She knew there'd be a bruise across the cheek where Resler had hit her, but she might get lucky and avoid the shiner. She shrugged. "You returned the favor so let's call it even." She should pull away from his touch, but there was something soothing about the heat of his palm on her cheek. Such gentleness from a man capable of terrible violence.

"No," he said. "We're not even. This was not for you to do."

"I only did what you did for Carnage."

"Pack protects pack." Something dark whipped up the storm in his eyes before he pulled away and his gaze slipped to the floor. "You're not a part of our pack. This wasn't for you to do." He wouldn't meet her eyes. Grief or guilt? "Stay away from us."

His rejection caused an almost physical pain. Silly. Angry, she bit back her urge to shout, igniting a fresh wave of pain in her cheek.

When she'd calmed, she spoke through the pain. "You'll find I'm not so great at following orders."

CHAPTER FOUR

The Dove
Earth Alliance Beta Sector
2210.149

Before going to see to Resler, Samantha stopped at her quarters to change shirts. If she'd gotten lucky and Drake and Resler hadn't noticed her Cirrillian coloring, she didn't want to risk another incident. Once her color had come up it was always easier to trigger it for a while. The two Roma men had a knack for making her angry.

By the time she got to the cramped med-bay, Drake had the other man stripped down to his briefs and feeling no pain. Eyes glassy, he barely registered her entry, but Drake didn't miss a thing. His eyes cataloged her from the toes of her boots to the fresh shirt and pearlescent salve she'd spread across her cheek.

"You okay?" His voice sounded oddly soft with none of the usual swagger and cockiness. His sincere concern was the last thing she needed when she wanted to hang onto the rage fueling her.

Samantha nodded to give herself time to swallow and work up enough moisture in her mouth to speak. "I used the med-kit in my room. It's not bad. How is he?"

"Better than five minutes ago." Resler was half sitting on the med-bed that had adjusted to something between standing and sitting to make it easier for him to climb on. With a grunt of effort Drake managed to lift Resler's legs onto the bed and push the man back into a seated position. Resler was too out of it to help. Drake had to shove the man's hips to get him properly positioned in the bed.

"What did you give him?"

"A standard blocker. Nothing that will interfere with anything we have to do to treat the leg."

There was disapproval in his eyes. He probably figured she'd leave him suffering given the choice and maybe he was right. "I was more worried about mixing a pain killer with the liquor in his system."

Samantha pressed the med-bed control to get the man laying flat then reached for the sensor array mounted above the bed.

"I should take a look at that cheek." Drake reached for her but she turned to block him.

"Really, I'm fine." She forced a tight grin onto her face and tossed a look over her shoulder. "Can you take the other side?"

Drake moved around the bed then helped her pull the array down and over Resler's legs.

Resler lurched up and grabbed Drake's hand, stilling his progress. "You make sure it gets done right. That bitch will leave me crippled, if you leave it up to her." There was drool at the corner of his mouth, negating the effect of the threatening tone.

Drake nodded and moved Resler's hand back to the bed.

Samantha pressed a sensor to his neck. "Lucky for you this is a pretty sophisticated med-bay for such a small ship. The equipment will be doing most of the work."

Drake pulled the mender out of its clearly labeled slot in the low ceiling above the med-bed, then positioned it over Resler's leg. Samantha could tell by the chime it made that there was a problem.

Drake studied the mender's interface screen then looked up. "Have to reposition the bones first." The words were said almost under his breath. If he'd waited on the pain killer they could've done a general anesthetic.

Samantha didn't have much sympathy for Resler, but cruelty was beyond her. "We could give him a scrubber to counter the painkiller and the liquor."

Drake shook his head. "He'll pass out when we get started."

Together they followed the mender's guidance to realign the cracked bone. Drake turned out to be right. The first time he put tension on Resler's leg, pulling it out straight, the brute went under.

Samantha looked across the mender to this pragmatic and efficient Drake and wondered where this side of him had come from. "You've done this sort of thing before."

"So have you." He answered with no bravado, no swagger.

After the craziness of the last hour Samantha struggled to adjust. "Basic medical is part of my training."

"That's right." Drake nodded. "As pilot you're responsible for the lives of everyone on board." He recalled her words with no venom or rancor in his voice. His eyes were on the screen. Without his perpetually sly look to harden his features, he seemed almost handsome.

It was a rare moment when she could genuinely say she didn't mind talking to him and she needed to smooth things over. It only made sense to try to make conversation. "So, where have you done this sort of thing before?"

He spoke without looking up. "I was born in the Mitna Refugee Camp on Denver3."

"That's attached to a mining colony, right?"

He made an mmm of agreement. "What medical care we had access to came at a high price—a debt to the Directorate—and that meant a stint in the mines."

"So how did you end up with Roma?"

"I hopped freighters for awhile. Working in trade for transport and board. Landed on Roma and never looked back."

His gaze lifted.

"If you focus on your job and get us where were going without any more of this kind of shit—" He waved a hand at Resler's mending leg. "Owens will compensate you well and you might even get a hand-up. The man has a lot of allies."

Not friends, Samantha noticed. He hadn't said Owens had friends. But then she'd lost her friends in an instant, so maybe she was the fool. "If I try to explain what happened, we're only going to argue."

"Probably."

"The man was drunk, Drake. You need to get him under control."

"You don't get it, Sam. Resler wasn't the problem here, you were." His glaze flicked to her bruise with a surprisingly concerned look. His lips turned white from being pressed together before he went on. "If you hadn't interfered, no one would've gotten hurt."

"Except Mercury. And Carnage."

The mender's task complete, the screen went dark. Drake moved around to stand beside Samantha as she guided the mender back into its storage slot.

"I don't want to fight, Sam. I don't want any of this keeping us at odds."

He reached for her wrist and brought her hand up as if he meant to press a kiss to her knuckles or maybe tug her in for something more. Stars, where had he gotten the idea she wanted any part of that? And why did it seem so offensively presumptuous when Mercury's touch that first day hadn't bothered her at all?

She tugged her hand away and tried to sound sincere. "Drake, I'm flattered, but—"

Cruel arrogance swept back onto his face as if the nicer Drake had been a holographic mask, easily dismissed. "Do you know what my job is with the Dogs, Sam?"

She had to think a moment, all the way back to Sevti's introduction. He and Resler hadn't talked much about their work in the time they'd been onboard. At least not in front of her. "You're a trainer."

"That's right. So, I know what I'm talking about when I tell you Mercury can take a lot more that Resler could dish out with a single stun-stick. The Dogs are tough bastards and Mercury is too well-trained to fight a guard." He huffed out a breath and shook his head, clearly realizing that recent events had disproven his assertion. "At least he never would have before."

Samantha took a breath and turned away to adjust the settings on the med-bed. "You'd expect him to just take the abuse?"

"It would be the smart thing to do. It would be over quicker that way and there'd be no repercussions. I chose him you know? Chose to work with him. Because he's smart. Aggressive, tough, but also trainable. I had to bust my ass to keep up with him. To find new tactics to keep them alive and winning. I researched military and history vids for hours every night. You have no idea how much I hate fucking history."

For a moment Samantha entertained the notion that maybe he cared for the Arena Dogs, that maybe he believed he'd been helping them. When she turned back around, he'd propped against the wall and his attention seemed to be focused on the past.

"I spent the last five years of my life working with those Dogs and they had to fuck it all up. Fuck up everything I worked for. Fuck up my career."

No. She hadn't been wrong about Drake. This was a man who saw only his own interests. Cared only for his own wellbeing. He would never have compassion for anyone or anything that stood in his way. Samantha watched him shake off the barely-leashed rage and head for the doorway.

And for once she showed prudence and kept her mouth shut.

When the hatch opened, Mercury was prepared to repeat his edict for the woman to stay away and he was oddly disappointed when it was Drake that stepped inside. Her willingness to stand-up to Resler on his behalf confused him. He could see no purpose to it, if she was allied with the whip-masters. A game? But why? She'd stopped him from doing more damage to Resler. But she'd seemed to believe she was protecting him. She'd rushed Resler like a young warrior, all courage and no thought for her own safety. He shook his head and studied the cold eyes of the whip-master.

If she was not allied with Drake, she was in danger and her failure to recognize the extent of the masters' cruelty only gave him more reason to warn her away. Such ignorance was dangerous for her.

He got to his feet slowly, watching the whip-master's hand tighten around a dart gun. Carnage panted heavily, sprawled across the floor of his cage, still hurting from the effects of the stun-stick on his healing internal injuries. With no food or medical care and nothing but abuse since they'd been sentenced to death, his injuries where healing more slowly than they should. In the cage beside him, Lo's muscles tensed. Mercury knew his pack brother was fighting against his fear. Lo feared almost nothing.

Almost.

But the drug in the dart, like other drugs the masters of the arena used against them, had the power to render a Dog helpless. That was the one thing they all feared and Mercury knew Lo had fallen to the drugs enough times to foster a fear so complete it coated his insides like a syrupy poison.

Drake's gaze raked over them, landing intensely on Mercury. A smirk slithered slowly into place, but his attention never wavered. Not even when his arm extended toward Lo and fired in one smooth motion. Lo slumped to the ground in a thump of dead weight. Drake's smirk slid back off his face when Mercury failed to respond. He knew Drake well enough to know what was coming and Lo wasn't the target of the whip-master's rage.

Drake's arm lowered, the hand holding the dart gun hanging against his thigh. "You know the penalty for injuring a guard."

Mercury nodded. "Death. But you're not going to kill me now."

"No. You're right. I need you alive at the end of this journey. So what am I going to do with you?" He tapped the gun against his thigh. "I could keep you unconscious. But then you wouldn't suffer the anticipation of your death. No. That's off the table."

Mercury remained silent. There was nothing to say. Drake had decided his punishment long before he'd entered the cargo-hold. Mercury could only be thankful Drake wasn't looking to target the others. Mercury had no intention of giving him any reason to hurt them. He would take whatever Drake dished out.

He heard Carn shift as if he might try to stand but he didn't want Drake's attention on his weakened pack brother. "And will you punish Resler for injuring the female?"

Drake ignored his taunt, walking directly to Carn's cage. He stood there watching the wounded Dog breathe for a moment before dismissing him.

Mercury knew why Drake wanted Lo unconscious—his cage was too close, but Carn was too far away to be a threat. He almost wished Drake would put Carn out as well. It would make what was coming easier on them both.

Drake stepped in front of his cage, pulling Mercury out of his thoughts. "You're right," said Drake. "I'm not going to kill you, but I am going to lash some discipline into that thick hide of yours. And you're going to cooperate because we both know there are worse things I could do to your buddy while he's out. Things you wouldn't enjoy watching."

Mercury's stomach twisted. And he could feel the twitch of muscles in his neck, where he'd locked his jaw.

Drake laid the dart gun on a nearby crate. Then he went fishing in his pocket, pulling out a flex restraint. "Step up to the front bars then turn around and reach your hands up through the top."

Mercury warred with instincts telling him to fight, hesitating for the briefest of moments, but he'd rather take the punishment himself than see either of his brothers suffer in his place.

The plasmold of the restraints slipped over his wrists and tightened.

The snap of the cage-lock releasing echoed loudly in his ears and the grating of alloy on alloy, as the front of the cage swung wide, scraped at his guts. In that moment, nothing more than a thin strip of plasmold stood between him and freedom and he knew that knowledge would haunt him. Thin, soft, malleable plasmold— a substance perfectly designed to be impossible to break by pulling. Experience had proven that hours of pulling with all his strength might make the plasmold stretch but it wouldn't break. Mercury had experienced Drake's lessons often enough to know exactly what to expect. So, he stood motionless and readied himself to accept the pain.

The first strike of Drake's whip crackled in the air and dealt a blow against his back that would have taken a human to his knees. But not Mercury. He visualized the pain rippling through his muscles and dissipating. He blew out his anguish and refilled his lungs with another deep, renewing breath of air. He waited for the next strike.

Focused as he was on the pain, he didn't hear the footsteps.

The press of Drake's hand on his shoulder blade broke his concentration and made his muscles jump in protest.

"There was a time," Drake's fingers traced lightly across his back as he spoke. "When I could count each strike I'd delivered by the scars left on your thick hide. Now there are too many. *Layers* of them."

Mercury fought the impulse to pull away from the touch. The fascination in Drake's voice crept across his skin like scurrying insects. The press of Drake's fingers disappeared as unexpectedly as they'd appeared and he was back in position, lashing out with the whip before Mercury could prepare. The strike was poorly placed—it wouldn't create as much of a gash—but it hurt as if it had been dipped in acid. The pain burned deep, spreading agony in a slow march in every direction.

The next two lashes faded in importance as Mercury pulled that place of peaceful resignation back around him like a familiar old blanket. Only now that he'd let the pain in, the blanket was threadbare, the pain more difficult to ignore.

The next time Drake approached, Mercury heard the footsteps, was ready for the touch. He'd added them to the things the blanket was meant to keep out.

"Why did you do it, Mercury? Why fight back now? Was it because you have nothing to lose? Do you want to go to your final hunt wounded and weak?" Drake's hand slipped along Mercury's ribs in a caress that made a mockery of tenderness and had his skin crawling. "Or was it the woman? Some kind of protective instinct?"

Mercury refused to answer, but he failed utterly at controlling his breathing. He couldn't help the panting that came from both pain and rage. The pain that had been dispersed by the blanket of his meditation now worked its way underneath and gripped him in aching pulses.

"You've never cared much for human women before. Or did moving Hera into your group's cell soften you up? Pretty, submissive Hera. Born and trained to please, yet I don't think you would have risked your neck or your flesh for her."

That's where Drake was wrong. He would have, still would, risk everything for Hera. Not because she was special to him, but because she was mated to Carn.

Crack. The next lash took him completely by surprise. It pulled all the air from his lungs. *Crack.* Fuck, he had to focus. *Crack.*

With each new lash Mercury channeled the pain into a moan pitched well below human hearing, so low that each one sent vibrations through his body and into the metal floor of the cage. Finally, he managed to drown out Drake's words and regain control. It was too late to stop the pain, but he could still keep his head high. Control his breathing.

Hide his agony.

Everything but the pain and his need for control faded away.

Distantly, he heard the clink of the cage door closing and he realized the lashes had stopped.

A yank on his hair tugged his head back. The movement sent spikes of pain through his shoulders and made him see spots. As his surroundings came back he smelled blood. His blood. The feel of it slick on his back and wet as it soaked into the waistband of his pants.

Drake's breath puffed hotly against his ear. "I may be losing you and your merry men, but there will be others to train. It could have been your *pup.*" He jerked hard, snapping Mercury's head back. "Owens wanted *you* to breed the bitch. He was even willing to sacrifice three good fighters to get them out of the way for you, but you had to screw it up. And now that Hera's proven completely useless, Owens has promised to give Hera to the trainers."

A different kind of pain hit Mercury deep in his gut and there was no way to control the gasp that accompanied it. He heard Carn's whimper, like the ghost of a sound.

Drake chuckled cruelly. "That's right. Hera is our fuck toy now…and our whipping girl." He released his hold on Mercury's hair and shoved his head forward. "At least that's one bonus."

Fuck, fuck, fuck. Not only had he failed his brothers, he'd been the cause of their deaths. And Hera alone in the care of the trainers—nothing could be more wrong.

Samantha woke, not with a start, but with a slow sense of dread. She uncurled herself from the small nook where she'd drifted off. Since Drake had left, she'd felt obligated to stay in the med-bay until Resler came around. He was a jerk, but even a jerk deserved the consideration of being told about his injuries.

As she stretched, a dull, grinding ache shuddered through her belly. Her head pounded and she couldn't fight off the urge to cringe away from…stars knew what. She didn't see or hear anything, but she felt *something*.

Samantha signed onto the med-bay terminal and did a remote check of the logs.

Nothing but nominal readings.

Listen to your gut, kiddo. Her father's voice whispered in her mind as she looked at the log. He might not have been much of a dad, but he'd been a good mentor. She let her fingers fly over the screen and started a more comprehensive sensor sweep running.

As the data scrolled up the screen, she searched for something, anything, that might explain what her gut was trying to tell her. Another wave of…whatever… washed over her, just as the reading jumped out at her. The signal detection sweep showed something in the sub-audio frequency range. An intermittent, low frequency burst. It had occurred several times in the last fifteen minutes. She couldn't have heard the infrasound, far below her hearing range, but somehow she'd felt the vibrations carried through the ship's skeleton.

She pulled it up as a waveform in one pane then arranged the raw sensor data in another. If the signal had been in the audio range, she'd have said it was an amplified vocalization. An incredibly loud moan.

The disorienting feeling hit her again she had to work to keep herself upright as she checked the read-out and tracked the signal to its origin point... in the cargo-hold.

The sound of her own boots echoed ominously as she strode down the corridor. She felt as hollow as the pale corridor sounded. She didn't have any expectations for what she would find, save one: it wouldn't be good. This trip seemed to be one bad thing after another. The hatch to the hold stood open and the crack of noise that shot toward her didn't call up any immediate images. The wave of discomfort that chased after it added nothing to her understanding. Neither fit neatly into any of her boxes. Not mechanical. Not a normal ship noise. Not something against the hull.

She reached the hatch and froze. The smell of sweat and something sharper clung to the air. Drake stood in front of Mercury's cage. His hands were on the bars and she heard the lock engage. He'd had the cage open. Why? Then she noticed his whip, hanging from the loop on his belt. The leather glistened wetly.

Her heart stopped.

Drake stepped aside and it was so much worse than she'd expected. Mercury hung from flexgrips pinning his wrists to the top of the cage. Slick, red blood coated his back. Defeat and defiance etched into the stiffness of his body. If she'd arrived a moment earlier she'd have tried to stop Drake, but he'd already stopped and there was nothing she could do to undo it.

Drake released the grips. Mercury dropped to his knees then lowered his chest to the floor in silence.

Drake's voice broke her concentration. "Don't worry. He'll be fine for now." He grabbed her arm to turn her. "I know what he can handle and I know what I'm doing."

Because he'd done it before.

All her doubts winked out of existence. No one should have to suffer the abuse Drake had carved into Mercury's back. No one. No human. No alien. No animal.

Resistance or no resistance, she would do whatever it took to free Mercury and the others. Whatever it took.

CHAPTER FIVE

The Dove
Earth Alliance Beta Sector
2210.155

Samantha stepped into the cargo-hold an hour later than usual. She'd wanted to be doubly sure that Drake and Resler were sleeping. They'd been traveling for ten days and visiting the cargo-hold had become a nightly ritual.

Mercury and Carnage both lay quietly. Mercury turned to watch her, stretching his body as he shifted, no trace of lingering stiffness or pain in the fluid movement. He'd healed incredibly fast and with nothing more than a sealer sprayed over his shredded back. As he got to his feet, she swallowed hard. He had a way of making every move mouthwateringly sensual.

Carnage kept motionless in a tight curl in the back corner of his cage, looking impossibly small for such a big man. Diablo huffed rhythmically as he gripped a bar running across the top of his cage and pulled his body up again and again in a slow, relentless rhythm. He couldn't get his head between the bars, so he tipped his head back, raising his chin to the bar, at the top of each motion. His lean musculature stood out in sharp relief as he lowered his body, then bulged with effort as he pulled up again. Tiny beads of perspiration made his skin shimmer with the movement.

She gave herself a mental shake and looked away. She was there to feed them, not ogle them. "Good evening, gentlemen."

Undaunted by the lack of response, she set her pack on the floor then dug out the rations.

Since the night after Mercury broke Resler's leg she'd been sneaking in ration bars. With everything else she was doing, her conscience wouldn't be pricked by breaking her word to Drake. She didn't understand why the caged men had gone back to acting as if the cargo-hold was a words-free zone. If she was going to help them she needed to gain their trust. At least they were eating.

She tossed an unwrapped protein bar first to Mercury then to Diablo, who stopped his exercises to stand near the front of his cage to catch the offered meal. She still kept well out of his reach. It was better, she reasoned, not to tempt him.

"Sorry, it's just rations again, but they're easier to get out of the supply stores and less likely to be missed."

Diablo's gaze tracked her as she moved to stand in front of Carnage.

"Carnage?"

His chest rose and fell, but not even a muscle twitched in response. It felt wrong to toss his food on the floor, but she didn't have time to consider other options. She needed to get to work.

Normally she brought her sandsilk and paints to work on, but tonight was different. Tonight she would set her plan into motion. Samantha pulled the tools she would need from the hold's tool locker then popped the cover off of the secondary access panel for the environmental controls. It was only meant to serve as a backup if the primary access became inaccessible, so nothing was in easy reach.

Holding a small circuit tuner, she slipped her hand between two fiber assemblies, brushing against them gently and with care. She didn't want to wreck the whole system.

There. The circuit buzzed against her fingertips as she worked the tuner into position then adjusted the phase, just off spec. Bracing her free hand on the wall next to the access, she turned her head and reached for where the next circuit board should be, stretching and twisting and working by touch. Good thing she had small hands.

Mercury fought the urge to ask Sam what she was working on. *Sam.* That's what they called her. It didn't fit. Nothing about her made sense to him. He lay on his back, chewing his protein bar and listening to the tiny noises she made, the in and out of her breathing.

In the cage beside him, Lo went back to his pull-ups. He hadn't heard Carn move, so he probably still lay in the corner of his cage where he'd been, unmoving, all day. Mercury's concern for his brothers multiplied with each day they spent headed for death and away from Carn's mate. He'd tried to convince Carn that Drake had lied about Hera's fate, that she was too valuable as a breeder, but how could he convince him of anything when he wasn't convinced himself. Hera had been with them for half a year without conceiving.

With nothing he could do to help them, his mind turned back to Sam. Every day she came. Normally, she would spread a piece of shimmering blue cloth across the floor, lay on her belly, and apply some type of coloring to the material. She'd said it was the only area big enough for the task, but her explanation was as thin as new ice. He'd warned her away, but still she sought them out and put herself between him and his enemies.

He'd tried and failed to believe she could be a temptress like the one who'd betrayed Lo. But the more he thought back over her actions the more he had to accept that her actions had shown her to be something he'd never expected to encounter—a woman who put his welfare and that of his brothers before her own.

He knew she wanted him to speak to her but he'd long ago developed a habit of talking to humans only when absolutely necessary. They always found a way to use his words against him. He'd accepted that she wasn't like the others, but some small measure of sanity warned she might be just as dangerous.

Dangerous, because he'd begun to look forward to her visits. Dangerous, because he'd begun to trust her presence. Dangerous, because thoughts of fucking her had become as automatic as the breathing.

Her voice softened when she directed her words to him. Females did such things to signal a willingness to mate. The thought tightened his muscles with eagerness. A frustrated growl rumbled in his chest at the unwanted response. Each night she came added to the agony of wanting that made his body ache more surely than any beating. If this was what Carn felt when Hera was near—

"Drake complained about his dinner again tonight."

Her voice broke into his thoughts. The sound of the whip-master's name on her lips angered him. He growled and she laughed. A sound that curled inside him and made him shiver with need. He wanted to feel her laughter against his skin.

"This time he actually had something to complain about. I made sure to overheat his meal. It was probably rubber."

She always made a point of mentioning the whip-master. It always made him growl. He suspected she did it just to hear him respond.

"I've been doing a bit of research." The clank of her tools against something inside the panel accompanied her words.

He closed his eyes, listening as much to her tone as her meaning.

"This planet we're headed for, it's some kind of private game preserve. They've taken your kind there before. I couldn't find anything out about what will happen though." Unmistakable notes of worry hid behind the quiet melody of her voice. "They've never brought any of them back."

He heard her shift and then a quick gasp of pain. He twisted, eyes snapping open, resolve gone—swamped by the need to assure himself that she was unharmed.

She'd already dismissed whatever small hurt she'd suffered and gone back to her task. Her hair was tied back in a knot, but the shorter strands around her face clung wetly to her temples. A fine sheen of perspiration made her skin glisten. She stretched and shifted to push up the sleeve of her jacket. The soft swell of her breasts drew his eye as she moved.

His body hardened at the sight.

He knew she wore the concealing jacket, always wore high necks and long sleeves, to hide the color that appeared when she grew angry. She'd claimed it had something to do with Cirrillian biology. He didn't know what that meant, but he knew it worried her.

She pushed at the sleeve again.

He snarled as his wisdom and caution failed him. "Take it off." He knew the words were barely recognizable, garbled by his growl, but his body burned with the need to do more than remove her jacket.

She'd gone still, not even breathing. Her hand clenched around her sleeve.

"Take. It. Off."

"What?" Her voice squeaked.

"The jacket. It bothers you. Take it off." He growled louder, making her flinch. "It bothers me also."

"My jacket? Oh. It's hot, that's all." Her voice lowered as she mumbled, "All part of the plan."

Her words were confusing, but he took them as a refusal and growled in the front of his mouth. It was an instinctive demand for her to submit. A sound any female of his kind would understand, but she wasn't one of their females.

Her eyes were wide, but she didn't scent of fear.

He breathed slowly to calm his anger. Control the animal instinct that made him want to claim her. He rose to his haunches then moved to the edge of his cage, wanting to be closer.

"Take off the jacket." Better, he thought. It had come out low, but without the growl. He didn't want to frighten her. He wanted to coax her to comply.

He understood that this Cirrillian business was a secret. He wouldn't like it if she kept a secret from him, but he liked knowing something of her that the whip-master didn't. Even if he didn't understand what it meant.

"I won't tell your secret," he promised.

Her face remained tight, but she tugged off the garment and went back to work. Barely noticeable bands of warm gold wrapped her slender arms as the muscles flexed, but she went silent. He didn't want that. He'd come to need her flow of words rolling over him.

"Where is your cloth?"

"In my cabin. No time for that tonight." Her arm disappeared in the wall panel and she held her breath before letting it out in a huff that relaxed her body and drew his eyes to her curves.

Mercury let out his own breath in a snort of frustration. "Tell me about the cloth."

She stopped, studying him, eyebrows raised in delicate arches. "Now, you want to talk?"

He nodded, not trusting his voice.

"Okay," she said. "I was just finishing this up, anyway." She tapped something inside the panel then closed it and put away her tools.

"In Haverlee—that's where I lived growing up—sandsilk is one of the few resources we have in abundance." She moved across the floor with athletic grace, to stand just out of reach. "It's not as valuable as real silk from old Earth, but there's a good market for it."

He knew nothing of sandsilk or old Earth. It didn't matter. He would gladly listen to her talk about them for the whole of their journey. "More," he said, afraid even one added word would give away how badly he needed her to continue.

She edged closer and sat in front of his cage. "The thread is made by sandsilk worms." She grinned. "I know it must sound weird, but the cloth is strong and soft."

Moving slowly to avoid startling her away, he rolled up on to his toes and crouched near the bars. He wrapped his hands around the cool metal. "Why do you put on the colors?"

"The paint? Well, when I was a girl I worked in the wormaries—that's where they cultivate the worms that produce the silk— and I got paid in silk thread. I was never good at dyeing and making the cloth so I learned to paint the decorations." Her tongue darted out to moisten her lips, leaving the soft pink flesh glistening. "It's the night sky over Haverlee," she said. "The pattern I'm painting."

She sounded suddenly hesitant. He hated the uncertainty in her voice.

"It's beautiful," he said. Her smile told him it was the right thing to say.

Once again moving slowly, he reached up and pulled at the knot of hair at the base of her skull. The lush mass of brown spilled to her shoulders, revealing strands of red and gold. He'd never seen anything like it. He pulled a handful to his nose and sucked in a breath, taking her essence deep into his lungs. "But not as beautiful as this." Her bright green eyes widened and her scent warmed, turning sensuous and receptive.

Lo moved to the corner of his cage and sniffed at her. Mercury growled a gentle warning. Sam flinched and Lo edged back. It shifted Sam's attention to Lo and the loss poked at Mercury's pride.

"The place we're going," he said. "We go to be hunted. To die."

She swallowed and her lips pressed together before she spoke. "I thought it was something like that, but don't lose hope."

He wanted to deny the possibility of giving up, but even as they spoke Carn's protein bar lay uneaten on the floor of his cage. The odds against them weighed more heavily on them every day. "The owners want us dead. Their greed is the only reason we aren't dead already. Humans will pay to be allowed to hunt us. They'll use human technology to track us and long range weapons to shoot us. We won't make it easy for them, but..." Mercury refused to accept the obvious conclusion.

"How can you know that?"

"Drake. He enjoyed telling us how it would be."

"Never give up." She looked suddenly serious. "Things will work out." She pulled her knees up and wrapped her arms around her legs, hugging them to her chest. Her scent changed with her mood and he regretted his words. He hadn't thought it through before speaking. He didn't want to cause her unhappiness. He wanted to soothe her.

"Tell me more about your cloth. You'll feel more relaxed and your scent will be better."

She scoffed. "Are you saying I smell bad?"

"No. Not bad. Your scent is always good. Sweet. Honey. Female. It's best when you're relaxed and talking softly."

"Charmer." She laughed with the word, but it wasn't humor making her eyes dilate.

He traced his fingers across her cheek, pleased when she allowed it. There was no sign of the bruise she'd gotten defending him. Her slender fingers traced the back of his hand, setting off sparks of need as urgent as if she'd touched his cock.

He traced a trail down the enticing length of her throat and across her collarbone then back. He let his fingers hover there as he watched the pulse in her throat race. It amazed him that she would allow his touch. Trust him with her vulnerable throat. It wasn't a submissive offering, not born of fear. Only trust.

He drew a curve that followed the edge of the scoop neck shirt that had been hidden beneath her jacket. The path took him across the swell of her breast. Her breath hitched and his cock jumped at the sound.

The bands of color on her arms seemed a more brilliant gold than they had minutes earlier.

He thought back to her earlier words and repeated them back to her as he traced along the edge of one of the stripes. "Do we have time for a *biology lesson*?"

She laughed, a loud joyous laugh that came from her belly and made her cheeks red.

A loud pounding broke the spell.

Samantha silently cursed the timing and scrambled to her feet. Finally, after days of trying, she'd started to build some trust with Mercury. They'd even had what could pass for a conversation. The pounding on the door doubled, making her flinch. She pulled on her jacket, sealed it to the top and twisted her hair in a hasty knot then jogged to the hold hatchway. She looked over her shoulder briefly to see that the men were all on their feet but looking calm, then keyed in the open sequence.

She bristled as Drake shoved past her, barreling into the cargo-hold. He came to a halt in the center, twisting around, looking for trouble and gripping a stun-stick in one hand.

"Why in hell was that door code changed?" Drake stormed toward her. "I should be able to get in here whenever the fuck I want."

His words rose and fell in the sloppy rhythm of a drunk. Sweat matted his hair and slicked his shoulders. He wore only baggy sleep pants, chest bare and sporting more muscle than she'd have given him credit for. Still, next to the Arena Dogs, he seemed small. Puny. But big enough to cause her some serious harm. He'd been an ass from the start, but the longer he'd been on board the more he seemed to be deteriorating. Apparently, the forced idleness of travel didn't agree with him. And since their discussion in the med-bay he'd started directing more of his venom in her direction.

Samantha pointed toward the auxiliary hatch in the corner of the hold. "I got some anomalous readings on the environmental controls and wanted to check them out. The environmental unit is through there."

"It's fucking hot in my quarters. Couldn't sleep."

And he'd clearly needed to sleep off the liquor and his foul mood.

"It's hot everywhere." When the resistance ship hadn't shown up, she'd decided to begin laying the groundwork for a slowdown. Maybe give them time. Now that Mercury had explained exactly where they were headed and why, she was doubly glad she'd set things in motion. "It's probably nothing, but I need to check it." She shrugged. "I changed the code and locked the hatch as a precaution, in case I find a bigger problem when I start pulling open access panels. Easier to keep things contained. Didn't want one of you accidentally opening the hatch while I was working."

"I told you before, you shouldn't be in here without me or Resler." Drake gripped her arm and jerked her closer. A chorus of growls went up and his grip tightened painfully on her arm. His pursed his lips in a calculating expression and studied the growling men over her shoulder.

"We've argued this to death, Mr. Drake." She jerked her arm free, drawing his attention back to her. "I'll do what I think is right where the ship is concerned."

The hold hatch still stood open and the commotion must have roused Resler. He came stumbling down the corridor.

Samantha returned her focus to Drake. "Haven't you told me those cages are secure? Besides, they," she indicated the men with a nudge of her chin, "seem to know I'm not a threat." She held her hands out to her side. "No stun-stick, no problem."

"No problem?" Drake's face twisted in a parody of a smile and he snickered. Samantha reared back away from his scowl and the sour breath that went with it.

"You're stupid if you're not afraid of my Dogs. They can turn on you faster than you can spit."

Samantha's heart pounded and her throat tightened. She'd never seen him so enraged.

He shoved her up against the bulkhead just out of arm's reach of Mercury's cage. "Yeah, I'll bet they think you look tasty." The liquor on his breath made her gag.

Samantha could feel the agitation radiating from the caged men as they growled their protest to Drake's rough treatment. She struggled, but she couldn't budge the man. Resler might have more bulk, but Drake knew how to use his strength.

Drake laughed at her efforts. "What do you say, Merc? You think she'd make a good snack? Or are you sniffing after something else from her?"

Mercury snarled and snapped in response. "You'd make a better meal. Perhaps when we reach the hunting grounds, you'll be the prey."

Samantha's gaze locked on Mercury, shocked that he'd respond to the taunts. Mercury barely looked at her. She could hear the others getting louder, then one loud howl drowned out the others.

Resler strutted to the farthest cage where Carnage's howl ended in a snarl. "Well, if it isn't our lazy Carnage coming back to life. What's the matter? You hungry? Or you done missing your bitch and ready to fuck anything with a hole?"

Mercury growled deep in his throat. "Come let me out of this cage, you coward, and we'll see who ends up fucked." The words vibrated out of his still rumbling throat.

Drake shoved Samantha down to the floor and stepped across her to reach Mercury's cage. She ended up on her hands and knees facing Diablo. He dropped to the floor, face less than a quarter of a meter away. Her racing heart stuttered and a shiver raced along her skin. She had a moment to wonder if he'd kill her or leave her scarred, then he spoke beneath the howling that filled the small hold.

"Go, little Sam." He spoke through gritted teeth, lips drawn back from his prominent canines. "Don't let Mercury's pain serve no one. Go. Now."

Samantha looked over her shoulder and saw Drake shove the stun-stick into Mercury's cage. Resler taunted Carnage with his matching weapon and a smirk on his face. The caged men backed away from their tormenters, but there was no room for them to escape the stinging weapon.

"Go now," Diablo growled. "Mercury is strong and we're used to such things."

Samantha looked into his eyes. The midnight black had been almost completely eclipsed by the flecks of blood red. His thin lips curled back to show his teeth and rage danced in the depths of his eyes.

Fear made her arms shake as she pushed up from the decking, but she wouldn't let any of them be tortured. Not again. Instinct had her launching herself at Drake, making a grab for the weapon. Drake shook her off, throwing her at Resler. The brute caught her around her waist, arms like steel cables. Luckily, the man was still unsteady on his injured leg. She swung her feet and kicked against Carnage's cage. Unable to balance her shifting weight, Resler dropped her.

Pain radiated up through her hip. Damn! What had she been thinking? She knew she couldn't take on both Drake and Resler.

Staying low, she reengaged her brain and scrambled past them. Mercury's snarls rang in her ears as she dashed through the hatch. She ran through the halls, slamming blast doors closed behind her to give herself time when they came after her. And they would. She'd make sure of it.

When she reached the pilot's station, she threw herself down into the seat. Still panting for breath, she hooked her feet under the bar beneath her chair as her fingers flew across the controls. The *Dove's* environmental system and grav-generators faltered in response. Anything that wasn't tied down tumbled across the deck, then the world dropped out from under her and everything started floating, suddenly weightless.

Samantha's lungs started to burn from the sudden drop in oxygen levels. The temporary outage might be drastic measures, but she'd promised herself she'd keep the Arena Dogs safe. Grateful for her habit of wearing her deck-boots at all times, she slogged her way back down the corridor. The moment the grav-generators came back on, she dropped to the floor. Gasping for breath, she counted the seconds until the oxygen levels normalized.

She needed Drake to believe she'd dropped on the way *to* the controls, that she hadn't yet made it to the pilot's station, so she pulled her body around until she lay face down as if she'd dropped on the way forward. That done, she lay there, gulping air, and waited.

After a few minutes it got easier to breath and the darkness at the edges of her vision receded. The sound of boots stomping toward her echoed along the corridor like the thumping pistons of a transgalaxy engine.

Drake lifted her up and set her on her feet. "What in hell was that?"

"Told you." She panted, exaggerating for effect. "Environmental contols are acting up. Help me get to the pilot station so I can take a look."

Lifting her arm over his shoulder, Drake dragged her to the empty seat and shoved her into the synth-upholstered polycarb. Drake cuffed her across the side of her head and she saw stars. "Get it fixed. We don't have time for delays."

She tapped in a few commands then realized he still stood looking over her shoulder. "I'm trying, so lay off."

"Get it stable," he said. "Then we're going to talk about your pointless stunt."

Samantha cringed. Damn it, if he knew what she'd done—

A loud thump jerked her attention back to Drake and the fist he slammed onto the console beside her. "What in the hell were you thinking, getting between me and my Dogs?"

"I-" Samantha stuttered, unprepared for the accusation when she thought they'd caught on to something far worse. "I didn't want to see anyone get hurt."

"You have no fucking idea what you're dealing with." He paced, hands raking through untidy hair.

"I swear they must put out some kind of pheromones. Women back on Roma fall all over themselves to get at them."

She didn't know what to make of that, so she counted to five then tried to ratchet down the tension in the room. "Listen. Let's calm down. I don't have time to deal with whatever drunken craziness is sloshing around in that whiskey soaked brain. I need to deal with the ship."

Drake's attention fixed on Samantha with a laser focus that made her squirm in her seat.

"Your sympathy is wasted on those animals."

Resler grunted from the corridor where he'd appeared. "Yeah, just ask that sexy brunette who tried to get cozy with Diablo. She was a knockout until he got a hold of her." Resler used his sleeve to blot away the smudge of blood on his forehead. He must have hit his head when the ship jolted. "Maybe we should throw this one in with that devil. We could make a bet on whether he slashes her up or fucks her."

Drake frowned. "Don't be vulgar."

Samantha wanted to shout *pot meet kettle*, but the sound of his own condemnation seemed to shake Drake. He leaned against the nearest wall, letting his head thunk back against the bulkhead.

Samantha watched, relief easing her breathing, as Drake smoothed hands over his hair, scratched at his beard and shook himself before standing straighter, all traces of the wild man of moments earlier gone from his eyes. It was as if Resler's crudity had snapped him back from the edge of some dangerous precipice.

"I'm a respectable business man," he said. It wasn't clear if he was talking to Samantha or reminding himself. "Just doing a job. I thought you'd respect that, Sam. We both know the value of hard work, you and me. I'm not the animal on this ship. Those Dogs are the animals and they're my responsibility, not yours."

He thought he knew her. He couldn't be more wrong. She wasn't like him—only out for himself. He'd read her file and thought that told him everything he needed to know. She might have come up hard, but her experiences had taught her first and foremost to value freedom and humanity. Humanity had nothing to do with being born human.

Keep your head down, Sammie. Don't go looking for trouble. Her father's words. But she wasn't her father. Maybe she relied too much on her gut as he always had. Maybe she'd suddenly developed his habit of letting attraction cloud her thinking. Maybe she was impulsive and took too many risks, but she would never look the other way and profit from the suffering of others. She would never be as cold as Drake.

"You're right. I do know about hard work and I have work to do, Mr. Drake. You should go back to your cabin and get some rest."

He scrubbed a hand across the back of his neck and gripped the edge of the hatch with the other as he paused on his way out. "Just do your job, Sam. Get us where we need to go and forget about the Dogs. They're already dead, but you still have a chance to make something out of this mess. I know I acted like an ass earlier and I'm sorry. I don't want us to be at odds. We could be a good team. Be smart. Stay out of things that don't concern you and stay away from my Dogs."

CHAPTER SIX

The Dove
Earth Alliance Beta Sector - Gollerra Border
2210.157

Two days.

Mercury paced in what space he had. Sam hadn't returned for two days.

"You should conserve your energy." Lo watched him from the closest corner of his cage.

Mercury stopped, wrapping his hands around the bars as he glared back. "You mean since she isn't bringing us food anymore?" His muscles burned with tension.

Lo dipped his head, not meeting his eyes, and made a low whine of apology in acknowledgement of Mercury's dominance.

Carn's voice rumbled up, sounding strained. "She's their pilot. I'm thinking a pilot is not property. Not owned. They won't kill her."

Mercury resisted the urge to throw his head back and howl. "They can do much harm without killing."

"Yes, but she'll live." Pain and sorrow muted the verve that once filled Carn's voice.

Mercury knew Carn was thinking of Hera. Lo's cage between them made it difficult for them to see each other clearly, but Mercury knew his friend would hear the regret in his voice. "I should have found a way to keep you together."

"The masters are too cautious, too well armed, too devious. There was nothing to be done."

Mercury choked back his shame. At least Carn was on his feet again. "I'd give my life to save any one of you."

Lo snarled. "It's not for you to defend us. We stand together. The female clouds your thinking."

He growled back instinctively. "She's also mine to protect."

Lo shook his head. "She brought us *all* food. You speak of her as if she's your mate. As if she's *your* responsibility. You take on too much."

Mercury feared Lo was right. That he was unworthy to claim a mate of his own. That he was unworthy to lead them. But he couldn't simply stop trying for them, not now when they needed him most. And his worry for Sam wasn't something he could easily let go. "You know what price she might pay for aiding us. They can do worse things to a woman than kill."

Carn spoke over their growls. "She's clever. She knows what she risks. That's why she hasn't been back."

Lo snorted. "She's not one of us, Merc. Don't forget that. Their females can be more devious than their males."

The urge to snarl and snap at Lo's accusations crawled up Mercury's throat, but he knew something of the unbearable experiences that had made his brother so mistrustful of human females. He couldn't judge his brother when he knew the man's rage was fueled by bone-deep pain.

Carn spoke up, clearing away the silence that had sprung up between them like a trap. "She's different. Perhaps she isn't human."

Mercury pulled against the bars, fear and rage like acid in his veins. "Two days." He couldn't stop envisioning the things they could do to his female in two days. *His* female? No! Maybe Lo was right to remind him of his responsibilities. He couldn't let himself think of her as his.

"I don't know what she is," Lo sounded calmer. "But I do know she's not from the arena. Not a Dog."

Carn shifted. "But she provided for us. And that lurch in the ship's responses when the whip-master attacked you—she tried to protect you, Mercury. Lo is wrong. She's not the enemy."

Emotion shredded Mercury. Relief that Carn would defend her. Fear for her safety. Rage that he couldn't protect her. Hunger to claim her. Useless emotion that brought him no closer to redeeming his past mistakes.

"What in hell?"

Sam lurched up, nearly falling out of her seat. Damn, she'd fallen asleep and at the worst possible time. Her passengers had taken to sleeping in shifts to keep an eye on her. Two days of nervous energy had finally pushed her to her limit.

A strong hand clamped her shoulder. "I asked you a question. What is that?" Sam recognized the voice without looking up— Drake.

The control panel showed the ship had dropped out of skipdrive exactly as she'd programmed it to do. "I don't know why we've stopped. Something must be—"

"We'll get back to that." He pointed to the external view screen, which had apparently been engaged while she slept. "First, you tell me what *that* is."

Samantha blinked her eyes and tried to clear her vision. A large hunk of equipment crowded out the space that should have been visible on the screen. Beyond that a nearby sun hovered. The sensor readouts showed several planets circling the Sol class star. She'd found it on one of the unofficial nav-charts stored in the *Dove*'s database. The planets hadn't come up on the commercial charts, so she was more than relieved to see them and their sun chasing away the darkness.

At first she'd only planned to create a delay to hope the resistance could still intercept, but as the tension on the ship had wound tighter, she'd decided to look for a delay spot that would give her more options.

She focused on the equipment visible on screen and made a show of initiating a fresh sensor sweep. She'd seen similar equipment enough to recognize its function, but the glyph-based writing on the hull didn't come close to any language she'd seen before.

"It's a terraforming platform. Inactive. Sensors don't show any signs of heat or electromagnetic fields, so it must be unmanned. Whatever company owns it probably parked it here waiting for their next project." She turned to face him and noticed Resler hovering at Drake's shoulder and looking ready to chew nails. "But we have bigger problems. For some reason we're smack in the middle of a solar system," right where she wanted them, "and I have no idea why we dropped out of skipspace."

Drake pushed past Resler and toward the section of storage compartments built into the back wall of the pilot's station. The sharp thwak of his fist slamming into one of the half-meter square doors made Samantha cringe. Resler shouldered his way next to her, hunching forward to put his face near hers. "The ship came out of skipdrive pretty smooth. Not like it was a malfunction."

"Unless you're a pilot, maybe you should let me deal with this and clear out of my way."

"I know a thing or two." Resler puffed out his chest like a cockle-bird strutting for dominance. "I worked at a lunar mining colony for ten years. I've flown plenty of shuttles."

"Shuttles!" She tried to play off the nervous energy bubbling through her circulatory system as anger. "This is *not* a shuttle."

Drake leaned back against the wall and crossed his arms over his chest. "Resler, you can check our position, right? You know how to read nav charts."

"Yeah." Resler leaned over the console. "But I can tell you now, if we were on track we should have dropped out in a shipping lane. Not a solar system." He lifted his face as if he were talking to the bulkhead above them. "Computer response."

The *Dove's* computer remained silent.

Resler glared at Samantha. "Voice control locked out, sneaky bitch." He reached across her and pounded away at the controls.

Samantha wanted to smack his hands away, but she knew it wouldn't do any good. Damn. She hadn't been prepared for them to have any real knowledge of the ship's systems. If she'd known, she would've locked it down tighter.

"Here it is." Resler shook his head. "Not even close to where we should be."

Drake humphed and shook his head.

"Wait." She swallowed past the tightness in her throat. "If the navs have been malfunctioning along with everything else on this cursed ship, we might be off course but it won't be by much. There's an auxiliary nav check at every skip-point in the course. Let me pull up the charts."

She reached for the controls, but Resler grabbed her wrist. Sharp pain spiked up her arm, but she managed not to react.

"Let her do it," said Drake. "But watch her."

Resler released her.

"Look, I'll do this real slow." She rubbed at the tender joint then called out the steps. She unlocked the skipdrive navigation then pulled up the charted course and their course log. "See. We're off track, but not by much. It had to be a small nav error at the last skip-point. The computer must've pulled us out of skipdrive when it detected this solar system in our path."

Resler snatched her up by the shoulders and shook her. "We're not going to fall for your crap."

Drake straightened and started pacing. "Let her go." He strode the length of the small pilot's deck then turned back to her. "And why should I believe you, Sam? Maybe you have us off course to rendezvous with a buyer. Maybe you want to steal my Dogs. They'd be worth a lot to the right people."

Samantha shivered at the thought of anyone selling Mercury or any of the caged men.

"Yeah," said Resler. "Maybe that's why she was spending time in the cargo-hold. Checking them out for resale value."

Drake pinned Resler with a look to freeze over a sun. "Shut up, Resler."

Samantha breathed a sigh of relief. Dissent between them could only aid her. And they hadn't realized the significance of their location on the Gollerra border. "Look. This job is a big break for me. No way would I intentionally screw it up. Not for any amount of money. This is my career on the line." Stars, she hoped she sounded convincing.

Drake smiled, a grim tug of his lips. "Your denials might be more convincing if you were getting us back on course while you made them."

She nodded. "Right. It'd be better though, if I ran a diagnostic first." There was still a chance that the rendezvous ship might find them if she managed to put out a beacon and stayed put.

"Just do it."

Samantha turned to study the view screen. "First, I'll have to maneuver us out of this system."

Resler sneered. "I'll fucking do it."

The next thing she knew, he was dragging her out of her seat. The air rushed out of her lungs as she hit the floor. She looked up from where she landed, but couldn't get enough air to shout out a warning. Before she could stop him, he took the standard drive controls. The ship lurched. Samantha slid across the deck. She heard Drake slam against something and curse.

At the screeching of the proximity alert, she scrambled to her feet and leapt for the controls. She tried to reach across Resler, but his bulky shoulders blocked her path and he resisted when she gave him a shove.

Something wet dripped into her eye from her forehead. She blinked trying to clear it. She'd been too panicked to notice, but she must've hit her head during her slide across the deck.

"Fuck me." Resler leapt out of the chair. He picked her up and slammed her into the seat. "Fix it." His voice shook.

She was still trying to clear her vision and when she did, she saw the terraforming platform now took up the entire view screen. "Hold on!" She flipped on the intercom to warn Mercury, Carnage, and Diablo. "Brace for impact!" Even as she shouted it, her hands flew across the controls.

"Turn us," Resler stammered. "Fucking turn us."

"I'm trying. This isn't a shuttle. She doesn't respond as quickly."

In the view screen a bit of space opened up. They were turning. Resler sighed as if in relief. He clearly didn't have a good grasp on the size of the *Dove* or how slowly she was turning. The nose of the ship might miss the platform, but her tail would never get clear in time.

Drake got to his feet behind her. Didn't anyone understand what brace for impact meant? Samantha reached back for her safety straps, looped her arms through, then adjusted them across her shoulders.

An obscene scraping sound echoed eerily along the port side of the ship and everything from the floor to the control station to the hatchways shimmied. A sudden jolt rattled her bones and the realization that the hull had buckled clutched her heart in a painful grip. The doors of the storage bins popped open and Samantha put her hands over her head to protect it from the flying debris. Anything that hadn't been bolted or lashed down bounced around the ship like dice shaken in a cup. A cacophony built and dragged on for what seemed like a lifetime but was probably about five minutes then everything went dead silent.

The knot in her chest eased.

She could still breathe and nothing floated around the pilot station so the environmental and grav drives had made it without critical damage. A quick check of the readouts showed the skipdrive at the far end of the ship wasn't even sending up data and hull integrity on the port side was down thirty percent. The emergency pods were on the starboard side, so they should be clear.

Her readouts streamed damage reports. One assured her life signs were stable for all six on board. She quickly weighed her options. She would either have to jump all-in on her determination to free the Arena Dogs or give up her plans and let them be killed. Decision made, she got to work setting things in motion.

It only took a handful of minutes to put her reputation, maybe even her life, on the line. The moment her fingers executed the last command, she used the view screen to check on her passengers in the cargo-bay then climbed out of her chair to check on Drake and Resler. They were on the floor out cold, but not showing any sign of serious injury. She grabbed the emergency med-kit and pulled out two doses of a restorative that would keep them under long enough for what she needed to do. Pulling the cord around Drake's neck, she slipped it free of his shirt. The green code-key for the cage locks pressed coolly against her palm as she pulled the cord over Drake's head. She administered the doses then left the men there and went back to work, blocking everything but getting the ship into orbit from her mind.

CHAPTER SEVEN

The Dove
Earth Alliance Beta Sector - Gollerra Border
2210.157

Mercury choked back a growl as Sam darted through the hatch. His worry had taken him to a special corner of hell the moment he'd heard her shouted warning on the ship's communication system. It seemed he'd been right to worry. A coppery tinge overshadowed her honey scent. Her hair was streaked with blood.

She stopped in the middle of the cargo-hold, her lips tilted in a half smile. "Everyone okay in here?"

Mercury nodded as he reached through the bars and held out a hand palm up. She flicked a cautious glance at Lo as she stepped forward. Everything inside him settled when her warm palm pressed into his. "You're hurt."

She pulled her hand back and pressed her fingers to her temple. They came away wet with crimson, but she shrugged it off. "I'm fine, but those idiots have wrought havoc on the *Dove*." She rubbed her fingers along her dark brown trousers, smearing away the blood as if she could hide it from him. "It'll be okay. I just had to make some adjustments to the plan."

"Plan?" He resisted the urge, the need, to touch her again, but he could feel it building in him like a thirst gone too long unquenched.

"We were supposed to rendezvous with a ship eight days ago.

They were going to help you guys get away from Roma. But things have gone straight to hell and—" She was talking fast and her eyes were everywhere but on him.

"Sam." Her name came out more bark than he intended, so he said it again softer. "Sam."

She frowned and he wanted to smooth away the lines that appeared on her forehead. He reached out and touched the side of her face. Her wince threw fuel onto the embers of his anger and he couldn't hold back his snarl. She flinched and he grabbed her wrist before she could move away. "Never. Be. Afraid. Of me."

She frowned. "Maybe if you didn't growl like that—"

"It's part of me," he ground out. "Deal with it." The words felt right when he said them, but grim pessimism rushed in to wash the feeling away and he wondered if she *could* deal with it—with him— an unnatural creature with the instincts of a beast.

Her arched brows shot up over wide eyes.

He pulled her closer and pressed his face against the bars. He drew in a deep breath letting her fill his lungs. She didn't scent of the whip-master. That cooled his rage enough to relax his hold and allow her to put a few inches between them.

"Speak slowly." He nodded encouragement. "You made a plan?"

She started to shake her head, but the movement was aborted, pain etched into her features. "No," she said. "It wasn't my plan. I was hired to get you to the rendezvous and look the other way when they freed you. Sorry I couldn't tell you before. They told me not to."

Mercury heard Lo and Carn shift in their cages. "Who would— "

"It doesn't matter now. They aren't here and we're going to have to improvise a plan B."

"Another plan?"

Her small teeth bit into her plump bottom lip. "Yes, and actually it's probably more of a plan C now."

He waited for her to continue, his joy that she would try to help them escape overshadowed by the dread of what cost she might pay.

"The rendezvous ship might still come," she said. "But they're over a week late. I'm taking that as a bad sign. The *Dove* is badly damaged, so we're not going far. If we wait here the help that comes might not be on our side, but I managed to put us in orbit around a small undeveloped world."

"Plan C."

"Right." A quick grin flashed across her face like the flicker of a glowbug, there, then gone. Its loss left his world darker, bereft after that tiny moment of light. "The ship is a mess and I think I can make Drake and Resler believe we're losing the environmental controls. I'll convince them to use the emergency escape-pod to go to the surface until help can arrive." She pointed to a hatch at the back of the hold. "There's another emergency drop-pod back there. It's meant for freight, but I think you can survive getting to the surface that way."

He nodded, shocked at the boldness of her plan.

"I need to ask you a question." She held his gaze, but her lips trembled and her jaw was tight. "Drake and Resler. I know you hate them. When you get out of these cages?"

She let the question hang between them, but he saw in her eyes that she knew what his answer would be. Cold washed across him as he realized how she might view the violence, the brutality, that had made him. He was a product of the arena. "I don't know much of your world, but my world offers only two choices. Kill or be killed."

She closed her eyes, shutting him out, and took a deep breath in through her narrow nose and out across soft, full lips. Her lashes fluttered then she was staring him down again. "They forced you to kill, but it doesn't have to be all you are. It isn't all you are." She reached a hand tentatively through the bars and he turned his face into her touch.

Even as he reveled in the gentle warmth of her fingers he worried she'd only done it to test him. To assure herself he wouldn't bite her hand off. That, given the chance, he wouldn't kill them all.

"I've done what was necessary to survive and keep my brothers alive."

She pulled her hand back and a tiny hint of her smile returned. "Are you going to tell me to deal with that too?"

His fists tightened around the bars of his cage. "I'd *never* hurt you."

"If you could be free?" She motioned toward Lo's cage with a quick tilt of her chin. "If you could all be free."

"We all wish for another life, but we cannot change what we are."

She nodded but there was still worry in her eyes. "I don't know where the others were going to take you, but we're not far from Gollerra territory.

"Gollera?"

"Oh. Of course. I wasn't thinking." A slight pink tinged her cheeks. "Roma is in the Earth Alliance territory—human controlled. Gollera territory is under the rule of a race called the Golley."

"Not humans?" The idea of a place where humans did not rule settled into his mind and started to weave into his reality.

"Right. I don't know what your status would be there, but I think you'd have a chance to be free."

Her words hung in the air. Small motes of hope that could surely choke him if he allowed himself to breathe them in.

"Roma won't know you got off the ship. I'll tell them you died in the collision—that the cargo-hold was breached." She backed away, stepping out of reach. She wrapped her arms around herself, as if warding off a chill that couldn't be blamed on her environmental controls. "When help comes, I'll go with them, but I promise I'll come back for you. There's just one thing."

He wanted to pull her to him, to wrap his arms around her, to ease her worries, but she was out of his reach.

"You can't..." She cleared her throat and when she spoke again her voice was steadier, her posture stiff with resolve. "You can't come after them on the planet surface. I know you probably want to hurt them and they deserve it, but it would ruin everything."

He hid the panic her words churned up in his gut. "Your plan is flawed, *courra*, my courageous one."

"How?" The tiny lines appeared on her forehead as she studied him.

"They'll try to punish you. I won't allow that."

"They won't know." She shrugged. "At least they won't be certain." She strode over to a stack of dull gray containers with the red Roma logo and started checking the labels as she spoke. "I'll have to rig the ship to blow out the cargo-hold, to support my story and explain why your bodies aren't onboard. I know it isn't a perfect plan, but it's the best I can do."

He wanted to shake her. The moment the whip-master no

longer needed her as pilot she'd no longer be safe from his twisted games. "You'll come with us. We'll keep you safe." He'd rather be stuck with her on a primitive world for the rest of their lives than allow anyone to hurt her.

"No." She started rearranging the containers, huffing with effort. "I can't. I need to be with them when help comes. And I could never survive the drop in the cargo pod."

"I'll protect you. You'll come with us." The growl was slipping back into his voice.

She shook her head. "There's no enviro in the cargo-drop. The three of you will survive the low oxygen environment to the surface. I'd never make it."

He wanted to howl. "Send them down to the planet and stay aboard with us. You can repair what you've done to the ship after they're gone."

She activated a switch on the hover-pallet beneath a stack of containers and pushed it toward the drop-pod. "The damage to the ship from the collision is too extensive to get her skip-ready and they'll never believe me about the rest if I don't go down with them."

"She's right," growled Lo. "They won't believe her."

Mercury snapped at Lo to silence him.

"Please," she said. "Trust me and be ready."

She stopped at the hatch to the cargo-drop and unlocked it. "I've programmed it so all you have to do is step inside. After it's launched I'll set the cargo doors to blow."

"And you?"

"I'll be long gone in the passenger pod before the explosion."

She pushed the pallet in, disappearing from sight for a moment before returning to stand in front of his cage, but still out of reach. "The supplies will make things easier for you on the surface. Now promise me, you won't come after Drake and Resler. That *none* of you will harm them." His brothers growled softly, but Sam kept her gaze locked to his, body tense as her voice dropped to a whisper. "Please. Prove you aren't the animals they claim you are."

Helpless to bend her to his will, Mercury keened low with worry and pain. She had no reason to think them more than the animals Drake had labeled them. Yet, she had protected them at every turn. That spoke more of her heart than her fear. This plan of hers was set and they had to see this through, but it would kill him if anything happened to her.

"I promise, *courra*. For me and my brothers. We won't harm them." Once spilled the words left a burning hole in his gut. He didn't blame her for the shrieking ache. She couldn't know how many times the whip-master's lash had torn through skin to strike at his pride. How many times watching it dig into the flesh of his brothers had left his heart in tatters.

She nodded, pulling out the code-key. "And you won't try to go after them now either? You'll stick to the plan?"

Her jaw tightened and her eyes searched his face as if she wasn't sure he would keep his promise. He didn't want to, but he had little choice but to rely on her knowledge of how to survive beyond the world of the arena. He nodded. "I've promised. Will you trust me, *courra*?"

"Step back away from the doors." She took them all in at a glance making it clear her command extended to them all. "It's going to be okay," she said, pressing the code-key to the lock.

She moved on to the other locks and Mercury fought instinct. His muscled trembled with the need to claim her and keep her safe. He wanted to shove open the cage door and pull her into his arms even more than he wanted to track his tormentors down and end their lives. The damn woman had him in knots, so he would keep his distance. There wasn't time for what he wanted. What he needed.

As she stepped back, putting as much distance as possible between them, Mercury finally stepped free of the cage and led his brothers to the cargo-drop.

The interior was lit in low red light. He walked inside and turned to see her with her hand on the door.

"You'll be fine," she assured, unaware that she was the object of his worry.

Somehow, he promised himself, he would get to her before Drake and Resler hurt her. As he watched, the hatch swung shut. The click of the lock sealing scraped against his sensitive eardrums like sandpaper.

A jolt threw him against a container. It knocked him off his feet and emptied his lungs of air.

A moment later, the floor fell out from under him. He scrambled for better footing. Bones rattling, oxygen deprived brain screaming in protest; Mercury knew Samantha had been right. She never would have survived the cargo-drop's rapid decent to the planet surface. His belly lodged somewhere near his throat and the vibrations were so intense the ligaments all through his body strained to keep muscle and bone together. Lo and Carn had to be experiencing the same sensations, but he didn't have enough air in his lungs for a whimper let alone a comforting howl.

When it finally came, the sudden deceleration proved no less agonizing. He huddled with his brothers in the center of the space, clinging to the cargo clamps and each other. The bottom of the drop seemed to have some mechanism to minimize the vibrations; if they were fortunate, it would be enough to prevent injury.

Mercury couldn't afford to be injured. Not when he needed to get to Sam as quickly as possible. He would honor his promise not to harm the whip-master or the bully that had tormented Carn, but that didn't mean he'd let them harm her.

The sudden stop of the cargo-drop put an end to his wandering thoughts. For a full minute, he and his pack brothers remained near motionless. The slight huff of their breathing the only sound.

"Ready?" He studied their faces, now back to normal, and could see they knew what he intended. Lo blinked his agreement. It was Carn who hesitated. Was he thinking of Hera? Did he think going after Sam too much a risk when they had to get back to Hera?

Carn dipped his chin in a slow nod.

Mercury pushed to his feet and studied the hatch controls. It wasn't meant for passengers so there was no obvious handle. He slid his hands over the smooth surface, stopping over a red shape. There was writing, but he couldn't read it.

"Why doesn't it open?" Carn's voice showed no trace of his earlier hesitance.

"Maybe it is not yet safe to go out," rumbled Lo.

Mercury's fingertips found a slight unevenness around the red shape. "I think there's something here." He pushed gently at first, then with more force. A small section of alloy sprung open to reveal a recess with a metal ring. The small curve would fit perfectly in the grip of a human hand.

Carn's boots scraped against the floor as he shifted his weight. "Doesn't red usually mean warning?"

"The air grows thin." Mercury knew they had no time for debate. He pulled the ring.

A heavy clunk sounded as alloy shifted inside the hatch. A pop as the seal broke took with it some of his worry. At least they wouldn't all die in a metal canister.

Mercury shoved the hatch wide.

Light filtered in, washing the small space in contrasts of bright and dark. The new scents it carried with it overwhelmed his sensitive nose, but the air was rich. It filled his lungs and cleared his head. He stretched and took a deep exhilarating breath.

Outside, the ground beneath his feet was spongy, but it didn't shift under his weight like the sands in the Arena. He stepped aside to let the others pass, watching as they too enjoyed the richness of the air. Carn stood tall for the first time in many days.

Awash in color, the vegetation surrounded them like a visual feast. Purple flowers decorated the nearest trees. Green and blue-leaved bushes spread across some areas like blankets tossed carelessly on the ground.

Unfamiliar sounds came at him from every direction. Small creatures moved along the ground or up and down the trees. Until he became accustomed to them and the sounds they made, he would have to rely on his eyesight.

Lo crouched down and lifted a handful of dirt to his nose then inhaled loudly. "Smells different here."

"Yes, but the air is good."

Lo nodded his agreement, but Carn shook his head. It didn't appear to be a sign that he disagreed. He looked more like he was shaking water from his ears after a dunking. "Carn?"

"I'm okay." But he squatted down and slumped forward.

Mercury moved to him and rested a palm on his back. "What is it old friend?"

"Can you hear it?"

"I hear many things."

"No." He grimaced. "A low thump, thump, thump."

"Low?"

"Yes. Very."

Lo crouched nearby. "Could it be a natural part of this planet?"

Mercury couldn't hear the thump, but he knew both Carn and Lo had better hearing in the lower ranges. "I don't know."

Of course, this was the first time any of them had stepped onto a planet surface outside the domes of Roma.

Mercury patted Carn's shoulder. "Let me know if it changes or gets worse for you."

Carn nodded as they got to their feet.

Mercury started a slow circle around the drop. Shattered wood covered the area behind the small transport device that had carried them down from a ship above the planet. His gaze followed the trunk of a tree. The cargo-drop had skimmed all the branches from one side as it had fallen to the ground. The top of the tree stretched high over head. Taller than any tree he'd ever seen. There were trees near the Arena Dogs' training grounds, but nothing like this living tower.

The sky overhead was a bright blue and impossibly far away. Somewhere above, the ship they'd fallen from hung in the vastness beyond the blue. He'd been told of space and the distant worlds beyond, but it hadn't been real to him. Standing in the place that was clearly not the same as the one he'd come from, his world had suddenly become vast.

"How will we find her?" Lo spoke from next to him.

Mercury started to speak but a flash drew his gaze to the sky. A puffy white trail of smoke traced across and downward. Mercury pointed. "There. We will find her close to where the smoke meets the ground."

He glanced at Carn again. The man looked stoic and paler than usual, but he stood straight and tall. Mercury could only hope his need to get back to Hera would drive him more than it hurt him.

"Let's go."

CHAPTER EIGHT

Roma Campsite, Planet G-45987
Earth Alliance Beta Sector - Gollerra Border
2210.157

Samantha brushed tree bark off her hands and took in a deep breath. It was the first planetary air she'd breathed in nearly a year and it smelled heavily of vegetation. Dense forest surrounded them on all sides. She'd managed to drop the escape-pod in a kilometer square patch of barren soil.

The cargo-drop Mercury, Carnage and Diablo were in had a much cruder propulsion system so she couldn't be sure exactly where they'd landed, but she'd tried to put them down in the same general area. She had their promise and it was the most habitable spot on the planet.

And her gut told her to keep them close.

Drake dropped another branch onto the small stack of firewood. "What do you suppose made this clearing?"

Samantha reached down and broke the seal on one of the bedrolls she'd hauled out earlier. "Probably the terraforming platform we saw." Or more accurately, crashed into. "There's three more positioned across the planet." The huge equipment had been visible from orbit and easy enough to spot since there'd been no vegetation, or anything else, around them.

"Why in the hell didn't you put us down near one of them? There might have been supplies."

"None of the others are functional as far as I could tell and the areas where the other platforms are located are not nearly as hospitable as this section."

Drake shifted the position of the last log he'd dropped. "Makes sense."

"Not really. It's like they were never activated, or they were shut down after stage one. But the one that was here must have run the full course. The vegetation here is way too advanced for recent terraforming. Who would install four terraforming platforms, activate only one, then let the planet and the equipment sit idle for fifty to a hundred years?"

"I think that's a mystery for another day." Straightening, he stretched his arms over his head with a grunt of pain.

"Hurting?"

"Feels like someone rolled me in a metal washtub and hung me out to dry."

Samantha huffed, surprised he'd admit to any weakness. "You need the med kit?"

"Just bruises. We should conserve the meds. I'll be fine." He hunched down and went back to arranging the firewood.

"That's good, because we still need more fuel for the fire." She used the back of her sleeve to wipe perspiration from her brow. The humidity gave the air a steam-like quality and made it difficult to breath. "From what I could tell from my scan of the planet, we can expect the temperature to drop dramatically with nightfall." She didn't like the idea of being soaked through when that happened.

"We could sleep in the pod, but I guess it's better to conserve the energy."

Samantha nodded in agreement. "Any idea why Resler disappeared?"

After what had happened on the ship, Resler had become quiet, moody, and scarce. When she'd returned from the cargo-hold, she'd found him dazed, but awake enough to help her haul an unconscious Drake into the escape-pod. When the explosion in the cargo-hold had rocked the ship, Resler had panicked. As soon as she'd landed the escape-pod safely, he'd started avoiding her.

"He'll be along shortly. I'm afraid he's not used to roughing it."

Samantha scanned the horizon.

The thick vegetation suggested there could be some small game to supplement the packaged emergency rations. It had to have been some sophisticated terraforming technology. She wasn't worried for herself or the men she'd brought down with her. It was the men in the cargo-drop that occupied her thoughts. They could end up stranded much longer.

Samantha spread out a bedroll where she'd cleared the debris from the ground. "Well, he should probably stick close to camp."

Despite Resler's panic, she'd been able to send out a distress call and set a beacon. When help came looking, they'd find the *Dove* in orbit. They had plenty of supplies to hold them until then, but the newly freed slaves would have far less and they wouldn't be getting off the planet when help arrived. They'd have to depend on her to beg, borrow, or steal a ship to get back.

Samantha stood and moved to spread out another bed roll. "I sent out a message to Roma before we launched the pod." She hadn't wanted to contact them directly, but it would have looked suspicious if she'd abandoned ship without sending something.

"That's good." Drake's voice came from directly behind her.

She fought instinct not to bolt away from him. She needed to keep things friendly. Samantha straightened and turned and found herself practically in his arms.

"I prefer a warm bed and good food myself," he said. "But we'll be fine. We've both been in worse places."

"That's right. The Mitna camp." He ignored her conversational volley, but maybe he'd said all he wanted to on the subject.

She'd been lucky on Haverlee—though she hadn't realized it at the time. The refugee camp had been safer than most. Since she'd signed on to her father's ship she'd seen a lot of ports. The wars of the last century had left displaced refugees scattered on both sides of the border. Most camps were scary, desolate slums. Mitna was one of the worst. When the Earthers had tried to push into the territory of the hive-like Rettans in that part of the galaxy they'd been soundly defeated. The repercussions ended in the destruction of several human colonies. Mitna had exploited the refugees unlucky enough to end up there. It wasn't hard to believe a place like that could turn out such a hard-hearted man.

"It must have been terrible growing up there."

The cockiness drained out of his face, his features melting into a blank mask. "Don't pity me, Sam. At least on Mitna we didn't have to live under the thumb of aliens. You of all people should understand that being born in a camp might be pitiable, but those of us that got out are different from the weaklings that stay there and wallow in the filth."

People with nothing, no education, no skills.

Despite her best intentions, his smug callousness grated on her nerves and her irritation colored her tone when she spoke. "You're always assuming you know me. Yes, I grew up in a refugee camp. Doesn't mean we're the same."

Anger flared, burning away the mask and revealing the side of him that frightened her.

"You're right," he said. "Despite that pilot's license, I've never met a woman so stupid."

She forced a smile. "You're welcome to your opinion."

She had no intention of letting him bait her any further. She was stuck with him and Resler until help came. All too aware of the precariousness of her situation, she tried to step back.

He grabbed her arms. "Don't be a fool, Sam."

"Take your hands off me, Drake."

"You look so pale, Sam. Don't worry. I'm not going to hurt you." There was no rush in his movements when he released her. His smile, when he stepped back, turned her stomach. "In fact, I'd be happy to make sure nothing hurts you. All you have to do is ask."

She didn't understand at first. Then she saw Resler over Drake's shoulder. He'd been watching them, waiting. As Drake turned his back on her and walked away, Resler stalked steadily toward her, intent clear in his eyes.

"Until then," Drake tossed over his shoulder. "I'll be inventorying the supplies. You and Resler can finish collecting the wood for the fire."

Samantha didn't see any sign of interest in wood gathering in Resler's hate-filled face. Back on the ship, while she'd been prepping the escape-pod, he'd ranted and shouted, blaming her for *setting-him-up* to crash the ship.

"Don't forget," said Drake. "All you have to do is ask."

Right. That was going to happen.

She kept her gaze fixed on Resler. His gaze fixed firmly on her breasts as he tugged his top free of his pants.

Without a weapon she'd have to let him get close if she intended to fight him. She might be able to stand her ground. He was an idiot, more brawn than brain, and still recovering from a leg injury. Maybe she could talk him out of the intent in that wild look, shame him into re-thinking his course of action. Maybe she could even out-fight him, but he came from a world that was all about combat. Did she want to take a chance?

Samantha ran.

Not toward Drake and the help with a price he'd implied. Toward the trees.

She kicked her legs and sucked in air. Resler's laugh rang out behind her.

She went for a crowded clump of trees where she might be able to out-maneuver him. She could hear him gaining ground behind her. As she broke through the tree line, vines snagged at her ankles and arms. Leaves slapped her face. She ducked her head, trying to keep one eye on the root covered ground and the other looking for a way through.

Behind her the thwap of brambles slapping against a stampeding body swelled. Saplings snapped, vines scraped along the leaf strewn ground. Resler had made it to the brush. She darted around a tree and sprinted in a new direction. Her lungs ached as she fought for the oxygen her surging muscles required to keep going.

Resler breathed just as heavily behind her. "Fucking. Bitch."

Too close. His voice had come from right behind her. Run. Run. She had to run faster.

Her head snapped back, the hand suddenly jerking her hair seemed to be trying to rip it out by the roots. Momentum carried her forward, pulling Resler with her. Her knees hit the ground as she came to an abrupt stop.

"Got you!"

The tug at her scalp loosened and she crashed forward. She managed to thrust her arms out to protect her face as she hit the ground. Then Resler landed on her, knocking the breath from her lungs.

She scrambled to get away, but couldn't break free. She swung back and her elbow connected with his jaw. He cursed and cuffed her on the back of the head. Her vision blurred and tears filled her eyes in an unstoppable flood.

She tried to make her body move, to crawl, to fight, but her muscles had stopped responding to her commands. Taking advantage of her momentary inability to move, he flipped her over and crushed her into the ground. "Fight if you want," he said. "That only makes it better."

Her throat tightened and bitter acid seeped into the back of her mouth. His arm pressed against her windpipe was making it even harder to breathe. He grabbed at her breast, squeezing painfully with his free hand then tugged at her top. Fabric ripped. The weight of his arm lifted off her neck and she gasped, desperate for air.

"Well damn. What's this?"

He spread her shirt wide and pressed a palm to her belly. She knew it would be an angry scarlet-gold. Too bright for any normal human flush of color. He tugged at one of her sleeves. The seam gave way at the shoulder, bearing the bands of color that stood out in vivid contrast.

"Fucking mutt." He spat at her then pressed his arm back in place and grabbed for the waistband of her pants with his other hand. Apparently, her mixed blood wasn't enough to change his plans.

She willed her muscle control to return, to let her fight. Her heart beat like a trapped hoverbird. The arm at her throat shifted enough to allow one deep breath. The darkness in her vision bled away and everything came back to sharp focus. She squeezed her hand into a fist, grateful when the command made its way successfully from her brain to her muscles.

Samantha put every scrap of strength she could muster into a swing. He dodged her fist but the movement gave her a small opening. She twisted under him and tried to drag, pull, kick her way forward.

His hand caught in her shirt. The ripped fabric pulled tight as he dragged her backward. His weight pressed across her hips and crushed her into the ground. A root dug into her belly. Damp leaves clung to her cheek.

"You're done... you little... bitch." Resler's labored breaths puffed against her temple. His heavy breathing drowned out any sound beyond their two bodies. Each shift of his weight, as he struggled to keep her pinned, as he groped her, created a new ache or jab of pain.

Samantha sucked in what little breath her crushed lungs could hold. The loamy smell of rotting vegetation filled her nose. Broken twigs pricked her palms as her fingertips dug into the moist soil beneath the rot.

She couldn't move and there was nothing more she could do to fight. She promised herself she wouldn't beg.

CHAPTER NINE

Roma Campsite, Planet G-45987
Earth Alliance Beta Sector - Gollerra Border
2210.157

Mercury crouched on a sturdy tree limb. He had a good view of the clearing where Sam was making camp. She moved easily— uninjured, healthy, fit and full of life. He didn't know how long he'd been watching. This new world was nothing like the domed city where he'd been created and trained, and his body had not yet learned its rhythms. Lo and Carn were close by and they would wait as long as necessary.

His ears flicked in concern when Sam's discussion with the whip-master turned tense.

Even though Mercury had known something would happen, rage burned through him when Drake abandoned her to Resler. The instant Sam's body broadcast her intent to flee, he exploded off the branch. The jolt of landing battered his body, but that didn't stop him from launching into a run.

His muscles caught fire as he surged through trees and across the open ground. His surroundings blurred. The scent of Sam, the scent of her terror, filled his head and guided him through the blur.

Then he was there. Sam was trapped face down on the ground. Resler on top of her. Mercury dug his fingers into Resler's shoulder and thigh. Satisfaction soared when he heard the man whimper and scented the stink of the man's piss as he wet himself. Mercury chucked him aside, aiming for a large tree—not so near the collision would kill the bastard, but close enough to provide a rewarding smack.

He shook his body in a head to toe shudder to rid himself of the need for further violence and turned his attention to Sam. He dropped to his knees beside her, bent low to shelter her with his strength, and reached for her.

She scrambled with her fingers and toes to get out of his reach.

"No!" She thrashed, forcing Mercury to dodge kicks and elbows until he slipped an arm under her belly and pulled her back against his chest to control her fear-fueled movements.

Fuck, he should have been faster.

He kept his touch unyielding, but careful not to dig into her already bruised flesh, as he growled softly to his courageous little female.

As her movements stilled he turned her in his arms, one hand cradling her skull. He pressed her face to his chest. Her hot breath puffed warmly against his perspiration-slicked skin, affirming that she was okay, alive and vital to his wellbeing. Nothing had ever felt better.

"Mercury."

"I'm here, *courra*. No one will harm you now."

Her fingernails dug small crescents into his skin as she clung to him. "How?"

He understood the question, but wasn't ready to answer. To risk her withdrawal.

All the times they'd spent with bars between them hadn't prepared him for the reality of her body pressed to his. He wanted to comfort her. To provide a safe haven. He also wanted to claim her. Every instinct screamed that he should bind her to him, punish her for putting herself in such danger. Soothe all her hurts.

He lifted her higher and buried his face against her neck. He pressed his lips low along her throat as he nestled his nose against her jaw line. He sucked in a deep breath, taking in her scent. He'd nearly lost her before they'd even begun.

His heart soared as she allowed his touch. She clung to him until he forced himself to loosen his hold, letting her ease back a few inches. Her hair spilled around her in a riot of color. Her skin began to fade from gold to pink as he watched. Her big green eyes studied him in that way she had. So different from other humans.

No greed. No calculation. No hate.

She blinked and looked around. Her gaze lingered over Resler's unconscious form before coming back to him. "Drake?"

He growled low in the back of his throat. His muscles tightened with annoyance that she would still worry about the enemy. "Carn will have him by now. He'll live. They both will. I remembered my promise. Even if they deserve worse than death."

He stood, setting her on her feet.

Mercury signaled to Lo. His brother emerged from the shadows as he made a chuffing noise in the back of his throat.

Sam clutched Mercury's arm as Lo's gaze brushed across her before he leaned down and pulled Resler over his shoulder. Sam pressed against Mercury's side as Lo padded back to the clearing with Resler's limp body.

Mercury wished he knew what was happening in her mind. Nothing in her scent provided a clue.

Samantha tried to take a step, but stumbled.

Mercury caught her then pulled her back into his arms. "Lo won't kill him."

She took the support he offered, letting him hold her. Relief and worry tangled in a ball in his gut.

"Talk to me, *courra*."

She stood silent. Her body no longer trembling, but still tense. He didn't know what to do, so he held her fragile body against him and waited for her spirit to return. Instead, all her heat drained away. The bands of color had turned ivory. He rubbed her arms, trying to chase away the chill.

"You're alive, *courra*. Alive and beautiful and strong."

She gave him a shaky smile, but something dark and lost still lurked in her eyes.

Mercury wrapped his hand around hers and led her back to the clearing. Carn and Lo had tied Drake and Resler, back to back. Carn still knelt next to them, wrapping a length of nylon strapping around Drake's feet.

Drake glared at Sam, his eyes hard as stone. "Lying bitch."

Mercury let out a low bark. Carn responded without hesitation, reaching up and backhanding the whip-master. The man's lip burst and blood spilled down his shirt in fat drops.

Drake spit blood, but didn't cry out. All the times the man had taunted him, urged him to show no mercy, rushed in and layered across his vision so he saw not only the man but every glare, every threat, every sickening smile of satisfaction the man had ever used to chip away at his soul. Mercury wanted to hear the whip-master whimper and every way he could make that happen rushed into his thoughts in a black surge of hate that made his muscles twitch and his pulse pound.

Resler had regained consciousness. He whimpered, one arm wrapped around his knee and rocking where he sat. His other arm hung limp. Blood seeped through what was left of his shirt sleeve and white bone glistened through a rip in the material.

Sam held herself still at Mercury's side. Would she reject him at the evidence of their brutality? This small hint of what he carried inside him?

She cleared her throat and he held his breath awaiting her verdict.

"Is everyone okay?"

Mercury stood spine-stiff. "Their injuries will heal. They'll recover, even on this unfamiliar world." He'd wanted to tear them apart, but he hadn't. "I deem them not harmed. I have kept my promise." He dared her with his eyes to dispute his claim.

She met his gaze squarely. "I was asking about the three of you."

He sniffed, searching for the scent of deception but found only lingering fear and beneath that, sweet honey. His throat tightened with the choking grasp of relief. "We're fine."

"I'm glad." She wrapped her free hand around his forearm and brushed her fingertips across the sensitive skin on the inside of his wrist. "You also promised to stay away."

Her whispered words turned relief into a knot that twisted and shifted low in his gut. "We didn't breach their perimeter until they threatened you."

Her fingers continued to stroke him softly. "But you must have been close."

The part of his brain that had become accustom to demands and obedience and the never ending threat of punishment heard censure and accusation in her words, but the reasoning, thinking part caught the thin far-away tone. His primitive male instincts thought only of the touch of her fingers across his pulse. It was a touch of submission and soothing—a mate's touch.

"It was necessary," he said, jumpy and confused by all the

warring parts of himself. "I knew they couldn't be trusted to keep you safe." He couldn't think clearly. Not when she was touching him that way. Not when he needed badly for instinct to be right. Not when she could turn on him at any moment.

Samantha reached up and cupped his cheek. "I'm glad you choose wisely in how to keep your promises."

The tight muscles along his jaw relaxed. The knot in his belly eased. He closed his eyes and reigned in the need to revel in the small victory. His instincts had been right or nearly so. They urged him to give into the need that had been building from the first scent of her. Instead he turned into her touch and pressed his lips to her palm. He wanted to lick, to nip, to taste, but there would be time for that later.

He turned back to the others. "Grab what you think we'll need, but leave them enough to survive. Destroy all their weapons."

"You're never getting off this fucking planet," Resler shouted. "You're all fucking dead."

Drake's voice was cool fire. "If the emergency rations run out we'll need weapons to hunt for food."

Mercury slipped free of Samantha's hand and strode over to Drake. He squatted down and got in the other man's face. "This world has plenty of grubs. Be grateful for what you have. Isn't that what you always told us?"

The stubborn bastard denied Mercury's need to see fear in his eyes. No, the whip-master wasn't done causing them trouble, but there was little he could do about that looming threat. Not without turning Sam against them.

It took only a few minutes to gather the things they wanted to carry and to dismantle and destroy the weapons. Mercury watched Sam closely. She moved with a heartbreaking deliberateness as she used the med-kit to treat the scrapes and bruises that marred her soft skin.

After she'd finished and packed it away, he led her over to the water supply and urged her to drink.

"You must drink while you can. With all we carry we can't carry the water, too."

She nodded and said nothing. She chugged the water as if downing a noxious medicine.

"Please, *courra*. Tell me what's troubling you.'

"Everything's changed." Her lips barely moved as she spoke

soft and low and with none of her usual spark.

The urge to shred something with his hands flared fierce and bright. He didn't understand what she was trying to tell him, but it rocked him to see her so lost.

"You regret aiding us."

"No." She shook her head in short, fast movements as if she couldn't negate the idea fast enough. "No. It's just…they know you're alive now and there's no way to undo that. I promised to get you off this planet and now I don't know how…" He watched as she stopped, collecting her thoughts. She reached back and braided her hair as if putting her appearance back together would give her strength. "There's no way to know who'll turn up to rescue us and what might happen when they do. Even if we figure that out, now Drake and Resler know that I'm part Cerrillian. My career is over. I know it's a stupid thing to be worrying about. Stupid and selfish."

Mercury flexed his shoulders, trying to escape the heat of his brothers' scrutiny. They all knew what needed doing, but he refused to break his promise. He caught her chin and made her meet his eyes. "It would be as nothing to us to take care of that problem." The cream she'd wiped across her bruises only made her seem paler. "Think of all they've done. All they would have done. It would be just."

"No." She spoke clearly, but her voice shook.

He swallowed back the need to demand she free him from the heavy chains of his oath. He hadn't expected her to agree, but he'd had to raise the option. At least she hadn't run screaming. He released her chin and pulled her hand up to study it. She'd used the sealer on the deepest scratch.

"Does it hurt?" When she didn't answer, he sniffed at her palm then licked a path along the angry red line that ran from the base of her first finger almost to her wrist. He swirled his tongue up to her pulse point and laved her skin. Mercury sighed in satisfaction when heat bloomed under his tongue and the color came back into her cheeks.

Lo edged closer. "If we're done here, we should go." Samantha jumped at the sound of his voice, but her spine quickly stiffened. She was still uneasy around Lo, but Mercury knew she wouldn't give in to her fear. He let hope flicker. There'd been no venom in his brother's voice and no question of whether they would take her with them.

Samantha would come to trust that Lo was not her enemy. Not now. Not after all that had happened. Lo might still be filled with rage and hate, but his loyalty was unquestionable.

Mercury strode to the edge of the clearing and waited for them to follow.

Samantha moved as quickly as she could. She didn't want to slow them down. The terrain beyond the clearing wasn't treacherous, but brush crowded beneath the taller canopy of trees. Where the brush thinned, roots gnarled the ground. She wished she had more grace, but her big heavy boots were designed for metal decking. Here they only weighed her down, making it difficult to step over vines and downed branches.

As they moved through the wilderness, she had the time to wonder at the beauty of the three men. They'd all been so sullen during the time she'd visited them on the ship. In motion, all the fluid beauty of their animal natures came to the fore. Alert and watchful, their movements seemed effortlessly coordinated. Despite the danger they faced, they seemed more relaxed than she'd ever seen them. Even Diablo. Lo—that's what Mercury had called the rage-filled man.

Back onboard the ship she'd done some research and learned they'd been part of a five "Dog" team that performed together. *Performed.* What a weak and awful word for what they'd been born and trained to do. They were killers and she could see the lethal power surging through muscle and sinew as they flowed across the ground like natural predators.

But they hadn't killed Drake or Resler and they hadn't hurt her in any way. There was a bond between the men that was as clear as the sky overhead. Despite the disparaging comments Grande Owens had made, their relationship was one of strong, abiding, loyalty—something she valued.

When they stopped by a creek to let her rest, the sun's light had grown dim and they could no longer see it overhead through the canopy. They looked as if they could continue indefinitely, but she knew they had to be feeling the strain. She had no idea how far they'd already traveled that day before coming to her rescue.

"My turn to feed you." Mercury handed over a standard issue emergency ration bar. His lips tilted up on one side in a half smile.

She took the offered food then dropped a purification tablet into the water pouch she'd found in one of the packs. "How did you find us?"

He took the container from her hand and studied it.

"For water," Samantha explained.

"Ah." He dipped it in the stream. "We landed first. We watched the sky," he said, "and saw your pod blaze overhead."

She nodded. "Where are we going?" They'd certainly seemed to be moving forward with a purpose.

"Back to the cargo-drop." Mercury passed the container back to her. "There are more supplies there."

"Makes sense." She swished the water in a slow circle to dissolve the tablet then took a small sip. "We must be close, right? It took you guys less than a day to cover the distance."

They'd made it to where the escape-pod had landed in plenty of time to save her from Resler. A twist of remembered fear roiled in her belly. If they'd landed too far to get to her in time... She shivered and realized it wasn't only that terrifying thought. The moisture on her skin ensured she couldn't ignore the cooler air coming with the sunset.

"At this pace we should make it in more than twice the time it took us to reach you. If we're able to find it again." Carn pressed another ration bar in her hand. "You must keep your energy up, Sam."

She smiled her thanks and offered the water to him.

His nose wrinkled. "You keep it," he said.

She chuckled. "That's the purification tablet. It will keep you from getting sick from the water here."

"Our physiology is resilient. I will risk drinking from the stream without your smelly chemicals."

She laughed and took another sip from the pouch. The slight bitterness of the purification tablet coated her tongue, but she'd had worse. "I guess your sense of smell and taste are more developed than mine." She shrugged and took another swallow. "Are we making camp here then?"

"No." Mercury drank cold stream-water from his cupped hands. "I wish to be farther from Drake and Resler before we stop."

Samantha tried not to be distracted by the ripple and flex of corded muscle as he scooped the water. "You tied them up. Do you think they could be following us already?"

"It's safer not to underestimate the whip-master."

She suppressed a shudder at the title. "You're worried because I'm slowing you down?"

Carn shook his head. "If they come, we can deal with them."

Mercury stood and held out a hand to help her up.

"So how did you guys get to the escape-pod so fast?"

"We ran," Lo spoke softly behind her and Samantha flinched but held her ground.

She'd lost track of him at some point. On the ship, he'd been impossible to ignore but now he seemed to melt away, a silent shadow hidden among the boisterous night creatures awakening around them.

"You must have incredible speed and stamina." Her voice sounded nervous and jittery to her own ears.

Carn nodded.

A sigh of regret escaped across her lips. They'd be better off without her. "Okay. I guess we better get moving."

Mercury shook his head. "You're still tired."

She couldn't argue. "And getting chilled. Moving will probably help that part." She attempted a grin, but knew they'd see through it. "Look, if I stay still too long, my muscles will probably revolt when we start moving again."

A tug on her braid startled her and she twisted to see Lo's fingers slip away. Her eyes widened at the seemingly playful gesture from the always-intense Lo. He stared back through eyes that had gone almost completely black in the low light. There was no growl, no fire, only the tip of his tongue peeking out to spread glistening moisture across his lips.

He reached for the pack she'd been carrying without a smile or any acknowledgement of that tug. "Allow Mercury to carry you and we'll make it to the cargo-drop much sooner."

Samantha turned to Mercury for confirmation and he nodded.

Carn added his own nod of encouragement and took Mercury's pack, then slung it over his shoulder.

"Are you ready, *courra*?" Mercury whispered the words as if he wanted to help her disguise her discomfort, though she knew they could all hear him.

She took a deep breath and put a hand on his muscled shoulder. "Okay."

Mercury turned to give her his back and bent his legs.

Samantha hesitated. "Are you sure about this?"

He growled in that odd way he sometimes did. "Now."

"Okay, okay." She wrapped her arms around his shoulders.

As he straightened to lift her onto his back, she pulled her legs up to let him position them where he wanted. Big hands gripped under her thighs and he seemed to sigh as she leaned into him. A quick nod to the others and they were off again, the heat of his body easing her chill—something she was increasingly grateful for as the temperature dropped.

They followed the path of the stream into the night. They moved more slowly after the sun went down, but they didn't stop until the moon also slipped out of sight. When Mercury finally set her on the ground, she couldn't see a foot in front of her. She heard Lo and Carn moving around, then Mercury was pulling her down to the ground. Instead of cold earth, her hands brushed against one of the thin thermal blankets from the emergency supplies. Mercury pulled her onto his lap and she went without hesitation, eager to press herself back into his body heat.

"N-no f-fire?" Her chattering teeth made it hard to speak.

"Not tonight." Mercury pulled her closer, tucking her face against his chest. "We'll keep you warm." Mercury nuzzled into her hair as he answered. "Rest."

She was surprised when he didn't lie down, but she was too exhausted to question. Another blanket settled around them and she heard the rustle of the synthetic fabric as the others lowered beside them. Somehow it seemed easier to let them get close in the dark. Still, she jumped when one of them tugged on one of her boots.

Mercury made soothing noises as the heavy weight slid off. She jumped again when strong hands tucked her cold feet against a warm torso.

"Be calm," Mercury whispered. "Lo only wants to keep you warm."

Lo. The man who'd seemed so dangerous was warming her feet on those washboard abs of his. And in the morning she expected to see the white rabbit her father had often warned her wandered around alien landscapes leading young girls into trouble.

She took a deep breath and relaxed, resting her head on Mercury's chest. None of them had hurt her. Lo hadn't even snarled at her since they left the clearing. She smiled in the dark. Maybe getting out of the cage had improved his disposition. She wouldn't count on it lasting.

"Sleep." Mercury's voiced rumbled softly near her ear. "We'll keep you safe."

It would be the first time she'd slept planet-side since her father's death. Samantha allowed herself a moment to think about the *Dove*, orbiting somewhere above them. This job had gone all wrong. It was supposed to put her back in control of her future. Instead it had taken away any hope of the dream she'd been working toward her whole life.

There'd be time enough to worry over that after they were found. Snuggling into Mercury's warmth, she let his heat relax her muscles and let her worries slip away. For now she would live in the moment.

This wasn't the time to worry about the white rabbit. Not when she'd already gone down the rabbit hole.

CHAPTER TEN

Arena Dogs Campsite, Planet G-45987
Earth Alliance Beta Sector - Gollerra Border
2210.158

"I can't wait to actually wash with real water." Stepping around a small crate of supplies, Samantha chuckled, happy with the thought.

With the added speed of carrying her, they'd made it to the cargo-drop only a few hours after sunrise. The creek that trailed alongside their path had lead to a river, ensuring they'd have water nearby. In under an hour, they'd hauled the most critical supplies up a small rise where they'd set up a makeshift camp. Shielded by a convenient arrangement of boulders, their campsite was completely hidden to anyone looking up from below but they had a clear view of the river and the cargo-drop landing site.

Carn straightened from where he'd been searching through the stores for more thermal blankets. "The river is wider and better for bathing a short distance upstream."

The muscles of Mercury's chest and arms flexed as he tugged on the waterproof tarp she was helping him lash over the shelter frame he'd built. "I'll take you there later."

"Sounds great." She tied off a knot on her side then traced her fingers restlessly over the rough seam at the edge of the tarp.

His gaze drifted from her face to her hand. The heat in his eyes made her want to snatch her hand out of sight. Ridiculous, as she wasn't doing anything to provoke that look.

Mercury growled and the sound was oddly suggestive. "Yes, *courra*. I want your hands on me and I can think of little else now that there are no bars between us."

Startled by his boldness, she stepped back and looked for the others.

Carn had been watching them, but he looked away as their gazes met. Before he did, she caught a trace of sadness in his eyes and remembered Resler saying something about Carn grieving for his mate. Carn's mate, not their mate. She hated that his grief—his and his alone—reassured her. The way Mercury talked to her, touched her, she couldn't deny she wanted to believe he felt something for her. Something more than gratitude or kindness. Something he wouldn't be feeling if the mate Carn was grieving was also his.

Despite her feelings, she wanted somehow to soothe his pain. Going on instinct, she went to him. She reached out and laid her hand on his chest. "Carn, I—"

He stepped back as if her touch burned him. His attention locked on Mercury ignoring her standing right in front of him. "I'll double back to check on the whip-master."

Mercury joined them and clamped a hand on his shoulder. "Observe only and return quickly, my brother."

One quick dip of his chin and Carn was gone, running back toward the Roma campsite.

Samantha squeezed her hand tight, cringing at the guilt that squeezed her heart. "I didn't mean to upset him."

Mercury pulled her hands to his face, rubbing them against his cheek. "You're not the source of his pain."

"He's mated," said Lo.

Samantha shifted her stance to look for him. She hadn't even known he'd come into the camp. Some kind of small animal, already skinned, hung in his hand. She didn't want to think of how he'd caught it. As far as she knew, they'd destroyed all of the weapons. However he'd done it, he'd been quick and he'd gotten back in time to see her exchange with Carn.

Carn, who longed for his mate. She understood the pain of longing. She'd seen a similar pain it in her mother's eyes every time she said goodbye to Samantha's father. Her mother had loved him more than he deserved and every parting had broken her heart a little more.

No matter how painful, she didn't see how it explained Carn's reaction to her touch, but maybe for them it did.

"Let's go to the river now." Mercury's rough voice pulled her out of her thoughts. "Lo will have the food prepared when we return."

His catch in hand, Lo stalked toward the neatly laid fire she'd started earlier. "You should wash before the light is gone and the cold returns."

He'd apparently already taken advantage of the river. His hair glistened wetly and hugged his head. Beads of water still traced down his shoulders to follow the leanly defined curve of his pectorals.

Samantha ducked under the tarp. "Uh, a bath now sounds good. Let me get a change of clothes." Luckily, the escape-pod supplies had included a couple of one-size fits all tops and bottoms. They'd be big on her but she'd manage. Unfortunately, *all* didn't include genetically engineered gladiators. Mercury, Lo, and especially Carn were too broad and muscular, so they were out of luck.

The walk to the water didn't take long despite the lush vegetation. The pungent mix of foliage and the gentle swish and splash of the briskly flowing river tumbled together to create an exotic oasis like nothing she'd seen before. For some species it would be a paradise and her vow to live in the moment let her bask in its beauty.

Mercury led her to where the river widened and reeds and willowy trees gave way to a grassy verge that led to a shoal, the perfect place to walk out into the current.

Samantha dropped down to the soft grass to pull off her boots and jacket. Mercury didn't even bother to take off his flex boots before wading out to the center. He only had the clothes he was wearing and they probably needed a bath as much as he did, but she'd been hoping to get down to her skin.

She eyed Mercury as he dipped below the surface then popped back up, shaking his head. Even with only his head and shoulders above water, his presence couldn't be ignored. She'd spent the day wrapped around him and a little turned on by the countless small touches he'd used to ensure her mind was focused on him as they hiked the alien wilderness. The way his hand would slip along her thigh or a finger would stroke along the sensitive bend behind her knee.

Samantha shook away the thoughts, but the lingering heat low across her belly wasn't so easy to dismiss. Stars, what was wrong with her? She'd never been sex-obsessed nor had she been prudish or shy. She huffed out a breath. Tired of over-thinking it, she pushed back to her feet and stripped down to her under-tank and briefs. Decent enough. She stepped into the cool water and waded out a few feet then moved down stream. She dunked her dirty clothes into the clear water and rubbed them briskly, wishing she'd brought cleanser.

"You're not bathing." Mercury had worked his way closer until he stood blocking the setting sun.

She looked up, but his face was shadowed, his body silhouetted against the brighter sky. "In a minute. Wanted to get these clean first so I could put them by the fire tonight to dry. We could be here a while and I only have one set of real clothes. The emergency gear is going to be like trying to wear a tent."

He reached down to her upturned face, still a shadow looming over her, and threaded his fingers through the lock of hair that had been falling into her eyes. He twisted it and smoothed it back from her forehead. "How long do you think it will be before someone comes to look for us?"

"I'm not sure." His question reminded her that she still had no plan for that eventuality. "I'm more worried about who they'll be."

"We'll deal with it when the time comes."

She nodded and returned her attention to her washing, glad he wasn't one to panic or fret. She chuckled under her breath at the thought of a fretting Mercury.

"What makes you laugh, *courra?*"

She looked up again and her retort caught in her throat. While she'd been lost in her thoughts he'd moved, letting the sunlight pour over him, and he'd stripped out of his pants. Her mouth went dry as desert sand. She'd gotten used to the men being bare-chested or at least learned not to stare too hard or too long no matter how enjoyable the sight, but Mercury in all his naked glory made her temperature spike. Knowing the bands along her arms would be shimmering with spreading flecks of gold did nothing to ease her discomfort.

She'd known the long, heavy muscles of his thighs were there, of course. His pants were form fitting and hadn't really covered much. But bare, those muscles drew her eyes directly to the part of Mercury that was wholly, impressively male.

She was silently thankful for the cool water. If he'd been fully aroused she might not have been able to recover. Unselfconscious, he squatted down in the water to mimic her washing technique. Now that he wasn't standing up, the water was deep enough to cover the most distracting parts of his anatomy.

Samantha managed to pull her eyes back to her washing. Mostly.

After a handful of minutes, he stood abruptly. "Enough clothes washing." He pulled the clothes from Samantha's hands and strode over to the river bank to deposit the lumps of cloth and his boots in the grass.

The view of him walking away was no less distracting. Firm muscles worked as he moved, making her think of how he'd feel beneath her calves if she wrapped her legs around him as he lay over her in a sexy reversal of the way he'd carried her that morning.

"Sammie," she muttered under her breath, "you've lost your mind."

She tried earnestly not to stare as he walked back. He didn't stop, only took her hand as he went past and led her into the deeper water.

Mercury turned her away from him and urged her to lean back. "You still have blood in your hair," he explained as he worked the water through the strands and gently rubbed her scalp. Samantha closed her eyes and let the gentle strength of his touch wash over her as the cool water moved around her in a wet caress.

His hands slid to her shoulders, stroked down her arms and brushed along her ribs. When she could no longer feel his hands she straightened and turned. He was as still as a boulder in the current. She let her gaze take in the tense muscles of his shoulders and the bob of his Adam's apple. He looked at her like the parched earth watched the rain cloud on the horizon, as if he could soak her in and have his thirst quenched.

He pulled her into his arms and she let him. "I hated letting you go with the whip-master and his bully. Hated watching you walk away to face them alone."

"You probably thought I was such a fool to believe I could handle them." She'd held her own in some of the most dangerous ports in the sector, but she'd badly misjudged her ability to manage Drake and Resler.

He cupped his hands around her jaw and urged her to meet his gaze. "I thought you were brave. You have the courage of a Dog."

His head dipped as if to press his warm lips against hers. Anticipation trembled through her. She hadn't been aware of wanting him to kiss her, but in that moment she couldn't think of anything she wanted more. He stopped a centimeter from touching her, keeping the small space between them, but breathing softly against her lips. Her need to have her lips on his, to stroke her tongue along his, swelled and became urgent.

His lips brushed hers as he spoke. "I thought you a worthy mate."

Samantha blinked, the word jolting her. "A mate?"

He stiffened and released her. "You don't want a Dog."

Samantha reached for him. "I didn't say that." Hurt etched severe lines in his face as she rushed to explain. "It's just that you're practically a stranger."

She struggled to explain the panic that had hit her at hearing the word—*mate*. "I know how seriously you take your bond to your mates. I've seen how Carn is tortured by it. I was surprised to hear you use that word."

The pain on his face was clear in the fading light. "I want you."

Her heart melted, twisted with yearning and thudded with a rote fear of reaching for what she wanted. "There's a difference between wanting someone and wanting to make a commitment to someone. You barely know me. "

He stroked fingers across her cheek. "I've wanted you from the moment I scented you. My people value every moment of life. When you face death daily you learn not to waste time."

He seemed so serious and sad. It tightened the need gripping her heart. "My people believe in building a relationship first."

"No," he said, shaking his head. "Human women often came to the arena kennels to be pleasured. They were from your world, but they didn't want to know us first."

Samantha cringed. "That's awful. Er, I mean…" She didn't want to insult him.

"You're right, it was awful. They kept us chained because they feared us, but they wanted to take their pleasure. When I was young, they would touch my body until my flesh was so hungry for release I couldn't resist. As I grew in strength and wisdom I learned to control my needs until they could no longer use my body against me."

Samantha wrapped her hand around his and pressed it against her lips. "I'm so sorry for the way they treated you."

"It doesn't matter now."

"Of course it does." She kissed his knuckles then twined her fingers with his. "But I can't change what happened to you. All I can do now is treat you with the respect you deserve."

"Pushing away what we both want isn't respect, *courra*. It's my choice to pleasure you and we aren't strangers. I know you, Sam."

"No. No you don't. You don't even know my name. No one who knows me calls me Sam. Someone I was going to—"

"Allow to pleasure you?"

"Yes," she agreed. "That person would know that and much more."

He released her hands and traced his fingertips up her arms. He lingered over the slight variations as his fingers found each of the smoother bands of golden skin. "I know you, Samantha Devlin."

She clutched at his ribs. "How?"

He smiled down at her. "Your friend introduced you to the whip-master the first time I saw you."

"And you remembered?"

He nodded then leaned down to nuzzle her jaw.

She strained on tiptoes, chasing the delicious sensation.

He spoke softly, his lips against her neck. "I've listened to you speak for many days. I've slept with your scent filling the air. I've dreamt of your smile. Tell me what name to call you and then I will be free to pleasure you with my hands, my lips, my body."

She closed her eyes at the images his words conjured.

"Samantha is fine." It slipped out before she could think it through. "But that doesn't mean—"

"I scented your arousal at the camp, Samantha." Her eyes popped open, appalled to see him looking confident and sure of her. "You'll allow me to pleasure you."

He lifted her off her feet, his big palm wrapping around her thigh and hitching it around his hip. The heat of his body pressed intimately against her chilled flesh, waking every nerve ending.

He pressed his lips to her forehead in a gesture both sweet and scorching. "I ache for you." Lusty agony laced through the quietly spoken words.

She cursed low. "Damn it, I can't think straight when you say things like that."

A rough chuckle rumbled in his throat as he lifted her higher then licked a path down to her collar bone. "There's no need to think right now, Samantha."

He was seducing her. The man who'd known nothing but violence was seducing her and she had to acknowledge she wanted to give in, to be seduced. His hands skimmed her thighs on their way to her ass. He squeezed, urging her to wrap herself more tightly around him. His hands felt huge on her body as he held her close and headed toward the riverbank.

She stroked her palms over his shoulders and the bunching muscles of his arms as he carried her out of the water. The moment he stopped on the grassy bank, he leaned in to take her mouth. It wasn't a light, easy, getting-to-know-you kiss. It was a kiss of pure possession. He licked her lips and pressed his tongue past them to stroke deep inside. She met the thrust of his tongue, needing everything he offered. He growled into her mouth and her stomach did a little flip in response.

Maybe he'd been right. Suddenly, thinking didn't seem so important.

Her whole body arched into him as she kissed him back, tangling her tongue with his. Her pebbled nipples were crushed against his chest. The sensation sent a jolt of pleasure down through her belly.

She broke the kiss and buried her face against his neck, panting for breath. Her dampening center begged for more sensation. She fought and failed to control the instinct to rock her hips, seeking relief for her swollen, needy flesh. He widened his stance and adjusted her body so his cock pressed more squarely between her thighs. The firm press of him proved how quickly he'd overcome the effects of the cold river. With the thin cloth of her briefs the only barrier between them, he had no trouble working his hard length against her with maddening precision.

She moaned, helpless to the sensual hunger. No man had ever taken her over so completely. Made her so needy that the world faded away and she could believe that having her meant more to him than simple release. That he might want her—the mixed-blood girl from a refugee camp—enough to care as much about giving her pleasure.

His fingertips traced up her spine with gentle thoroughness, as if taking inventory of each delicate vertebra. His other hand burrowed beneath her snug under-tank until his fingers found the hardened tip of her nipple. His fingers stroked and circled the nubbin, sending spirals of heat down to the soft flesh pressed against his hardness.

She rocked her hips again and he growled. Her stomach did another crazy flip as the growl softened to a rumble and he lifted his chin to give her better access to his throat. The sound vibrated against her lips where they pressed to the tight skin. A shiver raced through her. She opened her mouth and laved her tongue over the spot then licked along the cord of muscle. She followed it down to the vee at the base of his throat and dipped her tongue into the hollow.

His hands were suddenly back on her ass, gripping, controlling, encouraging the slow dip and roll. She clung to his shoulders as his body moved against her, grinding his cock against her swollen flesh.

He dropped to his knees in the soft grass, his arms banded tightly around her, and stopped. Their chests heaved as they both panted for air. Her head came up and he met her gaze, his big thundercloud eyes shining with intensity, the lines of his face strained.

"You feel so good, Samantha. I need my cock inside you, now."

There had been no question, but the alert, carefully leashed passion in his face spoke louder than his words. He wanted her, but he needed her permission. He would know how important it was for permission to come from her heart and her head. The body could be manipulated, fooled into unwanted pleasure, and he wouldn't do to her what had been done to him.

She slipped her hands down the muscled planes of his chest and gave a gentle push. His arms loosened immediately and she read anguish in his eyes until her hand continued down. Her fingers dipped briefly into his belly button, drawing a muffled groan as his abs jumped, before continuing on to wrap around his cock.

He moaned louder, thrusting into her grasp as she squeezed and stroked down and then up the long, broad length. His jaw tightened, the muscles in his neck straining in sharp relief, as if he thought she might be teasing him before turning him away.

"I want you too, Mercury." She smiled, remembering his earlier words about how he'd dreamt of the simple gesture. "I want to feel you inside me."

That was all the permission he needed. He tugged at her clothes, stroking her skin as he pushed and pulled. He turned her naked body away from him and positioned them with her back to his chest, his knees between hers as he sat back on his heels. She leaned back into him and wrapped her hands around his muscled thighs.

It was probably a mistake to have sex with him, but she couldn't deny them both. She knew his life had been cruel, but she'd seen for herself that he could be gentle and protective.

His hands came around to lift her breasts. "You're so beautiful, *courra*." He rubbed his palms over her nipples then lifted her breasts again.

As she tipped her head back with pleasure she realized he was tall enough to have a clear view of her body over her shoulder. His chin pressed against her temple as one hand stroked down to play in the wet heat between her legs.

"Tell me again you need me inside your body." His fingers stroked over her clit and pressed slow circles into the sensitized bundle of nerves.

She could barely breathe to get words out. "I need you. Please."

His fingers circled faster, relentless.

The pleasure was too intense and instinct had her bucking against him. She tried to close her legs against the unbearable pleasure but his knees were between hers and his body moved with her as she writhed.

"Please, Mercury. Please." She had never begged a man in her life, but with him there was no pretense, no walls between them. Mercury's raw, blunt need had swept her into a moment where nothing mattered but the demands of their bodies. And her body ached with a need only Mercury could fill.

He bent her forward until she was on her hands and knees then moved his knees outside hers, lowering his hips to match hers. The heat of his body never left her. The blunt tip of him pressed against her opening. She was beyond wet, but she had a moment of panic as he pressed forward. He was big and she was small.

He eased back, perfectly attuned to her body. "I'll go slow."

He adjusted his hips and pressed forward again. This time his cock stroked along her folds, brushing her clit.

She panted at the pleasure. A low rumble started in his chest and vibrated down her spine. He stroked across her clit again, then adjusted his cock and pressed against her opening. This time she was ready for the pressure, eager to be filled.

"Yes, *courra*. Open for me."

He eased in, her body stretching to accommodate him. He pulled back then eased forward again. And again. Her body took him more easily each time. Took him deeper. When his cock filled her completely, he pulled his hips back a few centimeters then shoved forward hard as if, after all that gentleness, he needed to claim her with one brutish thrust.

She yelped at the pleasure-pain of it.

He nipped at her shoulder, teeth scraping across delicate skin. "You're mine, Samantha Devlin."

He pulled out and thrust hard again.

His hips slapped against her ass.

It was too much. So much that she feared the pleasure would overwhelm her.

His voice roughened as he wrapped himself more tightly around her, sliding one hand between her legs to press two fingers firmly over her clit. "You're mine."

"Yes," she urged. "Yes."

His teeth nipped at her shoulder again, near the base of her neck, then clamped tightly around the narrow strip of muscle.

Her mind quieted and her pussy clenched around his cock.

A growl rumbled in his chest as he began to move in a steady rhythm that had her keening with pleasure until she thought her knees would no longer support her.

Pleasure swelled and pulsed like a bubble made of a thousand glorious colors and destined to burst. Orgasm washed over her, drowning her in sensation. Lights danced behind her eyes. Mercury fucked her through the powerful waves of pleasure, drawing it out until he lost his rhythm. He bucked wildly. His hands slid to her hips, keeping her ass pulled tightly against his groin as he straightened, threw his head back, and howled, his cock pulsing deep inside her.

This wasn't the mournful howl she'd heard before. This time the sound rang with triumph. Another howl echoed nearby. Lo wasn't far. At least close enough to have heard their moans.

Knowing Lo might have been witness to their passion did nothing to diminish her bliss. Later she would worry over how easily her lust drenched mind accepted the possibility. Chest heaving, pleasure still pulsing through every molecule of her body, she couldn't find the strength to be indignant.

CHAPTER ELEVEN

Arena Dogs Campsite, Planet G-45987
Earth Alliance Beta Sector - Gollerra Border
2210.158

Samantha lay languid, satiation lingering like the sweet aftertaste of fresh picked red-berries. After collapsing to the ground, she'd rolled to her side. Mercury pressed along her back, his body curved around her, his heat holding off the cold bite of the evening air. One hand stroked over her hip.

His breath brushed against her temple. "Are you well, Samantha?"

She reached back and stroked her thumb across his lips. "I'm fine."

"The bands on your arms are bright gold and your skin is warm and golden across your abdomen."

"It's normal for me." She glanced down to where his fingers traced lazy circles over the tender stretch of skin below her belly button. Her abdominal muscles jumped and twitched beneath his touch. Until the flush of gold faded she'd be hypersensitive.

He pressed a kiss in her hair. "Time for my Cerrillian biology lesson?"

She laughed, but as the feeling faded she realized she wanted to tell him about her past, her heritage. It wasn't something she shared with anyone outside her family and her father's crew, but Mercury wasn't just anyone. "My grandmother was Cerrillian." She took a moment to let the familiar surge of pride and sadness settle. "They're one of the humanoid species that populated this part of the galaxy before the Earth colonists arrived."

"I've never heard of them, *courra*." Mercury pulled her more tightly against his body and she knew he must have sensed the pain behind her words. "Where are your people now?"

"Gone or scattered."

She'd never even known her Grandmother, but she knew she died fighting. "Full blooded Cerrillians have slightly different coloring and a compound in their skin pigment that changes with the chemical surge that accompanies emotions. Other than that, biologically, Cerrillians and Earthers are a lot alike. I guess that's why they targeted Cerrillia for colonization. The atmosphere and climate were perfect for Earthers." The old grief threatened to choke her. "They were overrun by the settlers and very few escaped."

"I'm sorry, *courra*." His warm lips brushed against her temple. "This is why you hide your heritage?"

"If you have Cerrillian blood, you can't be a citizen of the Earth Alliance. Non-citizens can't hold licenses for anything. Everything from shop licenses to pilot's certifications are prohibited."

Mercury's forehead furrowed as he frowned. "You wouldn't be allowed to be a pilot?" His voice was a rumbly whisper, as if he were talking more to himself than to her. "You risked much for us."

Samantha turned in his arms. He looked so worried—it made her heart swell with affection. She nipped at his jaw then held his gaze. "I'd do it again. No regrets."

He nodded then pressed his lips to her forehead. They held each other tight, listening to the sound of birds give way to the hidden orchestra of insects. Samantha wanted to hold onto the moment. The closeness. But an inevitable chill rippled across her skin as the heat of their lovemaking seeped away.

"Come," he said, helping her stand. "We must return to camp."

She gloried in the easy way he helped her dress. His gaze appreciative, his hands guilty of a dozen seemingly accidental brushes against her skin as he helped her tug on the oversized top and pants from the emergency supplies. He rolled the hems of the too long pants and braided her hair, showing her a side of him that had been unavailable to her when he'd been trapped in a cage. It turned out his black, knee-length pants were made to dry quickly so he was able to put them back on without discomfort.

When they got back, Lo sat by the fire sinking his teeth into a golden brown hunk of roasted meat. The smell of the meal set her stomach to rumbling. She hadn't had real meat since—she couldn't remember when. She and Mercury sat across from Lo in companionable silence, enjoying the meal he'd provided.

After she'd eaten her share, she tossed her bones into the fire then went to wash her hands using water they'd brought back from the river. Lo's eyes tracked her every movement, stirring the familiar unease he generated in her so easily. But the more time she spent with the newly freed Arena Dogs, the more the nature of that unease changed. She was no longer afraid he'd hurt her, but her senses told her he was still a threat.

When a shadow fell across her, where she crouched by the water, she knew it was Lo even before he spoke.

"You should stretch before you sleep." His rough voice always seemed to be on the verge of turning into a growl. "You're not used to so much physical exercise, Samantha."

Inwardly she cringed at his use of her name. There wasn't any hint of innuendo in his tone, but she searched her memory, trying to recall whether Mercury had called her by name after they'd returned to camp or if this was his way of letting her know he'd listened in while she and Mercury had been making love.

"You're right," she said. "I'm not used to hiking planet-side, but Mercury carried me most of the way." Aside from the embarrassment she knew she should feel, she worried over how the new intimacy in her relationship with Mercury might affect Lo. She knew his anger hid some deep hurt and she didn't want do anything to cause him pain. His expression revealed nothing of his feelings. "You guys haven't been able to get much exercise the last few weeks either," she added. "The hike will probably be more of a problem for the three of you."

His head dipped in a nod. "I already spent time stretching, but you should let Mercury help you."

"Sure. Why not?" She shrugged. She knew ships top to bottom, but they probably knew a lot more about the body.

She was out of her element while they seemed right at home. Sure, she knew about living primitive. She'd cooked over a flame often enough in her youth, but she was more used to bargaining with an unscrupulous vendor at market than chasing after game in the woods. For Mercury and Lo, the chance to run free... Hell, this place had to be light years better than being a slave. Samantha stood and moved aside so Lo could wash.

As she returned to stand by the fire, she studied Mercury. He crouched atop one of the boulders, holding his palm up near his face. A glowbug had landed on the tip of his index finger. The glow of its body stood out like a spark against the night sky. They were the one creature that seemed to be on every planet in some form or variety. Mercury studied the tiny insect with as much intensity as she studied him. She wanted to climb up on the rock and wrap her arms around him, but she also wanted to soak in the sight of him there.

"We should probably talk about where you want to go after we leave here."

Mercury shook his hand and let the bug fly away before jumping down and meeting her gaze—direct and open. "We must return to RomaRex , Samantha."

"What?" Samantha's legs threatened to buckle and a sudden urge to vomit almost doubled her over, but she kept her back straight. "I did all this to set you free. How can you even think of going back?" She knew her voice was rising, but she couldn't stop it. "They were going to kill you!"

Mercury stalked toward her. "I can never convey how much I, we all, value your courage in helping us."

His words snuck through the prickly thicket of worry and anger that had sprung up between them. Unfortunately, she couldn't so easily dismiss either emotion. His revelation had doused her heart's defenses in quick-grow.

He gathered up her fists and cradled them against his chest. "But we must go back."

"Why?"

"Carn's mate. I swore I'd keep her safe." His voice had gone throaty and brittle. "We can't leave her in that hellish world. Besides, hiding, running while others suffer. That's not our way."

"But you can't storm the arena and free them all. Maybe if you explain to the resistance—"

"I gave my promise, Samantha. I swore to my brother I'd protect the life of his mate. Me. Not this resistance that hasn't even appeared. I can't leave Hera there."

"Carn's your brother?" Samantha twisted her hands as if she could ring away the emotions that swamped her. "He's your family?"

He shook his head. "Not as you mean. Carn and I don't come from a common bitch and sire. We aren't biological brothers." He looked thoughtful. "It's possible we share some genetic donors, but we can't be sure. It doesn't matter. We're brothers in spirit. We were raised in the same kennel and have stood together against all comers for all of our lives."

"You don't know who your family is?" Samantha freed a hand and lifted it to stroke away the tension that had crept into his neck. She squeezed, pressing her fingers into a thick ridge of muscle that crossed to his shoulder. "What did they do to you?"

"We were created to serve the masters of the arena. We were carried and birthed by surrogates. Female slaves from a distant world. They looked nothing like us."

"You remember them?"

"They stayed with us until we reached five years of age—until we were old enough to begin training for the arena. They weren't unkind, nor did they consider us their children."

"What happened to them?" Another race had been enslaved to create them. That had to be illegal.

Lo joined them by the fire, poking a stick into the flames. "We never saw them again after we were taken from the juvenile center to the kennel, but we were told they'd be used to birth more Dogs and after a span of years more Dogs were brought to the kennels."

It was probably the most words she'd heard Lo string together at once and all said without anger. That just seemed wrong. "You should stop calling yourselves dogs. Like you accept the way they treated you. You're not dogs. You're men."

Mercury smiled, showing his teeth. "We're what they made us—Arena Dogs—but we're also men and I'm glad you accept us as such, my courageous Samantha." He pulled her into his arms and kissed her. His lips were warm and confident. He should have been a broken man or a thoughtless beast. She didn't understand how he'd become the man that could kiss her as if touching his lips to hers was the most important thing in the world.

It started tender and gentle but quickly turned into a firestorm of want and need. His tongue plunged between her lips and claimed the moist recess of her mouth. She stroked her hands across his body, still fascinated by the smooth texture over hard muscle. His flat nipples pebbled at her touch and a rumble started deep in his chest. The vibrations against her palm made her own breasts tingle with awareness. She wanted to press against him, skin to skin.

Mercury pulled back, letting her catch her breath. Along with the air she pulled into her lungs came a rush of awareness. She'd forgotten they were standing in the middle of camp. Lo sat at the fire, watching them.

Stars, she'd lost her mind. She'd been ready to have sex with him again. A man that planned to return to hell and risk his life to rescue another woman. Pain twisted like a knife in her gut. She couldn't let him mean so much to her so fast.

She lowered her voice, knowing Lo would hear anyway. Somehow, truth could often be spoken more easily in a whisper. "I can't do this. And even if I could, I wouldn't in front of Lo."

"I can tell him to leave."

"No," she said. "Wait." She put a hand out to stop Lo who'd already started to slink away. He snarled at her touch and she jerked back and wrapped her arms around herself, suddenly chilled and feeling defeated.

Lo's features softened. Slowly, he extended a hand and brushed his knuckles against her cheek. His lips parted as if he'd speak, but in the end no words emerged. He let his touch speak for him.

Samantha unfolded her arms and took his hand. "We all need sleep."

Both men huffed at her as if they were equally incredulous. She laughed, despite the sadness that had seeped into her bones with the night air. "Sleep," she insisted.

Mercury sighed heavily. "Yes. Sleep."

She doubted any of them would rest well and it would have nothing to do with the cold.

CHAPTER TWELVE

Arena Dogs Campsite, Planet G-45987
Earth Alliance Beta Sector - Gollerra Border
2210.159

Samantha woke warm and comfortable despite the achy state of her body. Probably not as achy as she would've been if she hadn't given in to Lo and Mercury's badgering about those damn stretches before collapsing onto the pallet. Regardless, the warmth was good. With Mercury's big body wrapped around her and several layers of thermo blankets over them, her muscles were looser than she had any right to expect.

His heavy arm draped over her ribs and his fingertips had found the bare strip of skin between her tank and briefs. She tried to shift out from under his arm, but he growled softly and pulled her closer, her ass nestled against his groin.

"Sleep while you can, *courra*. The sun will rise soon."

"Where are Lo and Carn?" They'd made one big pallet, so Lo had crawled in with them and slept curled up on the other side of Mercury but he was gone now. She'd expected Carn to return before nightfall but he'd never crawled into the shelter—at least not that she remembered.

"They're close." He hesitated, rubbing his chin against the crown of her head. "If you can't sleep, I can pleasure you instead." He rocked his hips for emphasis and Samantha's heart sped at the impossible to miss press of his hard cock against her ass. His hand drifted lower on her belly and she grabbed his wrist to try to stop him. His hand didn't even slow. He stroked downward to slide across her briefs and cup her mound. She groaned and arched into his touch against her better judgment.

"Mercury, no."

He froze. "Are you injured?"

"No, I'm fine, but—" She struggled for words then huffed out her exasperation. "Where are my clothes?"

With a sigh, he released her and twisted to reach for her things. The blanket stretched across his hips, but it was easy to see he was still sporting an erection.

He followed her gaze as he pressed her clothes into her hand. He stroked one hand along her leg. "I want to pleasure you again."

Her stomach did a traitorous flip at his directness. She pulled her shirt on over her under-tank then flipped her hair free from her collar. Mercury relented, letting her move away. She scooted to the edge of the pallet and tugged on her pants and boots then twisted her hair into a quick braid while he dug through one of the packs.

Lo and Carn appeared out of the trees as she got to her feet.

Fatigue had smudged dark half-moons below his eyes and his hands hung limp at his sides as if he no longer had the strength to resist gravity. He lumbered into the camp, exhaustion weighing down every step.

"Stars," she swore. She strode toward him but stopped short, remembering his distress at her last attempt to touch him. "You need to rest and get some food." She pointed to the circle of crates where they'd eaten their evening meal. "Sit. I'll get you a ration bar."

Carn sat with all the grace of a mining platform trying to dock with an orbital tug. "They show no signs of coming after us."

Lo frowned. "That's not like the whip-master."

"You destroyed their weapons," Samantha pointed out, "and you reinjured Resler."

Mercury turned thoughtful. "They might believe they're better off waiting until help comes."

"True," said Carn, propping his arms on his thighs and leaning forward to let his head hang low.

Mercury brushed past her, the casual touch of skin like a secret caress that refocused her attention squarely on him. The whisper of touch reignited all of her nerve endings.

She strained to focus. "It will probably be a couple of weeks before anyone makes it to this system and comes down to look for survivors."

Samantha dug through one of the crates and handed Carn his meal. He took it, but she thought his wince and the lines etched in his face were less an aversion for her and more... evidence of pain. "Are you okay?"

He nodded unconvincingly then took a bite from the bar. Samantha sat down on the crate beside him, careful not to touch. "There's a med kit in my pack. If you're hurt, please let me help you."

He stared back at her, head titled to the side as if she were a strange bug who'd crawled into the middle of his dinner. The lines carved into his prominent forehead were deeper than she remembered. The ring of gold around his black eyes, wider than she'd seen. His ears, more rounded than Mercury's or Lo's, lay flat back against his head.

She forced a careful smile. "We're going to be here a while, but we *will* eventually get out of here. You need to stay strong."

His head swung back toward Mercury and his gaze landed heavily.

Mercury frowned. "The low-noise."

Carn's head dipped to hang down from his shoulders. "It never stops."

She'd been right. Pain. It sat heavily on his shoulders but the big lug wouldn't say the word out loud. "I'll get a pain blocker—"

Before she could get to her feet Mercury appeared in front of her. He crouched next to where she sat, his knees brushed hers and his broad shoulders dominated her field of vision.

"No drugs." His face was tight, leaving no room for discussion.

"Okay." She touched his thigh, some instinct driving her to reassure him—and nodded through her frown. "Is there something else?"

His face softened. "No, *courra*. We're used to pain. He'll be okay."

She scowled. "He doesn't look okay." Mercury's thigh muscle hardened under her hand as he slipped one of his knees between hers. A move guaranteed to focus all of her attention on him.

"Leave him to me. We take care of our own."

She rolled her eyes. "Oh, we're back to that. I'm the outsider again." She tried to move away, prepared for a good rant, but he gripped her hips and pinned her in place. He said nothing but the frustration still etched into the brackets around his mouth made it clear he had no interest in the fight she offered. It hit her then, the deliberate way he gently squeezed her hips and the measured distance, or lack of, he'd kept between them.

Samantha stroked along that tense thigh muscle under her hand. Was he feeling unsure of her because she'd ignored his offers of early morning sex? A part of her wanted to soothe away his concerns, but her head reminded her some distance might be called for.

"So what's up with this low-sound?

"Our hearing is different from humans. We can hear in a wider range. Carn is hearing a low pulse."

If quiet sounds made them ill, they'd all be sick all the time. "When you say low, you don't mean not loud, do you?"

"No," said Mercury. He tapped a spot near the bottom of his breastbone and growled out a bass note. "Low here." His eyes shifted to Carn and back. "I think this one is like a small tap." He lifted one had to brush a line down her nose then tapped three times lightly on her forehead. "Even a soft hit will cause pain over time."

"And he's been getting tapped since?"

"Since we arrived here."

She turned to Carn. "Sorry to be talking about you like you aren't here, but *stars* you big lug, shouldn't you go lay down or something?"

He laughed. Carn laughed. The rich sound eased the tension that has been thick moments before. Without a word he got to his feet and headed toward the shelter.

Across the campsite, Lo leaned with his but against a boulder— half sitting, half standing. He looked fine. Tightly wound, but that was Lo.

Samantha squeezed Mercury's thigh. "But you and Lo are okay?"

He nodded. "We aren't all alike in our abilities...or physiology."

His voice trailed off as if the uniqueness of their genetic make-up was disconcerting or maybe just a reminder of their genetically engineered status.

Samantha wrapped her hands around his jaw. "Maybe I should

call you snowflake."

"I don't know what that is."

"Well, I've only seen them once. They were beautiful. Millions of them. Ice crystals that fall from the sky. My father told me each flake of crystals is unique, but when you look at them together after they've fallen, they all make this uniform blanket of white that's spectacular."

Mercury kept silent, but his eyes had widened and they sparkled with wonder as he met hers.

"I hope I get to see them some day." Lo's voice drifted across the campsite like a lazy stroke. She looked up to see him staring at her as if she were the snow.

"Me too." She smiled hesitantly at him before turning back to Mercury. "I think you're talking about what I'd call low frequency or infrasound. You can make those kinds of sounds too, can't you?"

He frowned.

"Back on the ship, I detected a low frequency sound coming from the cargo-hold."

The wonder left his eyes and his checks flushed. She didn't bother to tell him that she'd somehow felt it. That part still didn't make sense. Sure she'd always been more sensitive to the vibrations ships made, but no way could she hear low frequency.

"Yes," he said. We can make them and Lo and I can hear them, but Carn's abilities in that area are much stronger."

"So, what are we going to do about this?"

"I don't know, *courra*. If it's part of this world, what can we do about it?"

He'd only ever been on Roma before and inside a habitation-dome, so it shouldn't have surprised her that he might think something like this was natural. "I suppose a planet could have a low frequency background noise for some reason, but you said it's a steady tap. That doesn't sound natural to me."

"You said the planet was uninhabited." Small frown lines creased Mercury's forehead and his thigh muscle tensed beneath her hand.

"As far as I could tell. I didn't see any sign of civilization. But somebody terraformed this world. That means someone was here at some point, even if it was just the terraforming crews." He seemed to be following and his frown lines had started to disappear, so she didn't stop to explain terraforming. "It could be some old piece of machinery causing the noise."

"Something we could stop," he said.

"Yes. And if Carn's this sick after two days…"

A look passed between Mercury and Lo.

Mercury put a finger under her chin and his eyes locked on to her face. When he looked at her that way she had no idea what he saw. All she knew was that he wasn't thinking of her as a hated human and it wasn't lust either.

The moment stretched out until she had to fight not to lean into him.

Lo shifted and made a chuffing noise. "When do we leave?"

"Carn needs to sleep," answered Mercury. "We should hide the supplies. We don't know how long we'll be gone or how long the whip-master will decide to wait before he comes looking."

"You could travel faster without me." Samantha did want Carn's pain to stop as soon as possible, but she didn't really want to stay behind.

"We stay together." Mercury's answer came quick as lightning. No hesitation. No indecision. "I have a feeling you'll prove useful."

She couldn't help but grin. "I was hoping you'd say that."

He looked skeptical. "Because you enjoy long hikes on unknown planets."

"It might just be some wreckage or space junk, but if it is something left behind by the people who terraformed this place, it's been here a long time. And the terraforming platform we ran into…it didn't look like any design I've seen before. I'm curious as a sand-cat about who they are and why they've left this place to sit so long."

He tapped her nose. "You do realize if we find it, we'll be destroying it?"

"Yeah. Of course." She sobered. "I don't want Carn to suffer any more than you do."

It hurt that he could doubt that. Setting them free may have earned her some acceptance, but that didn't make her one of them and she needed to remember that. Right now they needed her. Maybe Mercury even wanted her. But things could change. She'd learned that the hard way. They were smart and strong and they had each other. When they adapted to their new-found freedom, got off the planet, they might not need her. When they had a choice, their gratitude wouldn't bind them to her.

Samantha went through the supplies and pulled together what she thought would serve them best. She planned to distribute them between the packs they'd taken from the escape-pod. First, she distributed everything else among the indestructible, meter square cargo cases, making sure each case held a variety of supplies. That way, if some of the cases were discovered and stolen while they were gone they'd still have the things they might need. Mercury and Lo carried the cases into the woods in different directions while Samantha filled up their packs and turned off the cargo-drop's beacon. There was no real way to hide the bulky drop, but they worked together to pull limbs over and around it to make it less visible.

Samantha used the sleeve of her shirt to wipe sweat from her face. "At least they won't be able to spot it through the trees. They'll have to stumble across it."

Lo swept a small branch across the ground to scatter leaves and obscure the evidence of their efforts. "Even if they do, it will do them no good."

Mercury lifted the packs and slung them over his shoulder. "It is better that they have fewer clues for finding our supplies or setting a trap."

Lo growled softly in the back of his throat. "The whip-master would be a fool to try to take us now."

"Yes," agreed Mercury. "But we don't know how long we'll be gone from here. By the time we return others might have joined him and brought weapons. Never underestimate the opponent."

Lo scowled, his lips pulled back to display his prominent canines. "You use his words?"

"He's no fool and what he taught us is no less true now that we're nearly free of the man. It would be senseless to set aside those teachings now."

Lo humphed, transforming his face back to the less threatening Lo she'd been learning to appreciate. "True, but I don't need his words from your mouth just now. Reminds me too much of how badly I want to rip out his throat."

There was a brief moment of silence that made Samantha feel awkward and in the way. Mercury had to feel the same as Lo. Only he didn't say it because she was there. There was something wrong in that, but she wasn't sure exactly what. Did she think he was wrong to hate Drake? No. Drake deserved their hatred. Was it that she thought their easiness with the idea of killing made them evil? No, but she wasn't exactly comfortable with it either. She knew she couldn't expect them to think about things as she did.

Mercury's breath on the back of her neck pulled her out of her thoughts and focused her attention on the shiver of pleasure that skated down her shoulders.

"You're thinking too hard. Unless you are thinking of letting me pleasure you before we leave, it might be better to return to camp and help the others break down the shelter."

She looked around and realized they were alone. She hadn't noticed when Lo left and she hadn't noticed Mercury moving to stand behind her either. She turned to face him and looked up into those stormy eyes. The skin at the outside corners crinkled with humor. Sweat glistened on his skin. Just looking at him made it harder to breathe. She had to fight instinct to keep her hands at her sides when all she wanted to do was follow the contours of his muscles with her fingertips.

When she spoke her voice was less steady than she'd have liked. "Camp."

He put a hand out to indicate she should go ahead of him. She took her time climbing the slight incline to avoid the need for him to steady her. She could feel the weight of his gaze with every step.

CHAPTER THIRTEEN

Arena Dogs Campsite, Planet G-45987
Earth Alliance Beta Sector - Gollerra Border
2210.161

Mercury measured the path of the sun across the sky as Samantha had taught him. Midday. They'd been traveling for two days and those days felt as long as any he'd known in his life under the dome of Roma. Carn still lead the way, though both he and Lo could hear the pulse now. Even Samantha, who claimed not to hear the noise, clearly suffered its effects. The pain in her head etched tiny lines in her normally smooth brow. She'd claimed to have detected his moans of pain on the ship. Seeing her wince with each step, he knew it had been more than her machines that had detected his cries of pain.

Samantha stopped to catch her breath, putting her hands behind her head as she inhaled deeply. "Is it me or is Carn looking worse?"

Mercury looked down into Samantha's face. "He's lost much of his color."

"And I can't remember the last time I saw him hold down food or water." Her small hand rested on his arm as it had more and more through the morning. He laid a hand over hers.

"His physiology can handle the dehydration better than a human." Longer than one small female. But Carn couldn't fight off the inevitable dizziness and loss of consciousness forever. His steps were already clumsy.

Samantha accepted his judgment of Carn's condition and tilted her lips in a pained smile. "At least the ground here is level."

After a day and a half of steady climbing, they all welcomed the more level terrain. There were fewer trees and the underbrush was more sparse making it easier footing.

She looked in the direction they'd been travelling as if she could see a clear path instead of the next rise less than a day's walk ahead. "Seems like some kind of plateau."

"A plateau?"

She turned her attention back to him. "Sometimes I forget you've lived all your life on a flat rock under a dome. A plateau is a place in a mountainous area that has…well, level ground." She laughed. "Probably sounds silly to give it a special name, huh?"

He shrugged. She could call it whatever she liked. He cared little. But her smile put a salve on his worry over the fiery flush that dotted her cheeks and ringed her neck. He pressed the back of his hand to her cheek and found it several degrees too warm. "You need rest."

She rolled her eyes at him. "I'll be fine. And don't even think of offering to carry me."

Her gaze drifted to Carn and her smile faded. He knew she was thinking that she was no longer the one slowing them down.

"Carn grows weak, but so do you, *courra*." He cupped her cheek and forced her to meet his gaze. "We should turn back. You didn't feel the effects of the pulse back at camp."

"But Carn did."

He could see in her eyes that she understood the truth. Turning back might alleviate her pain, but only going forward to disable the pulse would help Carn. He knew, too, that she worried for his brother. Worried for them all. He wanted to tug her close and rub his face against her cheek. To press his nose behind her ear and fill his lungs with her scent.

"It was wrong of me to ask this of you."

"You didn't ask."

She stepped in close, so close he could feel the heat of her fever before she rubbed her cheek against his arm.

"Then I shouldn't have allowed it."

"What would you do?" She looked up at him, so close he could see the striations in her bright green eyes. "Would you sit back and watch him get worse every day? Maybe die?" She pulled her hand out from under his and twined their fingers together. "If you could do that, watch a friend die, you wouldn't be the man you are."

He'd never known a female with such a generous spirit. The submissive females of his race, like Hera, obeyed and served because they knew no other way. Their spirits were more broken than soft. The gladiatrix females among them knew the same bonds of loyalty as the males but they were few. He'd not even spoken to one since forming his pack.

One moment he was reaching out to pull Samantha into his arms and the next the ground shook under his feet. He bolted toward where Carn had stood seconds earlier.

He'd heard Carn's inrush of breath, his panicked scramble, and he'd reacted on instinct. Lo had responded much the same. Mercury passed him only a few paces before he reached the edge of the level earth, where the ground had opened up and swallowed their brother.

The ground beneath his feet gave way. Instead of fighting against the fall he dove into it. He caught his breath as he slammed, head first into the funneling brush and let it drag him forward. His heart beat like the swell of a blood thirsty crowd on arena night.

The earth closed in around his waist as he burrowed his arms deeper into the freshly loosened soil. The reassuring sensation of Lo's grip closing on his ankle kept him searching blindly for any sign of Carn long after his air had run out.

No! His mind raged as his body panicked at the lack of oxygen and he began the work of digging his way free. The moment he surfaced he sucked in a lungful of air, breathing deep. His gaze skittered across Lo and settled on Samantha. She lay at the edge of the collapse, one arm wrapped around Lo's leg. "Spread your weight out." Samantha strained with effort.

Mercury wanted to crawl up Lo's body and drag her away from the danger, but fear pinned him in place. He copied the arms and legs spread position that Lo, who'd likely already gotten this instruction, had assumed.

Mercury growled up at Samantha. "Get away from the edge."

"I will, if you'll climb back up," she bargained.

He had no plans to give up on Carn so quickly. He just needed to know she was safe.

"You need the rope." She started to edge back, as if she fully expected him to obey.

"She's right." Lo's eyes were dark with worry.

"Move slowly," Samantha shouted down. "And keep your weight as spread out as you can."

When he looked around him he saw nothing but freshly disturbed ground. Vines. Rocks. Branches. They all twisted up from the fallen earth like the skeletons of the restless dead. Carefully, he climbed upward, Lo moving beside him with equal care. When they reached the top, Samantha shoved the pack into his hands.

"He's alive," said Lo. "I can hear him."

"Conscious?" Mercury dug into the pack for the rope.

"I don't think so."

Despite the answer, Mercury called out using both standard and low sound. There was no response. Not even a moan.

Samantha, put her hand on his arm. "We have collapses like this in the dunes outside Haverlee. The dirt had to go somewhere. There's probably a void below us. Carn could have ended up in one."

He looked back to Lo. "Can you tell how far below you heard him?"

The other Dog shook his head. "Not close."

"There's a lot of earth to dampen the sound. It may not be as far as we fear." At Lo's skeptical look, Mercury indicated for him to back away.

"I'm lightest. I should be the one to go down." Samantha's fear laced voice came quick and breathy.

"No." He valued her concern, but he needed her safe and that need fueled the one clipped word.

She bristled as if she would argue, but seemed to think better of it. "Okay. But we've got to get him out of there."

He started tying one end of the rope around his ankle and passed the other end to Lo who started tying the other end around a stubby but sturdy looking tree. Mercury headed over the edge, belly crawling as the torn earth shifted and settled beneath him.

A tug on the rope let him know when Lo joined him. He didn't stop until the rope pulled tight against his ankle.

Lo scrambled over his back. "He's further down, but—" Lo rolled over and down below Mercury, gripping his hand with complete faith as he threw himself beyond the rope's reach.

"There's something here."

Lo began to dig one handed into the side of the ravine just below where Mercury lay at the rope's end.

"What is it?" Mercury couldn't see anything but Lo's efforts had sharpened to focus on a small area.

"A passage, I think." Lo's head and shoulders disappeared into the dirt or so it seemed from Mercury's position. He tightened his grip on Lo's hand. He breathed a sigh of relief when Lo reappeared. "Take my ankle."

Lo turned and Mercury grabbed the offered ankle, stretching his body to give Lo as much distance as they could safely manage. They both knew if it came to it, they'd simply lose the rope and go back to working without it. They were not prepared to lose another brother.

Lo scrambled back out. "There's a cavern below. It's large and I can hear Carn breathing. Roughly."

Mercury waited, knowing there was more. If it were that simple, Lo would already have gone into the cavern.

"I can't fit. This small channel is between two layers of rock." He twisted his body reaching a hand out. Mercury quickly switched from his ankle to his hand. "It's too narrow for my shoulders."

And if it were too narrow for Lo, Mercury certainly wouldn't fit. "We'll find another way."

Lo nodded. And crawled closer until they lay so close they could feel each other's breath. "Release me then." The whispered words had to be for Samantha's benefit. Lo could probably hear her moving around above. Mercury could hear little above the pounding of his pulse in his ears.

"Does it feel stable beneath you?"

"Stable enough. Release me."

Mercury forced open his grip and watched his brother scramble away.

"What are you doing?" Samantha's strained voice drifted down from above.

Mercury turned to release his ankle from the grip of the cord. He could see her on her belly above looking over the edge. He wanted to shout or snap at her, but he wouldn't risk startling her. "It's more stable down here now, but the edge is dangerous. Back away."

Her face disappeared, but he'd bet she didn't go far.

He scrambled on his belly again, this time following Lo's path.

"He's below here," said Lo. "Do we risk collapsing this area over him?" Lo's dark eyes telegraphed his trust and willingness to follow.

Nothing in the arena had prepared them for this. "It didn't collapse when I dug there before, but we can move to the side a bit. We have no choice but to dig."

Carefully they began to scoop the dirt away, hoping the weight of the dirt being moved wouldn't cause the very collapse they hoped to avoid. Mercury could hear Carn now. His breath was ragged and strained.

They dug and dug. The dirt had been loosened and moved easily, but there was a lot of it and every time the dirt shifted, more would tumble in to fill up the hole. They worked in silence as the sun overhead marched steadily down the sky.

He couldn't be sure how long they'd been digging when they heard Carn moan. His breath turned into a pant of panic.

"We're here, Carn. We're going to get you out." Mercury spoke loudly, but avoided shouting. The area around them had become less and less stable as they'd shifted the dirt around.

Carn calmed below, but he didn't answer. They dug faster…until they heard a shower of earth fall free below them. The surface where they lay didn't shift but they heard Carn sputter and spit.

Mercury tried for calm as he called out to his buried brother. "Are you okay?"

"Yes." The strained word drifted up alone at first. "The dirt above fell. Can you work faster?"

"If we do, more dirt might fall down. Can you move to the side?"

"No." Again the one word set heavily in the air for a moment. "Leave me."

Mercury had no intention of leaving him so he ignored Carn's command and continued to work.

"I won't be able to walk," Carn shouted up. "I'm safe where I am. Let me stay here and heal. " A cough interrupted his speech.

Mercury wanted to tell him to save his breath, but he knew Carn was no longer thinking clearly.

"Go and shut down the noise," Carn continued. "I know you can both hear it now. When I'm stronger I'll climb out."

Mercury gritted his teeth against the slow boil of frustration. "This is taking too long."

Lo tilted his head, ears flicking. "He sounds weaker."

"Fuck."

"He could be bleeding out." Lo's raspy whisper faded into nothing.

"Hey, guys?" Samantha's voice drifted down again as it had several times as they dug. The concern in her voice had changed to something more urgent. "Do you think you're going to break through anytime soon?"

"We have more digging to do."

"I was afraid you were going to say that. Watch out below, I'm coming down."

"No!" Mercury added his growl to his voice but it was too late. She was already over the side and moving down the rope. A small part of the edge collapsed in and tumbled down around them. Not enough to harm, but enough to make it clear that the area could collapse further at any moment.

Mercury belly-crawled over to the rope and steadied it as she crawled down ending in his arms.

"You shouldn't have come down."

"I didn't have a choice." He wanted to argue, but her fingers on his lips stayed his lecture. "There's a storm coming. I've been watching the rain moving our way for the last hour."

"Rain?" He looked up to see the trees shaking.

"Yes. The water will come pouring down here in an hour or so. We're running out of time." Her knuckles were white where she gripped the rope, but he didn't think it was a fear of falling that had her so tense.

"You can't be down here." He was grateful for her warning, but he wanted her safely back up the rope. "This area could collapse."

"I know," she said. "Right on top of Carn."

"If we dig faster we could create the same result."

"I heard Lo say there was a passage down here."

Up. Why wouldn't she go back up? She knew the need for speed. "The passage is too small."

"Let me try."

"No." The response came automatically, but her offer meant he could no longer dismiss the possibility he'd been unwilling to contemplate.

She took one hand off the rope and reached for him. "He could be bleeding or trapped. If I can get down there I could stabilize him. Maybe move him to a safer part of the cavern. Then you could dig faster. We don't have time to argue."

Mercury cupped her face. "My brave *courra*. If anything happens to you—"

"I'll be careful," she interrupted.

Careful. He doubted it. It seemed she was always jumping into trouble. If she'd been careful they'd still be headed to the hunt planet. "Spread your weight across the ground and wait until I free the rope."

Samantha's browse lifted. "The rope?"

"You're not going down there without some way for me to pull you back."

Mercury made sure she was in a stable spot then scrambled up the side of the rift. Working quickly he untied the rope and tossed it down to Lo, who'd moved into position near Samantha. He knew she was still uneasy with his troubled brother, but she fought to accept him. If anything happened to her... He had no idea how to finish the thought. She was human or close enough to have lived her life as one. She should mean nothing to him, but she had quickly come to mean everything.

Samantha waited impatiently as Lo tied the rope around her waist. "Where's the opening?"

"Just below."

As he released her he crawled down and over then reached out a hand to guide her. She hesitated only a moment. She no longer worried he might intentionally hurt her, but it was hard not to fear those claws.

When she took his hand, he guided her to a narrow hole that hadn't been visible from above. He moved closer pressing against her and increasing her heart rate.

"Don't be afraid. This area is more stable because of the rock."

She wasn't sure it was fear that made her heart pound. Every time he got near, her insides tightened and every place he touched her burned.

He tugged at her pack and she shrugged out of it. The opening was narrow and dark and too tight for her to wear it, but she clung to one strap.

"If he's hurt, I'll need the supplies," she explained.

He released it with a nod. "Push it in front of you."

His hands returned to her waist. She pushed the pack into the darkness then reached in and gripped the cool rock. The rough surface scratched her palms as she pulled herself forward. Strong hands slipped from her hips down her legs as she worked her way forward.

Her shoulders fit easily into the crevasse, but it was hard to maneuver. She had to wiggle like a worm until the passage turned sharply down. She froze and listened as her pack clattered downward. It sounded to be at least a few meters, but it did hit bottom fairly quickly. She reached down and spread her hands out. It seemed wide enough, but the drop continued past where she could reach. She considered backing out and turning to drop feet first, but she'd already wasted too much time and she had no idea what would be ahead after the drop.

"You'll have to let go now."

Lo had one hand around her ankle. The weight of it lifted away and then the slack in the rope at her waist disappeared. She moved forward slowly, the rope keeping her from dropping too fast. The space opened out and she couldn't reach anything, but she was able to get one hand wrapped around the rope. As her feet left the confines of the passage, she twisted but the rope kept her steady. Her feet ended up beneath her and she lowered several meters before they touched what she hoped was the ground.

As the rope went slack leaving her weight on her feet, something crunched beneath her boots. She cringed, visions of an army of insects crawling through her head. She squatted down and carefully spread her hands, searching for the pack. She sighed with relief when the cloth materialized out of the darkness beneath her fingers. She pulled the light out and switched it on casting a narrow beam against a rock wall a meter away.

Dirt swirled in the narrow beam like nightmoths drawn to the light, but she didn't see or hear the crawling critters she'd feared. She pulled the bottom of her shirt up to her mouth as a makeshift mask. Whatever had kept the earth above from collapsing the cavern had allowed enough of the dirt in to make the air thick with the stuff. She shifted her weight to stand and froze at the unsettling shifting underfoot. Slowly, she aimed the light down on the floor.

It bounced back at her, revealing the dirty white of bone.

Everywhere.

The bones of a hand lay crushed beneath her boot.

Her pack sat in the yawning gap at the center of a crumbling ribcage.

"Breathe, little female." Lo's voice drifted down from above, seeming much too far away, but she took his advice and forced air through her reluctant lungs.

Muffled voices and scrambling movements above gave her the moment she needed to recover her wits. She carefully shifted away bone fragments until her boots were steady on the solid floor then slung the pack over her shoulder and stood.

"Samantha? Talk to me, *courra*." The rough, growl couldn't hide the worry in Mercury's voice.

"I'm okay." She answered softly, knowing Lo would hear, and feeling less brave than when she'd volunteered to dive head first into a dark pit.

She swept the light across the cavern, turning in a slow circle and hoping whatever was responsible for the bones had long sense departed.

"Can you see Carn?" Mercury paused. "Your dark clouds are overhead now."

Samantha understood the gentle reminder for the need to hurry, but the dark was disorienting, so all she could do was to make a methodical sweep. "Not yet."

Where she stood, the cavern spanned three meters across. Bone dotted the floor—some recognizable as having belonged to a single skeleton, but others had been scattered making it hard to tell the number of dead.

The cavern ceiling formed a dome directly overhead, but the moment she started exploring it crowded down to only a few centimeters between her and what looked more like rotting debris than rock. She didn't immediately see Carn, but there was a bend in the cavern, which was looking more and more like a crevice or ravine that had been covered over in a land slide. She headed for the bend, picking her way around the bony remains.

As she cleared the corner the space between floor and earthy ceiling closed down to about two meters. A freshly fallen layer of mulch-like material covered the bones and the debris overhead bulged downward like a tarp straining under too great a weight.

Directly under the lowest point, a pile of debris and dirt created a mound. A mound with twisted legs.

Carn.

Samantha dropped to her knees and scrambled around the mound. She found his arms shielding his face. Luckily, he'd landed on, or gotten to, his side. His arms not only shielded his face but kept a path clear for air to reach him. He was breathing, but unconscious.

"Found him," she said aloud.

The bulging ceiling above shook loose another layer of debris. Samantha coughed and covered her face in her shirt again. When things settled overhead she dusted herself off and started scooping debris away from Carn's arms and shoulders. "This ceiling is shaky."

She couldn't hear a response, but there was no more movement above. She had him mostly uncovered when a voice drifted around the bend in the crevice. Reluctantly, she left him to get back to the tunnel she'd come down.

"I'm here." She shouted up. "Carn lost consciousness."

"Can you move him?" Mercury's voice settled the sense of doom that had been growing inside her.

She looked over her shoulder despite not being able to see him around the corner. She didn't need to see him to know he was big. And heavy. Still, if she needed to move him, she would. And she hadn't tried the med kit. A stimulant might bring him around. "Yes, but there's no way he'll fit through the gap up there."

"Agreed," he shouted. "But the roof here must be more solid. Safer." A gust of wind chased his voice through the opening. The heart of the storm had to be over them now.

She nodded to herself. "You're going to try to dig through."

"It's the only way."

It was also incredibly dangerous. One of the slopes above could slide down on top of them. Especially with the rain. But he was right. What choice did they have? "Has it started raining yet?"

"Yes." She was sure there was a lot that one word left out. What would rain be like for them if they'd never experienced it?

"I'm going to try a stimulant. Are there any medications that he'll react badly to?"

The answer was slow in coming. "No, but be careful. He might be confused if he wakes."

Samantha went back to Carn and dug through her pack for the med-kit.

She found a mild stimulant and applied it to the vein in his neck to try to get the fastest reaction. While she waited she pulled out her water and set it in reaching distance then backed up.

"Come on, Carn. Open those eyes for me." She could try to drag him, but—

He came around, sputtering and coughing. She wanted to reach out and help him sit-up, but she didn't dare. Not after the way he'd reacted to her touch in the past and not after Mercury's warning.

"Carn." She hoped she sounded calm. "It's Samantha. You fell, but you're going to be okay. There's water to your left."

He was already trying to push up. He leaned toward her, seeming to respond to her voice. When he lifted his head, he studied her face then grabbed for the water. After a big swig, he cleared his throat. "Mercury? Lo?"

"They're fine. They couldn't get down here without bringing it down on top of you. Right now we need to get you around that corner." She pointed. "The roof is more stable there and the sooner we move, the sooner they can finish digging through here. Okay?"

He nodded and untwisted his body. Small nicks and scrapes peppered his skin with bloody dots of color. Brushing dirt from his face and shoulders, he moved slowly but with purpose.

Samantha crawled toward the corner, leading the way with a glance over her shoulder. Carn panted with effort. Pain tightening his face into a ferocious mask. Crawling through the debris, filthy, and looking capable of chewing engine parts, he looked more animal than she'd ever seen any of the Arena Dogs, but beneath it all he was still Carn. A man plagued by worry and pain.

When the space over their heads opened up, he tried to stand, but failed.

Samantha edged closer. "Not much farther now. Will you let me help you?"

He nodded and she helped him loop his arm over her shoulder. He couldn't seem to put weight on one foot. Together they hobbled clear of the danger zone and beneath the domed stone ceiling where Samantha had come down.

"What is this place?" He stared at the bone littering the cavern floor.

"I'm not sure." She urged him on. "Let's get as far away as we can."

They stopped where the stone floor began to slope up and she helped him prop against the cavern wall then shouted up to Lo and Mercury.

She knew the moment they started to dig. The scrape and groan of shifting debris echoed off the stone walls. The noise of the storm outside kicked up. The muffled roar of the rain grew louder, punctuated by the whistle of the wind.

The temperature dropped.

She shivered.

"They'll be all right." Carn's certainty sounded as solid as a sand-break in a sandstorm and she wanted to shelter under its strength.

She met his gaze. "I know. I'm just cold." But it wasn't the cold making her pulse pound loud in her ears or drying her mouth beyond swallowing.

When they broke through, chances were high that the area would collapse further, bringing more sodden earth down on top of them. Mercury and Lo could be buried under more debris than she could shift.

"Thank you." Carn put a hand on her shoulder.

Confused, she waited for his explanation.

He smiled, a small smile, but a smile none the less. He shook his head and the explanation never came. The rustling crash of dirt and debris collapsing drew their attention back to staring down the cavern to the bend where instead of seeing the two faces they hoped for, they watched as dirt and dust swirled in the air and a stream of water trickled around the rock. It widened into a small rivulet that hinted of the danger, but disappeared into a crevice in the rock floor.

As the dust settled, Samantha's chest grew tight. Something at the back of her throat made her gasp for air. Her eyes stung. Too long. They had to have come down with the collapse. They should have been up and moving.

Before she made the decision to move she was running back. "Mercury! Lo!"

She dropped to her knees at the edge of a pile of mud and roots that nearly filled the space where Carn had been laying. She dug, dragging big handfuls of the stuff down and pushing it to the side.

A yawning gap loomed overhead. She could hear the storm above clearly now. The wind in the trees. The rain pounding the ground.

She was vaguely aware of the trickles of water plopping down on her from above and the moisture on her cheeks. Carn was there beside her. She didn't know how he'd made it back across the floor of the fissure when he could barely stand, but he was digging with purpose.

Something shifted in the now sodden muck where she'd just shoved her hands. She pushed in further until her arms were buried above the elbows. She felt firm flesh beneath her hand.

"Carn." A whisper, both hopeful and panicked.

His hand shoved in beside hers and he pulled back hard, knocking her to her ass. It didn't matter. Not one bit. All that mattered was that Mercury came up, clutching Carn's arm, gasping and shaking muck from his face. As his shoulders and chest emerged he scrambled forward, pulling Lo free behind him.

All four of them ended up in a heap, like the tangle of silk thread she'd always ended up with when she'd tried to learn to weave. Mercury was in her arms and Lo and Carn were there, too. For a moment she felt the sort of connection she'd always imagined she'd one day have with her father and his crew. She'd only known these men a few weeks, but she already felt a part of them. It had to be an illusion, a mix of adrenalin and euphoria. Like that heap of thread, one good shake and it would fall apart.

Alone, Mercury crouched in the wider part of the cavern while the others slept around the bend. He looked up to the gouge in the dark roof and the steady streams of muddy water trickling down. At least the chunks of muck and mud had stopped sliding down on top of the mound below. When he'd been lying beneath that pile of muck he'd had no fear of dying. He'd known they'd dig free, but Samantha hadn't known that. She'd thrown herself into action to save them. He hadn't been surprised when her hand brushed against his. Some part of him had known. Known she would offer aid. Known he could rely on her. She'd proven it time and time again. And that was something he'd never had from anyone except his brothers. The feeling left him uneasy.

"Can't sleep, brother?" Lo hunched nearby. That Mercury hadn't heard him approach said a lot about how unsettled he was.

Mercury shifted his gaze to the sky beyond the gap overhead. "I want to get moving as soon as the rain stops."

"It'll be slow-going with Carn's injured knee."

Mercury made a noncommittal noise in answer. He didn't want to think of Carn's injury or the competent way Samantha had diagnosed and treated the swelling. She was so damn competent at everything. They had relied on her for so much. Even here in this place she called Wilderness. "Samantha didn't take water or food when we ate."

Lo shifted his weight. "You think she can't hold it down?"

"I think she fears she can't. She gets worse every hour."

"She didn't want you to know." Lo tilted his head, ears alert. "Why?"

"She doesn't want me to feel guilty for pushing forward when turning back could end her suffering." Her attempt to ease his guilt was wasted effort. He hated the choice he'd had to make.

"Perhaps," said Lo. "Or perhaps she does all to gain your trust for her own reasons."

"Reasons? What reason could she have for any of this?" He held out his hands to indicate the obvious lack of comforts. "What profit could there be for her that would be worth this risk?"

"I don't know, but that doesn't mean it isn't true."

Anger became a choker tightening around Mercury's throat. "Do you really think she's capable of such a plot when she is more apt to jump head first into every dangerous situation?"

No. Mercury didn't believe the woman who recklessly tackled a guard to spare him pain or fought her fear to climb into a hole to save his brother could be calculating enough to plan their downfall. But in moments of too much thought, he also questioned why she would do so much for them. Could a woman with so much skill and knowledge and passion truly care for them or was it simply in her nature to aid those in need? He hated the insecurity that made him need to be special to her. To know that she saw them as more than animals to be set free. Worthy only of her pity.

He hated that tiny seed of doubt, but the doubt in Lo's eyes lurked as large as the mountains of Wilderness. "What did she do to hurt you so deeply?"

The shutter that closed off Lo's emotions fell so fast Mercury knew Lo understood they were no longer talking about Samantha.

"You know what happened." The pain hidden in the slow

cadence of his words extinguished Mercury's anger.

"No," he said. "I only know she betrayed you. I don't know how?"

Lo's face tightened, drawing attention to his powerful jaw. "Now? You ask me this now?"

"I think it's time, brother."

"Grah." Lo shook.

He'd been bottling up his hurt so long he must need to howl, to run, to fight, but none of those options were available to him. When he spoke it was through a clenched jaw.

"It had been months since she'd asked for me at the Ladies' Wall. She'd been bribing one of the guards to give us time in one of the training rooms. She no longer needed the drugs to have me panting after her like a prize." Lo's eyes glazed over as if he were back there again, lost in the memory. "I was chained to the wall when I saw her. Owens was there and another human female. A patron I didn't recognize. Rachel brought them there to watch, to prove to them I'd fuck her without the drugs, without the chains to keep me from hurting her. They'd still chained me, but as she explained her plan she freed one of my hands."

Mercury was tempted to stop the flow of words. In truth, he didn't need to hear the details, but he knew Lo needed to give them. To get them out of his heart where they'd been lodged for months. "Her plan?"

"If I performed," he spat the words, "as she'd promised. Owens would send me to the pleasure suites for three months. Rachel would get a share of the premium they'd earn from it."

Fully trained gladiators were never sent to the pleasure suites where their more submissive counterparts were given to patrons for sex. The submissives had no will to fight, but once trained, the gladiators were too dangerous to leave unattended with a patron— even chained down.

Mercury waited. The worst still hid behind Lo's shuttered expression.

"She said it would be easy work for me. That all I had to do was lay back and get fucked by the grandest patrons on the planet. She said..." He swallowed as if the next words had formed a jagged rock to cut at his throat as he forced them out. "She said she promised they'd all have skin as soft as a whisper. They all laughed when she said it. Owens, the guard, even the female. It was a thing

I'd said to her when we were alone together and she threw it back at me for all to hear. I wanted to kill her."

"Instead you marked her."

His eyes shifted away "Mercury—"

"I'm glad you fought your instinct. Not because she didn't deserve a slow and painful death."

"Merc—"

"Because if you'd given in, they would have taken your life. If I had a chance I'd kill the bitch myself."

"Mercury."

Finally, Mercury understood Lo's warning. He turned to see Samantha standing at the bend in the cavern. She stepped forward to stand between him and Lo, but a full pace back from them both. She smiled...and it broke his heart. The smile was brittle. Her pale limps trembled.

"Samantha?" How long had she been there? Long enough at least to hear his blood lust.

She didn't meet his eyes when she spoke. "They're the same people who terraformed the planet."

His mind couldn't follow whatever leap she'd made to move the conversation beyond betrayal, humiliation, and killing. Was it mercy or disgust that led her to change the subject? "Who?"

"The skeletons. They must have been the same people who terraformed the planet." She lifted her hand to reveal a thin disk of metal cupped in her palm. "I found this with one of the more intact skeletons." She traced the disk with the tips of her fingers. "I saw this symbol on one of the terraforming platforms."

He wanted to snatch her fingers away and draw them to his lips. He wanted her in his arms. He wanted to make her forget the ugliness of his past, his and his brothers, a past she couldn't—shouldn't know.

She might not belong in his world, nor him in hers, but he wanted to remind her of how well their bodies fit. If nothing else, at least they had that.

He held out his hand to accept the disk she offered and set his mind to her words. "How do you think they died?" Had these people been trapped by a landslide or did their customs call for a single burial site for all?

Lo stood quiet and grim as Mercury watched her flip the disk over in his palm. A scorch mark marred the metal.

"This mark was made by a plasma weapon," said Samantha. "Someone killed them."

CHAPTER FOURTEEN

Planet G-45987
Earth Alliance Beta Sector - Gollerra Border
2210.162

There'd been no more rain since they'd crawled out of the ravine that morning, but the air seemed thick and heavy with moisture. Mercury held Samantha as the mid-day sun beat down on them. Her belly heaved beneath his hand as her stomach tried again to rid itself of food and water that wasn't there. He'd carried her all day while Lo had drug the hastily made litter that carried Carn, so Mercury knew she hadn't even attempted to drink water.

"Stars." Samantha pushed back to stand upright and attempted a tired grin. "I can't remember the last time I felt this bad. I must look like death."

Mercury brushed the backs of his knuckles across her cheekbone. "You look as beautiful as ever—just a little more green."

She started to laugh and then she was bending forward again with her belly heaving uncontrollably. He'd been teasing her about the green, but he would welcome the sight of any of her colorful nature, even green. Her complexion had actually grown dull and colorless.

She'd been small and slight from the beginning and he knew human bones were less dense than those of the Arena Dogs, but her personality had a way of convincing everyone around her that she was tougher than those facts allowed. She'd charged Resler, fought with Drake. Now that he held her, the slender ridge of her ribs beneath his fingers, it seemed impossible she could have done those things. He cringed at the memory of how he'd fucked her like an animal. He'd tried to be gentle, but he never should have touched her. He shouldn't have, but he had and he wanted to do it again. First, he needed to stop this damn signal that was making her and Carn sick.

He helped her sit up again and wiped perspiration from her brow. "We need to keep traveling, *Courra*."

She nodded. "I know." Her gaze drifted to where Carn lay unconscious. "The last time he came around he seemed delirious. That's seriously not good."

"No," Mercury agreed, aware that her condition was deteriorating faster than Carn's had. Another day and she'd be as bad or worse.

She reached out and rested her delicate hand on his arms. It was the first time she'd reached out to touch him since that awful moment in the cavern when he'd confessed his desire to kill Rachel. They'd both pretended like it hadn't happened, but he'd been waiting for her to push him away every since. She'd let him carry her, but there had been nothing offered—until this.

"Lucky for us that you and Lo are okay," she said. "We'd be in real trouble if we were all feeling like Carn."

"True." He turned to let her wrap herself around his back. By the time he got to his feet she'd already leaned forward to lay her cheek against his shoulder.

He gave Lo the signal to move and watched as he lifted the handles of Carn's litter then fell in behind them. As they slogged forward, the next rocky rise loomed larger and larger. When they reached the end of the plateau, dread became a stone in his belly. He'd have to leave Carn and Lo behind. Trying to get the litter up the rocky, slope didn't make sense.

Lo must have come to the same conclusion. He dragged Carn over to a small cluster of rocks jutting up. "This is a good defensible spot."

"We don't know if there's water nearby."

Lo's ears twitched. "I'm hoping you won't be gone so long we'll need to find it, but I think there's water near. I hear a noise like the creek we followed some days back, only bigger."

Mercury knew if Lo heard it then it was there. "I hope you're right on both counts. We'll return here as soon as we can. And I know Samantha will want a bath." Thoughts of their last bath together heated his blood.

Lo slapped a claw-tipped hand over Mercury's heart. "Return soon, my brother."

Mercury mirrored the movement. "Be safe and well."

Mercury decided to pick up his pace when he started up the rise. He wouldn't be able to maintain it long, but instinct told him they weren't far from the source of the pulse. The increase in pace made for a rougher gait. Samantha woke, tightening her clasp around his shoulders.

A sudden jerk rippled through her body at his back. "Where are Lo and Carn."

"Not far. At the base of this slope."

She turned as if to look behind them and he had to adjust for the shift of her weight. He bent his knees and pushed through to leap up the next outcropping. This time when she clung tighter she pressed her body tightly against his. The pleasure in that served as a welcome distraction from the ache in his muscles and the growing pain in his head.

He leapt again, reaching for what appeared to be a ledge. He gripped the rock edge tightly and strained to use nothing more than upper body strength to pull them up. At his back, Samantha didn't so much as breathe until he swung his legs onto the ledge.

"Show off," she teased with a playful squeeze of his biceps.

Despite his pain, joy soared within him at the reminder of her unflagging spirit. He started to tease her back, but the words froze in his throat at the sight in front of him.

The ledge cut further into the slope than he'd anticipated. It looked almost as if something had sliced away a section of the incline. The ledge reached about ten meters into the slope ending in an unnaturally smooth cliff. Hand and foot holds had been carved in the rock making a ladder at one side. Symbols had been painted in a deep blue color all along the cliff. At the center of the ledge a two meter tall spike had been driven into the rock. Atop it sat a multi-sided object with more symbols etched into its surface.

"Samantha?"

"I see it. Help me."

She pulled free of him as he set her on her feet. On shaky legs she stumbled over to the strange object.

"What is it?" He caught himself whispering as if the owners of the object would appear out of the rock face.

"A pentagonal cupola."

"That sounds as if you're speaking another language."

She grinned through her pain. "That language would be geometry. It's a twelve sided shape. I haven't seen one outside a three dimensional navigation chart, and that only back in my time cramming for the pilot's exam. I think it's also our transmitter. And who knows what else."

"The symbols—"

"Yeah. They match the ones from the terraforming platforms and that metal object we found in the cavern."

Hesitantly, Mercury stepped up to the object and studied the symbols as she ran her hands over the surface.

"Ah, here." She said the words almost to herself as she did something with her fingers.

One of the sides sprang open to reveal a small lit panel.

Samantha crouched down to study the small screen. "If it's as old as the terraforming platforms, it's hard to believe it still has power, but it does. This panel looks like an interface of some kind."

"Something to turn it off." It had to be. Something so destructive clearly needed a way to be stopped.

"More than that. It's way too complex for a simple on and off switch."

"But turning it off is all we need to do."

"Right, well good news there." She stopped and stepped back. "This interface panel is not as tough as the outside covering. Now that it's open you should be able to smash it. Looks like you didn't need me here after all."

"You figured out how to open it."

She shrugged. "You'd have managed."

Mercury put his hand around the spike to see if he could pull it free of the rock ledge. A symbol caught his eye and stopped him still.

"What is it?"

"I know this symbol." Mercury pointed to the one he

recognized.

"Something from Roma?"

"Yes and no." He closed his eyes and the image came back to him—a blue-black finger, drawing the shape in the dirt. The Mothers kneeling around it to mumble a chant."

"Mercury?"

Samantha's voice drew him out of the memory. "The surrogates."

"Seriously?" Her eyes had grown wide and round.

"I wouldn't joke about this."

"I know, I just meant… The odds of finding a connection to the surrogates here." Her brows drew together. "Then again. We're at the edge of the sector and so is Roma. And I did find this planet using an unofficial Roma star chart."

She stumbled and Mercury steadied her.

"If this is connected to the surrogates," she said, "you can't just smash it."

He frowned. "You believe you could learn something from it." He was curious about the surrogates, but his curiosity didn't matter when he needed to see to her wellbeing.

"Maybe. I have to try." She put her hand to her forehead and rubbed as if she could rub away the pain. "If we could find them, the people who made this place, they might be willing to help your people."

Mercury searched his memories of the surrogates. They hadn't been true mothers, but they hadn't been unkind. Who could blame them for not wanting to grow attached to children they knew would be taken away from them? "If they had the strength to fight Roma, wouldn't they have attacked when their females were taken?"

"Maybe. Or maybe not. Who knows how far they came to colonize this place. The people that were here might have been an advance team or the terraforming technicians. Their homeworld might not even know what happened to them."

She looked so pale and her body trembled with pain. "That doesn't mean they would help us."

"The Cerrillians have an old saying. *A common enemy makes for fast alliances.*" Samantha wrapped a hand around his arm to steady herself. "Any civilization that built those terraforming platforms has to be big and technologically advanced. If there's even a chance they could help you free all of your people…" Her words trailed off.

Mercury pulled her into his arms, but she pushed against his chest, resisting.

"Give me a minute. I can figure the damn thing out. I just need to breathe. The altitude must be getting to me."

He brushed sweat-dampened tendrils of hair away from her face. It wasn't the altitude and she wasn't going to get better with a few minutes of rest. He stroked her small nose with his fingertips. She had done a good job of convincing him that the Mothers' people might help. He even believed she could figure the object out if given enough time. But it didn't matter. He couldn't let her die or suffer long lasting effects of continued dehydration. He wouldn't let her suffer even one more minute.

Mercury lowered her to the stone beneath his feet protecting her head as she gave into the fatigue and pain. He strode over to the object and jerked it free of the spike holding it in place. He turned it over in his hand as he looked closer, committing the symbols to memory. It could be a link to his past and future. It wasn't worth losing Carn. It wasn't worth Samantha's life or her suffering.

He squatted down and held it over his head then brought it down to the rock in one powerful movement. It smashed in his hands, breaking into countless tiny pieces.

He let the remains fall from his hands and returned to Samantha. "Rest, *courra*. Regain your strength. I'll keep you safe and we'll soon be bathing in Lo's water noise that is bigger than our river."

CHAPTER FIFTEEN

Planet G-45987
Earth Alliance Beta Sector- Gollerra Border
2210.163

Samantha kept her eyes closed and stretched. The bedroll beneath her didn't provide much cushion from the hard ground, but she had a sense of having slept well for the first time in days. She scrubbed her hands over her face and eased open her eyes. She didn't remember making camp or lying down to sleep. Had she lost a day? She guessed the time at late afternoon, the sun seemed to be hidden behind one of the nearby mountaintops.

"There's water beside you." Carn's voice drifted to her from outside her field of vision.

She sat up to find him propped up against a stack of their packs. There was no one else around. "Where are Mercury and Lo?" The words scraped her throat as they went by. She reached for the water, took a sip, and coughed.

"Slowly. Sip slowly. Lo and Mercury are getting a better look around the area."

Samantha nodded then pulled her legs up and crossed them for balance. Not only were Mercury and Lo not around, she didn't recognize where they were. She rubbed at her head trying to bring things back into focus in her mind. Slowly, it all came back. Her head still ached, but that was the dehydration. The pulse had been silenced and she didn't remember doing it at all, but she did remember finding...

"The artifact... " she started then looked at Carn . If Mercury had destroyed it without telling them—

"He smashed it to stop the pulse. There was nothing left." Carn looked sad. "It was the right thing to do."

So Mercury *had* told them. "I wish I could've had more time."

"There's no use spending energy thinking on something that cannot be changed."

His gentle dismissal eased her guilt over failing to save the object. "Whoever named you had you all wrong."

His eyebrows lifted. "What do you mean? I can wreak havoc and leave a wake of carnage when the circumstances call for it."

She laughed, almost spitting out a mouthful of water. "I'm sure you can. But I still think Owl would have suited you better."

He frowned and she laughed again. He joined her with what might pass for a chuckle, if she were being generous with her chuckling standards. The moment passed too quickly and she found herself sitting with a man in pain. Suffering, not just from physical pain or fatigue. It was something much softer squeezing his heart.

"What sort of name," he asked, "is Owl?"

She couldn't contain her grin. "A big Earther bird my father taught me about. It had enormous eyes and could hear its prey from a kilometer away. It could turn its head all the way around." She made a big eyed face and circled her finger in a spinning motion.

"You compare me to this monstrous creature?" He didn't look bothered as he said the words.

Samantha sobered. "It's also credited with great wisdom."

He dipped his chin to his chest then met her eyes, looking solemn. "I'm honored."

Samantha studied the big man. His body was covered with fresh scratches layered over old scars. She knew none of those injuries and scars mattered to him. The only wound that mattered would be the one left if he lost his mate. "Will you tell me about her?"

His jaw flexed, making the scar that cut across it stand out in white relief. "She's not like you."

"Of course not."

"I mean she's not a fighter. She's strong in her own way, but she has few defenses."

"Really? I'm surprised your women aren't enhanced the way you are."

"Some are," he admitted. "The strong females fight and die in the games, but Hera was not made for the arena. Some of the females and even some males were created to be submissive and docile so that they could be safely used to entertain the patrons."

Samantha remembered Lo had said something about pleasure suites. It had to be prostitution. Or was there a better word considering they had no choice and received nothing in exchange? Rape. Abuse. Yes, those were the right words. She didn't know what to say to Carn so she waited.

"In the past only fighter females became mates and there are not many of them. The guards did not start bringing the submissive females to the kennels until a year ago. They wanted us to breed them. This is when we realized something must have gone wrong with the surrogates. No young dogs had been brought to the kennels in too many years."

"What happened when they brought the women to you for…" She couldn't even say the word.

"We refused at first, but each time we refused they punished the females. I couldn't bear to see her hurt anymore. Some of the males snapped the necks of the females to end their lives quickly, but I couldn't."

"Of course you couldn't. That's crazy." The thought made her queasy. Had Mercury or Lo done that?

"Don't judge them harshly. Many of the females welcomed such a death."

"I can't imagine choosing death. There's always hope." Her hands tightened around the water container. It was something her father had taught her. Her gentle mother would have said joy could be found in any life.

"Easier to say when you don't live your life in a cage."

She blushed, ashamed. "I didn't mean to judge anyone."

"I know," he said. "It's your way to be optimistic."

Optimistic or always chasing after the future, like her father?

"I can see how that might change, if I'd been through everything you have."

He shrugged. "It was the only life we knew." He adjusted his injured leg and sighed at the relief of moving. "It's a life that taught us to enjoy the moments we could and to seize every opportunity."

Her mother would approve the sentiment. "And Hera made you happy."

He dipped his head. "When she chose me, all my worries and doubts became nothing."

"I'm glad." Samantha took a long sip of water. "How long did you have together?"

"Only six months, before I was marked for death."

"You mean the hunt?"

"No. Before that. We didn't understand it at the time. We were forced to divide our pack and fight against each other. Mercury and Lo against Me, Jupiter, and Senneca. I was made to fight without armor."

"Someone stacked the cards against you."

"They wanted me to die that day and Hera will pay the price for my survival."

"What do you mean?"

"On the ship, the whip-master told Mercury Hera will be given to the guards. They'll make an example of her for others who don't cooperate." He hung his head and his shoulders slumped. "I fear she won't survive it."

"I'm so sorry." She wanted to wrap her arms around him and hug him as her mother had always done for her, but she didn't know how he'd react.

"We have to go back for her." Fierce determination hardened his jaw line. "Before it's too late."

"Yes. I know."All three of them would go back and risk their lives for Hera. She hated it. The thought of losing them put a painful ache in the vicinity of her heart. "Was it after you were sent to the hunt that Mercury vowed to help you?"

"No. That was when Hera first came to live with us. They—" Carn's head lifted, alert and listening. "Mercury is back."

She saw him then, breaking out of the woods that wrapped around the base of the slope.

She got carefully to her feet and met him half way. He lifted her in his arms and pressed his face to her neck. As he set her on her feet and took her hand, he waved to Carn with the other.

"Feeling better, *courra*?"

"Much." It felt so good to have her palm pressed to his, she couldn't remember why she'd been keeping her distance.

"Come," said Mercury. "I have something to show you."

Samantha heard the rumble long before they reached their destination. He led her along a winding path that meandered through boulders and trees the likes of which she'd never seen. Bright green moss topped chalk-white boulders. Pink strings of color swirled through the stone like silk ribbons frozen in a timeless dance. Small, tightly packed vines covered the path, releasing a sharp herbal scent each time she stepped on the small, but hearty, plants.

"Careful here," Mercury warned, lifting aside a thick strand of flowers that dropped down from one of the many trees blanketing the area.

The flowers grew on wandering vines that seemed to live in harmony with the foliage it wove through. Each time a breeze shook the trees, the flower vines were dragged across the ground making a rustling noise, but it was quickly overshadowed by the insistent roar.

When the source of the noise came into view it was still some distance away. "A waterfall," she breathed in awe. "I've seen them on vids but I've never actually seen one in person."

"A first for us both, then. I'm glad I could share this with you."

Mercury pulled her further from the trees and toward the river.

"I can almost feel the water swirling in the air," she said. Three channels of foamy white water rushed over a cliff face and spilled into the river below with varying force.

"The center channel is too deep to stand," he warned.

Samantha accepted the warning with a nod. "Even if I knew how to swim, that water is moving too fast to be safe."

"Yes. It's safer along the sides."

She'd been so preoccupied with the power of the spilling water she hadn't taken in the odd formations in the rock along the edge of the river. "The water must have carved the gullies."

The shallow channels and dips worn into the white rock funneled water into the center of the river, but not before making an elaborate network of clear pools.

"Some further up on this side are warm. They seem perfect for bathing." Mercury pushed loose strands of her hair out of her face and brushed his knuckles along her jaw.

A shiver of pleasure raced down her neck at his touch. His

hands were rough, but the texture only added to the sensation. The memory of their last bath sent heat rushing to her cheeks and across her chest.

She met his gaze and looked into the piercing silver, searching for some hint of what he was thinking. She knew he wanted her, at least in the moment. She knew lust was a factor, but it couldn't be the only one. There was tenderness there, too. She only wished she knew if he would look at her the same after they got off the planet and she introduced him to a world where females weren't rare and she was just another ordinary woman.

Enjoy the moment, Sammie. The moment might be all she had with this incredible man. He was accustomed to living without luxuries, but he'd found her a warm bath in an uninhabited wilderness. It was no small thing to her way of thinking. "Show me the way."

He led her along the edges of the network of pools, steadying her footing as they went. "It's slippery," he explained.

"Must be algae," she muttered, still feeling awed by the riot of color and texture and sound.

As they grew closer to the cliff and the thundering fall of water, she saw the warmer pools he mentioned. Steam hung over the water like a miniature cloud. The heated pools sat along the base of the cliff, but far enough to the side to be out from under the fall.

One of their packs and several strands of flowers sat beside the pool where they stopped. Mercury crouched down to dig through the pack. He came up with cleanser. "I have clothes for you to wear after your bath."

She couldn't help the flush of color that came at the thought of how good the steamy water would feel against her skin. "This is going to feel so good."

Mercury made a noncommittal "*mmm*," as he pressed the cleanser into her palm then tugged at one of her boots. She let him pull them free, one at a time, then watched as he slipped off his flex boots and laid them beside hers.

"First," he said. "We need to get the mud from your clothes." He led her toward the closest section of the waterfall. Positioned to the side of the main channel, the water trickled over in what compared to a steady rain. He urged her onto the rocks that dotted the area in front of the fall and kept her moving to the far side—closest to the center channel. "Here the water flowing over does not feed the bathing pool." He pointed at the seemingly random pattern of gullies and she realized he was right.

It was a beautiful sight, but the charm of it was quickly forgotten when Mercury pulled them both directly under the falling water.

Even as the water chilled her, Mercury's grin warmed her inside. It was the wide, carefree grin of a man with nothing but play on his mind. It exaggerated the lines at the corner of his eyes and called attention to his generous, sensual lips. "You're insane!" Her teeth chattered with the words.

His grin only widened. "Hurry, *courra*."

She had no argument with that idea and she quickly pulled her shirt off over her head. The mud caked into the material had dried, making it stiff and awkward. He tugged down her trousers. She kicked them off and started scrubbing herself down with the cleanser. The dirt and mud slid off and washed away with the water. Mercury helped her briskly brush down her arms and legs then he was tugging at her tunic and briefs. She struggled playfully at first, but then gave in because she understood he'd let her go back to the warm pool once she was free of the muddy garments.

The moment she kicked free of her briefs, she scrambled away. She made a dash for the warm pool, splashing in, then wading to the far side where she could watch Mercury standing under the waterfall...unabashedly nude.

Stars, he was beyond words. Powerful muscles, sleek lines.

He soaped his inky black hair and turned his back to the spray. Samantha followed the suds with fascination as they trailed across his shoulders and down his ribs to follow that masculine vee that led down from his hipbones.

When he finished washing he carried their things back to the pool where she waited, near the point of drooling over him. He tossed in the cleanser and strode into the mist topped water like a mythical god.

As he crossed the pool, he scooped up handfuls of water to pour over his body. It kissed his skin like a misty lover. She couldn't tear her gaze from the sight. She followed the water down the planes of his pectorals and down his flat belly to pool in the small dip of his navel. The mist swirled around his muscled thighs leaving only one place for her gaze to rest. Despite the chill of the waterfall he'd made a speedy recovery. He was aroused—the thick column of his cock stood straight and tall, the plum tip stretching toward his navel—but the grin on his face was still playful and light.

He lowered the appealing planes and hollows of muscle and bone into the water with a masculine sensuality that fogged her already muddled brain.

"I'm glad to see your color again, *courra*." His low chuckle broke the spell and she splashed water in his face for laughing at her.

"Hey!" She tried to fend off his hands when he made a grab for her, but she ended up pulled against him—her back to his chest, his legs cradling her, his arms wrapped around her and both of them laughing. When the moment settled into ease, she sighed in pleasure and wrapped her arms over his. The tips of her fingers brushed across the scar tissue that ringed his wrists. He'd survived such horror and become so strong. With the memory of his laughter fresh in her mind, she laced her fingers with his. "This feels nice."

"Mmm." He pressed his lips to her neck, laving a path downward with sucking kisses and quick nips that accelerated her heart rate.

She tilted her head to give him complete access. Her blood rushed frantically through her body as if every cell raced for a chance to pass through the artery beneath the damp stroke of his tongue. "That's almost too good. Maybe we should finish washing before we forget why we came here."

"My memory is excellent," he boasted, but he eased back and pushed his hand through the water around them until he found the cleanser. "Ah, here it is."

The top snapped open and he worked the cool gel through her hair, strong fingers messaging her scalp, stroking down her neck.

She lifted her hand to make a cup. "Let me help." He poured cleanser into her hands and she used it to clean first her own legs then his as she leaned forward giving him access to her back. He worked more cleanser around to her belly as she pulled his foot into her lap and rubbed her thumbs into the arch of his foot. He made a soft rumbling sound and rested his chin on her shoulder as she repeated the process with his other foot. The powerful intimacy of washing together, stroking soap-slicked skin, wrapped in the warmth of the water and each other, seemed at once natural and impossible to comprehend.

Samantha leaned back against him and relaxed into his embrace.

"Never in my wildest imagination could I have ever dreamt I'd be here today on an uninhabited planet, bathing in a natural pool under a waterfall with flowers everywhere and I'd be doing all this with the sexiest man alive."

Mercury chuckled. "I'm glad you find me sexy, *courra*. I also find you sexy."

The word *sexy* sounded odd in a mouth made for rumbles and growls instead of sultriness. Her cheeks caught fire, but she was too relaxed to respond to his teasing.

He filled his hands with her breasts like a blind man relying only on touch to learn her. When her breasts began to ache and her nipples were tight nubbins under his fingers, he slid his hands down her belly and to the feminine folds between her legs.

"I didn't dream of this either," he said. His fingers stroked along her sensitive folds. "But after this, I think my ability to dream may be much improved."

He slipped one finger inside her and she sucked in a breath, arching her back like a contented cat. No. She wasn't contented yet, but she trusted Mercury would see to that eventually. There was no rush.

He stroked her lazily, playing in her folds and dipping a finger insider her then pulling it out again, with no discernible pattern. The result was blissful and frustrating and made her body shake with anticipation. She pushed back against him and the growing erection that promised so much. She was beyond ready when he added another finger to his game. She couldn't stop herself from clenching down on those filling fingers.

"Relax, *courra*. I won't hurt you."

"Oh, I'm not so sure," she breathed. "Frustration can be its own kind of hurting."

"Then I'll have to give you what you're wanting," he whispered. His hands slipped around to grasp her hips. He lifted her and positioned her at the edge of the pool.

She was ready and he slipped inside her easily from behind, filling her with hot, hard cock. She braced one arm against the icy stone edge and reached back to pull him closer with the other. The curved slope of the bottom of the pool put him at the perfect height to fuck her in a sensual in and out slide that had her whole body tight and burning with pleasure.

Her fingers clutched against the slick skin across his ribs, coming up empty, but the rest of her was full of him. Full of that heat and hardness.

She hung onto the edge as long as she could then plunged into orgasm.

His moist breath against her cheek, became a pant.

His hips jerked in a less steady and more powerful rhythm as he gave into his own needs, and filled her with his release.

Samantha could have stayed in the warmth of the pool all night, but not long after they'd both recovered from the sex, Mercury started urging her to the edge of the pool where the pack sat.

"There is still one more thing to show you," he said.

She let him move her about like a rag doll, as she indulged in naughty speculation about what else he might have to show her.

"You're grinning and golden," he accused.

"Me?" She tried to sound surprised and playfully offended, but in the end she couldn't stop either the grin or the coloring, so she nodded. "You're right. I totally am."

He lifted her out of the water and sat her on the stone edge.

"Yikes. That's cold." She realized then that the sky had turned the pink and ginger of twilight, but the white of the rocks reflected what light was left and made the area glow in a rainbow of colors.

As Mercury pulled his body out of the water, she made a grab for her tanks and briefs.

"The other pool I want to show you is cooler but those won't keep you warm. You don't need them.

Samantha looked around. "What if Lo or Carn decide to come down for a bath?"

His brows drew together and his flat nose scrunched, but then he shrugged and picked up his own pants.

Samantha stepped into her briefs. "I suppose, living together, you aren't used to having much privacy." Or, being a slave, allowed any modesty.

Mercury didn't answer and she took that to mean he didn't want to think about his years of captivity. She tugged on her tunic and started to grab the rest of her clothes.

"That's enough. More will weigh you down in the water. The other pool is larger and deeper."

"Okay." She helped him pack their things then followed him

back the way they'd come. He brought along the flower vines, tickling her curiosity, but she managed to hold back her questions.

"This is it." Mercury stopped and put down their things. "Wait here."

She sat on the edge of the pool as he took a strand of flowers and waded into the pool.

Samantha pulled her legs up to her chest and huddled against the cooling night air.

Mercury disappeared below the surface of the water and she leaned forward. He was a dark mass against the lighter rocks and a trail of glowing pink light moved through the water beside him. It swirled in a whimsical pattern and she followed it, fascinated and giddy as a child by the time Mercury surfaced and pulled her into the water with him.

"It's beautiful," she breathed. "It has to be some sort of bioluminescent reaction," she said as he pressed the vine into her hand. "How did you discover it?"

"Last night, Lo and I found some of the flowers that had fallen into one of the pools." He tugged on her hand. "Go ahead, *courra*, paint for me."

She chuckled. "I guess it *is* like painting." She made a large circle, trailing the vine through the water and was rewarded with a pink glow following her pattern. A burst of pure joy had her stopping to share the feeling with him. "I love it. Thank you for showing me." But her voice fluttered like feathers and it wasn't joy that shook her.

He was beautiful with a smile on his face and delight, a sparkle in his eyes. She pretended it was the cold that started her trembling and she stepped into his arms. It should have been a happy moment, but fear and cynicism and longing had twisted into an achy ball that burrowed into her chest. Her eyes threatened to overflow with barely restrained tears.

She wanted to find some way to keep him from going back to Roma. To keep him from risking his life. But selfishness would do her no good. He wasn't hers. She could so easily fall in love with him, but too much was uncertain. Even if he survived his rescue attempt, his whole life, everything he'd know was changing. This wasn't the time to expect him to make any life altering decisions or new commitments. This was a time to enjoy every moment they could.

"Samantha?" Mercury's warm breath tickled along her neck, starting another wave of shivers. "Your cold, we should get back."

"No." She ducked under his arm and pressed her chest to his back, wrapping one arm around his shoulder. When she hitched a leg to his hip his hands were there in an instant. Large warm hands under her thighs. She twined the fingers of her free hand with his-- their two vines of flowers trailing in the water. She pressed a kiss to his shoulder. "Paint with me."

CHAPTER SIXTEEN

Arena Dogs Campsite, Planet G-45987
Earth Alliance Beta Sector - Gollerra Border
2210.167

Samantha sat cross-legged and barefoot in a patch of grass on the slope down from the cargo-drop campsite. The breeze rustled in the trees and some sort of insect provided a concert of clicking noises. They'd arrived back at their original campsite early the day before. Lo had continued on, to check on Drake and Resler. Mercury and a still limping Carn had disappeared into the woods at sun-up. It seemed impossible Carn had been able to hike on that knee so quickly—genetic engineering at work.

They'd been gone for hours, but she wasn't worried. Once the urgent need to stop the low frequency pulse had been met, they'd become more interested in exploring this new world and she knew they wouldn't be so far that they couldn't get back if she ran into trouble.

She studied the collection of objects she'd pulled together—a scrap of thermal material, a small emergency toolkit with a cutter and a sealer, and packaging from supplies they'd already used. She'd never had a need to make shoes before, but she wanted something besides her deck boots to wear around camp.

Samantha tugged the tool-case open and peered inside. She had the cutter in her hand when she realized she was no longer alone. Lo stood like a living statue under the nearest tree. Only his chest moved. He had one hand pressed on the trunk of the tree, the other against his belly. The muscles of his arms and chest were sharply defined in the dappled sunlight.

He stood there, watching her, even after he knew she'd seen him. His teeth hid behind his lips, but the tip of his tongue peeked out.

Sometimes he took her breath away.

What did that say about her? Her feelings for Mercury had grown so strong she could barely contain them. She shouldn't even be noticing Lo. She'd grown fond of them all. How could she not? But that didn't mean she should get hot and bothered by two of them. She wasn't her father. Stars, she couldn't be that faithless and weak.

Something broke the spell and Lo strode toward her in long fluid movements. He crouched in front of her, but kept nearly a meter between them. "All is well, little Sam. I'm no threat to you."

She reached out and waited for him to put his hand in hers. "I know, Lo. I know."

His touch burned hot against her palm. His claws were barely visible. His presence dominated her field of vision. So close, it was impossible not to notice his raw sexuality, but she refused to acknowledge her reaction.

It had been a mistake to touch him.

She slipped her hand free and wiped her sweaty palm against her thigh.

Lo followed the movement and she considered trying to explain, but he tipped his head back and howled.

"Calling the guys," she guessed.

He nodded then tilted his head to the side and twitched his ears. "They'll be back soon."

"Great," she said with more enthusiasm than she intended. "I wasn't making much progress on my shoe project anyway."

He looked down at her collection of materials and frowned. "Is *that* what you were doing?"

Samantha sighed. "I hadn't really started yet."

He pushed to his feet, but didn't offer her a hand to stand and she didn't ask for one.

They walked in silence back to the cluster of boulders. Samantha tucked away her supplies and took a seat on one of the containers. Within a few minutes, first Mercury then Carn jogged back into camp.

The men greeted each other with small touches—a clasp of an arm, a pat on a back, a brush of shoulders—as if they needed the physical contact to reassure each other that they were all together again. When Lo and Carn found spots to sit, Mercury settled on the ground near her. He pressed his arm against her leg, instantly making her feel one of them.

She hadn't realized until he did it that she'd been envying them as she watched the small ritual. She put her hand on Mercury's shoulder and something tightened in her belly then eased in her chest.

"They remain in their camp," said Lo. "But I saw the whip-master speak into a panel on the escape-pod."

Mercury peered up at her. "Could he be trying to call for help?"

"No." Samantha shook her head. "He couldn't use the pod to contact anyone. It doesn't have that kind of range." She tried to think, but she was certain the Roma men didn't have the skills to rig up a relay with the *Dove*.

"What's the range?" asked Carn.

"Pretty good in deep space. Not so good with the interference of a solar system close by. From planet surface, it wouldn't reach beyond a high orbit."

Lo bent forward to rest his forearms on his thighs. "He didn't look as if he was repeating a message. Seemed more like a conversation."

Carn made a sound, something like a whimper, and his eyes widened. "Could it be the rendezvous ship?"

"Or," said Mercury. "Someone responding to your distress call."

Samantha refused to calculate the odds someone helpful would respond. "If anyone is out there they would've found the *Dove*. They might have moved into orbit to look for survivors."

Mercury frowned. "In which case they could be more help to the whip-master than to us."

"I was hoping," she said. "That the call might draw help from the Gollerra system."

Mercury blinked slowly. She could see the possibilities turning in his brain. "Could someone from that system have reached us?"

"Yes. There are transports that could make it in about three days, if there was someone willing and ready to respond right away." Willing to cross the border, too. She'd sent her distress call on the main shipping frequency and included her indie call-sign hoping someone friendly might hear it. The problem was, she didn't know how many friends she had left among the indies. "But it's also been long enough that someone could have made it from Roma. I'd have thought two more days-but if they had a fast enough ship…"

"Then we have to be prepared that it might be them," concluded Mercury. "If it is someone friendly, can you make contact from the cargo pod?"

She thought about it. "Yeah. Damn it. I should have thought of this before. I'll have to rig something. The thing is only equipped with a beacon, but I can make it work."

Mercury's nose flared and she knew he was trying to read her scent. Good luck to him. She wasn't even sure what she was feeling herself. Letting herself care for him was crazy when she'd been confused by her reaction to Lo less than an hour before. Thinking about the future, their future, seemed like a really bad idea.

She was startled by the fingers that tugged on the fist she'd tightened around the cloth of her shirt, right over her heart. She hadn't been aware of doing it, but he'd seen it and the determination on his face as he pulled her to her feet, promised he wouldn't be pushed away.

He sent Carn to patrol the perimeter around them and told Lo to get some sleep, then he led her to the cargo-drop. He observed, intent, as she worked on the transmitter. It wasn't easy without the proper tools, but she wired up a simple receiver and got to work altering the beacon transmitter to meet their needs.

"Do all pilots have such skill with modifying systems?" His voice broke into her thoughts.

"Hardly." She laughed at the thought, more than a little pleased to see him looking as interested and intent on her work as when she started. "Most pilots are too arrogant to get their hands dirty." And most men were too easily bored to sit around watching her work.

He moved closer, propping against the side of the drop. "Then how did you learn to do this?"

He was close enough to touch, making it harder to keep the emotional distance she'd been aiming for between them. "My father had a small freight hauling business. Strictly indie, that means independent—not part of a large company, but he had a good reputation." At least with clients. "He taught me to pilot, but before that his crew taught me to work on the ship."

"Why would you seek out this skill when your father could teach you the other?"

She tried to keep her face blank. "It was never a sure thing that he'd let me on his ship, let alone teach me to fly. Mom and I lived in a refugee camp, Haverlee. My folks never actually married."

"I don't know this word."

She looked up at that. "Married? It's a commitment when two people decide to share their lives, be with only each other."

His lips thinned and his tongue slipped out to briefly flick across them. "It's like mates then."

The Arena Dogs probably didn't have any legal options, she realized. They'd been slaves with no hope of anything better. They'd made the best of their situation.

"Your father and mother had a child together, but weren't mates," he said. "Were they forced to breed?"

Samantha's stomach twisted. He looked so grim. "Have you ever been forced to father a child?"

"Forced breeding is something they started only recently and no children have been conceived." His face blanked as he spoke, all sign of emotion gone. "Hera was sent to us, but Carn wanted her." He shook his head as if he thought he could shake away the thought.

A knot formed in her stomach, as she considered what might have happened if Carn hadn't wanted Hera. "I'm glad you weren't forced."

"What of your parents?" His tone rang with a demand to move the conversation forward.

She turned her attention back to her work, connecting the power circuit to the voltage regulator. "My parents weren't forced either. They wanted to share sex. I think having me was a mistake. Dad had women in every port he worked. He wasn't awful about it though. He brought my mother funds when he came around. And he did come around."

"And..." The softly spoken word encouraged her to continue. To dive back into the old memories as she completed her work.

"I knew he was my only way out of the camp so when he came to visit Mom I hung out with his crew. I was just a kid, but I was his kid, so they treated me well. Taught me things." Probably, her old man had told them to keep her busy so she wouldn't be in the way of him getting busy with her mother, but mentioning that might be over-sharing. "So I learned to work on ships around the port and he eventually falsified citizenship papers for me and paid for the tests so I could get certified. I signed onto his ship and he taught me to be a pilot, too."

"You no longer work with your father."

She had to swallow a lump of regrets before she could answer. "He died last year."

Mercury stroked her cheek with the back of his fingers. "I may not have had a true blood family, but we made our own." She'd understood that much and been awed by the strength of heart that had allowed them to survive in such brutality without losing their humanity. "We made packs to protect one another, to stand and fight together. Just as Carn and Lo are my pack brothers, there were others who are gone now. We mourned their loss and still feel it with each breath." Maybe it was the loss he wore like a gravity-suit that had made it so impossible for her to ignore him. It was something they shared. He slipped his fingers under her chin and lifted her face to look into her eyes. "I'm sorry you lost this man who was your father. You honor his memory by using these skills he taught you."

Something moist dripped onto her lip. She licked it away, tasting the saltiness of tears. She hadn't known she was crying. She'd never cried for her father before.

She scrubbed the moisture from her eyes. "I hated him. I loved him, but I hated him too. My mother loved him, always. Every time he came around she'd light up and then he'd leave again. She never cried in front of me, but her light was gone when he left." She scrubbed at her eyes again to make sure all traces of her tears were wiped away. "I swore I'd never cry for him."

Mercury pulled her into his arms. His deep voiced rumbled softly in her ear. "You wanted to hate him, but you couldn't hate someone who gave your mother joy, gave you life, gave you skills to make a life for yourself."

She pulled away choking on a laugh. "Sure. Side with him. Just like a man." Her laughter faded quickly, leaving a raw ache in its wake. "I thought I'd become important to him, but when he died he left me nothing. Not even a part interest in his freighter. He left that to his crew chief."

"I have nothing to give you," he said. His eyes narrowed as his stormy gaze met hers. "Nothing but myself. But I'll never stand against you or leave you behind. I'll fight to keep you with me always."

His words were too perfect, everything she could hope for... and impossible to believe. "When would that be? After you rescue Carn's mate? Or after you free all the slaves?" Stars, she sounded like a selfish shrew.

Mercury didn't bristle as she expected—as some terrified corner of her soul hoped he would. A fight would be easier to handle than more of this weak, clingy creature that had taken over her body. But the solemn expression on his face never wavered, never gave way to anger.

"You're right," he said. "I'm not free to devote myself solely to your happiness, but seldom in our world are things as we would wish."

His easy agreement doused the fuel for her ire.

She couldn't even imagine the life he'd endured. The cruelty and hate. He came from a world that seemed terrible and incomprehensibly horrifying.

He didn't scoff at her grief. A grief that should have seemed trivial through his eyes. Eyes that had gone silver for her. As if he stood ready to fight her battles. How could she do any less for him?

She couldn't find the words to tell him how she felt. Even if his intentions were the best, letting herself love him would give him the power to crush her.

The crackle of the cargo-drop's newly adapted receiver saved her from failing, utterly, to protect her heart.

"Drake? Come in Drake." The voice coming across the recently modified circuits was unfamiliar, but the person obviously knew the Roma men.

Mercury stilled, barely breathing.

"This is Drake." The voice that answered filled Samantha with rage. "You get them?"

"We retrieved the tracking receiver from the *Dove*. We're coming down for a low pass now. We'll land when we've completed the sweep. Should be first light in your location."

"We'll be waiting," said Drake's voice over the receiver. "We can start the hunt as soon as your ship is down."

"Hoowa."

The transmission went quiet and Samantha let out the breath she'd been holding. "That doesn't sound like a rescue."

"Hunters." Mercury growled in the back of his throat.

"We must return to camp and tell the others." Mercury threw back his head and howled. The others joined him, howls echoing faintly in the distance.

By the time they made it back, Carn and Lo were there, waiting for the news.

"The hunters are here. They hunt at daybreak." Mercury's voice had gone all snarly in a way she hadn't heard since they'd left Drake and Resler behind.

"We'll be ready." Carn sounded calm and confident.

Lo spoke directly to Samantha. "Will you be able to fly their ship?"

Finally, something she knew she could handle. "If they can land it here, I can pilot it."

Mercury squeezed her hand. "You'll remain in this camp. We'll come for you after they're dead."

She had no intention of waiting in safety. She might be a coward, but she wasn't that kind of coward. And she'd really hoped they could avoid any killing. "They said something about a tracker. They'll know where we are, by now." She looked up to the cloudless aqua expanse overhead and in her mind's eye she could picture the ship skimming the planet's atmosphere.

"She's right," said Carn. "The camp may not be safe."

Lo spoke up. "If they can track us, they'll know we're coming to them. They'll have the advantage."

"Maybe not." Samantha met Lo's fire-flecked gaze. "If they needed to run the scan before landing, then they aren't sure it will work once they reach the surface. It may be designed to bounce off a satellite—something this planet doesn't have. Then again, the pilot could drop them off and return the ship to orbit. The ship could relay the info down to the men on the surface."

"They'll be too arrogant and too eager to hunt to believe that would be necessary," said Lo.

"Tomorrow," Mercury growled, "we take the fight to them."

She knew her next words wouldn't go over easy, but they had to be said. For Mercury, for them all. "You can't kill them."

Lo snarled. "You don't know their cruelty." His words were bitten off with remembered pain. Samantha flinched at the sound, but she knew now that his anger wasn't directed at her. It only made her want to find a way to undo every terrible hurt done him.

Mercury wrapped a hand around her arm and spoke more quietly. "Do you care so much for them?"

She jerked her arm out of his grasp and huffed as angry heat flushed through her. "No! I don't give a damn about them, but if you kill them, you'll be wanted men. You'll never be free." And it would be more violence to weigh on their souls.

Lo's growling faded. "We're already escaped property to them, little Sam."

She shook her head. "But maybe not in Gollerra. There's only one crime the Golley-Alliance treaty recognizes as cause to hand someone over, and that's the murder of each other's citizens. "

Mercury reached for her slowly, cautiously, as if she were a sand-viper. He drew his palms down the length of her arms until he circled her wrists. "Then perhaps we steal their ship and leave them here, alive. Can we prevent them from alerting Roma?"

She took a deep, relieved breath and exhaled her agitation. "They've probably already alerted them to what's happening now, but yeah, we can keep them from finding out you're on your way back for Hera. The real question is, do you have a plan once you get there?"

"We'll find a way. A way that will keep you safe."

"We're not far from Haverlee port. We could get help." She realized she was pleading. It wasn't as if she wanted them to abandon Carn's mate, but it wouldn't do the woman any good if they got themselves killed trying to get to her.

"We," Lo raged, voice dripping with venom, "don't need the help of humans."

Mercury released her and put himself between her and the others. "We'd still be in cages, if this human hadn't helped us."

Samantha could hear Lo panting with anger. She squeezed Mercury's shoulder and edged around him, stopping within touching distance of Lo.

She rubbed her hands on her pants legs to keep from reaching out. "I only wanted to help."

"You're different," Lo snapped then shook his head as if clearing his thoughts. "I didn't mean to frighten you."

"I wasn't afraid." From the moment she'd realized his anger served to shield his pain, her fear had started to lessen. She didn't know when it had disappeared completely, but she knew now that it was gone.

He frowned, tiny lines disturbing the beauty of his features.

She pressed her lips together, biting her lip as she searched for some way to reach him. "I can't pretend to know what your life has been like, but I do understand the hopelessness of having all roads to a better existence blocked against you. I understand going without the things others take for granted. I understand betrayal." She took a deep breath. It was important that she think about her words before she said them. When she made a promise she made sure it meant something. "I'm nothing like the people who hurt you, Lo. I'm not perfect, but there's one thing you can count on, I'll never betray your trust."

Lo reached out and took her hand. He glanced over her shoulder to where Mercury stood at her back then pulled her hand to rest over his heart.

Mercury directed everyone to prepare for tomorrow. Samantha slipped easily into the rhythm of the team as they worked in silence. A silence that gave him plenty of time to contemplate the coming challenge and all that was at stake. He had time to reflect on the determined set of Samantha's chin as she'd spoken to them from her heart of loyalty and betrayal.

She'd help them free Carn's mate. She'd help them learn how to survive in her world, she'd face danger at his side. She was beautiful and courageous. In his heart she was already his mate. A more perfect mate than he could ever have dreamt of. So much more than he deserved.

He'd seen so many of his people die in the arena, unable to do a thing to help them. In the kennels he'd done all he could to protect his pack brothers, but still two were gone. After years of standing strong together on the training grounds and in the arena, Jupiter and Senneca were dead. The thought made him want to howl out his grief.

He'd been shocked by the offer in the glance Lo had given him as he pressed her small hand to his heart. He'd never thought to see the implied offer of loyalty to Mercury's mate from his troubled brother. It was something he'd been afraid his brother would never be able to give. It made him breathe easier and created an ember of hope in his gut.

Tomorrow they'd slip into the enemy camp and steal a ship. Something could go wrong. They could face death. If not tomorrow, then when they returned to RomaRex. He could be killed and he couldn't leave Samantha to face the consequences of aiding them alone. Lo's look assured him that was no longer a worry. Even if death took Mercury from her side.

It was the way of the Dogs. The way of the packs. The only way they'd found to stay sane in a life full of danger and death.

A man always had brothers. He always knew that, should he die, they'd stand together and survive. A mate to one became bonded to the pack and they'd give their lives to stand beside her. Females of their kind were so rare, no pack had ever been given two, but Carn was already mated. That left only Lo to bond with Mercury's mate. He might harbor a deep distrust of human females, but Lo would stand with Samantha should Mercury fall. Tonight, he'd seal the bond between his mate and his brother. If he fell in battle, they'd stand together. Samantha would not be left alone.

CHAPTER SEVENTEEN

Arena Dogs Campsite, Planet G-45987
Earth Alliance Beta Sector - Gollerra Border
2210.167

Samantha decided not to wait for sundown to get some sleep. The three males sat near the fire talking strategy. Lo had caught dinner sometime during the day. They preferred fresh meat over ration bars—not surprising as their animal natures were so close to the skin. Mercury had already informed her they'd hike away from the camp before sunrise. She didn't have their stamina so she curled into the bedding on the pallet under the tarp.

She woke hours later to Mercury climbing into her den of blankets. The sun had set and the night was growing colder, but he'd hung a low camp-light on one of the posts. "Where are Carn and Lo?" They'd only made one pallet and they'd all been sharing the space and the warmth.

"Carn will keep watch tonight. Lo will join us later." His voice was soft and serious. She wanted to see him smile again.

He'd moved closer but hadn't yet touched her. His dark hair hung loose around his shoulders. A black so luminous it was almost silver had eclipsed the thundercloud gray of his eyes.

She let her gaze trace across his broad shoulders and down his sculpted chest and abdomen to find he was completely bare and aroused. Just the thought of him buried inside her, as close as the two of them could be, created a wet heat that threatened to bathe her thighs. She wanted him. That fast she was ready to take him into her body as if it were the most natural thing in the world. But it had never been like that for her. Not with any man.

He held her gaze as he moved closer. "I want you, *courra*. Say yes."

"Yes." She knew what she wanted. He wanted her and she wanted him just as much.

He took her lips in an aggressive kiss and she met him stroke for stroke. Their tongues fought eagerly until they were both breathless. She bit at his lip to make him back off.

He moaned an encouraging sound, but slowly he eased back. He panted, his whole body moving with the labored breaths. When she pushed on his chest he rolled to his back easily and pulled her over him. Hands on her hips, he centered her over his erection, surging up into the damp material of her briefs. His hands slid back, slipping under the material to squeeze her ass. She nipped at his chin, pressed kisses to his jaw, rubbed her cheek against his. They rocked together, building the anticipation until it grew too large to contain.

Samantha sat up, pulling at her under-tank, tossing it aside as she freed her breasts. She palmed them, needing the contact on the sensitive tips. Mercury groaned as if her hands were on his flesh instead of hers. His eyes turned slumberous with arousal. His hands pushed hers aside and molded against the soft mounds. When his thumb scraped across the cinnamon-toned flesh, she moaned and he repeated the touch. He watched her nipples harden with the fascination of an artist discovering a new mix of patterns on an artscreen.

She leaned forward, seeking a firmer sensation and the resulting pressure sent a spike of arousal swirling down through her body to settle into the swollen flesh between her legs. She rocked her hips and it was suddenly Mercury groaning. His hands slipped across her ribs as he reached for her briefs then he rolled her beneath him, working them down and off.

The moment she was free of the material, he came over her, settling between her thighs as if he'd always belonged there. She wrapped her legs around his hips and circled his neck with her arms. He felt incredibly right pressed skin to skin with her. For long, delicious moments he held her. Nothing more. Just an embrace, tight and relentless, as if he understood her need for that feeling—that he would never let her go. She needed it more than she needed orgasm. But his body quivered with a more carnal need. She pulled a hand down from his shoulder and slid it down his chest. She coasted over all those formidable muscles, the strength he'd never use against her.

Her finger dipped in the indention of his navel, seeking the jump and quiver of his response, but she didn't stop. Not until her hand found the hard silk and steel length of his cock. She palmed the broad crown then wrapped her fingers around him and stroked. When he jerked against her hand, she pulled up to the tip and thumbed across the slit, spreading the drop of fluid pearled there. She swirled it around then moved just enough to let her moistened thumb work around the flared ridge. Her thumb brushed a spot along the underside of his cock and his whole body shook. She played her thumb there, glorying in the strain in his body as he fought to allow the intense touch for as long as possible.

His urgent moans made her pulse race as if they were two parts of one being, his pleasure feeding hers. And then he was tugging her hand away. He pulled her other arm from his neck and threaded his fingers with hers, holding them immobile near her head.

He adjusted his hips and his cock was suddenly there, right where she needed it. Another nudge and she gasped at the pressure as he breached her entrance. He stopped, giving her time to breathe, scattering kisses against her temple, her ear, her cheek.

She took a deep breath and urged him inside with the grasp of her thighs. This time, he edged forward, centimeter by centimeter, not stopping until he was as deep as he could go.

He fucked her slow, letting her feel every sensuous slide as he watched her with those intense eyes.

"You're mine," he whispered. "Mine to protect. Mine to provide for."

She wanted the intimacy to last forever. Or she thought she did until the urgency reclaimed them both. His thrusts became quick, deep, hard. They bowed her back with pleasure, building until her orgasm crashed through her, carrying her away and taking him with her as her body rippled around him. He threw his head back and howled as his release filled her.

Samantha came back to herself minutes later, renewed pleasure already coursing through her body. She didn't bother to open her eyes, unable to find any reason to resist the delicious lassitude. Mercury's hand played between her thighs, drawing lazy circles in her cream, touching everywhere but the now over-sensitive bud. Warm lips nuzzled at her belly, trailing kisses up to the lower curve of one breast.

A warm tongue trailed back to her belly button, circling it in a slow wet lick.

She stretched, arching her back and spreading her thighs wider, seeking more of the decadent sensations. Mercury responded, immediately giving her what she needed, stroking her clit with firm pressure. Her hips bucked in response to the agony of a gratification so intense it perched precariously on the border between pleasure and pain. She stroked her hand across the silken head at her belly. Her eyes fluttered open as she gasped with pleasure.

Mercury's silver eyes met hers...but he was above her—not beneath her fingers.

Confusion, followed by shock, sent ice water through her veins. She fisted her fingers in the silken hair beneath her palm and jerked the unexpected second lover away from her. Lo came up with a snarl. Even in the dim light, she could see the flecks of red fire dancing in those night black eyes.

"Breathe, Samantha." Mercury spoke in soothing tones as his hand gripped her thigh, where she'd jerked her knees together. "All is as it should be."

"No. No, I'm pretty sure this is wrong." She released Lo with a shove and struggled to sit up. "What in the stars is going on?"

With a sigh, Mercury let her go. "It's all right. Lo would never hurt you. I told you he would join us tonight."

Samantha vaguely recalled Mercury saying he'd join them later. She tried to think clearly. Whose hand had been between her legs? Aw hell, as if that was all that mattered. "Join us to sleep, not...this." Her stomach sank as she remembered Owens' words. They shared their females. But their actions had told a different story. Right up until she'd woken with both Mercury and Lo touching her.

Samantha wrapped her arms around her knees and pulled them

to her chest for modesty's sake. When she glanced around for clothes there were none in sight. Lo had backed to the edge of the sleeping pallet like a dark shadow.

She turned her attention to Mercury. "Can you hand me my clothes?" Her voice shook.

Mercury edged closer and she scooted away instinctively. Underneath her confusion, a deep sense of betrayal lurked, waiting to swallow her up when she got safely dressed and far away from him.

"Let me hold you, Samantha. You're trembling. Don't be afraid."

"I'm not afraid. It's shock and the cold. Why, Mercury? Why would you do this?"

"This is our way. You're my mate and Lo is my only unmated pack brother. He must seal the bond."

Samantha decided to leave aside his claim that she was his mate. "I don't get it. You share your women? Owens said that, but after being around you guys, I didn't believe it." Her stomach clenched, but she knew it was more nerves than disgust. Shouldn't she be disgusted? No, she'd never been one to judge the practices of other cultures.

This time when Mercury edged closer, she held her ground. He pulled her into the shelter and warmth of his body and the heat of it eased her tremors.

He lifted her chin, forcing her to meet his gaze. "We have few women. When we take one as mate, our unmated pack brothers vow to protect her. Sharing pleasure seals the bond. This is our way."

"It isn't my way, Mercury. You should've talked to me about this. Among my people having sex with someone else is being unfaithful. It's disloyal."

He frowned. "Our lives are different in many ways, my Samantha. For Arena Dogs, every day could be our last. We fight in the arena, often to the death. We must ensure our mates are protected if we die."

She wrapped her hand around his wrist, needing the physical connection between them. "You're not in the arena anymore."

"We still face danger. Let me keep you safe, Samantha. Lo is the only brother I have left to offer you. You know he won't harm you."

Offer her? Like a gift? The idea was crazy, but in a weird way she understood what he meant and how important it was to him. The sincerity was plain on his face. This was normal for him. He didn't understand why she resisted.

"Lo is my pack brother," he said. "I wish you to bond with him. It wouldn't be disloyal if it's what I want."

"It's not what *she* wants." Lo's voice startled her. Soft and mournful, it seeped out of the shadows. She'd never heard him like that. Lo was always angry, but not now. Her rejection hurt him.

"Lo, please understand this isn't about you. It's about me. The way I feel about Mercury."

He shook his head, but he didn't meet her eyes. "Mercury wants us to bond. This is not about him. It doesn't matter. I pledge my protection for my pack brother's mate." Finally, he lifted his head, but it was Mercury he looked at. "I swear it. She set us free. I owe her my life. I won't force the bond on her."

In a flash of movement, he was on his feet and stalking away from them. Pain radiated in every movement.

Samantha turned to Mercury to find him watching Lo with sad eyes. "I'm sorry. I didn't mean to cause him pain."

"I know." He pressed his forehead to hers. "He'd been without hope for so long. He cares for you. That's why this hurts him. Please, Samantha, go to him and ease his torment. His pain is my pain. I'd find only joy if you could ease my brother's misery as you have mine."

She had no intention of having sex with Lo, but she could try to make him understand that she wasn't rejecting him. She eased back and took a deep breath. "I'll talk to him."

Mercury stroked her cheek. "Thank you, my generous mate."

"When I get back we should talk about this whole mate thing," she said. "First, I need something to wear."

CHAPTER EIGHTEEN

Arena Dogs Campsite, Planet G-45987
Earth Alliance Beta Sector - Gollerra Border
2210.167

Samantha pulled on the tent-like top Mercury handed her. She considered making him hunt up her real clothes, but it hung low enough to cover all her girl parts, so she went with it and crawled off the pallet. She padded quickly across the clearing and slipped between the boulders where Lo had disappeared. She saw him heading into the trees at the bottom of the slope and went after him at a jog.

At the tree line she had to slow down. The ground there was covered with brambles and she was barefoot. She grimaced as fine thorns pricked at her tender skin. Lo had to have heard her follow. He'd either allow her to catch him or she wouldn't get near him no matter how fast she moved.

She stepped on a particularly nasty patch of underbrush and her foot snagged on a vine. One minute she was falling right into the brambles, the next she was in Lo's arms. He came from behind her. He'd obviously circled around. She sighed. Probably following her to make sure she didn't get lost. She really was out of her element in this place.

He stood behind her, his arms a loose circle as she got her feet back under her. At her back, he sniffed.

"You're injured?" His voice was full of concern as he turned her, his clawed hands carefully gripping her slender arms.

She wanted to put him at ease, but she couldn't hide her uneasiness with him. "Thanks to you, no."

His inky brows drew together and his nose made a cute little scrunch. "I smell blood."

"I have a few scratches on my feet." She could almost feel the distance between them ease as she watched him fret over her. He was still scowling, but it seemed more adorable than threatening. The tension was still there, but she could breathe easier. "It's nothing s-serious." Her teeth had started to chatter and it was getting harder to ignore the cold.

In a move too quick to counter, he slipped an arm under her thighs and lifted her into his arms. "It was foolish to come into the woods without your boots...or a blanket."

She expected him to carry her back to camp, but without another word he strode deeper into the woods. She knew he wouldn't hurt her, but he might have misinterpreted her actions in following him.

"Where are you taking me?"

"There's a clearing. It's not far." He didn't look at her when he said it and she became very aware of the heat of his body along her side and the hand gripping her leg, just above her knee.

"Lo, I—"

He didn't let her finish. "I assume you followed because you wish to talk."

She was reminded of Mercury's claims that her scent changed when her moods changed and wondered if that accounted for Lo's seeming ability to read her mind.

"I'll listen," he said. "If it will ease your discomfort."

Her discomfort? "Gee, thanks."

"You're welcome."

She laughed. He was too smart to miss her sarcasm. Somewhere, buried deeply, Lo had a playful side. It hurt her heart to think of the pain that had buried that side of him so deeply.

Lo stepped into the clearing. The moon washed the small ring in a soft light, creating a silvery sanctuary. The lingering aroma of flowers drifted in the air. In the daylight, the spot would be full of color. He set her on her feet in a patch of soft grass. She stood her ground, not stepping back. Choosing instead to reach up to caress his cheek.

"Please look at me, Lo."

She waited until those devil eyes met hers.

"I never wanted to hurt you."

He said nothing.

"I don't know how to explain it right," she said, the cold beginning to seep back into her. "I've always believed loving someone means ch-choosing to be only with them."

His features were closed again, but he nodded, one sharp dip of his chin. "You love him."

For one moon-drenched moment her heart stopped.

She loved Mercury.

Her heart pounded hard in her chest. "I do." She swallowed hard against the lump in her throat. "I can't believe I t-told you that. I haven't even told him. I'm not sure I should. None of you realize how much things could change when we get back to civilization. When you get Hera back."

"Dogs don't often think of love or spend time trying to predict the future. We think of life and death. Mercury wants to spend whatever life he has with you and he knows you feel the same."

"Presumptuous," she said, but there was no heat in her voice and she nodded in acknowledgement.

He pulled her hand from his cheek and moved it to his chest over his heart.

"You're in both our hearts. I don't have a whole heart to give you as Mercury does, but I have room there for you. I'll keep my pledge. No matter what the future holds."

Her heart ached for him. She wrapped her arms around his ribs and pressed her cheek where her hand had been. He skin smelled of the spring fed river and the night. His arms came around her, pulling her more tightly against his muscular frame and his warmth. They stood that way as she listened to the steady thud beneath her ear.

One of his deadly hands wove through her hair and the other stroked her back with more gentleness than she thought him capable. Her body responded to the heat and shelter he offered. She sucked in a breath. It filled her lungs and pressed her breasts more firmly against the wall of hard muscle. It sent a jolt of pleasure to her feminine core.

How could she want him so much when she'd just admitted she was in love with Mercury? She tried to will away her reaction, but

she refused to push away from him, unwilling to shatter the peace
they'd made. Her hands stroked the lean muscles of his back,
fingers hesitating over the scars that told the story of a life lived in
hell. They'd named him Diablo, the devil, but they'd failed in their
attempts to turn him into his namesake. He had anger, but he also
understood tenderness and loyalty. He'd never betray Mercury.

But Mercury wouldn't see their having sex as a betrayal. He
wanted her to take away Lo's pain. He wanted them to bond. She
wondered if Lo, with his heightened senses, could smell the arousal
dampening her thighs. "You can't possibly want me," she
whispered. "I'm not sure you even like me." The words slipped out
before she could think better of it.

His body stiffened in response. The hand in her hair fisted tight,
pulling her head back, as he gripped her ass to pull her off her feet
and up his body. The evidence of his desire was hard and
undeniable and pressed nearly where she needed it.

"I want you," he said. "More than I have wanted anything
since... I haven't fucked a female for my own pleasure in a long
time."

She should probably be offended that he might want her just to
ease his horniness, but her body responded to the longing and
hunger in every syllable. And she knew behind his words there was
a truth he was unable to speak. She wasn't one of the greedy
women who'd used his body with no care for the man. He'd
chosen her. She was something he wanted for himself. The
knowledge was intoxicating.

She wrapped one leg around his hip, instinctively seeking the
pressure she needed to appease her heated core. His hands shifted
and he adjusted her, drawing her legs more firmly around him and
rocking his restrained cock against her aching pussy. He buried his
face in her neck. Licked the pulse point. Growled deep in his chest.

Samantha moaned and ground against him.

Lo's hands shifted again, pushing aside her shirt to squeeze her
bare ass. He boldly traced the valley with the fingers of one hand.
His hands were firm, but there was no prick of claws as he touched
her. Her heart raced as one careful finger dipped slowly into her
wet flesh, but in that moment, she trusted him with the most secret
parts of her.

"I want to taste you," he whispered. "I want to taste his seed on
you."

She shivered at the thought. Cringed at the reminder of the man she loved. Was she really doing this?

"Lo—"

He nipped at her lips, silencing her protests as he carried her across the clearing and to a blanket stretched across the ground.

When her eyebrows shot up, he explained. "This is where I went earlier when Mercury was fucking you." He lowered her to the blanket then traced a finger across her forehead, easing the signs of a frown. "Don't worry, he'll be glad of this." He grinned— the first happy expression she'd seen on his face. "He'll be glad as long as you're well pleasured and there is no doubt of that."

She believed his boast. His face was all arrogance. He was sure of his ability, but there was no malice in that knowledge, no intent to use it against her. If her desire for him had been nothing more than lust she could have left him there and gone back to Mercury. But it was more than lust. She didn't know if that made it less or more of a betrayal, but she let the tender feelings bubbling up inside her tug the corners of her mouth into a smile.

Lo dropped to his belly between her legs. Large hands gripped her thighs, pushing them wide and preventing any attempt to thwart his purpose. He turned his head and licked at the soft skin over trembling muscle, a long wet lap of his rough tongue that had her squirming. He tended to the other thigh in the same way, lapping away the evidence of her earlier bout of lovemaking with Mercury and the cream of her more recent arousal.

"You taste as sweet as you smell." His words rumbled up from somewhere deep in his chest. The next swipe of his tongue burrowed between the lips of her sex and stroked directly across her clit. Lightning shot through her, bowing her body. The next stroke of his tongue followed the same path and all thought was swept aside. The only thing in her thoughts was the wicked sweep of Lo's talented tongue and the vague thought that she needed to talk to him about the proper pace of foreplay. But maybe not. She felt tender and swollen, needy and hot. Relentless, he stroked her to the edge of orgasm.

And then the pressure was gone. She wanted to weep at the pain of the loss. She blinked him into focus. He hadn't gone far. He stood in the moonlight, fighting his way out of the tight pants to bare all of his beautifully masculine body. His cock stood up, hard and full, the tip shimmered with pre-cum and the length jerked in anticipation of fucking her.

He dropped back to the blanket. He turned her to her hands and knees then thrust into her. Already wet, her flesh provided no resistance. In that one stoke he was fully, deeply inside her. He withdrew and slammed home again. She screamed her pleasure. He wrapped his hands around her hips and set an unyielding pace, fucking her hard. He was wild and reckless and she didn't want anything else in that moment. The hard pounding shook every cell in her body, without providing any hope of relief. It was as if he needed to fuck out his pent up pain—something that could give them both searing pleasure, but not release. Release was not something he wanted for this tortured part of himself.

As his cock surged in and out of her he found all the dark corners of her soul. Places that denied her any pretense of fucking Lo because it was what Mercury wanted. Places where she was forced to acknowledge she wanted Lo only for herself and she gloried in the wild freedom of the physical. Later she would worry over what he'd touched inside her. What she'd allowed him to uncover. But not now. Not when the pleasure was a blaring horn in her head, drowning out any rational thought.

When he finally slowed, her arms were shaking, her thighs trembling. Panting hard, he leaned over her back and wrapped one arm around her hips. He held her tight against his groin as they both took a moment to catch their breaths.

Lo rotated his hips in one sensuous, grind then eased out of her. She wanted to protest but couldn't yet form her thoughts into anything coherent. She was far more compliant than she intended as he repositioned his knees along the outside of hers and slipped his cock back between her thighs. But he didn't enter her, instead he slipped the head of his cock against her clit. She gasped. Her back arched and she threw her head back.

His cheek pressed against her temple as he moaned. Her thighs were forced tightly together by the position, making a tight wet channel for him. He thrust against that sensitive nubbin in short strokes that kept him surrounded in her slick heat and supplied her with a constant, unbearable pressure.

Instinctively, she started to fight to free herself, but he only wrapped more tightly around her, controlling her and the need to fight died away as pleasure stole her will and left her limp and stunned. Just as the world went black at the edges, she heard him throw back his head to howl and felt the hot splash of semen against her belly.

In the distance a second howl joined Lo's throaty bay... Mercury.

CHAPTER NINETEEN

Arena Dogs Campsite, Planet G-45987
Earth Alliance Beta Sector - Gollerra Border
2210.168

Mercury looked down at his sleeping mate. She'd been nearly boneless when Lo had carried her back to him. Lo had pleasured her well and she'd eased Lo's pain. The change in his pack brother had been clear in every line of his body, every line of his face. How this had changed his mate would be harder to see.

Time would tell.

Worry stalked his thoughts like a hulking beast with impossible reach, ready to pound him with dismal scenarios. Its boisterous roar warned that she might not be able to accept their ways. That asking this of her when she wasn't even ready to accept his claim, to call him mate, might have broken something between them. But they hadn't had the luxury of time. She was strong. She would adapt and he would find a way to make things work.

His mate was worth any struggle. He traced the tip of his finger along her narrow little nose with its curved shape as she slept. She'd driven his lust higher and made his heart swell with happiness as Lo had put her on her feet near the sleeping pallet. The necessity to stand on her own had pulled her out of her well-fucked haze. She'd immediately looked for him and he'd met her gaze, doing his best to look attentive but emotionless, unsure what she might be feeling and how his own emotions would affect her.

Lo's blunt declaration that they were bonded had sent a thrill of deep satisfaction through him. His mate was safe. Should he die, she wouldn't be left alone and unprotected. He'd gone to her then and she'd gone into his arms without hesitation. He'd pressed his lips to her ear and whispered his gratitude then urged her to the pallet. He'd pressed his body along one side of her and Lo had taken his place on the other side, his face pressed against her side. His mate had turned her face into his chest, but her hand had stroked Lo's hair before she'd fallen asleep, bone-tired.

He wanted to let her sleep longer, but they had to leave soon if they were going to catch their enemies off guard. Carn stood by the fire, waiting, impatient. Mercury looked down to Lo to see him awake, but still curled tightly against Samantha.

"It's time."

The sound of his voice woke Samantha. Lo pressed a kiss to the underside of her breast as she stretched into wakefulness then he rolled away and left them.

Samantha's eyes batted open. "Time?"

"Time to go find you a ship to fly."

She smiled, but something sad lingered in her eyes. "Right."

"How are you feeling?" He studied the tiny muscles of her face and breathed in her scent. The smell of the pack on her was distracting, but not enough to overlook the tension around her mouth.

"A little sore. Nothing a good hike won't work out."

One look ensured Lo and Carn backed off enough to give them privacy. "Samantha—"

She pressed fingers over his lips. "I'm fine."

He took her fingers, moving them away and threading his with hers. He bent down to press his forehead to hers as he wrapped one arm around her, pulling her tight against his body. "Today, I go into battle knowing I've already won, for you are mine."

She wrapped her arm around him and hugged him then pushed away gently. "Let's just get through the day without anyone getting hurt, okay."

He nodded. "That's my plan, also."

She laughed. It transformed her face. Cast off the shadows. "Good," she said. "Then, now that we're agreed, let's go find a ship."

Basking in the warmth of her laughter, Mercury knew he was

the luckiest of Dogs. Samantha was special. He would find a way to give her happiness. But first they needed to get off this world. "Lo and Carn will accompany you to find the ship. We expect it will be near their camp."

Samantha nodded. "And you?"

"I'll lead a false trail for the hunters then join you."

She folded her arms across her chest, all the laughter gone from her cheeks. "So you make yourself the bait. Take the biggest risk."

"I'm fastest. I can lay the trail and get back to you long before the hunters double-back."

Her lips pressed together in a bunch then the tension eased and she licked her lips. "Be safe," she said. "And don't be long."

"Nothing," he promised, "will ever keep me away from you for long."

Mercury breathed deeply, filling his lungs with the scent of his enemies. He turned his head and moved forward taking in another breath. Teasing out the direction of a scent on the wind as he was approaching them was far harder than tracking a scent trail behind them, but the stakes were high, inflaming his senses and driving his determination.

Another deep breath and Mercury had the whip-master's scent in his nose. He worked his way into Drake's path, then laid a trail to lure him away from the other hunters that stalked the woods with him. A broken twig, a scuffed trail in the dirt, crushed brambles beneath his boot.

He stopped, hugging his body to a wide tree and listened. There, the scrape of a branch against the whip-master's coat. Confident Drake followed, Mercury circled around. This time his steps were light. Not even the ground noticed the weight of his tread. He fell into step behind his enemy.

He followed the man past the edge of the trail he'd laid. A satisfied warmth seeped through his muscles as he watched him grow frustrated with no more trail to follow, then Drake stopped abruptly. He stood there, stone still for nearly a minute.

Drake cursed low then raised his voice. "Impressive, Mercury." He turned slowly to face him. "But I always knew Owens underestimated you."

His hand edged toward the whip coiled on his hip.

Mercury snarled. "Don't make the same mistake."

"You can't think I'm going to lie down and die, because you're feeling puffed up on this temporary freedom."

He said he'd fight, but his hand halted.

Mercury held his distance. "I don't plan to kill you."

Drake's brows shot up. "Turning into a pacifist? That woman is clouding your thinking."

Mercury grinned, a growl vibrating in the back of his throat. "Are you asking me to rip your throat out? Offer me your throat. Tempt me. I may not be able to resist." He wanted Drake to do exactly that. Give him an excuse to break his promise. It wasn't Samantha clouding his thinking, it was his own rage.

Drake's hands slowly lifted to his sides. His face paled, but beyond that small tell, he remained indifferent. The whip-master was notorious for his unemotional way of dealing with the Dogs.

"You control your fear well." He thought of Drake's earlier words, then added, "Impressive."

"Fear? I'd say it's more a healthy respect for your ability to kill efficiently. You're a predator, Mercury. I haven't forgotten that, even if you've fooled Sam."

"Don't even think of her. Don't speak of my Samantha." Mercury instantly regretted the words that told Drake more than he had a right to know about his feelings for his mate.

"Your Samantha? So, she's playing it that way. I bet you think she actually wants you."

Mercury tamped down the rage coursing through him and drew on the icy, calculating mien he'd perfected through years of battle. "Are you brave or foolish to goad me?"

"Maybe there are some things you should know about Samantha Devlin." Unfortunately, the sudden drop in temperature didn't work as effectively on Drake as it did in the arena. The bastard had seen Mercury use the look many times. "After all," Drake taunted. "Roma chose her. Owens never hires anyone without knowing everything about them."

They hadn't known everything. They hadn't known she'd aid him and his brothers. But Mercury couldn't speak of that. He intended to let this man live and he couldn't give Drake anything more to use against her.

Drake smiled, the same cruel twist of lips he wore as his men chained up a Dog for him to whip. "Owens and Sam Devlin are old pals, you know."

"That's not true." Even as he spoke, Mercury realized there was no point in listening to Drake. The man was ever a skilled and shameless liar, but he could smell the lie.

"Oh, not Samantha. Her father, Samuel Devlin. I guess the apple fell farther from the tree than we expected. Her old man would never have tried to steal a shipment out from under Owens. He'd never have lived so long."

"We'll see who lives longest. Today you live, but we'll take the hunter's ship and leave you here to anticipate the day I do come for you. Anticipation—isn't that what you called it when you taught us to drag out an arena match for the amusement of the fans?"

Drake's grin confused Mercury. Drake had to realize Mercury had led them away from their ship while Carn and Lo dealt with whatever men they'd left behind. With Mercury's speed he'd make it to the ship hours before they could get back.

"Do you think because I have no plan to kill you now that you have no reason to fear me?"

"That's not it at all." Drake smirked. "But do you honestly think I didn't plan for something like this? Did you forget who oversaw your training? Who lashed the lessons into your back when you failed?"

Adrenalin flooded Mercury's body as his muscles twitched. Of course Drake had set a trap, but Lo would keep Samantha safe. He had to trust in that.

"I have a message for our girl," said Drake. "In case you do get off this rock." Drake's smirk widened into a full smile, but his hands remained still, held out to the sides. "Tell her to take good care of you. We want you in good shape when she's ready to sell you back to us. After spending all that money, Owens will want to make sure he turns a profit off your sorry hide. Will triple the cost for the privilege to hunt you down."

Mercury ignored the man. He only wanted to return to Samantha and leave the whip-master and his boasts behind. The surge of strength as his muscles readied for the run back, made him restless to move, now. "We'll leave enough supplies for you to survive. I wouldn't want you to die out here before Owens can find you. I don't suppose he'll be too happy that you let us escape in one of his ships. Enjoy whatever life you have left..."

Drake's smirk faded, no doubt disappointed that Mercury didn't respond to his taunt. "Oh, I plan to enjoy it and maybe, when Sam stumbles into my men, I'll enjoy her too."

Mercury let his rage power the blow he struck against Drake's body. Watched the man fall, curling his arms around his vulnerable belly.

Drake sputtered and held out one hand as if to stop Mercury from attacking. "Wait." He spit out blood. "You don't have time for this. Unless you don't care about Sam after all."

Mercury crouched down and snarled. "Don't even speak her name."

"Wait. Let me." Drake moaned as he tried to move. "There's a receiver on my belt, take a look. We've been tracking you."

Mercury hesitated. If they'd been tracking them all day, they'd know exactly where the others were. He took the small device with a colorful screen and blinking lights.

In the center a red and a green dot flashed close together. That had to be him and Drake. One more green dot flashed with two more red. That had to be Lo and Carn with whatever man had been left to guard the ship. Half a dozen more green dots moved toward Carn and Lo…and Samantha.

His rage spiked and his vision clouded. He was on Drake before the rage cleared. Holding back his strength he tapped the man on the head and watched his eyes roll back and his body go limp.

It was little salve to his thirst for vengeance, but for now it would have to be enough.

He leapt to his feet and headed back toward the others.

CHAPTER TWENTY

The Kestrel, Planet G-45987
Earth Alliance Beta Sector - Gollerra Border
2210.168

"Let me in, you overblown excuse for a security protocol."
Samantha adjusted the algorithm on her hastily compiled hack
program then leaned back in the pilot's chair to watch it run.

When they'd reached the area where Drake and Resler had
made camp, Lo and Carn had quickly located the sleek Raptor class
transport vessel and the man left on guard. He'd been sitting on the
ship's entry ramp, not exactly subtle. Carn had taken the man out
with a single throw of a fist sized stone. The big bear of a guy had
quite an arm on him.

A flash of movement on one of the view screens caught
Samantha's eye. She swiveled, putting her full attention on the
exterior views. There. A shadow at the edge of one of the screens.
It could be nothing. Or one of the men who knew this ship. Knew
the vid coverage.

Carn had taken the unconscious guard to the Roma campsite
and Lo had gone to patrol the woods. Neither would have a reason
to skirt the visual sensor arrays even if they knew where they were.
If the hunters were back, what did that mean for Mercury? Lo? She
couldn't think about that now. They were safe. They had to be.

She jumped to her feet and spun in a circle. She needed a
weapon. Until she could complete the security hack she couldn't

get the ship on her side. It would let them in without a fuss.

"Where would they keep weapons?" In the cargo-hold? In their sleep cabins? On their hips, definitely. There'd be no need to stow any in a pilot's station, but she quickly searched every bin and locker. Her gaze jerked back to the hack.

Still running. "Damn it."

Samantha sprinted down the corridor, eyes searching every square meter as she flew past. Smooth walls everywhere. Then a turnoff opened up and she slung herself around the corner. She spotted the four steps down to a slightly lower compartment and jumped, landing at the bottom. Hope spiked her energy levels as she saw the neatly labeled doors along both sides of the hallway. They had to be the crew cabins. She slammed her palm against the sensor next to the first door. It stubbornly remained closed.

Samantha doubled over, hands on her knees and panted to catch her breath. "Emergency response!"

"State emergency." The computer had a slick, almost human voice. Nothing but the best for murdering scumbags.

"Open all hatches."

"All public spaces are accessible," the calm voice responded. "Sealed hatches indicate areas not available to passengers."

"I can't find the crew," she improvised. "I need the hatches open so I can conduct a search."

"Sensors indicate crew not on board."

"You've got a sensor malfunction," she said, hoping the hack would help along that lie. When there was no response, she pounded on the door in frustration. "This is an emergency. Comply!"

"Acknowledged. Running a diagnostic and releasing all hatches."

She didn't know if it was the hack or bad emergency response programming but she wouldn't complain over her good fortune.

"Hallelujah." She slipped through the door as it slipped open. The floor was hidden beneath piles of clothes and empty bev tubes. The room smelled like a stale reminder of a days-old hangover. She checked the storage drawers then shoved aside a blanket hanging half of the bunk and bent to look underneath for any supplementary storage. Nothing.

"Sensor diagnostic complete, no malfunction found. No crew currently aboard. One unregistered and two registered passengers identified."

Two. Where had they come from? If anything had happened to Mercury—the sound of the doors engaging sent Samantha dashing for the next doorway, but all the doors slid shut. Stars, she needed the hack to kick in. If the security protocols were still functioning, whoever had come back to the ship could use them to locate her.

She headed up the steps to the main corridor. Left would take her back to the pilot's station, probably the first place they'd look. Right would take her to the commons, but anyone coming in the main hatch would also have to pass through there to get to the pilot's station. Between her and the commons were a lot of dead ends and several turns. If she was lucky she might make it to the one cross corridor she'd seen before they found her.

She dropped to the floor and removed her boots, then went to the right, moving quickly but cautiously. The metal decking felt cool and smooth beneath her feet as she followed the corridors into the body of the ship. The telltale thud of booted feet warned her they'd already made it past the commons and were headed right for her. She spun around and sprinted back along the corridor, sliding at the turns like a drunk on an ice plane.

She rounded the last corner between her and the pilot's station and ran smack into a solid male chest. Damn, where had he come from? His arms closed around her like a vise squeezing the breath from her heaving lungs.

"Well, look what I cornered." The hunter spoke to someone over her shoulder. The other one must have caught up.

"No points." The voice behind her was jovial and relaxed. "That was luck."

"Being in the right spot is a skill," the hunter protested.

Samantha struggled against his hold. She tried to get a knee to his groin but he held her too tight.

"Hey, mister lucky?" Getting his attention was the only tactic she could think of to get him to ease his grip. The moment he looked down to her, she wrenched her head back and then forward, clipping his chin with her forehead.

"Shit," the man shouted. He was pissed. It hadn't exactly felt good to her, but it worked. His hold loosened.

Samantha grabbed for the stunner at his waist and dropped to her haunches, letting her body fall like dead weight. It broke his grip and she scrambled.

She came away with the stunner and got in a shot as she did a one handed crab walk away from him. He dodged. She tried to adjust her aim, something slammed into her, flipping her over and flattening her against the deck.

A sharp, jarring pain shot through her shoulder. She couldn't get air and before she recovered both men were on her. One lay with his torso across her, the other wrenched her arms over her head and tried to twist the stunner out of her hand. She fired. He yelped and released her. The high, shuddering whimper told her she'd gotten him good. Not enough to take him out, but enough to throw him off his game.

The guy still crushing her to the decking wasn't distracted by the blast—he was too busy shoving her face into the floor.

She was trying to get her arm back around to get a shot off at him when she saw Lo coming down the corridor like the devil they called him. There was no sound, except her labored breathing and the grunts of the man pressed against her. Lo's eyes flickered with red flames and he sprung into the air and flew at her attacker, claws extended. She saw it as if time slowed. She braced for the blow of Lo's weight coming down on them, but it never came. His momentum carried him over them and he plucked the man off her as he tumbled past. The quiet, swift movements gave Samantha an eerie chill. She tried to push up to a sitting position, but her hands slipped in wet crimson. She hadn't realized Lo had drawn blood but the evidence was soaking into her top.

The second man was trying to get a stunner in his left hand. The right hung limply at his side. The awkward movements slowed him down. She scrambled to get to him before he could aim. They both froze as a loud growl rolled down the corridor.

Mercury.

A blur of motion whooshed past in a quicksilver flash of heat and energy. She shivered as cool, ship-controlled air sucked back in to fill his wake.

Everything stopped.

The hunters, both injured and unconscious, lay barely breathing on the floor. Lo and Mercury crouched over them, hands bloody, chests heaving. They watched her and waited. Waited for her reaction. Waited for her to accept or reject them. Waited, unrepentant, for her to pass judgment. They needed her to go to them, to reassure them. She tried, but something between her brain and her body had broken.

The aftermath of suppressing her fear washed over her, leaving her trembling. Another flash of movement and Mercury pulled her into his arms. She buried her face in his chest and breathed him in. The subtle spice of him cleared the tang of blood from her nose and settled her nerves. She pushed back and slid her hands up to frame his face. "When they came, I thought something had gone wrong. That maybe you were hurt, or worse."

"I'm fine and Drake lives.

"Carn is with the others," said Lo. "They all live."

"We're all safe." Mercury pulled her back into his arms.

She stretched out her hand to Lo. "Come here."

He didn't hesitate. He settled his big body against her side and wrapped his arms around them both as he pressed his nose against her neck.

They sat that way, quietly reassuring each other, for a full minute before Mercury shifted. "We must get these men out of here and help Samantha ready the ship."

"I'll take them," said Lo. "You stay here and help her. Carn and I will return shortly."

"Be careful," said Mercury. There are at least four more in the area."

"Just two. I ran into two in the forest. That's why I headed back here."

Samantha cleared her throat of emotion. "We'll be ready when you get back."

Everything moved quickly then. By the time she got back to the pilot's station the hack had completed and she had full access to the ship's controls. The moment Lo and Carn stepped back onto the ship she sealed the hatch and started the launch sequence.

The familiar rhythm of the work and the force of the ship shooting toward space fit like the comfort of old work boots. As they cleared the atmosphere, Samantha saw the *Dove*. "Bastards." The damage was far worse than it should have been for the small directed charge she'd triggered in the cargo-hold.

"Samantha?" Mercury appeared over her shoulder.

She wanted to turn, to see his face, reach out to touch him, but until they cleared the planet's influence she had to stay focused on the controls. "You should be resting."

He dropped a hand on her shoulder. "Tell me what's wrong."

She pointed at the view screen. "When the hunters boarded looking for that tracker they made a mess of her boarding hatches and scattered the remnants of the cargo-bay blowout." Maybe setting off an explosion hadn't been such a good idea. "The debris field surrounding her will make it impossible to dock. We won't be able to salvage a thing."

His hand squeezed gently. "You hoped to salvage your personal possessions? Your mother's cloth?"

"No," she said. No, it had been nothing as sentimental as that. "I was hoping we could siphon some fuel from the *Dove's* auxiliary tanks."

"Fuel?"

"Yeah, this beauty was designed for speed, not efficiency." She tapped the readouts on the control panel. "We only have enough fuel for one Skip and that won't get us back to Roma."

"Why would they travel without enough fuel?"

"They must've spent extra fuel getting here so quickly."

As the ship moved out of range of *G-45987*, Samantha quieted. She checked navigation and set a course to take them out of the solar system.

"There are two refueling ports in range," she explained. "We're on the border between Gollerra and Earth Alliance territories, but the closest fuel depot is on the Alliance side." She swiveled far enough to look at Mercury. "If Roma sent out a bulletin on you guys it could be dangerous to go to the depot on the Alliance side."

"Drake wouldn't have admitted his loss to anyone outside the company. He wouldn't have believed we could evade recapture."

She considered his words and her own feelings. She couldn't let her own concerns and needs delay their return to Roma. "Okay, but, in an abundance of caution, let's say he did. Or he tagged my credit accounts. I might not be able to pay for the fuel."

Mercury nodded. "Our other option?"

She sighed, but held his gaze. "Haverlee."

He reached out and ran a finger along her jaw, stoking under her chin. "We go to Haverlee, then."

"I'm sorry, Mercury. I know Carn won't be happy about the delay."

He pulled away his hand and she immediately wanted his touch back. Had she become addicted?

"He'll see the logic of it," he said, for once unaware of the reason for the tumult inside her.

Logic had little to do with the jumble of her emotions. "I hope so."

CHAPTER TWENTY-ONE

Haverlee Port, Krena
Gollerra Sector
2210.170

Samantha yawned as Haverlee's controller confirmed her account, finalized the portage and wished her well. Handling all the ship's systems herself had made it a short but punishing journey. Before Samantha closed the communication channel she checked one more time for any response to the encrypted relay she'd sent out for Sevti, but there was nothing.

She stood and stretched, pushing her worry away. She could only hope Sevti was okay and being cautious. No use in assuming he'd been caught when she was too far away to help him. Besides, after a year away, she was back in Haverlee. Surely that earned her a few hours of peace before she had to start worrying again.

Turning to leave the pilot's station she found Mercury watching her with intent eyes. She brushed her fingertips across his cheek and enjoyed the warm rush of affection that heated her skin when he pressed a kiss to her palm. His tongue traced a circle across the kiss dampened skin. Her pulse skipped and pleasure zinged outward to all her more feminine places.

She pulled her hand free. The last thing she needed was to face the Chief with her brain floating on a cloud of lust.

"I need to go speak with the Port Chief. He's the local authority. He controls everything in Haverlee. I need to explain about the ship in case it comes up on a port bulletin."

"I'll go with you." He crossed his arms over his chest, presenting an appealing show of strength and determination.

"You should all wait here. Haverlee is a multi-species port, so I don't think you'll stand out so much, but—"

"There could also be a bulletin on us—stolen property."

She cringed and patted his bicep. "I'll talk to the Chief about that, too."

He didn't budge to move aside or let her through the hatchway. "I'll go with you. Carn and Lo will stay here."

Over his shoulder, she could see the two men standing in the corridor.

"You should all stay here. I grew up in Haverlee, I'll be fine."

A rumbling growl reverberated in Lo's chest.

Carn looked somber. "We listened to the ship's data entry on this port. There's a traveler warning posted."

She couldn't help the eye roll. Why had she taken the time to teach them how to use the ship's com interface? "There have been warnings about Haverlee since I was no taller than your hip, but nothing truly bad happens here. I promise."

Red fire sparked in Lo's eyes and a muscle in his jaw twitched.

Mercury wrapped his hands around her arms, stroking with his thumbs. "If you don't let me go with you, I won't be able to keep Lo from following you. He doesn't seem in a very agreeable mood. It'd be better if you let me stay at your side."

Samantha humphed. "You think I'm falling for that?"

He nodded, face carefully neutral. "It's true."

Damn them. She knew she was being maneuvered, but she also knew Lo would do exactly as Mercury warned.

"Okay. You win this one." She strode over to Lo and put her hand against the sleek expanse of his muscled chest. "You stay here. Mercury will go with me."

The rumble quieted beneath her palm. His lips tilted in a half smile that pressed his prominent canine teeth against his lip. The man didn't know how to look anything but deadly. She turned in a slow circle. What was she thinking? None of them could look anything but lethal.

She shot Mercury a grin. "Come on. First stop, we find something to cover you up. No way are you walking around out there with all those pretty muscles on display."

His eyebrows lifted. "Pretty?"

She traced a finger down his sternum. "I call 'em like I see 'em."

Ten minutes later, he walked at her side through the bustling port and into the market that sprawled right up to the gate. They found a hooded jacket for Mercury and arranged to have two more delivered to the ship in an hour. With the hood up, it covered Mercury's ears and shadowed the distinctive features of his face, but there was nothing she could do to disguise his size.

The chief's assistant led them into his office. Port Chief Pillar sat behind an ancient but tidy desk. A window looking across the port stretched across the wall behind him, like his own personal backdrop. The older Golley had the blue-tipped, silver hair that put his age well into his senior years, but to her he'd always looked old. The wrinkled gray skin and rounded shoulders were typical Golley, but as a child she'd thought him just another elderly human. That was back before she'd had access to the port. Most of the Golley worked and lived within its walled shelter.

Samantha sat in the faded chair across from him and Mercury stood behind her, one hand reassuringly on her shoulder. "It's good to see you, Pillar."

"And you, Sammie." The chief eased his chair back. "You here to file a claim on the *Bucket*?"

Samantha shook her head. "No. My father left it to Shred. I've accepted that."

His bushy brows shot up. "Shred doesn't seem so sure."

Samantha adjusted her boots beneath her seat. She didn't want to talk about Shred. "I told him as much, last I saw him."

The chief tapped crooked fingers against the arm of his chair. "Shred and the rest of the crew seem to think you'll put in a claim to cut them out and throw them off."

Samantha frowned. "I'd never do that. The *Bucket* is their home." Of course it had been her home too.

"So you're here for something else then."

A miniature of the Earther scales of justice sat on the corner of the chief's desk. A strange artifact to find in a Golley port office. On Haverlee he was judge, jury, and jailer should the need arise. He'd been on Halston before Haverlee and Golley Minor before that. He was more than a backwater caretaker, or had been. Samantha lifted the figurine in her hand.

"I need your expert knowledge of the Gollerra judiciary."

He smiled, nodding his head in a way humans couldn't duplicate. It was more like moving his head up and down rather than tipping it forward and back. "Clever start, acknowledging my ex-par-tese and appealing to my sense of self-importance. Go on."

"This is a hypothetical."

The chief waved one hand in sharp little circles, urging her to get to the point.

"How exactly does Gollerra law determine who is a person?"

The chief leaned forward letting the legs of his chair slam forward. "Now *that* is quite a question. You're going to have to explain that one."

"I mean, if someone claimed someone else wasn't a person, that they were property, more animal than humanoid, how would they go about deciding it one way or another?"

The chief's attention shifted briefly to Mercury's shadowed face, before he turned serious and met her gaze levelly. "Well, it isn't something that often comes up. It'd have to be basic sentience testing. Self-aware, able to communicate on some recognizable level, capable of comprehending complex social structures. But, if the person can question the claim of ownership and be understood, that's evidence enough of sentience."

"No genetic requirements? Nothing about DNA?"

He frowned, doubling the number of wrinkles across his forehead. "No. We have our share of prejudice, but it is usually more cultural than species related."

"What about a claim of ownership...or creatorship?"

"Ha!" He let out a puff of amusement. "Parents create their children, doesn't mean they own them."

Samantha reached up to lay a hand over Mercury's on her shoulder. "Good. Perfect."

Pillar's gaze tracked the movement. "I take it this hypothetical has some basis in reality?"

Fabric rustled from behind Samantha as Mercury pushed back the hood of his cape. The chief wouldn't be able to miss his less human features. "This is Mercury."

"The Roma Company created my people through genetic manipulation." Mercury gave nothing of his anger away in his tone. "They have deemed us animals and claim ownership."

"Roma?" The chief's face scrunched with derision as he said the word.

"They own a small planet," Samantha added. "In the Earth Alliance Beta sector."

"I know the company, but they have no legal standing here." The chief got to his feet and extended a hand to Mercury. "Welcome to Haverlee and Gollerra sector."

Mercury hesitated for only a moment before he stepped forward and took the man's hand. "Thank you."

Samantha cleared her throat to draw Pillar's attention. "I should also tell you that the ship I arrived in may have been reported missing or stolen."

The chief settled back into his chair. "How did you end up with it?"

"I was hired to pilot some freight for Roma."

"Your friend here?" He indicated Mercury with a tilt of his head.

Samantha nodded. "I took an unconventional route. When they realized that, one of the idiots they sent along tried to take over the pilot's station."

His brows lifted again, like two fuzzy caterpillars trying to walk off his face. "He thought he could fly a transport?"

Samantha shrugged. "To skip ahead a bit, we took the escape-pod to the surface of a planet and the fellows on the ship I brought here came to rescue the Roma men. They didn't have any intention of the rest of us getting off the planet alive. Taking their ship was the only way we were getting back."

"Hmm...They...and Roma might not see the logic of that. Those men on the planet, what exactly happened to them?"

"We left them there with supplies. Roma knows where they are. It was habitable. Lush even. I'm sure they'll be fine."

"Well, then. You best make this an official report so your side of the story is on record before they can twist the facts around."

"I can do that. Pillar, I need a favor."

The caterpillar brows crawled toward each other as his face scrunched. "Oh, Sammie. I hope you're not going to—"

"I need you to hold the report locally for a few days."

His hands fisted around the arms of his chair. "You're not thinking of flying that ship back out of here."

"I promised Mercury and his brothers that I'd get them where they need to go."

"I'm sorry, Sammie. I have to impound the ship. If you hold

onto it, no one will believe you're not a thief."

"I'm willing to risk it."

Pillar shook his head. "No. This is my port, but I can't control every bit of news or gossip that gets out. Someone will have noted your landing and your launch. And no other port is going to clear you inbound without your license number."

"That won't be a problem." Samantha hadn't expected it to be easy to convince him.

"Where—? Never mind, don't answer that. Probably best I don't know too much of what you're planning, but I can't let you pilot that ship, Sammie. Keeping that ship would cause you nothing but trouble. And I don't want trouble coming back my way."

The floor beneath her boots shook as she got to her feet. Through the window, she saw a Golley freighter in the distance, lumbering skyward. "I understand, Chief. We'll find another way."

"Twenty-four hours, Samantha. I'm impounding the ship now, but I can hold the paperwork until tomorrow. Give you one peaceful night's sleep." He reached across the desk as if to take her hand but stopped when Mercury growled a low warning. "Sorry, I can't do more."

"There is one more thing."

His head dipped with interest. "Yes, if I can."

She dug the metal disk she'd picked up from the bottom of the ravine and handed it to him. "Have you ever seen anything like this before?"

His lips pursed and slid right and left as he thought. "No, don't recognize it, but I can try to identify it. Would take some time."

Samantha had already done a complete scan of the object so she decided to leave it with him. "That would be a great help. Thank you."

"No trouble," he said. "I like a good puzzle."

She and Mercury turned to go.

"Sammie." The chief's voice stopped her.

She looked over her shoulder. "Chief?"

"What you're doing for these men. Your father would be proud."

She spun on her heel, not sure why his misguided attempt to be kind made her so angry. "My father's first rule was to stay beneath the notice of powerful people."

The chief sighed. "He learned to be careful to protect those in his care. Back when he was relocating refugees, flying beneath the radar was the only way to stay alive."

Samantha shook her head. "My father was never a refugee runner."

Pillar smiled. "It was when you were a tot. Before he started spending more time here."

She frowned. "More time?"

"He told me he went to visit your mother once and realized you'd gone from being a baby to being a person. He made a point of working this port more after that."

Samantha blocked out his words. She didn't want to hear that she'd ever meant anything to her father. In the end he'd proven what she meant to him. Exactly nothing.

"We should get going," said Samantha.

"One more thing." He held up a finger as if to reassure her he knew her hold on her emotions wouldn't last longer than that one more thing. "Shred's been in my office checking on you every time the *Bucket's* been in port this last year. More than any other year I can recall."

"Checking on me?"

"Asking if you've been by to clean out your dad's lock box over at the Treasure. Seems only next of kin, a blood relative, can clear the box."

"I didn't even know he had one."

"Well Shred did and it sure makes me wonder what he thinks you're going to find in there."

"I'm wondering that myself. Thanks, Chief."

He acknowledged her gratitude with a nod. "Give my regards to your mother. And do let me know what you find in that box."

CHAPTER TWENTY-TWO

Haverlee Refugee Camp, Krena
Gollerra Sector
2210.170

Samantha considered Pillar's claim that her father had been a refugee runner on the way back to pick-up Carn and Lo. Why wouldn't he or her mother have told her if it was true? No, she would have known.

Pushing all thoughts of her father aside, she let her feet follow the path they had trod a million times before. When she finally led all three of the males through the market she realized the tension in her muscles meant she was nervous. She stopped at the gateway to the refugee camp. It was on a rise with the shantytown where she'd been born spread across the slope below. Beyond the camp, the desert stretched out in all directions.

Near the entrance to the trails that led out into the warren of temporary homes, the buildings were made of salvaged materials, the hulls of derelict ships mostly. It made for some odd shaped structures and the conditions in them were often the worst in the camp. The buildings had no cooling units and the metal roofs made them nearly unlivable during daylight. The areas to the right of the gate huddled around the port's safety perimeter. The structures there were small, flimsy, and tightly packed. It had changed over the years, taking in each new wave of refugees until they could establish some safer section on the border of the camp and build more permanent homes. Directly ahead and beyond the older scrap-built structures, there were sections with rows of prefabricated emergency housing and areas dominated by rows of colorful tents.

She had no idea how Mercury would see the camp. They hadn't talked much about conditions in the place he referred to as a kennel. She hoped it wasn't as bad as it sounded, but knew no matter the conditions, his life had been hell.

Her mother's tent was luxurious compared to what they'd had in the early days, but even then she'd had her mother's love and a sense of community.

Steeling her courage, Samantha looked up to the men's faces. Their ears twitched with curiosity, their noses flared as they took in the rich array of spices that perfumed the air, their eyes took in the bustling jumble of people. These were the refugees of destroyed worlds and forgotten cultures. Gollerra hadn't always been a peaceful sector and the camp had already been well established when her mother's people had made their way here. They'd crossed the border to get out of the reach of the Earth Alliance.

Mercury must have felt the weight of her stare. He looked down and his lips tilted in a smile. "There are many different species here."

"Yes," Samantha confirmed. "Mostly humanoid, but from many different worlds."

"We'll be able to blend in." At Carn's low growl he added, "Until we leave to free Hera."

Lo stepped closer, gently tugging a handful of Samantha's hair. "Show us the way, little Sam."

"Right. This way."

She gave a nod to the nearby group of men playing Fret, an informal group of sentries that kept an eye on who entered the camp's safe zone. She led Mercury, Carn, and Lo through a tidy, wide trail to a long established part of the camp. Her mother's tent was smaller than some, larger than most. Colorful stripes showed where it had been expanded when she was a child.

The entrance stood open, the cloth door tied back. Samantha started to step through, but Mercury held her back. Lo ducked inside then straightened. His ears twitched and his nose flared and then his body relaxed as he motioned her forward.

Samantha stepped quickly inside, sure Lo's appearance had

scared her mother speechless. She should have known better. Her mother stood near the meal table. It was covered with food. A warm smile curved her lips and her face radiated a golden glow.

Samantha flew into her mother's welcoming arms.

"Welcome home, daughter."

"Mom." She sunk into the sage and desert-dahlia smell of her for a moment before pulling back.

"You were expecting us."

Her mother's smile widened. "This is still a small community, daughter. Messengers came from the port to let me know the moment you landed." She turned her attention to the men. "They said you traveled with three large males, so I prepared food to make them welcome."

Samantha introduced her mother and briefly explained the circumstances of their visit. She left out any mention of the more intimate part of those circumstances. It wasn't something she was ready to explain, but her mother would know. She'd sense it.

It was Mercury who approached her mother, bowing his head like a supplicant. "Thank you, Moira, for gifting our lives with your courageous daughter."

Her mother's laughter filled the tent like musical bells. "Her father called that particular trait recklessness. I've always thought it an extension of her generous heart. I'm glad she was able to help you. Please sit and eat. You all look too long without a proper meal."

Moira led them to the table and the men ate as she filled Samantha in on all the news from the camp.

Samantha peeled a citrus fruit and handed it to Mercury who broke apart the sections and shared it with Lo and Carn. "We won't be here long. We have to find Carn's mate. He's very worried about her."

Her mother's golden hue flushed to a dull copper. "I'm proud of you, daughter. But also afraid."

Mercury stood and went to Moira, kneeling at her feet. "I'll do all in my power to keep her safe."

Moira reached out a hand and stroked his head as if he were just a boy. "I believe you."

Surprised by the exchange, Samantha cleared her throat and stood to start clearing the table. "Is Felzaf still working in the clinic?"

The men took their cue from her getting to their feet and helping her clear away the remains of the meal. They'd all discussed it during the journey and decided their first priority had to be getting rid of the tracers that had allowed Drake to hunt them.

"Yes." Her mother's glance bounced from person to person. "Is someone injured?"

Samantha could feel Mercury's questions in the air, but he remained silent. She hadn't thought to explain that Felzaf was more medic than technician. "Everyone is okay, but we think Mercury, Lo and Carn may have tracker implants. I'd like to get that taken care of as soon as possible. Roma could have contacts at the port. If Owens sends someone after them, I don't want to make it easy for them."

Her mother nodded. "I'll send word you're coming."

Mercury stroked a hand down Samantha's back. "Do we endanger your mother, by staying here?"

Moira had moved to the opening to call a messenger from the path. "There are no maps of the camp and no one would help an outsider, even one from the port, to find my home."

The men still seemed tense.

"It's true, guys," Samantha assured them. "You'll be safe here, as soon as we get rid of those trackers."

A young boy stepped up to Moira, who greeted him by name.

Sometimes Samantha was struck by how fortunate they were—how different Haverlee was from the camps she'd seen on the Alliance side of the border. "Mom, the guys need clothes. Could you send a messenger to the market, too? I'll give you my account number."

Moira shook her head. "I have plenty in my account from what you last sent."

Samantha swallowed to wet her throat. "You should hang onto that. I'm out of a job for awhile."

"Don't worry," her mother soothed as she glided back across the room and took Samantha in her arms. "Things will work out."

She hoped her mother was right, but there were so many obstacles in their way. All she could do was take it one thing at a time.

CHAPTER TWENTY-THREE

Haverlee Refugee Camp, Krena
Gollerra Sector
2210.170

Mercury walked beside Samantha as she navigated through the warren of lanes with ease. He'd liked her mother's home. Textures and colors filled the space like a sensory feast. The cloth walls blocked the heat of the sun, but were easily pushed aside. Any wall could become an exit. He found the freedom of that appealing.

The large building ahead of them had to be where she was taking them. It dwarfed the much smaller structures crowded into the area around it and the homes beyond it looked hastily built with many types of building materials, all in bad repair.

He didn't recognize the hard material that formed the walls of the larger building, but he didn't like that it only had one way in and out. A half dozen bright red symbols hung over the solitary doorway. Samantha led them into the cool and well lit interior. The smell of the place raised the fine hairs on the back of his neck.

He wrapped a hand around Samantha's arm to still her movements. She looked at him with concern. "Something wrong?"

"This is a medical facility."

"Yes," she said. "Oh." Her face fell. "I didn't think. I should have explained."

Behind him, Lo and Carnage had gone on alert. He could tell without looking that Lo had gone up on his toes and his claws had slipped free.

"If this is where we must be to remove the trackers, then this is where we must be."

He made the words loud and firm for Carn and Lo, but he knew he wasn't on firm ground here. He was on edge. They needed to do this and have it over.

While Samantha spoke with the Cerrillian female that seemed to be in charge, Mercury studied the colorless cloth drapes that hung from the ceiling to divide the space. The place looked too much like the staging area at the arena. If the medics were going to drug them before a match, it always happened there.

Instinct urged him to put as much distance as possible between them and this place, but he had to trust Samantha. So, he let Samantha walk away to speak with Felzaf and followed as the female led them to a three meter square section where they were to wait. Whispery voices came from all directions. They swirled around them and wound him tighter and tighter.

When Samantha walked into the room with a human male, Lo lunged for the man. Mercury had to hold him back and it was that need alone that saved him from being the one to tear the man apart. If it hadn't been for Lo, Samantha would have seen a demonstration of his true nature—primitive, animal, barbaric.

To his credit, the brown haired man with the round features atop a slender frame held his ground.

Samantha jumped between them. "This is Felzaf."

"My patients don't normally want to kill me *before* their treatment." Felzaf tried to chuckle at his own joke, but the man's voice shuddered as he tried to breathe normally.

"Everybody calm down," Samantha urged.

Lo snarled, but let Mercury push him back. His eyes flashed as he spoke. "You expect me to allow this human to cut into me?"

"We must trust Samantha." He believed the words, but his instincts roared in complaint.

"I've known him for years," Samantha supplied instantly.

Felzaf stepped out from behind Samantha's protection and this time Mercury couldn't hold in his growl.

Felzaf kept his hands open and carefully out to the side in plain view. "Samantha told me about your situation. I'm not like the other humans you've known. My ancestors were some of the first to leave Old Earth and settle the new worlds. We tried to live in harmony with the indigenous people we found, but that meant we weren't well fortified generations later when the Earthers came out to settle the galaxy in the name of the allied corporations. They drove us out just like they drove out the other races."

"Please," urged Samantha. "Give him a chance."

Mercury fought his impulses, but what would happen when she finally did see his instincts get the best of him?

She stepped closer and rested a hand over his heart. It thudded hard beneath her palm.

"Please," she said again. "Trust me."

Mercury calmed, backing away, and the others followed his example. "Forgive us. We haven't had the best experiences with human medics."

"I understand." Felzaf crossed the room to a cot at one side. "I've worked with other refugees that went through some bad things. We humans like to pretend we're civilized and above petty cruelty, but the truth is, we can be some of the biggest bastards in the universe." He stood less than a meter from Mercury. "All I can say is I'm willing to help. Whether you want my assistance or not is up to you. You let me know what you decide."

Mercury looked to Lo and Carn then turned back to the medic. "We would be grateful for your help."

"Good." Felzaf smiled broadly and patted the cot. "I'll need one of you up here."

As leader it was his choice who would go first, but there were no good options. Carn was weak and mated. Lo, despite his outward calming, was terrified.

Mercury climbed up on to the cot and sat quiet as the man pulled a scanning device out of his pocket.

Felzaf had no trouble identifying the trackers Roma had used on the three men. Unfortunately, it was in their blood stream and the only way to neutralize the signal was a dangerous chemical cocktail.

Samantha hadn't been surprised when Mercury had insisted on going first to make sure it was safe for the others. The cocktail had done its job but left him weak. He and Carn were both sleeping off the effects. Lo had insisted on going last.

He lay on a medical cot with an intravenous line in his arm

feeding him a simple nutrient rich, immune boosting fluid. Felzaf had insisted on treating their malnutrition before giving them the chemical that would scrub the tracers from their blood. Samantha had given Lo her hand and he still gripped it in a death grip.

"I'm sorry I didn't think to explain about Felzaf before we came here."

Lo huffed. "The human arena medics couldn't be trusted. They would drug us often. Aggression drugs to make us fight more viciously. The crowds had to be entertained." He snarled the last sentence.

"This bothers you more than Mercury or Carn."

He looked away. "From the first year I began to fight in the arena, I was often selected to service the human females who paid for the privilege of fucking one of our kind—the females who wanted a dangerous Dog from the arena instead of one of the submissive males available in the pleasure suites. They gave me drugs that made my body react as they wished and clouded my mind so I couldn't think clearly enough to fight them. The drugs didn't work as well on Mercury and Carn. They weren't drugged as often."

Samantha stroked the length of his arm, her heart breaking over the awful things he'd been through. "I'm sorry, Lo. They should all be punished for what they did to you."

He released her hand to reach for the multicolored strands of her hair. He gave a little tug. "I see now where you get this. Moira is even more colorful."

She understood that he wanted to change the subject. "Her mother, my grandmother, was full blooded Cerrillian."

"She changes color," said Lo.

"Yes. It changes with emotion." She tried to smile for him, but all she could think of was the past. Moira had always been at her most golden when her father was around. "Lo, why did Mercury act so...deferential toward her?"

He slipped his hand back to hers. "We never had true mothers. He considers her special. And she's important to you." He hesitated. "You should've told her Mercury is your mate. It hurt him that you didn't claim him when you introduced us."

Samantha's heart thudded heavily. That sluggish organ already belonged to Mercury, but that didn't make them mates. There were too many obstacles standing between them. "I didn't mean to hurt him. It's just that…none of us know what the future holds. I'm not sure I can be what he needs and when you have Hera back…" And she wasn't sure he'd want her once it sunk in that he could find a more suitable mate on any block in Haverlee. Her throat squeezed shut as if a slither-constrictor had coiled around her neck, making it difficult to breath. Confronting what she might or might not mean to Mercury invariably left her heartsick. "I don't know how to explain things to my mom."

Lo squeezed her hand, stopping the flow of words. "Because of me?"

"That's part of it. It hurt her so much that my father had other lovers. But that isn't all of it."

"She'll see the truth of things." He rubbed his thumb across the inside of her wrist. "Will *not* claiming Mercury make it any better in her eyes?"

She shook her head. A week ago she would never have dreamed he could be so wise. "You always surprise me, Lo."

"It's fair then."

"Fair?"

"You're also a surprise to me." His voice dropped to an awe filled rumble. "A prize I never imagined."

"Lo—"

"When Carn took Hera as mate, I refused the bond." His muscles tensed as if he'd confessed a terrible sin…or a dangerous truth.

"Why?" But she wasn't asking why he'd refused. She knew he had a terrible past where women were concerned. And she knew he'd bonded to her because he was the only one left of Mercury's pack brothers who could. "Why tell me?"

His ears flicked. "Go to Mercury now. I hear him getting up."

She stroked one of the velvet triangles and watched him tremble with pleasure. "I'll get Felzaf. Then I'll be back. Mercury wouldn't want me to let you face this alone."

He closed his eyes as if her words wearied him. It sent shards of doubt through her. She had never been good at relationships and she'd never let it bother her, but this time she was navigating the trickiest of waters and she was afraid she'd tip the boat in the wrong direction and all of them would drown.

CHAPTER TWENTY-FOUR

Haverlee Refugee Camp, Krena
Gollerra Sector
2210.170

"Will you open your father's box in the morning?" Mercury had already pulled off his new clothes and crawled into the collection of stuffed mattresses they'd stretched across the floor of her old bedroom. A strategically placed blanket prevented her from drooling over him—too much.

"I don't know." Samantha pulled the comb through her hair one last time then set it aside. "It doesn't really matter. Nothing in that box could change the way he lived his life."

Though Samantha was beginning to see that just because she didn't understand something that didn't make it wrong.

"Moira speaks of him with happiness in her voice."

"She always did." She crawled into the bed still wearing her tank and briefs. The others would be joining them to sleep. Somehow it had seemed wrong to ask Carn to sleep in the other room, and then there was Lo.

"You should speak to her about it." He leaned against her, nudging her temple with his jaw.

She shrugged. "Maybe."

He nipped at her lips then stared her down. "Maybe?"

She was saved from having to answer when Lo stepped into the room. He'd taken off his boots, detracting from the more civilizing effects of the clothes he still wore.

"Carn is walking Moira down to visit with one of her friends for a few hours." Lo stood very still by the door.

Samantha looked from Lo to Mercury. Both men watched her as if she were a star with nova potential. "You arranged for her to be gone?"

Mercury stroked a hand down her back. "You're uncomfortable with your mother knowing about us."

So he'd made it possible for them to have sex without her mother hearing. "I'll explain it to her in the morning." Because she didn't want him thinking she was ashamed of him.

She could see her promise made him happy.

Mercury looked up to Lo. "Come closer."

Lo didn't budge. "It must always be her choice. Not yours."

Samantha realized then they intended to make love to her together. Lo hadn't gone with her mother because he wanted to be included. He was hovering by the door because he waited for her to welcome him into her bed for more than sleeping. Both men waited, tense, for her response. She could see that Mercury wanted Lo with them, but he wouldn't force the issue.

She'd been too busy and too exhausted to do more than sleep on the transport ship, but there was no more reason to put off dealing directly with what she'd done. She'd taken them both as lovers. She hadn't planned it, but they needed to know she didn't regret it either. She might not be comfortable with it, but she didn't want to undo it.

She reached out a hand toward Lo. "Come here. Please."

He moved in a blur of motion. In the next breath she was on her back with Lo over her, his face buried against her neck.

She heard Mercury laugh—a low, gravelly sound that flooded her body with anticipation. He shoved Lo off her, but it was a playful gesture. Lo rolled with fluid grace, to lie beside her.

Mercury leaned over and kissed her lips, nipping gently then tracing the tender area with his tongue. She followed his lead, using her teeth and tongue and got lost in the back and forth of it. Mercury could always do that to her, overwhelm her with just a kiss.

Her breasts ached and tension coiled low in her belly. She arched her back, needing his touch. He reached for her, one big hand firmly stroking. Stroking from her belly button to her ribs. He palmed her breast and gently squeezed.

"More," she pleaded.

"Yes, *courra*, we'll give you more." He pushed at her top and she helped him pull it over her head.

The spell Mercury had woven broke long enough for her to be aware that Lo hadn't gone far. He lay close, watching. He'd stripped his clothes off and had his cock in his hand. Seeing him stroke his thick cock made her pussy clench.

Mercury ran a fingertip down her nose, tempting her thoughts back to him. His eyes darkened, eclipsing the silver almost entirely. She reached for him and he came over her, nuzzling her neck. He trailed kisses down to her breasts. Wet heat engulfed one nipple and expert fingers teased the other to painful attention. She squirmed with pleasure.

Samantha traced her hands over Mercury's chest. His skin was hot and touchable over hard muscle. She flexed her fingers digging into resilient flesh. He growled around her nipple, sending pleasure vibrating through her body. He liked firm handling. The evidence of that pressed against her hip then lifted away as he moved lower and began to pull at her briefs.

She lifted her hips to help him. Lo yanked away the blankets that had been tangled around them. Presumably, because they'd been blocking his view. His eyes were on her now completely bared body.

She had to close her eyes and concentrate on her breathing to control the strange hitch that thought had caused in her pulse.

"Samantha?" Mercury sounded concerned, but she didn't know how to respond.

He'd moved to lie alongside her. The heat of his body warmed her, but he didn't touch her other than the undemanding press of skin. It must have taken some doing to keep his impressive cock from pressing against her.

He was trying to be considerate. How did she tell him that was the last thing she wanted him to be?

He wrapped his hand around her neck and squeezed gently. "Samantha?" His tone was sharper this time and her eyes shot open.

"It's okay. Just—" Lo watching Mercury strip her naked had seemed both terrifying and exciting. What would they think of her if they knew the idea of Lo watching Mercury slide his cock into her made her damp and needy. She knew it had to be what they wanted, or at least part of it, but was she supposed to want it to? "Stars, this is confusing."

She heard Lo shift and knew he'd leave. The sadness in Mercury's stormy eyes gave her the excuse she needed to twist and make a grab for Lo. Her fingers dug into his hip and he eased back toward them in response.

"Don't go." And she meant it, one hundred percent. Mercury was all her heart needed, but that didn't mean her heart didn't welcome Lo. The rest of her body had no objection at all to him being a part of their lovemaking.

Luckily, she didn't have to ponder it for long. Mercury touched his lips to hers and she was lost in him again. He pressed quick kisses across her lips, cheeks, jaw, and then it all changed when he got to her neck. Big, open-mouthed tastes made her squirm beneath him.

His tongue traced along her throat and she clutched at his biceps, trying to pull him over her. The bulk of him didn't budge, but she could finally feel his hard length against her thigh again. Stars, his cock was big. How had he ever gotten inside her?

She'd have turned her body to press along his, if she could have, but he easily held her in place until his hand slid down the front of her body. Then she no longer wanted to move.

His hand trailed down further, molding over her curves and ending with the firm press of his hand between her legs. There was nothing she could do to stop the movement of her hips as she arched into him, needing more pressure, more contact, more anything.

"Please," she urged.

He obliged her with enthusiasm. His fingers dipped between the folds of her sex, shooting sparks of electricity through her nervous system.

"Is she wet?" Lo's voice sounded eager and dirty and it made her want to spread her legs wider, to give Mercury more room to explore.

"Very." Mercury confirmed it between kisses as he slipped a long finger into her damp heat. "It feels so good," he spoke against her skin. "I want to push my cock into her now. I almost don't want to wait."

But apparently, almost wasn't enough to deter him from his

chosen course. And hearing them discuss her as if she wasn't needed in the conversation they were having didn't cool her need. It only made her more wound up.

Mercury had to know she was ready for him, but he didn't make a move to shift further over her. He added a second finger then pressed his thumb over her clit.

"Stars, yes." Her voice shook with need. Both men moaned at hearing her.

Mercury seemed to remember exactly how she liked to be touched, what rhythm drove her wild. He put that knowledge to work, bringing her quickly to the point of orgasm.

The tip of his cock dampened her thigh. She needed to do something to get him inside her. She didn't want to come around his fingers. She wanted that thick cock filling her up. When had she turned so greedy?

Samantha reached for him, but he had her pinned exactly how he wanted her and apparently letting her touch his cock wasn't part of his plan.

Lo made a noise, half chuckle and half groan. "I think she wants you to fuck her, Merc."

She looked over to him. He was still stroking his cock. His hand squeezed the long length as he pulled slow and steady. The tip had gone dark and the slit was weeping with moisture. She knew Mercury would look much the same, pressed against her hip. She groaned.

"Yes," said Mercury. "She wants me to fuck her. She's small inside and tight, but she's so wet I could get all the way in her with one stroke."

She was glad Lo didn't feel the need to inform Mercury that he'd done exactly that when they'd been together. Instead he made another half laugh, half groan sound.

"Do it," he said. "I want to see you shove your cock in her nice and hard. Let her feel how big you are for her."

Mercury nipped at her chin, drawing her gaze back to his. "Is that what you want, *courra*? You want me to fuck you nice and hard?"

"Yes." It was beyond her ability to formulate anything more than that one word. "Yes." Since it was all she could get to come out, she said it again as if he wasn't already more than certain of how badly she wanted him.

He nipped at her lips and whispered against them. "I'm going to fuck you hard, but I'm going to do it slow and I'm going to keep space between our bodies so he can watch. Is that okay for you, *courra?*"

"Yes." Again she was stuck with the one word and she hoped he wouldn't be too shocked at her easy compliance.

The thought slipped away as Mercury put his words into action. He moved over her but kept his arms extended. His cock slipped along her folds. All three of them groaned and Samantha looked down to see what Lo was seeing. Mercury's cock was even harder and more engorged than she'd imagined and it now glistened with the moisture from where he'd stroked it across her.

She started to reach for him but he moved again, sliding into her, unerringly finding the angle he needed. He shoved forward in a hard thrust that she felt all through her body. She gasped and he leaned forward to kiss her open mouth.

When he pulled back, he slid his cock out slowly then started a pace that was sure to kill her. Her hands slipped along his ribs and his muscles jumped in response. He growled and the strain on his face assured her he was torturing himself along with her.

He was huge inside her and the slow, thorough strokes were going to driver her crazy. Watching his body work, the thrust of his hips, the flex of muscles, made her feel swollen with need and on the edge. It wouldn't take much. She just needed—she slid one hand down toward her clit. The slightest touch forced a moan across her lips.

Mercury snarled again. His gaze snapped up to Lo. "Hold her hands."

"No. Please." She wasn't above begging at this point.

She would owe Lo some huge favor because he seemed to be on her side.

"She needs it, Merc," he said.

"Not by her own hand," Mercury protested.

They were talking over her again. This time it was Samantha who growled. Mercury looked back to her and he must have seen the desperation in her eyes. He lowered his body, wrapped his arms around her and rolled, putting her above him.

He barked-several small noises that seemed to set Lo in motion. Suddenly, he was behind her. Strong, warm hands wrapped around her ribs and he pulled her up to sit astride Mercury's hips. Mercury was still lodged firmly inside her. The change in position shifted the pressure in a way that made her moan. Lo pressed close behind her, a blazing fire at her back. His fingers stroked across her ribs sending waves of sensation rippling across her skin. Lo banded one arm around her, holding her in place, his other hand dipped down between her legs and—oh. He pressed right where she needed it.

Her pussy clenched around Mercury's cock, drawing a groan from him. He thrust up and, hands on her hips, pulled her solidly against him. He seemed to be trying to push as far as possible inside her then he retreated, dragging his cock out until only the flared crown stretched her opening. He pulled her down slamming them together again. The strokes were short but intense and every pull moved Lo's hand on her clit.

"Careful," said Mercury on a thrust.

"I am," answered Lo.

She thought they must be talking about his claws, now positioned near her tender flesh. She didn't feel the claws at all but the small circles he'd started, those she felt to her toes.

Her orgasm broke over her out of nowhere. One moment she was on the raggedy edge the next she was flying apart. Mercury ground their hips together while Lo's touch drew her pleasure out as long as possible. When her body went limp, he wrapped himself more firmly around her and lifted her off of Mercury's still hard cock. He edged back and settled her on his thighs. Somehow he rearranged things until they were between Mercury's spread thighs.

She might have protested the idea of leaving Mercury unfulfilled if her arms and legs weren't limp as noodles. For a moment she let Lo's strength support her, but Mercury still lay beneath them, lungs working like bellows, cock looking painfully hard. That didn't seem right. No, not right at all, but Mercury didn't seem worried or in a hurry. He looked pretty damn pleased with himself as he watched her, limp in Lo's arms, Lo licking along her shoulder.

Licking? Yes, he was definitely licking.

About the time control of her limbs seem to be returning, Lo urged her to lean over Mercury, her lips brushing against the damp tip of his engorged cock.

Lo said, "Take him in your mouth."

She blinked, uncertain. She wouldn't want to place any bets on her chances of getting him very far past her lips, but Lo added, "No one's ever done that for him." She knew then that she'd give it her best try.

The suggestion prompted another groan from Mercury. It hadn't left her unaffected either. She steadied herself with one hand near his hip. She wrapped her other hand around the base of him and licked up the length. She laved her tongue around the crown and looked up to see him watching her with rapt attention. Her pussy clenched in response as if she hadn't already had her pleasure.

His hands gripped the blankets under him as if he might be fighting the urge to fist his hands in her hair and she wished he wouldn't hold back. Or maybe he knew Lo would take care of it for them all. His hands were suddenly there, tight in her hair guiding her to take Mercury inside. His other arm still wrapped around her waist, keeping her ass snugged back against him. The hard length of Lo's cock slipped between her thighs and pressed to her entrance.

He let her work Mercury into her mouth to a point she could handle, then he slid his cock into her channel in one luxurious thrust. He managed to wrap all of her hair in one hand and trailed the other down her spine. For the first time, his claws brushed her skin, just enough to send prickles spiraling out across her back and tracing along her rib cage. Each thrust of his cock filling her up demanded she take Mercury deeper in her mouth until the velvet swell of the tip worked against the soft, sensitive palate at the back of her throat. She fought her gag reflex. She didn't want to stop.

What they were doing had all three of them desperate for release.

It didn't take long.

Lo shifted his hands to her hips just as Mercury howled and filled her mouth. Lo changed the angle of his thrusts, pushing her off the edge to follow Mercury—her second orgasm a warm wave rolling through her. As her pussy clenched around Lo's cock, he groaned, a throaty sound of satisfaction. Howling in perfect harmony with Mercury, he pulled out of her then coated her thigh with the sticky evidence of his pleasure.

Together they collapsed on the bed in a pile of tangled limbs. It took a while for Samantha's pulse to slow. Her mind was blank as if all the other parts of her body had taken all the oxygen and left her brainless—and for the moment, that was fine. On a purely instinctual level she knew she was safe. Someone passed her water and she drank. The lamps flickered off and she was wrapped up by two strong bodies. Nothing in her life had ever been so right. A tiny voice in the back of her mind whispered that it wouldn't last. That it wasn't real. But the voice was small and far away—a small stone beneath the overstuffed mattress, easily ignored.

CHAPTER TWENTY-FIVE

Haverlee Refugee Camp, Krena
Gollerra Sector
2210.171

Samantha jolted awake as Lo launched out of her arms and Mercury pushed her behind him. Lo took the man at the door to the ground. Carn had joined them to sleep sometime in the night. He leapt over Lo to dart into the main room.

Samantha peeked around Mercury to see Lo snarling and snapping at a man in the drab gray of independent spacers and wearing freighter boots with silver toned straps—Knock.

"Wait!" Samantha tugged at Mercury's shoulder. He snarled in response. She wrapped one of the blankets around her body and struggled to get to her feet. She tripped over a pair of trouser that had been thrown off last night. One of the guys', not hers, unfortunately. Mercury caught her.

The volume of Lo's snarling dimmed. Knock had finally smartened up, freezing stiff.

Samantha resisted Mercury's efforts to again push her behind him. "I know him," she explained. "He's not a threat."

Mercury released her and made a barking sound she hadn't heard him make before. Lo responded, easing back then off his chosen prey.

"Uh, can I move now?" Knock, with his familiar spiked white hair and narrow features, spoke without moving an extra muscle.

"Sammie!" She recognized the desperate shriek as a stressed version of Mikal's voice. He'd apparently waited in the next room.

"Oh dear." Moira's voice trailed in. She appeared in the doorway her eyes wide. "I'll, ah, put out some food, but you should tell Carn to let Mikal go. I've never seen him so pale."

Mercury let out another bark and an answering bay came from the other room. Her mother disappeared as quickly as she'd appeared.

Knock sat up, but stayed on the floor. "I can see now why I wasn't man enough for you, Sammie. Three men? I'm sure one of the guys would've been willing for a threesome but I can't say I'd be willing to go farther than that."

Lo launched himself at him again.

"Knock, you idiot." Samantha scrambled over the pile of bedding to put a fist in Lo's hair. She pulled his head back. Red fire danced in his eyes. "He's not a threat and you're not going to kill him for being an ass."

Lo growled a wordless response that communicated frustration.

She grinned at him. "You know..." She spoke softly, not wanting Mikal or her mother to overhear. "Your eyes looked just like that the first time you were inside me." Lo's snarl died away and his features softened. She let go of his hair and stroked his head. "Let him up, please."

Lo eased back and was on his feet in another blur of motion. He put an arm around her and pulled her to his side. Samantha glanced back to Mercury. His look was approving. He was still alert and wary of Knock as the man held his hands up and muttered an apology.

"Joking," he said. "Just joking."

"Mercury, Lo, meet Knock, a member of my father's crew. The man in the other room is Mikal, the tool slinger on the *Bucket*." She started to introduce Mercury and her throat tightened. She knew what he wanted her to say, but she couldn't. She swallowed hard and took a steadying breath. "Knock, this is Mercury and his pack brothers Lo and, in the other room, Carn."

Mercury pressed along her back, a quiver of emotion rippling through his body.

Knock held his hands out in a show of surrender. "Sure, sure, whatever, but can you tell them to put something on, or at least cover up those monster dicks." He made a shivering motion. "All that meat swinging around gives a man the willies."

Samantha chuckled. "Jealous?"

"Hell yes. After this I may develop a complex or something."

Samantha remembered that Carn had actually been wearing something as he'd flashed by on his way out of the room. That was some consolation, since her mother was out there with him.

She sent Knock out to wait with Mikal and Carn, then pulled on her own indie-gray pants and paired them with a soft yellow top that clung to her curves. She fingered the soft material. One of the perks of coming home was a vast improvement in her wardrobe. She tugged on her freighter boots and smoothed the trim that matched Knock's. Her father had bought his whole crew new boots as a celebration a week before his death. Knock and Mikal's visit meant the *Bucket* was at the port. She couldn't help but wonder if Shred still wore the same boots.

Samantha helped Mercury and Lo with the unfamiliar clothes her Mother had secured for them. They looked almost normal in the full length trousers and loose shirts. Mercury pulled his hair back with a small tie. The effect was startling. He looked more civilized and less human. Without the fall of hair around his face all the angles of his face appeared sharper and more pronounced.

Civilized or savage, he became more a part of her every day. What would be left when he ripped those parts away?

"Why are you here?" Samantha put her hands on her hips and stared Knock down. He sat at her mother's table, stuffing a biscuit into his mouth. He had to work it down and chase it with fruit-water before he could answer.

"Moira, I never understood how you always seem to have the best foodstuffs from Serona." Knock wiped his mouth with his sleeve.

His comment struck her as funny, considering it was her father's connections that ensured her mother's regular shipments from Haverlee's sister city—an Eden nestled on the planet's most verdant continent.

He shifted his focus to Samantha and stopped eating. "Sammie, I came to say I was wrong. Wrong to let Shred leave you behind. Wrong not to tell you so sooner." He smoothed his hands along the table, until he realized what he was doing, then he stopped and held still. "Aren't you going to say something?"

She straightened. "Sure. I'm going to say, if that's all, you're done and you can go. "

"You're skeptical." He put a hand to his heart. "I'm hurt."

"You're a soft spined letch with a hard head and no common sense, Knock. I doubt I could hurt you if I dropped a skipdrive on your head."

"Now that's mean, Sammie. I'd have thought you'd be in a better mood after..." He waved a hand at Mercury and Lo who flanked her.

"I want a serious answer, Knock."

He leaned so far forward he almost landed in his plate. "I mean it, Samantha. I tried to talk Shred out of it before and I tried to talk him into going back after. I left the ship at the next port."

"I didn't," said Mikal. He looked much the same as she remembered, tall and rangy with a face that had seen too many bar brawls. The streaks of gray had nearly taken over his once auburn hair—that was new. "Sorry Sammie, but work is work. But you should believe him." He nodded to Knock. The idiot even spent his own credits to go after you. Leastways, he said he was going to. He did leave the ship for a few months. That much I know."

Samantha sat in one of the chairs and reached for the sugared grain and nut mix her mother had set out. "Is that true, Knock?"

He frowned, drawing his browse together and puffing out his slender cheeks. "For all the good it did me. You'd already gotten off planet by the time I got there. We were friends, Sammie. Real friends. You know I never had anybody give a damn about me before your dad and you."

Mikal cleared his throat, but left a ring of sugar around his mouth. "Chief told us you might be looking for a ride off this ball of sand."

"He had no business telling you anything." She poured cream over the grain and nut mix and passed it to Mercury who'd taken a seat between her and Mikal.

"Look at you—" Mikal snickered. "Feeding your man. I didn't know you had any of your mom's domestic, man-pleaser genes."

Samantha froze. His words had a chilling effect on the entire room. She met Moira's gaze where she hovered next to a storage chest. "Be careful how you talk about my mother. I'd be damn proud to be half as strong and wise as Moira." She wouldn't admit aloud that she saw her mother's relationship with her father as weak. It had been her only weakness. And Samantha wouldn't explain that she peeled the fruit or poured cream over the grain because the food at her mother's table was unfamiliar to Mercury and his pack brothers.

"We were talking about helping Sammie." Knock piped up. "In case anyone wanted to get back on topic."

"Right," said Mikal. "So we heard you scuttled one of Roma's ships and stole a Raptor class transport."

"Chief didn't tell you that."

"No," said Knock. "That's in all the latest Alliance bulletins."

This news rang in her ears like the reverberation of a hangar door slamming shut.

Mikal swallowed a mouthful of the grain and nut mixture. "We were worried about you, Sammie."

"Right." She laughed, a mirthless sound that came more from grief than humor. Mikal had been the first one of her father's crew to acknowledge her. He'd taught her tool slinging and made it possible for her to join her father's ship. "Like you were worried about me on Sydney-3?"

"I was worried. But I'm not a young man and I knew when your old man died my retirement plan died with him. I needed the job."

"Right. Gods forbid anyone get in the way of your retirement. " Samantha pushed away the year old hurt. The touch of Mercury's hand steadied her. "Okay. Let's pretend for one minute you really came because you were worried about me, or what was the first excuse, oh yea, to ask for my forgiveness. Well, you can see I'm fine and forgiveness isn't in the cards for today, so feel free to leave any time."

Knock fingered the edge of his plate then pushed back from the table. "Okay, Sammie. You have good reason to be furious with us all." He got to his feet and swatted Mikal on his way past. "Come on."

Samantha stood to watch him walk out, but he stopped at the opening to Moira's tent. "One more thing. You should check your father's lock box. Whatever's in there has Shred worried. And keep it in the back of your head that, if there is ever anything you need, anything, I won't let you down again."

Mikal surprised her when he faced her with real emotion on his face. "And don't forget, the indies are here for you, too. We were all sad when you joined up on one of them fancy corporate haulers. I mean, don't expect anything from Shred, but just about anyone else would spin a moon for you. We all loved your old man and you're the chip off the block."

Samantha closed her eyes as they left. Her mother's scent filled the tent and her gown swished softly as she moved. Blinking rapidly, Samantha opened her eyes to take in the subtle hues of color decorating her mother's skin. How many times had she wished to be more like her serene mother? Instead she became more and more like her father. Even Mikal could see it. Ironically, she was no longer sure exactly who her father had been.

CHAPTER TWENTY-SIX

The Treasure, Haverlee, Krena
Gollerra Sector
2210.171

Most buildings outside the port itself had been made of scraps or converted from one purpose to another. The Treasure was housed in a building that had once been a gambling house. The previous owner had installed extra security measures to keep the place honest and to protect profits. Now it protected whatever the indies who frequented the port considered valuable. For some it was credit markers or account numbers. For others it was halo-vid projectors or alien artifacts they hoped would be worth something one day. Samantha didn't know what her father had considered valuable, but she was about to find out.

She didn't recognize the guard at the door, but she recognized the one inside.

"Jebedi." She'd been prepared to be ignored or looked at with pity, but he did neither. His face scrunched in a grin.

"Hey short stuff! Been too long." He reached over to rub her head the way he had when she'd been thirteen and hanging around the port after her shift at the wormarie.

Mercury tensed beside her, but he managed to let Jebedi finish the motion and withdraw his hand. It was a good thing Lo had waited outside.

"Jebedi, this is Mercury." She reached over and squeezed

Mercury's hand. "Jebedi has worked here as long as I remember."

Jebedi laughed, rocking back on his heels. "Surely, not so long as that. I remember you already had engine grease under your nails by the time I first laid eyes on you."

The familiar teasing went a long way toward putting her at ease when she hadn't expected anything about clearing her father's box to be easy. "You're probably right about that."

Mercury shifted to edge between them. "We're here to open her father's box."

"So much for easing into the process," Samantha muttered.

Jebedi kept his smile in place, but he crossed his beefy arms over his barrel chest. He'd picked up on the disapproval of their reminiscing that was radiating from Mercury like a soundless warning siren. "Well, nothing to fear in that box, short stuff. Even if your father stuck a sand-viper in there it'd be dead by now. Those boxes have an airtight seal and no one's been in his box for at least a year."

A year. Her father had been gone more than a year. "Is that your way of telling me I put this off too long?" And she'd probably have left it forever if she'd stayed on the *Reliable* slinging tools for some mammoth corporation.

"Na." He sobered. "You have a right to take your time with something like that."

Mercury huffed. "Well she's made up her mind to do it and it's best to get on with it now that we're here."

His hurry surprised her. She didn't ever recall Mercury rushing her about anything. Even when Knock brought up the topic of the box, Mercury had seemed interested only in so far as she cared.

His voice softened. "Once it's open you'll be able to deal with it and your fear will be gone."

Of course. He could probably smell her apprehension and he always knew what she needed. He was right. Once she knew what she was dealing with, there wouldn't be anything left to fear. "Good point. Let's do it."

"Back wall," said Jebedi. "Number fifty-two. It's all set for you."

She swallowed and nodded.

Samantha led the way. Rows of small doors reached from floor to ceiling. Each one DNA coded. She scanned the numbers and found the box. "This is it."

She put her hand in position just millimeters from the pad.

She pulled her hand away. "I don't think—"

"Will it hurt?" Mercury looped one arm around her waist and pulled her back to press all along his chest and thighs.

"Just a prick."

"Good." He bent down to speak directly against her ear. "We'll do it together."

"But—"

Before she could get anything else out he'd seized her hand. He pulled it up to the pad, laid his hand over hers and pushed forward.

She never felt the prick. His hot breath tickling her neck and the subtle thrust of his hips rubbing his length against her ass distracted her until the box's seal released with a whispered whoosh.

Mercury pressed a kiss to her temple and stepped back just enough to break the seal of warmth that had connected their bodies. "Time to see what's inside."

She pulled open the drawer, holding her breath as if she did expect that sand-viper Jebedi had reassured her wouldn't be jumping out. He'd been right about the viper, but the neatly organized carrier bit her as surely as any slithering reptile. She could feel the poison spreading under her skin. All that was left was to determine how deadly it's effects.

She lifted the carrier out. Through the transparent material she could see the title to the *Bucket* and a data-strip with her name. Tears welled in her eyes and threatened to fall, but she managed to swallow down the sudden surge of grief and regret. And then she saw the rest--a half-dozen keys each labeled with a familiar name.

Mercury's heat returned and his hand settled low on her belly as he looked over her shoulder. "What is it?"

It took her befuddled brain a moment to realize he had no idea what he was looking at. "It's the *Bucket*. It's mine." If she could manage to reclaim it.

"What's wrong, *courra*? You're shaking. Doesn't this ease your doubts about your father's feelings for you?"

"I wasted so much time being angry."

"Yes, but you cannot change what is past."

A startled bubble of laughter escaped her tight throat before the mirth dissolved under the weight of her regret.

Mercury turned her in his arms. "I didn't mean that to make

you laugh."

"Oh, I know. You just reminded me why I lo—" She choked on the word she had no right to say. Not when she was sharing her bed with two men and had feelings for them both. Two men who might be in her bed, whether they understood it or not, because they needed her. Two men who planned to risk their lives for another woman.

He wrapped his arms around her and pulled her tight against his chest. "Something else in the box is making you sad. Tell me."

"Key codes for my father's lovers." Her voice broke on the end of the sentence. Her father had cared for her, but he had cared for them all. She wasn't jealous of them, not for her own sake. It wasn't that at all. But she expected Mercury to come to that conclusion.

He stroked a hand down her spine. "Talk to me. I know you're hurting and I want to understand."

"They don't know," she tried to explain.

"Of his death."

"No. I mean…I did make sure they were all notified. All the ones I knew off. But the key codes. If he left them credits or property…"

He cupped her face in his palms. "Don't blame yourself, *courra*."

He understood. Her self-pity had caused others to suffer. To think her father had forgotten them and maybe to go without support they'd relied on.

"They were his responsibility, not yours."

"He counted on me and I let him down."

"No. He let you down by not making sure you knew how he felt about you."

Just as she was doing to Mercury. Stars, she was her father's daughter and making all of his mistakes.

"You can't change the past," he said again. "You must change the future."

"Is that what you're trying to do?"

"Yes. I let my brothers down. I acted rashly when the counted on me to be clever." He pulled her close again. "Because of me, my brothers were condemned to die. Because of you, I have a chance to make things right."

"We all make mistakes."

"Yes," he said. "We do."

But when, she wondered, would she stop making them.

Her father's ship—no. Her ship...was parked somewhere in the port. A part of Samantha had wanted to hunt down Shred and kick him off the *Bucket* the moment she realized the truth. Ironic since she'd told Chief she'd never do such a thing.

When her anger cooled she realized there'd be no point anyway. "Even though the *Bucket*'s mine," she explained to Mercury, Lo, and Carn as they headed back to her mother's home. "I'll never be able to fly her legitimately again. I could take her, to get us back to Roma. Pillar would back up my claim. But the *Bucket* isn't a speedy ship. It would take us over a month to get there."

Carn protested immediately. "We can't leave Hera alone there for another month."

"I agree," she reassured. "Besides that, Owens would be suspicious if the *Bucket* turned up in the Roma port."

"Agreed," said Lo.

"Explain about you not being able to fly the *Bucket* again," said Mercury.

The man didn't miss a thing.

"Right now I'm wanted for theft on the other side of the border. And the minute Drake or Resler reports my Cerrillian heritage to the Earth Alliance authorities, they'll pull my license. I can't even own property of any kind on that side of the border."

"What about here, in Gollerra territory?"

"I can own the ship, but there's no work for her here. The Golley have a monopoly on all freight and transport in this sector. They only accept non-Golley ships at the border ports. Shipping anything from here to further inside Golley territory can only been done through one of their authorized carriers."

When they stepped into her mother's tent, Moira sat waiting at the table. She had a sealed packet in her hands. Shades of blue and indigo swirled across her skin—a mix of grief and other emotions, but Samantha had never seen this exact combination.

"Mom?"

The tense smile that appeared on Moira's face aged her. "Come, sit with me."

Samantha turned to see Lo and Carn backing out through the opening and Mercury waiting for her attention. "We'll be outside."

She nodded then sat with her mother. "You know what I found."

Moira shook her head. "I don't know for certain, but I can guess."

Samantha reached out and clutched at her mother's hand. "The title for the *Bucket*. He left it to me. Shred kicked me off my own ship."

"You allowed it, Samantha." Her mother's voice socked her in the gut. "You let your anger at your father blind you."

Samantha didn't know whether to feel betrayed by her words or sad that she'd let this happen. "Did you know?"

"He never spoke of it, but I knew he'd never have left you with nothing."

"Why didn't you say something?"

"You needed to figure it out for yourself. You've never been able to see him clearly."

"You're right," said Samantha. "My opinion was always clouded by the knowledge of how he'd hurt you."

"I never complained," denied Moira. "I never blamed him for not being able to stay with us."

"You didn't have to. I could see your pain every time he left."

"Yes, I suppose any woman who loves a man is sad when he leaves. Maybe I should have talked to you about it more so you could understand, but you were so angry. You didn't want to listen."

Samantha searched her feelings for her father. There was such a jumble of love, respect, animosity. "I'm listening now."

"I knew your father would never be one to settle on a planet when I met him." Moira smoothed her hand over the packet. "I allowed myself to become involved anyway. That's why I never blamed him for leaving. Space, his crew, his ship...they were all a part of him and I loved him as he was."

"What about the other women? I know you knew about them."

"Of course I knew," she lowered her head for a moment, as if the weight of it bowed her spine, then she straightened. "He asked me once to live with him on his ship, but I couldn't. It wasn't the place for me. It was after I turned him down that he began seeing the others. I can't tell you it didn't hurt. Your father wasn't a perfect man, but he was a good man. He did so much for others. For all of us."

"What do you mean, Mom?" Samantha's heart rate accelerated.

Her mother squeezed her hand then let go. She lifted the packet in her hand and opened the seal. "It was enough that he loved me. Made me feel for someone when the wars had made me numb." She pulled a handful of encrypted stills. She traced her fingers over the corner of one and the view sheet leapt to life. The still showed young versions of her father and mother standing close. Her mother shimmered with gold. Around them dozens of people crowded together. They all looked weary, but relieved. She could see transport bags on the ground at their feet and the Haverlee dunes stretched out behind them.

"This was the group I was in. We were no longer on Cerrillia by then, but the Alliance had bounty hunters out looking for us on the Alliance side of the border. They were afraid we were building an army." She grinned and flushed more golden. "We would have if we could, but there just weren't enough of us. When Aurilia—the planet where we'd been hiding—became too dangerous, your father smuggled us to Haverlee."

Her father truly had been a refugee runner. Emotion dropped on Samantha's head like a confused mass of sand-cats, scratching and scoring her as they purred their way into her heart.

Samantha pressed her nose against Mercury's neck. They sat on the side of a sand dune far enough out of the camp to guarantee a little privacy.

"I feel like my life has turned upside down in the last week. It seems I was wrong about everything."

Mercury tipped her chin up and rubbed his thumb across her lip. "Tell me what I can do to make it better?"

She shook her head. "I'm not even sure I want to make it better—or at least not to change it back to the way things were."

She could see he didn't understand. He looked at her with those storm cloud eyes, letting her talk. Trying to give her what she needed when she had no idea what that was.

"A few weeks ago," she explained. "I was alone. I mean, there where people around, but I was still alone. I thought the indies, my father's friends, had abandoned me as surely as his crew did when they left me on Sydney3. Now I don't know what to think."

"Chief Pillar was right about your father's past."

"Yes. I need to let it soak in, to figure out how I feel about it."

Mercury frowned. "I thought that was a good thing."

He might not understand the history and politics of the Earth Alliance, but he knew when things made her happy and sad. For him that was all he needed to know and as far as she was concerned it was more than enough.

"Yeah," she agreed. "That's a good thing. It means he wasn't as selfish as I thought. But he never told me. And it doesn't make up for everything else he did."

"Drake claimed your father was a friend of Grande Owens." Mercury offered up the slight with no malice, but Samantha bristled at the thought of it.

"No way would he deal with that dune-slug." That she was sure of.

"I didn't think so either," he said. "I know his daughter and such a woman could not have been born to a man who accepted the suffering of others."

She cupped his hand where he still held her. "It isn't important what he did in the past. We have plenty to worry about in the present."

"But your father—"

"Yeah." She sighed. "I thought he was a complete bastard. Turns out it was my own insecurity that was the real problem." She held his intense gaze for several minutes and he allowed it, letting her think her way through to what she needed to say. That was Mercury. He always knew what she needed. In his eyes there was complete acceptance. Complete confidence of who he was. Stars, she didn't want to lose him. Not to Roma and not to her own fears. She looked down and studied her knees, unable to face him with fear choking her. Her heart pounded and she couldn't breathe. "I don't want to make the same mistakes with you."

He pressed his forehead to hers. "Don't be afraid..."

She pushed back, needing to gage his reaction to what she wanted, no, needed to talk to him about. "I know you made a promise to Carn. But you're going back, taking that risk, it's about more than that isn't it? You're pack bonded with his mate."

He turned her in his lap and wrapped both big hands around her face. "*You* are my mate." When she started to protest he silenced her with a look. "I know you don't believe it yet, but it's true."

She pressed her lips together to stop the protests she wanted to spew out. She wouldn't be distracted. She needed an answer. "But you're bonded?" This time she made it a clear question. Demanded an answer even if she knew the answer and didn't want the confirmation.

"I was bonded to her, but nothing comes before mates. Carn knows this. Hera knows this."

She swallowed against the lump that formed deep in her throat. "It was the one thing I swore, Mercury. That I'd never fall in love with a man who couldn't give me his whole heart. Who wouldn't be with only me. I know it isn't fair after I had sex with Lo... but I couldn't bear it if you were with someone else. I couldn't."

"We're mated," he said. "I'll never touch another. Think, Samantha. Think of Carn. He's my pack brother and he cares for you, but he doesn't touch you. He can't touch any female but his mate. This is our way. I need no one but you."

She wanted to believe him and she was terrified to let herself believe. Maybe if she didn't believe now it would hurt less if— No! She couldn't think that way. She loved Mercury whether she wanted to or not. He'd never lied to her. She had to trust him or end it and she knew she couldn't leave him now.

"Okay." She took a deep breath. "I've been wrong about a lot of things lately. Maybe there's one more thing I've been wrong about."

He sat quiet, waiting.

"Maybe I've been wrong about not having any way to help you get back to Hera. I think it's time I go back to the port and make a few calls."

CHAPTER TWENTY-SEVEN

The Mug and Grub, Haverlee, Krena
Gollerra Sector
2210.171

Mercury had walked proudly at his mate's side all day as she'd
worked amongst the Golley at the space port, contacted old
friends, and called in old favors on his behalf. He'd thought he'd
seen her strong and confident when he'd watched her through the
bars of his cage as she took on the whip-master and his guard.
He'd thought he'd seen her at her most courageous when she'd
crawled down the side of a collapsed ravine and gone head-first
down a dark hole to save Carn's life. He'd thought he'd seen her
clever and competent when she'd exhausted herself, single
handedly flying the unfamiliar, low-on-fuel transport to Haverlee.
But he knew now he'd been wrong.

The woman beside him was the one who'd snuck into the port
as a child and changed her future. He suspected this woman was
stronger, more confident, more courageous than he'd yet seen. The
events of the morning had led her back to herself and a fierce joy
for her wrapped around his heart, even as it fed the doubt in his
gut. Doubt that he could keep her with him after they freed Hera.
Doubt that she would accept his mate-claim. Doubt that she would
ever find him worthy.

When they arrived at the backdoor to the Mug and Grub, a
small crowd waited outside in the twilight. The humans all had

mugs in their hands, several were propped against the exterior of the building. As they approached, the humans fixed their attention on Samantha. They all dressed alike in shades of pale blue and gray and wore heavy boots similar to the ones Samantha and the men of her father's crew had worn.

"Do you know them?"

"Yes," she said. "I haven't seen them in years, but yes."

He urged Samantha forward and signaled Lo with a low-sound bark. The command went unanswered, but Mercury knew Lo lurked in the shadows. "You should introduce them before Lo decides to shred them."

Samantha hurried forward and he thought he heard her whisper the word *friends* under her breath as she approached them. Her voice sparkled with happiness as she called each of them by name, three males and two females. Mercury forgot Lo's discomfort and bristled with his own when she allowed the males to hug her. He wanted to knock them away and then he wanted to strip her clothes off her and roll around with her on the silken bed sheets in her mother's tent until she smelled only of him.

The hugs were over before his possessiveness got the better of him. He settled as she introduced them to him and to Carn and finally to Lo as he materialized out of the darkness.

As she spoke Lo's name with her hand resting softly on his arm, Mercury realized he didn't mind at all if she smelled of Lo. It was their way, but the more time he spent in her world the more he understood how she might have trouble making sense of things he accepted without question.

The humans turned out to be from the *Gwendella*, the ship she'd contacted that afternoon. Samantha had explained that she'd done some of her pilot's training there. He'd only been expecting this meeting to be with the captain Samantha had asked to help them and he hadn't been entirely comfortable with the idea. But this was her world and he had to trust her judgment.

The plain door into the building's back room had no markings and had to be opened with a code. Samantha had explained that customers entered through the front, but the captain had arranged for a private meeting. Inside, dozens of dimly glowing, fist-sized balls lit the interior. Scattered across the tabletops and the counter that ringed the small room, their combined output left much of the room in shadow.

The chairs sat empty for the most part. Samantha led the way to a large table at the center of the room where the room's only occupants, two females and a male, got to their feet. He recognized the man as Knock, the man who'd thought he had a right to walk into Samantha's bedroom that morning. He bristled at the man's presence.

The younger woman dressed differently from the others. She was the bar worker, he realized as she disappeared through an interior door, leaving only the older woman to greet them. The appearance of the woman, who had to be the captain, startled him. He'd seen dark skinned humans before, but none as dark as her. The resemblance to the blue-black skinned Mothers was undeniable, but also meaningless. She was clearly human. Her tightly curled silver hair covered her skull, unlike the Mothers with their slick skulls. And her figure registered as typical human. Her clothes seemed more formal than the others and she wore a shiny silver star on her collar.

"Mercury." Samantha's hand rested on his arm as she pulled his attention back to her. "This is Captain Amanda Artane, owner of the *Gwendella*."

He lifted his chin in acknowledgement and the woman held out her hand. He knew what she wanted, but it was a gesture made amongst humans. She kept her hand out, unbothered by his hesitation, until he accepted the gesture. She shook the hand he offered and gave him a warm smile.

"Good to meet you," she said.

Mercury released her hand and breathed deeply, subtly searching her scent for deception, but found none. "Samantha tells me you helped her gain her skills as a pilot."

Lines crinkled at the outside edges of her eyes. "I suppose I did."

"You have my thanks then."

The captain's mouth opened as if she would speak then closed.

Samantha motioned to his pack brothers, but didn't move aside to allow them to approach. "This is Carn and Lo."

They exchanged nods of recognition and then the captain sat back down and motioned to the chairs nearby. Her crewmembers went to the far end of the table where the young woman had returned with a pitcher of drink and began to refill their mugs.

"It's good to see you, Samantha." The older woman crossed an ankle over the opposite knee and rested one hand on her boot. "I was sorry to hear about your father."

"Thank you, Captain." Samantha's spirits no longer darkened as they had before when her father had been mentioned. "And thank you for coming."

The woman's lips turned downward, making her face seem sterner. "We were about to leave Sedona when I got your call. Between my respect for your father and my affection for you, delaying departure by a day was an easy call. Especially since I'd seen this." The captain slid a thin flexible sheet across the table. "This bulletin is bad news. You and your friends are in a heap of trouble, Sammie."

Knock sat silent on the other side of the captain.

Samantha touched the corner of the sheet and it lit up with images of each of them and some text Mercury couldn't read. Samantha huffed and her spine softened. She looked up to the captain. "I don't think there's anything we can do about this, but I have a more important favor to ask you."

"The one you mentioned in your call."

Samantha nodded.

"Okay, tell me. The whole thing. Even the parts you think I can't help with. You might be surprised what I can do."

"First, Captain. I'm sorry, but why is Knock here?"

The captain bristled as she turned and frowned at Knock. "He was waiting at the port when the shuttle brought us over from Sedona."

Knock leaned forward. "I have almost as many connections in this port as you do, Sammie. I heard you were up to something and I'm here to help. If I can. And to warn you that Shred knows you're here. He's prepping the *Bucket* for departure first thing tomorrow."

Samantha frowned, but she nodded then turned her attention back to the strip of flexible material. "It's even worse than this, Captain. Even if I could clear this up, I'll be losing my pilot's license. They know I'm part Cerrillian."

The captain slammed a fist against the table. "If it was that cretin, Shred, I'll—"

Samantha gasped. "I didn't know you knew." She visibly shook off her surprise. "No it wasn't Shred. Two of the Roma employees found out the old fashion way. Observation. And if they haven't spoken up about it yet, it's only because they haven't had an opportunity. You can be certain they'll speak up when they get the chance."

"Well," said the captain. "Looks like the only way to fix this is to get you a new identity and to get your friends here as far away from Roma as possible."

Samantha jerked as if she'd been struck by a lash. "Are you saying...?"

"That I can get you in touch with the person who helped your father forge your papers the first time?" The lines reappeared at the corner of the woman's mouth. "I wasn't always old and conservative. Your father and I had to walk on the wrong side of the law a time or two when we were younger."

Samantha fell back in her chair, with a laugh. "You and he were runners together. I had a feeling."

The captain nodded. "But I don't like to let that part of my personal history get around. Earth Alliance still has open warrants for anyone who helped the refugees during the refugee uprisings. The fewer people that know a secret, the easier it is to keep."

"Of course, but I have to tell you that's part of why I contacted you."

"So, tell me what you need, Sammie. Whatever it is, you'll have it along with a new identity and transport for your friends."

Mercury's guts twisted. "We aren't going anywhere without Samantha." He wasn't letting anyone separate them. Only Samantha could do that and he didn't think he'd be able to allow it. The captain offered her a way to return to being a pilot. Why would she choose to stay with him when he could offer her only danger and a life of struggle?

Carn stood, his chair scraped loudly across the floor as he shoved away from the table. "We aren't being sent anywhere."

The crew members at the far end of the room all got to their feet, but the captain remained seated and waved them off. "It's an offer gentlemen, not an edict. You're free men here. You'll do as you choose. I didn't help relocate thousands of refugees because I was looking for folks to oppress."

Samantha turned to face Carn. "I know you have no reason to trust me. I know I'm not a Dog. But I do keep my promises, Carn, and the captain may be able to help me do that."

Carn eased back into his seat. "I didn't say I don't trust you."

Samantha stilled as if his words struck her unaware. It squeezed Mercury's heart to think she didn't feel certain of their trust after all they'd been through. He stroked a hand along her thigh to urge her to continue.

She nodded, almost to herself then turned back to the captain. "I can't tell you how much your generous offer means to me. What we need most right now is a way to get back to Roma without being seen."

Knock pounded a fist on the table, making it shake. "Why in hell would you want to go back there?"

Samantha scowled. "Seems someone got left behind." Mercury let satisfaction slip over him as her careful word choice scored a hit on the man. Knock's mouth tightened. Real regret or anger that she wouldn't let him off the hook?

"Okay," said the captain, drawing everyone's attention back to her. "What's your plan?"

"I've heard a lot of the runners had a captain's closet. If the *Gwendella* had something like that, I thought it might give us a chance of getting into the port undetected."

"All of you," asked the captain.

Samantha nodded. "Plus one more on the outbound journey. It should help that your last port of record will be Sedona instead of Haverlee. I doubt Owens or many of the Alliance port workers would even know Sedona and Haverlee are on the same planet."

"Allendson's Port Chief there now." She narrowed her eyes. "But you knew that."

Samantha licked her lips. "I don't expect him to be a problem."

"No," said the captain. "I don't expect so."

The serving woman brought another pitcher of whatever the captain and her crew had been drinking and extra glasses. The room went quiet as she poured out glasses for Samantha, him and his brothers. The woman put a hand on his shoulder as she leaned across him to fill his tankard. He shifted his shoulder to discourage the woman. She moved on to Lo, but not before Samantha noticed the woman's touch.

When the serving woman left the room again the captain sipped her drink then spoke again. "I do have a closet and it should meet your needs. We're not scheduled into Roma, but I can arrange something. Roma's not so far off our route that it would raise suspicion for us to detour there."

"Perfect." Samantha's response to the news that her plan was coming together seemed subdued.

He reached for her, but she avoided his touch in favor of adjusting her mug as if the precise angle of the handle required all her attention. Was it Hera on her mind or did she think him so fickle as to be distracted by the serving woman's touch? He didn't know how to reassure her, so he returned to the task at hand. "You didn't mention this closet before," he said as softly as his rough voice would allow.

"I wasn't sure and I didn't want to count on it." She wrapped her hands around her mug. "Some indies have a smuggler's hold—a compartment built into the floor of the ship's decking. It's hidden and shielded so goods can be smuggled without being detected even by sensor sweep. The closet works on the same principle, but it's built into the walls and it's hooked into the environmental controls. For carrying people, not cargo."

Mercury said, "We could hide in this closet?"

"Yes. Even if Owens sends in a search team, we'd be safe."

Satisfaction warmed his veins. "Good. That is very good."

"Now," said Samantha. "We just have to come up with a plan to get to Hera and get her out."

"Leave that to me. We'll handle that part of things."

"I might be able to help with that," said Knock. "I'm pretty good with a security hack."

He didn't like the idea of Knock becoming involved, but when he looked to Samantha she nodded. "He's better than me...by far."

"Very well." Even as everything was coming together better than he could have hoped, Mercury's spirits flagged. They'd left Hera twenty-six days earlier. If Drake had told the truth, she might already be dead. If he'd lied then she might have been given to another pack for breeding. They might have to kill more of their kinsmen to re-claim her. And if neither case were true, there was still the impossible task of freeing her. Even if all went perfectly, he might lose Samantha. He knew she didn't expect to stay with them after they were truly free. No, there was little to celebrate.

When the planning was done and they headed back to Samantha's childhood home, she held him back to speak with him in private.

"There is something I want to talk to you about."

"What is it, *courra*?"

"On the *Gwendella*, things will be different."

He held his silence, not sure of her meaning.

"The *Gwendella* has a large crew and plenty of space. I'll take a crew berth, they'll expect it. I'll make sure the captain arranges for a guest suite for you, Lo, and Carn. This will be better for everyone."

She wanted to keep him at a distance. He'd thought they'd been getting closer, but perhaps the thought of having a new identity changed things. "This will not be better for anyone." He wanted to demand she acknowledge his claim to her, but he knew that would do no good. "But, it is your choice." After they had done what they must he would convince her that she belonged with him, with his pack. They would find new ways. Ways that she could live with. Because he no longer wanted to live without her.

CHAPTER TWENTY-EIGHT

The Gwendella, Roma Orbit
Earth Alliance Sector
2210.184

Ugly. Mercury studied the barren planet hanging bellow the *Gwendella's* observation port. It was the first time he'd seen the entirety of the planet where he'd been created, birthed, and trained. It didn't surprise him to learn the owners had been too impatient and too greedy to complete the terraforming process. The network of domes covering the only inhabited section of the planet reflected the starlight of space like scraps of metal tossed in the mud.

On one side of him, Carn stared at the view unseeing, his mind on his mate, while Lo watched Samantha, the woman who'd become everything to him. Samantha stood centimeters away, but the gap seemed achingly wide.

She spent time with him and his brothers every day. They ate meals together. She taught them a game called ping. And her eyes studied him as he exercised in the ship's gym. It would have pleased him if her fascination had been with his body, but only fear filled her eyes. He didn't understand why she feared him now, only after they'd reached her homeworld. But there was one thing he did understand—the more time she spent in the shoes of her old life the more out of his reach she became.

Beside him, Samantha watched the shuttle that carried Knock

up from the surface. The light colored craft seemed to grow steadily in size until its trajectory took it out of sight. She pivoted to face them. "The shuttle-bay is on the other side of the ship. As soon as Knock's on board the captain will start the landing sequence. We'll be on the surface and free to move around in a couple of hours."

Mercury and his brothers had already changed into the training pants and boots they would wear to blend in at the kennel. He acknowledged her words with a nod. He wanted to pull her close and taste the lips he dreamed about night after night, but he could feel her uneasiness like a prickly wall between them. He hated not knowing how to scale that wall and he wanted more than anything to tear it down. As long as she didn't push him any further away he would be patient. He could wait until she was sure of him. He would wait as long as it took.

Carn shifted from one foot to the other behind him. "When will we know if Owens will send a team on board to search?"

Samantha's eyes lifted and she focused over Mercury's shoulder. "According to the captain, back during her runner days she smuggled people safely through hundreds of searches. Not one search team ever discovered the captain's closet."

Mercury took Samantha's hand. "Let's go then."

There was no one around when they reached the Ward Room, where the entrance to the closet had remained hidden for decades. A large table took up the bulk of the space, but left enough room to move around. The side walls were covered in rows of square display screens. Across the room from the main entrance another door led to the captain's quarters.

While Lo and Carn pushed aside furniture and opened the complicated mechanism on the door to their hiding space, Samantha pulled him aside. She helped him shrug the holyrobes on over his training gear. They'd rely on the disguise to get through the port and through the public square. She stepped close and pulled him down to press her forehead to his. He rumbled in satisfaction.

"We won't have time to talk much after we land and there's something I want to tell you."

He said nothing, giving her time to arrange her thoughts. "You once said it was my courage that made me a worthy mate."

His heart stuttered. This might be the moment when she would finally accept his mate-claim or she might once again deny him. Whatever she needed to say, he would hear her out.

"I know," she said. "You think you failed your brothers in the arena when you led Lo to attack the patrons."

Stunned by her choice of topic, Mercury straightened. Her hands trailed down his chest, but she wouldn't be discouraged. Not his brave little mate.

"If you hadn't done that, we'd never have met. And if I hadn't taken a chance to help you escape we wouldn't be here, together, today. When I was headed down to the planet in the pod with Drake and Resler I can tell you I was worried that my impulsive decisions had gotten me into a bad spot."

"You act from your heart, *courra*. It's one of the things I like most about you."

She smiled, that mysterious now-I've-got-you smile she sometimes used when they were sharing pleasure. Damn how he'd missed pleasuring her.

"And I want you to think about something," she said. "What you did that day in the arena, it may have seemed like a mistake at the time, but you went with your heart and your instincts that day. You lost two brothers, but not because of anything you did. If you hadn't done it, Carn might be dead too."

And he would never have found her and had a chance at freedom. "In battle it's cool reason that most often wins the match." He knew this to be true, but her words also had merit.

"Carn and Lo depend on—"

She pressed her fingers to his lips. "Carn and Lo don't follow you because you're smart or clever or great at strategy. They follow you because they know you would do anything in your power for them."

She smiled again, but this time the smile was sad and the sparkle in her eyes dimmed. He could think of nothing to say.

The door to the external corridor flew open and Knock stormed into the room. "Sorry it took me so long to get here." The man panted as if he'd run the whole way from the shuttle-bay. "I've got the security grid map and the lock overrides as promised. But I've also got something you're really gonna like." He looked from face to face. "Hey, did I interrupt something?"

"No," said Samantha. "Show us what you have."

He held out his hand and three tiny-metal cylinders sat in his palm. Each secured to a slender chain. "Personal scatter-shields. They'll make it harder for them to see you during scans, vid or sensor."

He passed them around then stopped in front of Samantha. "We should be getting inside now. Give me a hand."

Samantha allowed Knock to help her into the closet and he and his brothers followed her inside. Once they were all inside the narrow space, the door snicked shut, leaving them in total darkness.

CHAPTER TWENTY-NINE

The Gwendella, Roma Spaceport
Earth Alliance Beta Sector
2210.185

"Just staying here, waiting, is going to kill me." Samantha paced the length of the *Gwendella's* rec-room. Knock's eyes followed her as if she were the ball in a ping match. Everything had gone to plan, but that was no comfort when Mercury, Lo and Carn were out there risking their lives.

Knock tossed a ball in the air and caught it. "Nothing else we can do until they get back. Until the commotion starts."

"If they're caught, I'm not leaving." She would find a way to get them out. She wouldn't leave them. She couldn't.

"Don't borrow trouble. They have the shields and the overrides I rigged. They'll be fine."

Knock got to his feet and stepped into her path. Momentum had her crashing into him before her brain could give up its worrying enough to respond to the movement. "Damn, Knock."

He set her away from him, but kept a grip on her arms. "Sammie, we've been all through this. Covered every contingency. All we can do is wait. You wearing out the decking isn't helping a damn thing."

The *Gwendella's* duty officer appeared in the hatchway. "Sorry to interrupt, Ms. Devlin, but there's a woman demanding to see you."

Everything that could go wrong crowded into her thoughts.

Her pulse surged. "She asked for me by name?"

The man fidgeted with his jacket as he answered. "Samantha Devlin."

"Damn. She alone out there?"

"Alone, yes. Out there, no. She begged me to bring her in," he explained sheepishly. "She looked scared to death."

Samantha and Knock exchanged a glance and Knock left. Samantha knew he'd make a sweep for surveillance and tracker tags and monitor the hangar for transmissions.

"Well, then. Bring her in. Maybe she's in the mood for some Ping." Samantha propped a hip against the Ping table and crossed one booted foot over the other.

The officer led the woman into the room. She gave her name as Rachel. Samantha took note of the mink brown hair she wore loose around her shoulders. She held her head in a way that made the hair fall artfully over one side of her face, but scars snuck out of hiding to trace across her nose and lips. Someone had clawed the woman's face. Some Dog. She had a terrible feeling she knew exactly who.

Even with the scars, Rachel was attractive. The slashes had been shallow, at least where Samantha could see them. They hadn't done any structural or nerve damage. The woman wore an evening dress that bared a lot of cleavage. It might have been a tactic to distract people from the scars. The dress synched tight around a narrow waist and a slit in the skirt showed enough leg to have the *Gwendella's* officer acting like a schoolboy.

Samantha didn't offer to shake her hand. "I've never understood how women manage not to fall out of dresses like that."

"Practice. And Adhesive." Rachel's gaze swept the room before coming back to Samantha. "But I didn't come here to talk fashion."

Samantha said nothing, leaving the other woman to fill the silence.

Rachel adjusted a bag that hung from her shoulder. "I know you're the one who freed Diablo, Mercury, and Carnage."

Samantha shrugged, all cool on the outside. Inside her mind spun, searching for a plan. "That's what the bulletins claim, but you shouldn't believe everything you read. Can I ask how you found me?"

"I know they're here. I saw Lo and I knew you had to be the one to bring them back. I checked all the ships that landed today. I did some cross checks and this seemed the most likely one."

A fist twisted in Samantha's chest. "You saw Lo?" She shoved her hands behind her to hide the fact she'd started to shake.

"Near the kennels. I don't think anyone else saw him. They're going after Hera aren't they?"

"Hera?" Samantha fought to keep her expression blank.

"Carn's mate."

"He has a mate?"

Rachel shook her head. "We don't have time for games. Owens expected they'd try to get Hera out. I don't think he expected you to come so soon, but the point is—"

Samantha pushed away from the ping table and crossed her arms over her chest. "A point, that would be good."

"He moved her. Hera isn't at the kennel anymore."

"And?" And Samantha knew there would be no way her men would come back empty-handed. Funny how they'd all become hers, even Carn. She hated her fear over how things might change when they brought Hera back. They had to come back.

"I can take you to her."

"Me?" Samantha laughed, but she knew it sounded hollow. "And I'm supposed to blindly follow you? Owens must think I'm stupid."

"I didn't tell him when I saw Lo." Rachel tapped the toe of her pointy shoe. "If I had, they would have everything on lockdown. Owens would've already dragged you off this ship. But he doesn't know about the Dogs being here and he doesn't know that your father was pals with the owner of this ship. He hasn't bothered to look that deeply into your background."

"But you know, because?"

"Sevti. I'm working with the resistance." Rachel fingered the strap of her bag again. "I can help you. And unless you have some way to contact the Dogs without alerting Roma, you're going to have to be the one to do this. I tried to get the resistance to help, but Sevti was my only contact and he broke transmission before I could explain. Now he's missing. They're likely questioning him. You might not be safe here long enough to wait for the Dogs to find her on their own."

Samantha pushed her fear for Sevti aside. She would tell the captain, beyond that she could do nothing to help him. Samantha uncrossed her arms and reached for a ball from the Ping table. She closed her hand around the cool green surface. They were unlikely to reach Mercury—a downside of the scatter-shield. She wasn't yet ready to trust Rachel, but she might not have a choice. "Lo gave you those scars."

Rachel pulled her hair forward in a gesture that looked subconscious.

Samantha twisted the ping ball in her hand. "You betrayed him."

"I needed him to attack me, so I provoked him." Rachel shifted in her fashionably hazardous heels.

"Why?" Samantha set the ball spinning on the table. She wanted to slug the women who'd used Lo so callously.

"Owens was beginning to suspect me. When Lo attacked me, it put all of his suspicions to rest."

Samantha huffed. "You're insane."

"I'm determined." The fist she'd wrapped around the strap to her bag had gone white with tension. "You haven't seen the arena up close and bloody. You haven't seen the kennels." Rachel swallowed hard. "You don't know what it's like to watch someone you love be drugged out of his mind so he'll rip out the throat of a Dog he fought beside the night before or fuck any bitch that's willing to pay."

Tears rolled down Rachel's cheeks. Samantha's gut twisted in agony. She was talking about Lo. He'd told her, but she hadn't had to watch. She'd filed it safely in the past. What would she be willing to do to keep that from happening to Lo, or Carn, or Mercury?

"We have to get Hera out," said Rachel. "I know where she is now, but they're going to move her again. They won't risk losing her."

"You make it sound like she's more important to them than recapturing the guys."

"She is." Rachel studied her as if she were a flash flood that might jump the banks in a change of course that could drown her at any moment. "Hera is pregnant. It's the first natural pregnancy they've been able to produce."

The world had spun away and, selfish as it was, all Samantha could think was that it might be Mercury's child. It was a miracle and all she could do was stand there with her heart in her throat. A child. She wouldn't risk the life of an innocent. It didn't matter if it was Carn's child or Mercury's, she couldn't pretend it didn't exist.

"Okay," she said. "Tell me what I need to do."

Rachel opened her bag and pulled out a roll of bright red cloth. "You can start by putting on this dress."

CHAPTER THIRTY

RomaRex Arena
Roma, Earth Alliance Beta Sector
2210.185

Samantha had never felt more uncomfortable than now, wearing the tiny scrap of a red cloth and more glittery make-up than a veil dancer. There was even glitter in her hair. Glitter and something that made it stand out in spikes and ringlets. Rachel had at least provided reasonably sensible shoes. "In case you have to run," she'd said.

She'd left Knock to try to get through to the guys and followed Rachel out of the port and through the throng of the passenger terminals. They slipped through a grate in a storage bay in one of the terminals and followed an underground tunnel to the underbelly of what turned out to be one of Roma's luxury accommodation establishments. For someone who said she had proven her loyalty to Owens, she sure was taking every precaution.

When they finally slipped out of the building, Rachel guided her onto an elevated moving walkway that carried them to the gates of the arena. A steady stream of brightly dressed patrons moved through the entrance in anticipation of the show. In the center of the walkway, a line of familiar looking cages stood tempting the crowds to stop and gawk at the Arena Dogs on display. Here the cages were safely behind security fields, keeping the slaves from reaching out while giving the illusion of danger for the onlookers.

On the level below a massive crowd of more drably dressed spectators jostled and shuffled their way through another gate leading into the standing-room sections near the arena floor.

Rachel led her to a guarded door marked private, then led her through a lounge where privileged guest gathered to drink before the event. The gowns and cosmetics they wore made her look sedate and boring, which was fine so long as it didn't make her stand out and get her caught. The far wall was completely transparent and looked over a labyrinth of partitioned spaces.

Rachel punched in a code, opening a door to a narrow metal walkway. "This is the staging area. Come on."

Across the space, Samantha saw a crisscross of similar walkways. She nodded at a small group of men dressed in evening attire on an adjacent path. "What are they doing?"

"They're looking over the gladiators that will perform tonight." The men talked among themselves, occasionally pointing to the area below. "There trying to get an edge on the betting by seeing what condition they're in."

"Oh." It was awful. She could see the men being held below in chains. Some were being strapped into leather gauntlets. Others were being oiled down. "How do you stand this?"

"This is nothing," Rachel's voice was light, easy. "Toughen up. It only gets worse from here."

They crossed to the far side of the staging area and through another door, then down a level. Rachel walked them right up to a cluster of uniformed men, standing near a transit tube. "Manny," she called. "Can you give me and my friend an escort out to the Owens Kennel?"

Rachel had explained that to get to the tunnels that would take them to Hera they'd need to get inside a well guarded area of the kennel. Going in as privileged guests was the most reliable way.

As Manny separated from the crowd and led them to one of the transports, Samantha noticed that the men wore subtly different uniforms.

"There are five different kennels," Rachel said. "They were established by the four men and one woman who created RomaRex."

"Playing tour guide tonight, Lady Rachel?" Manny spoke politely as the transport pulled out of the station and moved them outside and along the tube-track. The land around them was open, flat, and empty and it flew by at dizzying speed. There wasn't a soul in sight. Clearly a restricted tract. If Rachel had seen Mercury, Lo, and Carn at the kennel they must've made it across safely. If they were still there she might be able to connect with them and they could help her get Hera out—assuming she could get Hera back to the kennel once she found her. It was a damned big assumption.

Mercury crept along the rafter, edging his way in silence. The guards patrolling the corridors wouldn't hear him, but the eyes of the Arena Dogs in the cells below tracked his progress. They'd have smelled him the moment he entered this wing of the kennel. He found the cell he wanted and settled his body against the cool metal to wait for the two guards to reach the optimal distance in their patrol pattern. It helped that it was an arena night. The guards were spread thin.

He barked a low yip and waited for Saber to respond. The massive male leapt to a narrow bar that had been hung in his cell to provide exercise. He swung his body up and balanced there, much as Mercury did with the rafter. The others in the cage watched in silence.

Saber got right to the point. "You've come for Carn's mate?"

"Yes. I need your help."

Saber's unblinking stare gave none of his emotions away. "You shouldn't have come."

"Carn is my pack brother. I couldn't ask him to abandon his mate."

The big man dipped his head in a slow motion of acknowledgement.

"We need a distraction. Lo and Carn are spreading the word through the kennel." The others wouldn't make a move without Saber's leadership.

Scowling, Saber shook his head. "I must think of the good of all. If you breach the kennel defenses, they'll tighten security."

Why would security be important to Saber? The implications flared through Mercury's brain like the snap of a glow-stick. "You have a plan to free our people?"

Saber said nothing, but his silent stare was answer enough.

The possibility was an ember of hope that Mercury would hold close to his soul, but he couldn't abandon his promises to Carn in hopes Hera would be able to escape in whatever scheme Saber was working. "Carn won't leave without her. We only need the guards distracted. Our transport has room for a few more. We could take some of you with us."

"No," said Saber. "We let Owens believe this ends with you." Tipping his big head back, Saber growled.

An answering growl sounded in the distance. Several howls sounded from other areas of the kennels.

Saber sighed. "We'll do what you ask, but Hera isn't in the kennel."

Mercury steeled himself against what might come. "The guard's quarters?"

Saber snarled. "I don't think so, but Owens wants us to believe she's in confinement. It's a trap. They've put on an elaborate show, but none of us has scented her in days."

Mercury breathed out a careful sigh of relief. The trap was a worry, but knowing Hera hadn't been subjected to the guards eased his guilt.

Lo's scent reached Mercury before he heard him. He shouldn't have heard him at all. He was supposed to be in the east wing. Lo bounded from beam to beam, landing precariously in front of him.

"Samantha is here." The words rushed out and worry danced in the red flames of Lo's eyes. "She was with Rachel and one of the whips." Lo's chest heaved as he spoke. "They were headed toward the Lady's wall."

Mercury's world stopped for a heartbeat. He met Saber's eyes and dropped the override Knock had made for him through the bars. "Be ready."

"Good luck." Saber's whispered words faded away as he and Lo raced toward the scent of his mate.

Rachel giggled loudly then leaned in to whisper in Samantha's ear. "You remember what to do?"

"Yes." Stomach roiling at the sight of the men—the Arena Dogs—stripped bare for any cruel human that would pay to see them this way, men like Mercury and Lo, she wanted the whole thing over. "You go first."

Rachel giggled again. She traced her fingers over one of the muscled creatures chained to the tilting contraption. She gripped his already engorged cock drawing a moan. She pressed her body close and lifted one leg as if she'd climb him.

She'd been right about the guards. They were all too busy watching Rachel to notice when Samantha pressed the small mask over her mouth and nose, biting hard on the mouth piece. She slipped the small air delivery strip from beneath her belt. Her arm swung out in an arc, spraying them all with the anesthetic.

They dropped quickly. She reached out for Rachel and managed to soften her fall. Easing Rachel to the ground, she made sure her limbs weren't twisted.

"Thank you." She knew the woman was unconscious, but she hoped somehow her appreciation would get through.

Samantha wished she could free the chained men, but freeing them might only get them killed. She quickly divested the guard of his weapon. She traced her fingers over the patterned walls until she found the seam of the hidden door Rachel had promised would be there. At her touch the mechanism released the latches, letting the door swing freely. Samantha shoved through then climbed down the ladder leading into the darkness. As she dropped the last few feet she found herself in another transport-tube station. This one was underground, cramped and obviously not recently used. Tubes led out in several directions and a map, a stunner, and a uniform lay in a shadowed corner, right where Rachel promised they would be. She pulled the uniform on quickly and transferred all of the gear she'd carefully hidden on her person into the pockets of the uniform. The fit was terrible, but it only needed to fool the guards from a distance.

Samantha slapped the map-display against her wrist and turned on the projection. The map flashed into life and Samantha set out to find the juvenile center and Hera. She quickly worked her way through the tunnel system until she could see the platform that the map had been programmed to find. There had been surface access shafts at regular intervals along the path and she stopped under the last one before the station and began to climb. Rachel had warned that the shafts were secured by metal grates, but Samantha wanted to try to get a look around before walking into the station.

At the top, she was able to get a glimpse of the compound above. The quiet three story building, mostly abandoned now, sprawled across a barren plain.

Halfway between the grate and the building, a high charged

fence surrounded the facility. She couldn't see any guards, but they'd be there. A minimum of three, according to Rachel. Satisfied that everything was as described, Samantha climbed back down into the tunnel and made her way to the empty station. The doors to the stairs had been welded shut, but one blast from her purloined weapon on full force managed to break the hinges on one side. Samantha squeezed through the small opening then moved quickly up the stairs.

She waited at the top, listening for any sign of the guards. She wondered again what she thought she was doing. She had no business going after Hera. What if she made things worse? She should've waited for help. No. According to Rachel, Owens had plans underway to move Hera tonight.

She heard Mercury's voice in her head. How many times had he called her courageous? She had to do this for him. For all of them. She gave the last set of doors between her and the juvenile center a gentle shove and cringed at the racket it made as it slid open.

She squeezed through the gap and pushed the door back into place. A quick look around showed no sign of patrols. Rachel had promised the surveillance cameras weren't operational. If she'd been wrong she'd know soon enough. Samantha sprinted down the corridor to the first turn and stopped, back pressed against the wall, waiting for some alarm to sound or for a group of armed men to come charging out, but she heard nothing.

The rooms on the ground level all appeared to be schoolrooms. Instead of miniature chairs and tables, stacks of gear and wrestling mats sat in a corner waiting for children to need them again. If she had her way, not another child would be allowed to grow up in those dreary rooms.

Once she felt confident there was no guard at this end of the building, Samantha headed for the stairwell that led to the second level. The moment she got to the top she heard the guard patrolling the corridor. Samantha waited for him to round the corner and get a good distance away then headed for the nearest window. She took in the narrow ledge and decided it was better than a wide hall where she'd have to face at least one guard.

She made her way along the ledge and to the bedroom window of the building's only resident. She found Hera sitting on her bed—no evidence of the child in the shape of her body.

Hera wore familiar black pants and a matching tunic. Her long, ebony hair had been pulled back from her face in a tight braid. The severity of the style emphasized her high cheekbones and wide, black eyes. Her nostrils flared as Samantha dropped into the room. Holding a finger to her lips in the universal sign for quiet, she approached the woman and sat on the bed.

"I'm a friend of Carn's. I'm here to help you."

"You shouldn't be here," Hera whispered, panic flaring in her eyes. "Carn can't come here. Don't let him come here."

"He doesn't know where we are. We're going to have to go to him, okay?"

"I can't leave. There are guards and a fence and no way off the planet. Please go before they find you here."

Samantha had known Hera had been created and trained to be submissive, but she hadn't expected her to be timid to the point of refusing to participate in her own rescue. She put her arm around Hera's shoulders.

"I know you're afraid, but you have to be brave. We need to get your baby out of here. Okay?"

"Baby?" Hera's eyes widened as she edged away from Samantha's touch. She stopped at the end of the bed, but continued shifting like a tethered camule unable to get out of the path of an approaching sandstorm. "There are no babies here."

Samantha allowed her eyelids to slip down over her tired eyes. Why would Rachel have lied? Or had Roma used her to bait a trap?

Samantha pushed to her feet. If it was the latter, she was in real trouble. "We have to get out of here now. Is there more than one guard on this floor?"

"I don't know. I'm sorry."

"It's okay." Samantha considered the window ledge, but this time she chose speed over stealth. "I'm going to go stand over in the corner. When I give the signal, you call out. I'll stun them when they come in." And she'd have to hope catching them by surprise was a big enough advantage. "As soon as the guard is down, you have to be ready."

"The fence?"

"I have a different way out. You follow me."

"Okay." Hera visibly straightened. "I'm ready."

Samantha stepped softly across the room and froze as a symbol carved into the wall caught her eye. She traced her fingers over the rough etching. It was one the symbols from the terraformers back on G45987. Mercury had been right. The terraformers and the surrogates must have been one and the same. She stored that bit of knowledge for later.

Turning back to Hera, she gave the signal. Hera shouted out for help. The door banged open and a uniformed guard strode through.

Samantha waited. If there was more than one, she wanted them both to come through, but no one followed and the first guard was already starting to turn. Samantha fired. He fell to the ground like a stone and she wanted to jump for joy, but there would be time for celebration later.

Samantha took a deep breath then peered into the hall. No one. Could she be that lucky?

She started to wave Hera forward, but instinct told her to be methodical, take every weapon available. She dashed over to the fallen guard and dropped to her knees. She took his weapon first then rifled through his pockets and came up with some keys and a remote unit that looked right for the fence. It was always good to have more options. She shoved the remote and keys into her jacket pocket and pressed the weapon into Hera's hands.

"I couldn't."

"It's point and shoot. Easy."

Hera shook her head frantically. "Please, I can't."

"Okay." Samantha shoved one of the weapons into her belt and kept the other and the stunner in her hands as she led Hera into the hall. They made it to the stairwell and down. Her pulse was pounding so loud in her ears she knew she wouldn't be able to hear a guard patrolling if there was one. She'd have to hope Hera would have the sense to warn her, if she heard something.

The hall was clear.

She led Hera back to the station entrance, a ball of worry growing in her belly. It was too easy. Too quickly they reached the door down into the station.

Samantha stopped.

She pressed her shoulder against the smooth surface.

She looked back to Hera wanting reassurance that Hera wasn't hearing any movement.

Before the panic on Hera's face registered the door was shoved against her. She'd been right there and the guard had shoved the door hard. It knocked her off her feet. The pistol went skittering across the floor.

The guard came at her, smooth and efficient. He kicked the stunner from her right hand. Pain exploded through her knuckles and wrist. She bit her tongue to hold back her scream. She didn't want to alert any more guards and she didn't want to frighten Hera. Carn's mate had stepped back and plastered her body against the wall.

The guard made a grab for Samantha, but she rolled away and pulled herself toward the stunner that lay just out of reach.

A booted foot crushed the weapon then connected with her ribs and something snapped. For a heartbeat she stopped, unable even to breath. All the oxygen had been sucked out of her lungs and she couldn't get anything back in. The pain eased then throbbed again as the guard pulled her up by the back of her collar.

Samantha reached blindly behind her, sliding the heel of her hand down his body until she found his cock. She dug her fingers into his balls and tightened with all her strength. He released her so fast she nearly fell. She got her feet under her and spun. Dots of light danced in her vision as she pulled back a fist and punched him hard in the nose.

He collapsed to the ground, not out completely, but dazed.

She pulled her last weapon from her belt and held out a hand for Hera. "Come on."

The woman's fingers trembled as they slid into hers. "There are more down those stairs," Hera warned.

"Damn!" Samantha trusted Hera's nose and hearing so she tugged the woman toward the nearest door out of the building, pain in every step. They'd have to find another way. Samantha pulled her through the door, muscles tensed and ready to run.

"No," Hera warned, but too late.

CHAPTER THIRTY-ONE

Owens Juvenile Center, Roma
Earth Alliance Beta Sector
2210.185

Samantha stumbled as Hera slammed into her back.

She reached behind her to steady the clinging woman.

"I tried to tell you," Hera murmured.

Less than fifty meters away, Drake and two guards stood between them and the gate in the high pulse-fence. In the back of her mind, she'd been thinking they could get out that way, but that was no longer a possibility. The guards only carried stun-sticks, but Drake had a pulse-pistol aimed at them, negating any advantage they might have gained from the distance between them. A smile spilt Drake's face and he held his trademark whip in a loop in his other hand.

Samantha jerked her gaze away to search for another way out.

"Don't even think of making a run for it," Drake shouted. "Even if you could make it before I shot you, you'd be out the moment you touched the fence."

This couldn't be happening.

Had Rachel set her up or had Sevti broken under interrogation? She didn't want to contemplate what they might have done to him to get the information. And Rachel...if she was working for Owens, there would be no one coming to help.

"What are we going to do?" Hera's voice trembled.

"Do you see anyone outside the fence?" Samantha kept her voice low.

"No," said Hera. "No one."

"Stay behind me," Samantha whispered. "Keep me between you and Drake."

She pointed the pistol in Drake's general direction, knowing the time had come to make the sort of life and death decision Mercury had faced over and over in the arena. Kill or be killed. If it were only her life, she might make a different decision. But Hera stood terrified behind her and Carn would never get over her death. Carn. Wise, kind Carn.

"Oh, no." In a flash of insight, Samantha understood. Realization stabbed hard in her belly. It slithered under her ribcage and slogged upward, like a writhing snake forcing its way up her throat. Mercury hadn't come back to Roma for Hera. He'd done it for Carn.

Samantha could hear the whoosh of her pulse in her ears. *Mercury had come back to Roma for Carn.* That bit of wisdom echoed loud above the sudden surge of her heart rate. She shut it away for later consideration and focused on the moment.

As long as there weren't any guards beyond the fence, getting over it seemed like their best option. Beyond the dangerous barrier, the land was bereft of foliage, but it wasn't level. A ditch or a rise could serve as cover, either for a rescuer or for them, if they could clear the fence.

"Be smart, Sam," said Drake. "Put the weapon down."

"I don't think so."

Drake's pistol was the real problem. The guards would have to chase them down to use the stun-sticks and Samantha was willing to bet Hera could make it to the fence before they could close the distance.

The thought of what she was about to do made Samantha lightheaded. Her belly clenched and bile rose up the back of her throat.

Samantha pressed her lips together.

She lifted the pistol higher and took aim at the center of Drake's chest.

She squeezed the trigger.

And nothing happened.

Frustration and...relief warred in her gut. Her hands shook

with the reality of what she'd been willing to do. For Mercury. Not for Hera. Not for Carn. For the man she loved more than her own moral high ground.

Drake shook his head. "Sam, I'm so disappointed. Did you really think I'd let you get your hands on a functioning weapon?" Smug confidence etched his features like the macabre grin of a slither-constrictor with a squirming rodent halfway down its gullet.

Sam dropped the gun and held her hands out.

"Rachel." Against her will, the name came out with all the grief she was feeling. Grief for what the woman had put Lo through. Grief for the chance that help would come that had just slipped away.

If the gun was a plant, the remote might be, too.

Drake laughed—a cruel sound. "Poor, ugly Rachel has no idea what she's done. She doesn't even know we've been watching her for months. It was easy to make sure she overheard exactly what we wanted her to and even easier to swap out the pistol she left you. She led you right to us."

Samantha sucked in that bit of information like a fire chasing after fuel. If Rachel hadn't been working against them, she might still be able to send help.

Drake started walking toward them to close the distance. "It's time to be sensible. If you cooperate, I can guarantee you won't be harmed."

Samantha shook her head. "You'll let me go? I don't think so."

"I'll hand you over to the Alliance law officers and you'll get a fair trial," he promised.

He knew she had Cerrillian blood. That she could never get fair treatment from the Alliance authorities. She wanted to laugh at the absurdity, but she needed to keep him talking so she could think. "What charges?"

"I'm not negotiating here," he shouted back. "I'm offering you a way out of this that doesn't end in you never leaving this estate." Drake shoved the pistol into a sheath hanging from his waste and tapped the whip against his hip.

Samantha's heart raced right into her throat. Drake's arrogance might have given them a chance. Samantha pitched her voice low again, for Hera. "Reach down to the pocket on my left thigh." Drake was watching Samantha and paying no attention to where Hera's hands were. "There's a sparker—a small metal strip. Pull it out and when I say, snap it and toss it ten meters in front of us, but don't look at it." She raised her voice for Drake's benefit. "Why should I make it easy on you?"

"Because things can always be worse." Drake started uncoiling the whip in his hands.

Hera, bless her, managed to get the sparker out of her pocket without freaking out.

Under her breath, Samantha said, "can you get over the fence, if I bring the power down?"

"Yes, I think so."

Drake was close enough to speak without shouting and his face said his patience was at an end. "What are we doing here, Sam?"

"What's the hurry?" Samantha shrugged and slowly lowered her hands in the direction of her jacket pockets.

Drake grinned. "I know you don't have any more weapons. You can't fake me out, Sam."

"I wouldn't even think of it," she said sweetly. She slipped her hands into the folds of fabric and carefully fingered her jammer and the remote she'd taken off the guard. If she could trigger the remote, and it was for the fence, then she could jam the signal to keep it from going back up while they climbed. "Look around, your real targets aren't anywhere to be seen. Isn't Hera supposed to be the bait? Why don't we wait and see if anyone else turns up?"

He frowned. "I have to say, I wasn't expecting the Dogs to send *you* after the bitch."

"I didn't have anything better to do."

"I see them." Hera's whispered words were laced with excitement. "Mercury, Carn, Lo. They're coming."

The news was bittersweet. Drake was getting close. Odds they could both get over the fence weren't good. Samantha tightened her hands around the remote. "Tell Mercury—"

"No!"

"Shh. Tell, Mercury, this is my choice. I knew what I was doing when I came after you. Tell him this isn't his fault. Promise me."

Hera made a yipping noise then nodded. "I promise."

Samantha triggered the remote and watched the red light at the top of the fence posts go dim. She triggered the jammer. "Okay. Now!"

Hera tossed the sparker and they both turned and ran. Even with her back turned, the light flashed in her vision and the crackle and pop made her ears ring. With any luck, Drake would be temporarily blind and disoriented.

Samantha pumped arms and legs, adrenalin helping her ignore the pain in her ribs, but she couldn't keep up with Hera. The woman might not have the aggression of the males of her species, but she clearly matched them for strength. She went up and over the fence without looking back.

Samantha knew she wouldn't make it up the fence in time, but she continued to struggle forward, her mind unwilling to accept that she might never again see her mother's smile or lay in Mercury and Lo's arms. She hadn't gotten enough of either.

The slap of Drake's whip against her boot shot bolts of fear through her body, but Samantha didn't stop. She put her whole heart into pushing forward. A brutal tug yanked her foot back and her body slammed hard against the ground. A sickening snap and a flash of icy cold gripped the arm she'd thrown out instinctively to protect her face. She would've screamed, if she hadn't lost her breath from the impact.

Samantha pushed up with her good arm and searched for Hera through the fence. She'd made it out forty meters where the men had run out to meet her. Mercury was in the lead, that amazing speed of his, but Lo and Carn were close behind.

Hera threw herself into Mercury's arms. Samantha watched as her love's arms closed around the female he'd bonded with then a tug on her boot jerked her back again. Her arm gave out and her face slapped against the hard packed ground. Lights flickered behind her eyelids as pain radiated out from her cheekbone but it couldn't compare to the pain in her heart.

Hera and the others would be safe. Satisfaction pushed her fear and her grief aside for a moment and she clung to it, let it fill her heart.

As the weight of Drake's shadow fell over her, she closed her eyes and imagined them all happy, living together, looking out for each other. Drake's boot came down on her wrist and he dug into her pocket and came up with the remote.

He fumbled with it for a moment before growing frustrated. "Fuck."

Samantha took pleasure in the momentary victory. He couldn't get the fence back up as long as the small device still in her pocket was transmitting.

"Give me your stun-stick," he barked to someone outside her field of vision.

"Sir?" The guard sounded confused and uncertain.

"It'll fry whatever jammer she's using. Hand it over!"

His boot lifted off her wrist and she tried to push up, get to her knees.

"Faster than searching her," he said.

Lightning struck her ribs. Her muscles twitched—all of them tightening in agony at the same instant. Fuck, how did Mercury stand it? The pain blazed through her brain and time slowed. When the worst of the agony faded, pain still washed through her like water sloshing in a shakily held bowl.

Howls filled the air in a sweet chorus that settled against her heart like a balm and terrified her at the same time. They sounded close, too close. Why weren't they running far, far away?

With the realization that she couldn't yet give into the pain, she fought the lingering weakness. She could almost feel the surge of adrenaline. Her breath came easier and control of her limbs slowly began to return. She pulled her usless arm tight against her body. Her fingers pressed lightly against the cool metal of a low tech blade she'd taped to her belly. It had been the only weapon she could carry hidden beneath that skimpy dress.

"That's right, Mercury." Vile expectation slithered beneath Drake's voice. The remote was in his hand. "Come on over the fence."

Mercury's answering howl rang with frustration. Stars, he was so close. He had to know the moment he touched the fence Drake would trigger the pulse system. He'd be stunned and Drake would have him back in a cage before he recovered.

"Put down the remote." Mercury's voice vibrated with menace. "*Then* we'll come over."

"He's afraid to face us," Lo growled. "Without chains and bars between us."

Something squeezed a fist around Samantha's heart. She took a fortifying breath and lifted her head. Mercury crouched just beyond the fence, beautiful storm cloud eyes locked onto hers. "I won't leave you." His voice was so low and rumbling she doubted anyone could have understood, but she knew him. Knew his voice. Knew his soul. He'd promised her once. It was the only thing, he'd said, the only thing he had to give her. His promise not to leave her behind.

"It would be smarter to leave me." She whispered, but she knew he heard.

"Sometimes," he said. "It's better to go with your heart and your instincts."

He used almost the same words she'd used back on the *Gwendella* and there was absolute certainty in his face. He finally understood. She groaned with a heart full of love and grief. Why now, when she needed him to be smart instead of giving into his emotion and instincts? He wouldn't give up now, even if it got them all killed.

Lo paced like a trapped animal, searching for some flaw in the fence that would allow him to get to her. "Be the man you claim," snarled Lo, stare fixed on Drake with a laser focus. "Toss away the remote and let us in."

Samantha had been willing to give her own freedom to save Hera, to save them, but she wouldn't allow Mercury or Lo to be put back in a cage. If they were willing to fight for her, she had to find a way to help them.

Her hand closed around the blade handle and yanked, tape and all. Thrust it hard into Drake's booted foot.

"Fuck!" The remote hit the ground with a soft thud. Drake dropped to his ass, grabbing for the handle of the blade and pulling it free. "Fucking bitch."

Samantha batted a hand at the remote. She struck it with a rewarding amount of strength. It flew across the ground, well out of reach of Drake or any of the others.

Mercury and Lo flew up the fence with the grace and power of dancers. They dropped to the ground in one, two, heavy thunks that sent dirt flying into the air.

"Fucking, hell," Drake swore as he scrambled toward her.

A fist in her hair jerked her head back then pain exploded in her temple. Drake screamed. Mercury snarled. He pinned the whip-master to the ground. She tried to blink them into focus. Mercury's hands held Drake's head. He looked ready to crush the man's skull.

And then he hesitated. His muscles went slack. He landed in a pile atop Drake, who shoved him to the side and scrambled to his feet.

Lo lay a few meters away, equally still.

Tears welled and her belly revolted. What little she'd eaten that day came up and spilled onto the hard packed ground. Her belly heaved again, but there was nothing left inside.

Samantha pushed away from the mess and rolled onto her back. Her energy drained away as the adrenaline rush faded and her injuries roared into her awareness.

Through the blur of her own tears she saw two shapes form out of the shadows of the juvenile center's roof. Blobs became columns—human columns with rifles cradled in their arms. They'd never really had a chance.

What had she done?

CHAPTER THIRTY-TWO

RomaRex Arena Medical Center, Roma
Earth Alliance Beta Sector
2210.185

Everything hurt. It was the first thought Samantha had. Her head ached like a herd of cattle had trampled across it. And she couldn't remember where she was.

"I want her on her feet and ready for the arena in an hour." She recognized that voice. Drake. She forced her eyes open to see a woman with ice-blue eyes and short blonde hair leaning over her. She wore a white med-coat.

Samantha was in a med-bed, but she didn't remember how she'd gotten there. As she tried to bring it back, grief swamped her.

"Mercury. Lo." The words cut free of her chest and across her lips like blades cutting through a fleshy scabbard.

"They're fine." The woman spoke with confidence. "They were sedated using dart rifles. They're being taken to the arena staging area," the woman explained.

Relief surged up and nearly took Samantha back under. Something pricked her arm. Gentle hands applied something cool to her cheek and temple. Across her lips. Slowly she became aware of distant cheers and low thuds from above. They must be directly under the arena.

She tried to speak and nothing came out. She swallowed and tried again. "What will happen to them?"

"You should be more concerned about *your* situation at the moment," answered the medic.

"Please."

The woman shot her a sympathetic look. "Owens is slating them into the arena schedule tonight. He wants them back in the arena one last time so that everyone can see they're back where they belong."

"Then what?"

"Oh, I don't expect there'll be a *then* anything. Owens doesn't like to lose an opportunity to make profit, but he wants them dead and there's no way he'll risk anything going wrong again."

"He wants you there." The man attached to the voice came into view. Short cropped hair and a med-coat. Another medic. "He'll want you on display for the crowds. To show that no one gets away with stealing from Roma."

"Abel," said the woman. "Don't upset her."

"She'll find out soon enough," said Abel.

Yes, she needed to know as much as possible, if she was going to find a way to stop it. *Never lose hope.* That's what her father had taught her and she was finally ready to accept she was her father's daughter.

The medics moved away. Samantha didn't think they'd gone far, but her head hurt too much to move, so she lay still staring at the ceiling.

"Look at this," The female medic whispered. She was speaking to Abel though. Not to Samantha.

"Damn. Is that right?"

Samantha decided she'd risk the pain. Slowly, she turned her head until she could see them huddled over a screen. The pain of moving was every bit as bad as she expected and she still had no idea what they were looking at. She glanced toward the door. No guards. Her desire to escape won over her curiosity. She lifted a leg a centimeter off the med-bed experimentally. She might have the strength to stand.

"This could change everything," said the medic.

Samantha was working up the energy to roll off the bed when Abel was back by her bedside. "You don't know that it's one of theirs." He was still talking to the other medic.

"She's been with them long enough."

Abel huffed. "Let's stick to things we can do something about."

Sam made a useless grab for his arm. "What are you talking about?"

He pulled a mender down over her chest. "Hold still now. I'm going to stimulate regen on that broken rib. It shouldn't hurt. Tell me if it does."

Samantha felt the tingle in her chest from the mender doing its work. "What could change things?"

"Don't talk."

The female medic came around to Samantha's right side and pressed an injector to her wrist. "This will numb your hand while I work on it. The good news is, this isn't as bad as it must feel."

"Answer my question," Samantha demanded. She was aware as she did that some of the pain in her skull had already started to fade. They must have treated it before she regained consciousness.

The medic tilted her head and studied her like a specimen under a scope. "Have you been intimate with the Dogs?"

"What?" Samantha sputtered at the too personal question.

Abel put a hand on her shoulder. "Be still and quiet or I'll sedate you."

Samantha lay in defeated silence while the two medics worked. When they'd done all they could for her injuries, Abel stowed the mender and the other supplies while the woman held her hand.

"You're a tough woman," said Abel. "That whip-master needs a beating with his own whip. Why in hell did you go after Hera by yourself?"

Samantha bristled at the implied criticism. "I thought she was pregnant."

Abel shook his head. "I heard they'd been putting out that rumor, but I can assure you she's not."

"I know that now."

The female medic patted the back of Samantha's hand. "Her lack of pregnancy is the reason they were so determined to get rid of her mate."

Samantha thought of the conversation she'd had with Carn back on *G-45987*. "Carn thought the match had been rigged."

"Finding a way to make more Arena Dogs is critical to Owens. If there's a chance Mercury, Carn, or Lo is the father of your baby we have to get you out of here."

"What?" Her baby? Shock left her dazed.

"Chelle!" Abel's shout startled her.

"We can't hand her over to Owens," said Chelle. "Not if there's even a chance. If Owens knew human women can carry their children, there'll be no stopping him. We have to get her out of here. And we need to do it before Myers and Mallow come on shift."

Chelle squeezed Samantha's hand and looked down at her. "You should be feeling a bit better now."

"Please," said Samantha. "You're not making any sense."

"You didn't know." A sad smile ghosted across her face. "Hera isn't pregnant, but you are."

CHAPTER THIRTY-THREE

RomaRex Arena Staging Area, Roma
Earth Alliance Beta Sector
2210.185

A familiar pain radiated through Mercury's shoulders. He couldn't feel his hands. For once the chants of the crowds, dully pulsing somewhere overhead, were a welcome promise of relief. If he was expected to fight, whatever he was being punished for would be forgiven.

He forced his eyes open. Lo was by his side. The dull gray drapes that divided up the staging area blurred momentarily and the shadow of another place fell across his field of visions. It twined around the pillars and slipped along the ceiling like a ghostly phantom, painting his world with memories of a dream. A dream so sweet he couldn't fathom how it could have come from his imagination. He had no frame of reference for a human medic that would treat him with respect and a woman who would stand at his side with courage in the day, then hold him in her arms through the night.

"Samantha."

"You say her name like it's some fucking prayer." Drake sneered then shoved him from behind to set his body swinging.

The pain spiked, but not enough to steal his consciousness and send him back into the blackness. Not enough to distract him from Drake's words. Not enough to disperse the intense anguish that came with the return of reality.

Samantha was no dream. She was real and, because of him, she was in the hands of the worst of monsters. He'd brought her here. He was to blame.

Mercury snarled at the man who'd been his trainer and his tormentor. "Where is she?"

"Don't worry," said Drake. He circled them as if he were tethered to them as surely as they were tethered to the cold metal rings over their heads. "I'll make sure she has a good view of your match."

Lo's snarl snapped Mercury's attention to his brother and the whip-master taunting him from a safe distance.

He didn't see Carn or Hera. He could only hope they'd managed to evade recapture. They'd be free. But at what cost?

"Will this match be as fated as the last?" He still remembered the horror of watching the Game Master's thumb dip down.

"Oh, much worse," said Drake. "The medic will be here with the drugs shortly."

Lo shuddered. Normally, Drake would have jumped on the opportunity to torment him and draw out his fear, but he was focused inward and he continued speaking.

"Grande wanted me to whip you first. Try to get you to tell us where Carn is hiding. I convinced him that would be pointless. Pointless and bad for our image. The crowd should always see you looking strong."

They'd heard that axiom often enough.

Mercury coughed up a bitter laugh. "Still trying to earn your way into your master's good opinion? I'm surprised he let you live after how badly you failed."

A flush crept up Drake's neck. If his features tightened any further his face would crack. He turned and stalked a few meters away.

Mercury locked gazes with Lo. "She told me you didn't follow because of my strategies or my success. After stumbling at every turn this day, I'm thinking she must have been right."

"She *is* right." Lo yipped. "She wouldn't want you to waste time blaming yourself."

Mercury dipped his chin in acknowledgement. "We have no time for regrets."

"No regrets," echoed Lo. His voice dropped and turned wistful.

"I regret nothing."

"She also said there's always hope, brother. We won't give up now." Mercury howled and Lo joined him. All around them, other voices rose up and merged into a song of grief—an expression of agony known to all Arena Dogs.

Drake spun around to face them. "Shut the fuck up!" He turned in a small circle and shouted the command out to all the Dogs being prepped for matches. "Shut up!"

Mercury let his howl fade to nothing and the others followed. "We are Arena Dogs!"

"We are Arena Dogs!" The shout came back to him, clear and strong with the power of every Dog close enough to join in.

Mercury sucked in air and shouted again. "We are strong!"

"We are strong!"

Mercury's heart surged with the combined will of all Dogs. "We will be free!"

The chant thundered back to him. "We will be free!"

"We will never give up!"

"Never!" Their voices drowned out the arena crowds as they broke into howls and hoots and discordant cheers.

Mercury met Drake's blood-red complexion with a smile of satisfaction. He wouldn't give up. Samantha would not die on Roma, nor would she live under the thumb of the owners.

Mercury forced all his energy and breath into making a low-sound alert. Many of the others joined him. He took another breath and dove back into the silent booming of their infrasound calls. It had to be enough to alert Saber. It had to be enough to give them some small opportunity to fight back.

CHAPTER THIRTY-FOUR

RomaRex Arena Medical Center, Roma
Earth Alliance Beta Sector
2210.185

Could it be true? Samantha's hand went to her belly. "I had a blocker. It should be good for another year."

"I double-checked the test results," said Chelle. "Just four weeks. It is their baby, isn't it?"

"We've always suspected the males had sturdy swimmers," said Abel.

Chelle scowled at him.

"Uh, sorry. We've suspected for some time that the females are the problem."

Samantha had no reason to trust them. "Why should I tell you anything?"

"Because we're on your side," said Chelle. "We're going to help you get out of here."

"You can't do this," said Abel. He pulled Chelle around to face him. "Think what you're doing."

"There's nothing Owens wouldn't do," said Chelle. "If he knew. Nothing would stop him from breeding a whole new generation of Arena Dogs."

The implications were terrifying, But Samantha couldn't think about that now. If she was going to have a baby, she wasn't going to raise it without the father. "I'm not leaving without Mercury and

Lo."

"Don't be stupid," said Abel. "Chelle is already—"

Another look from Chelle shut the man up. "Abel, don't you see. It really is theirs. She's trying to save the baby's father."

"Leave that to me," said Abel. "I'll do my best to get them out."

Chelle shook her head. "If I get her out, security will be tightened. The usual way won't work. I have to do this."

Chelle took her hand and squeezed her fingers. "I'd like you to let the leaders of the resistance know I wouldn't have blown my cover for any other reason."

"You shouldn't do it at all," said Abel. "You have any idea how hard it's going to be to get any more of them out of here without you?"

"What are you talking about," asked Samantha. "What usual way?"

Chelle smiled sadly. "Not all Dogs that die in the arena stay dead. Abel and I save some of them, like Mercury's pack brothers."

"They're alive?"

"We got them out to the resistance. After I'm gone, Abel will have to find a way to carry on without me, but that will take time. I'm afraid that's not an option for Mercury and Diablo."

Samantha didn't want Chelle to risk anything for her, but she didn't have a lot of options. "If you can get us all to the port, we can take you with us."

Chelle smiled like she was dealing with a naïve child. "Let's focus on getting you out first."

Two guards burst through the med-center door, dragging a bulky Arena Dog into the facility. Chelle urged them toward a second med-bed. "From the Arena?"

"No," said one of the guards as they lifted him onto the table. "There was a brawl in one of the kennels. This one is alive, but we can't get him to come around. He may have a head injury."

Chelle stepped over to the table, watching as Abel fitted the restraints and strapped the Arena Dog down. "Thank you," said Chelle to the guards. "We'll take it from here. You can wait outside."

The men were barely out the door when Abel released the restraints and the big man on the table pushed up and looked right at Samantha.

Chelle stroked the large man's arm like she was stroking a pet.

"Saber. Thank goodness you're all right."

"Mercury and Lo were recaptured?" He spoke without dropping his gaze from Samantha.

"Yes," said Chelle. "I'm afraid so, but Carn and Hera haven't been found."

The man called Saber gently pushed the medic aside and jumped off the table. He approached Samantha like a wild animal approaching an offered treat. She kept still and waited. The medics clearly weren't afraid of him and he seemed to know Mercury.

"You're hurt," she said, choosing to focus on the obvious. "You should let the medics help you."

He lifted his arms and looked down his torso, crisscrossed with claw marks. Blood welled along the marks. Raising his arms also showed off his lean, muscular frame. His torso was as lean as Mercury's but those broad shoulders made him seem much bigger.

"This is nothing but scratches," he said. He big shoulders rolled and he dropped his arms. He stepped closer, bent over her and inhaled deeply. Scenting her, no doubt.

"Who are you?" Saber's browse wrinkled.

Samantha knew exactly what response she needed to give. Not for him and not for the medics, but for herself. "I'm Mercury's mate," she said. "My name is Samantha."

"You don't scent of him." Saber stated it matter-of-factly.

"It was a long journey…and we were separated for most of that." And she was a fool. That she left unsaid. She pushed up into a sitting position and swung her legs over the side of the bed, grateful that the pain and dizziness didn't knock her back onto the bed. "Now that we're acquainted, there's only one thing I need to know." She closed her eyes and took a shallow breath before facing him again. "Are you going to help me rescue him?"

"Saber," said Chelle. "We have to help her. She's pregnant with his baby."

Shock painted his face a shade lighter. "Does he know?"

"No," said Chelle. The medic stepped over to a counter and started preparing two dosing-wands. "Drake will be here any moment to escort her into the stands and I'm supposed to make sure the match doesn't go well for Mercury and Lo. I'm replacing the usual drugs with a performance booster, but I'm not sure what else to do." The medic shoved the two prefilled wands into the big pockets of her white coat. "I'll do whatever I can to help."

"There's no way to get any help this quickly," said Abel.

"Oh," said Samantha. "Rachel. She's in trouble. They know she's working for the resistance."

Abel nodded. "I'll try to warn her."

The big Arena Dog sucked in a breath and released it in a loud huff. "Go with Drake. I'll do what I can to help your mate get up into the stands. I can do nothing beyond that."

"I understand. Thank you. Thank all of you."

Saber climbed back onto the bed and Chelle returned to Samantha's side. She held up a small instrument. "I'm going to insert a sub-dermal data-slip in your arm. It has information that will help you contact Haven."

"Haven?"

"It's the base of operations for the resistance. I don't know more than that."

"How do I know this isn't a tracker?"

"You can trust her," grumbled Saber. "She has freed many of our kind."

Samantha nodded then held still and Chelle touched the instrument to the soft tissue on the inside of her arm. When she'd finished, she wrapped her arm around Samantha's waist. "Can you stand?"

Samantha pushed her legs over the edge of the med-bed and borrowed some of Chelle's strength to get to her feet.

"Well done. Now let's go wait for Drake in the hall so Abel won't have to put Saber's restraints back on. He hates that."

Chelle's calm unnerved Samantha. She supposed it took guts to work as an undercover operative in a place like Roma, but her Zen-like state seemed almost inhuman.

"Samantha," Saber's growly voice stopped her speculation and she looked over her shoulder to where he sat on the med-bed.

"Yes?"

"Mercury," he said, "chose his mate well."

CHAPTER THIRTY-FIVE

RomaRex Arena, Roma
Earth Alliance Beta Sector
2210.185

Drake tugged Samantha up the ramp toward the light and noise beyond the end of the tunnel. It should have been evening, but she blinked at the brightness as they emerged into what looked like mid-afternoon.

"Doesn't it ever get dark around here?"

"Sure. But right here, not until after the games. Look." Drake pointed at the sky.

She hadn't expected a real answer, but her gaze followed the line of his arm up to the bright blue dome overhead. She couldn't see the horizon. They weren't high enough in the stands. But she could see the imitation sky began to fade to a pale purple beyond the reaches of the arena. "Owens must feel like a god around here."

Drake dropped his arm and shoved her toward a transparent polycarbonate wall. "Owens and the other owners *are* gods on Roma."

Beyond the barrier she could see the sandy oval and the throngs of people crowded into the stands. Some areas were packed tight with people, while others were fitted with semicircles of luxury. She looked back to the arena floor, dreading the moment when she'd see Mercury and Lo out there. She could see areas where the sand had been stained a ruddy brown with blood during earlier matches. Near the center, the remains of some sort of cart had been spilled over and twisted into shards of painted metal.

"Showtime," said Drake.

Samantha blinked as the light intensified around them. She looked up to see that directly above the blue dome had brightened into a white so bright it gave the effect of a spotlight. Drake turned his back to the wall and lifted his gaze as an amplified voice called for attention from every speaker around the arena.

Samantha turned, too. The next level up sat about two meters back. The transparent barrier sat in a gilded frame and beyond it, Grande Owens stood next to a man in what could only be described as a toga. Above that, a large screen showed vid of the men standing many meters tall. A hush spread through the crowd like a wave drowning the voices in silence.

"Good friends of Roma, we have a special event for you tonight! I'm sure you've all heard the rumors that House Owens lost some of its gladiators…and not in the usual way."

Pockets of laughter exploded in the audience.

"We're here to bring a close to this badly-handled publicity stunt. I bring to you, the Master of House Owens himself… Grande Owens!"

The toga draped man stepped back and Owens stepped forward, bringing his hand down for quiet.

"You may know," he said. "That I'm known for having a bit of a competitive nature, as do all the Heads. Perhaps this time we oversold our storyline a bit." Sprinkles of laughter followed his attempt at humor. "But never let it be said that House Owens doesn't do things in a big way."

This time the laughter sprang up like weeds after a rain, covering the crowd in giggles and half formed laughs.

"Let me start by introducing you to the woman we hired to play the part of our thief…the half-human–half-alien actress, Samantha Devlin.

Suddenly, Samantha's face appeared on the screen and she was standing alone. Alone with Drake and two burly looking guards standing just out of the light.

The crowds roared, half cheering, half booing.

She still wore the guard's uniform Rachel had left for her in the underground tunnel to the Juvenile Center. That had to add credence to his claims. Owens might be willing to cover up much of the truth of what happened, but he intended to ensure *her* secrets were out.

The light shifted and Drake stepped up beside her, his smile that of a sand-viper after striking prey, waiting for the poisonous venom to take effect.

"And for our match tonight," continued Owens. "We have two of our...missing...gladiators!"

Cheers swelled louder, this time all in complete accord. They wanted to be entertained.

"I give you a death match," said Owens. "Mercury and Diablo against the behemoth champion of House Bonita!"

The large screen shifted to the arena floor and a darkened tunnel. The crowd's cheers spiked, creating a cacophony that seemed sure to shatter the structure of the city's dome.

Drake jerked her around to once again face the center of the arena. At eye level a three-dimensional holo projection flickered to life. Hanging in the air above the arena floor, a large holographic projection showed Lo and Mercury. The mammoth structure of light being projected from various points in the arena ensured everyone would see the action of the match in 3D as it happened.

Samantha scanned the arena floor and found them where they had just emerged from a tunnel directly below where she and Drake stood. Mercury and Lo jogged toward the center of the oval.

Heavy chains shackled their feet, but not so much that they couldn't keep the easy pace. Running, however, would be out of the question. A leather binding strapped Mercury's right forearm to Lo's left.

Panic began to eat at the edges of her thoughts. She couldn't stand by and watch them die. She had to *do* something. "Why are they chained?"

Drake smiled with a trace of pride. "Because independent freedom of movement would be enough to give them the match. Even a behemoth couldn't survive against those two."

She considered asking, but she wasn't sure she wanted to know what exactly a behemoth was. And then she didn't need to ask. From further down the arena wall, a large creature lumbered into the light. Its legs were short and thick. Its long arms ended in blocky hands that touched the ground when it stooped forward. It wore leggings and a tunic, making it horrifically clear it wasn't just a beast. It also had intelligence. Intelligence and size. Dust flew up around it with every step, creating a cloud of sand that would irritate his opponents' eyes and hinder their breathing. Short bony horns sprouted from it skull.

"Roma created it." Samantha could hardly believe it. She wanted Drake to deny the obvious.

"You didn't think they would try only one DNA combination did you? What would the arena be without beasts to slay?" Drake stroked the narrow beard that hugged his chin. "They didn't have any tigers or elephants handy. Those creatures have been extinct for centuries."

In the arena Mercury and Lo climbed through the wreckage of the cart. The crowd had taken up a chant. "Fight, fight, fight…"

"Idiot crowd. They think the Dogs are trying to hide." Drake chuckled. "Owens should have had that chariot wreck cleaned up before the match. They'll find a way to use the sheared metal to cut up the champion."

The boasting tone of his voice shocked her. "You're proud of them."

"Mercury and Diablo? Of course. If they weren't drugged they might even have a chance to win."

A spark of hope flared. If Chelle managed to switch out the drugs they might survive. But for what? More slavery? An execution? "Is that all you care about? Winning?"

"It's all I can afford to care about."

Drake was right about Mercury's tactics. The behemoth had been steadily swinging at them and getting sliced up in the process. The beast managed to swing through a chunk of the wreck and caught Lo in the head.

Samantha gasped. Her heart beat like a hyper-motor, ready to speed out of her chest at any moment. She leaned against the wall for support as her legs quaked. This had to stop.

It had to stop before she lost one or both of the men she loved. *Stars, she loved them. Both of them.*

Her heart wouldn't slow. Her stomach cramped with fear. Frantic, she searched for someone familiar in the sea of faces. If wanting could make something happen, there would be an army of help in that crowd, but she knew Captain Artane too well. The captain wouldn't risk her crew in what could be branded an open act of terrorism. Artane had plenty of courage, but she wasn't foolish and she took her responsibility to her crew seriously. No, Samantha wouldn't find help in that direction.

The crowd drew in a collective gasp. She jerked her gaze back to the arena floor. Mercury and Lo were wrapped around the beast's back. Out of its reach, they jabbed at it with relentless repetition.

The creature turned in a circle—a macabre dance—as it bled from dozens of cuts and punctures. Suddenly, it reared up with a roar and rammed backward into the wreckage. All three went down in a heap amidst the twisted metal.

Mercury and Lo climbed free of the tangle while the behemoth still struggled.

"They should be getting weaker." Drake's confusion added another spark to the quietly building fire of hope in Samantha's belly.

She put a hand over the spot. Was she truly pregnant?

Motion drew her gaze to the guards standing to the side and to the crowds beyond them.

Knock!

His face came into focus as he slipped back into the crowd and disappeared. She looked away, not wanting to draw attention. Knock was out there, waiting for an opportunity to help.

The noise in the arena spiked and more guards spilled out of the tunnel below where she and Drake stood. In the center of the arena, the behemoth lay unmoving. Mercury and Lo climbed to their feet, leaning heavily on one another. "They won."

"Fuck!" Drake grabbed her arm and pulled her toward the tunnel they'd emerged from before the match. She looked up catching site of Grande Owens beaming out at the arena with a smile too wide to be anything but forced. As they headed into the tunnel, the roar of the chanting crowd followed them. "Live, live, live…"

More guards waited at the distant end of the tunnel and she realized this was not the direction she wanted to go. Mercury and Lo were in the arena and Knock was somewhere in the crowd. Samantha balled her hands one over the other and swung hard for Drake's face. Smack.

"Bitch!" Momentarily stunned Drake released her to pinch his nose as blood spurted out in a dripping mess. Surprise must have been on her side. She had no intention of wasting the advantage.

She dug in her heels and ran back out into the light. The guards that had been holding off the crowds lay at Knock's feet.

"Come on." He held out his hand.

Samantha grabbed for it and let him pull her through the noisy, distracted crowd.

They were half way around the oval when he started to drag her toward an exit tunnel.

"No!" She screamed to be heard over the chanters. "I'm not leaving them."

He grinned. "I know. I've got some equipment near the opening of this tunnel. Cutting tools to get us through the barrier and climbing gear to get them up into the crowd."

She wanted to hug him, but they were already running toward the small space between the tunnel archway and the adjacent seating area. The entire arena was on its feet, so no one paid any attention to them.

Knock reached into the shadows and pulled out a colorful bag. He pulled the strap over his head and settled it diagonally across his chest. He slapped a cutting laser into her hand and she sprinted to the nearest section of polycarb. The cutter hissed to life in her hand as she heard a shout of alarm.

She ignored it and kept cutting.

As she worked, the arena floor was a blur beyond her focus, but she could tell hell had spilled onto the sand. A battle between Dogs and guards played out for the entire arena to see.

"Maybe now they're entertained," she muttered as she worked.

She slid along the barrier then started the next cut. Beside her, Knock struggled with an unwieldy bolt-hammer in one hand and a plasma pistol in the other. The audience around them scattered, scrambling for cover or the nearest exit. Guards came at them from every direction, but most carried stun-sticks or shock-whips, not pistols, and none were close enough to stop them...yet.

The instant she completed her cut, Samantha rocketed to her feet. She grabbed the bolt-hammer, positioned it, stepped on the anchor points, and leaned her weight into it. She pulled the trigger. The recoil, as the preloaded bolt drilled into the walkway, reverberated through her muscles and nearly threw her off her feet. She shoved aside the heavy piece of equipment and took the rope and gloves Knock pushed into her hands.

She dropped to her ass and started rigging the rope to the bolt.

Time seemed to crawl and she was sure the guards would be on them any minute, but experience told her they'd managed the whole process in under ninety seconds. She'd cut into dozens of hulls in her day and the rest hadn't been much different than setting up a freight tie down, something they'd both done a hundred times. The rope had come out of the bag connected to an auto-repel, so setting that up took no time at all.

She kicked out, sending the cut section of the barrier tumbling to the ground below. She had one foot over the edge when Knock grabbed her arm. He handed her a small hand held stunner and the cutting torch, which she shoved in her pockets.

"You might need it," he said with a shrug. "I have a med-services transport on the verge between the arena and the public transport station outside the main entrance. I'll meet you there."

She leaned forward, kissed his cheek, then went over the side and down the wall.

CHAPTER THIRTY-SIX

RomaRex Arena, Roma
Earth Alliance Beta Sector
2210.185

Samantha hit the sand with a heavy thud. Okay, so maybe the automatic part of the auto-repel wasn't ideal. She was in one piece and that was really all that mattered.

She pulled the stunner out and strapped it to her hand, then turned and jogged toward the mini-war being waged between Arena Dogs and guards. She spotted Saber, first. The tall man was surrounded by uniformed men, but holding his own. A small figure in white flashed in and out of view—Chelle. Together, they must have freed every Dog in the staging area.

She wove through the pockets of fighting until she saw them. Mercury and Lo, still chained together and steadily working their way back toward the tunnel.

She lifted her arm and shouted. "Mercury! Lo!"

They looked over and saw her. They were both battered and bleeding, but they were alive and they were hers and she was theirs.

"Over here!" She turned to lead them back to the rope, but someone snatched her off her feet. Lo and Mercury ran toward her, their eyes promising swift death for the person who'd dared to grab her, but before they could get to her a group of guards swarmed them.

Samantha's captor had grabbed her from behind and lifted her off her feet. She kicked back toward his shins, wishing for her boots. She swung her head back, hoping to break his nose. He squealed and dropped her. *Bingo!*

Most of the group of men that had charged Mercury and Lo lay at their feet unmoving.

A wave of dizziness slowed her down when she tried to get to her feet. She'd nearly forgotten she had a head injury. She knew she should stay down and think of the child she should be protecting, but the baby wasn't real to her, yet, and Mercury and Lo needed her. Despite her drive to get to them, the pain kept her down. She curled into a ball until the dizziness passed then forced herself up again. Mercury and Lo were still fighting, working their way toward her. A guard came around the corner right next to them.

Samantha shouted out a warning, but it was too late.

The guard jabbed Lo with a stun-stick. Lo's body jerked, but he managed to slash bloody gouges into the guard's shoulder before Mercury tossed the man aside. And then he was there kneeling in front of her. *"Courra?"*

"I'm okay." She dug the cutter out of her pocket. "Let me get that restraint off you."

He and Lo knelt together letting her work as they remained alert. Saber and Chelle and the other dogs managed to run interference for them long enough for her to free them.

Mercury lifted her into his arms, folding himself around her to protect her.

"We have to get up into the stands," she mumbled against his neck. "There's a rope."

"The stands," he repeated. He looked down the length of the wall and found the gap she'd created. "Wrap your arms around me," he urged. He barked then took off toward the rope.

His hand slid under her bottom to support her and she slid her legs over his hips. "What about Lo?"

"I'm here, little Sam." He shouted it from a few meters away.

Every Dog that could disengage was following, then running ahead. Samantha twisted to see them forming a living launching pad. Mercury never slowed. He launched them toward the other Dogs. The next thing she knew they were flying through the air. She didn't know how Mercury did it, but they came down solidly on the walkway.

He set her aside and hunched down near the edge.

Snarls and shouts still rumbled below them, but on the walkway all was quiet. Most of the visitors in the section surrounding them had already fled.

Samantha looked over to see Saber serving as a launching platform for Lo who came flying at them. Lo slammed into the edge and with a groan Mercury pulled him onto the walkway.

Samantha looked for Chelle and her stomach heaved when she saw her. The guards had followed them across the sand. They had the group surrounded and Chelle lay face up, glassy eyes wide. Her head lay at an unnatural angle, neck broken.

Samantha heard a whip crack below. For a moment she thought she'd see Drake at the end of that whip, but it was another man. The whip wrapped around Saber's arm.

"Go," Saber shouted. "Go."

Mercury pulled her back from the edge.

Samantha resisted his tug. "We can't leave Saber behind."

"He won't go without his pack brothers, *courra*."

The truth of his words settled her. She understood, because she couldn't leave without Mercury or Lo.

"We'll find a way to get them out," she vowed.

"We will," Mercury agreed. "One day, we will."

Mercury pressed his forehead to hers, his hands framing her face. They were shaking. "I'm never letting you out of my sight again."

"A good idea," said Lo. "But we need to go. Now."

"Since when did Lo become the sensible one?" Sam shook her head as Mercury released her and they all headed down the tunnel.

"I don't much like the role," answered Lo. "So you two had better start thinking clearly."

Samantha somehow found the strength to chuckle. She buzzed with hope.

She turned and led them toward the exit tunnel. As they came out, spilling into the path of people streaming out from other areas of the arena, the people closest got a good look at Mercury and Lo and screeched, then scattered like sand-cats in rain.

"Which way?" Lo ran to the outside wall and looked over. "Too far," he said.

"Knock has a transport waiting," she explained. "But we have to get to it without being seen."

"There will likely be guards waiting for us at the exits," Mercury warned.

"When we are low enough we'll jump or climb down," said Lo.

"So how do we make it that far?" Samantha turned in a slow circle, desperate for some safe route to magically appear. She spotted a set of doors along the interior wall and they looked very much like lift doors of some kind. "Wait." She charged toward them and slid to a halt as the doors slid open.

Drake stood in the doorway, blood staining the front of his shirt from where she'd injured him earlier. More importantly he was holding a plasma pistol and pointing it in her direction. His finger was already on the trigger.

"I'll blow a hole in her if you so much as move."

They all know his speed wouldn't match Mercury or Lo's. He might get one shot off, but he'd never make two. Still, as long as he had her in his sights, he could control them.

Keeping the pistol ready, he strode directly to her and spun her around. He put an arm around her throat and tugged her back against his chest and there was nothing she could do to stop him.

"Now that's better. Time to talk," he said, facing off against Mercury and Lo. "You can't get off this planet. Cooperate and Sam won't be harmed. I give you my word."

Mercury and Lo both growled and snapped, but neither moved closer.

Samantha's mind raced. She still had the cutter. She just needed to get it out of her pocket. "You don't think they're going to fall for that, do you Drake? Didn't you teach them better than that?"

She locked her gaze on Mercury's and pleaded with her eyes for him to help her distract Drake. To her surprise, he held out his hands as if waiting for restraints.

"I will do as you ask," he said. "Just don't hurt her."

"Incredible." Drake shook his head and laughed.

Samantha slipped her hand in her pocket and pulled out the cutter. She flicked on the control and swung out toward the hand holding the blaster.

"Fuck!" The blaster hit the floor with a metallic clink. "Fucking bitch."

Mercury and Lo flew toward them in a flash of grace and power.

"Fucking hell," Drake swore as he scrambled back, his arm tightening around her throat. As she struggled for air, the pain in her head swelled as if her skull had been filled with the expanding foam she used to plug holes in engine chambers. She slammed her fist into his groin and the pressure eased. She yanked free and fell on her ass.

Drake screamed. Mercury snarled. He pinned the whip-master to the floor a meter away. She tried to blink them into focus. Mercury's hands held Drake's head. He twisted the man's neck with a vicious snap, silencing the screams.

Samantha stared at the body of the man who hurt her and the men she loved over and over. His relentless drive for vengeance against them had virtually guaranteed his death. Maybe she should have let them kill him back on Wilderness.

Mercury stroked hair out of her face with gentle hands. "Samantha?"

She tried to speak. Coughed. Swallowed.

His hand tightened in her hair. "I want to kill him again."

"Okay," she agreed.

He chuckled, a choked, desperate sound.

She heard Lo yip and she reached out a hand. He was there pressing her hand to his bare chest. "What do you say we go look for our ride back to the port?"

"Our ride?" Mercury wrapped an arm around her and helped her stand but the world spun.

Samantha swayed. "I think I may have overdone it a bit."

Mercury pulled her into his arms. "I'll carry you, *courra*." He urged her to wrap herself around him and she did. Even standing had begun to feel like a chore.

Mercury and Lo surged through the corridors until they found an exterior stairwell. They slipped inside and slipped in and out of the shadows.

"Samantha?"

Mercury urged her to look over the edge of the protective barrier. She searched for the med-transport. There were several.

"*Courra*, we must know where to go."

"I'm looking," she stalled. Three of the transports had the doors open, loading people. "That one." She pointed to a transport with no signs of activity.

"Look," said Lo. "There are more stairs like these, over there."

"We have to do this fast," said Mercury. "It looks as if more guards are moving up the ramp."

"Let's go," said Lo.

Mercury kept Samantha wrapped around him as they worked their way to the transport. They climbed along ledges and jumped from level to level on exterior features of the Arena building. Silently, she willed the idiot guards to continue to fail to look up and for the acid in her stomach to stay down.

The moment Mercury and Lo touched ground in a soft patch of grass, Samantha pushed at Mercury. "Put me down," she whispered in panic.

Mercury set her on the ground just in time for her to drop to her knees and heave. There was nothing in her stomach to come up, but she heaved until the cramping in her belly stopped.

"How bad are your injuries, *courra*?" Mercury spoke as he pulled her deeper into the shadow of a bush.

"I do have a head injury, but the medic treated it. I should be fine."

"You don't seem fine," accused Lo.

"Maybe I don't like climbing down buildings and jumping from ledge to ledge."

They both stared her down, unappreciative of her sarcasm.

"We don't have time for this," she pleaded.

Both men spun as two guards practically tripped over them. One of the guards caught Mercury with a stun-stick. Samantha scrambled back out of the way and Mercury had the man pressed into the ground in a blur of motion. Lo had an arm around the neck of the other guard and he squeezed tight until the man went limp.

Mercury pulled her back into his arms and ran, hunched low and using as much cover as he could find, taking her to the transport. And then they were there.

A click and a thunk signaled the moment they crawled into the transport. Mercury and Lo curled in a ball around her behind the seating. The passenger door swooshed open and she heard voices. Captain Artane! She was saying something about a twisted knee. Two other *Gwendella* crewmen climbed in to the transport in the guise of patients.

When the doors slid shut and the engine started, Samantha whispered, "Too easy."

Lo laughed—a rusty sound.

Mercury stroked her cheek. "They were unprepared. Nothing

like this has ever happened before."

She lifted her chin and let her determination show in her eyes. "We'll make sure—"

"It happens again," finished Mercury. "Rest now, *courra.*"

She eased back and let her muscles relax. It was time to trust the others to see to their escape.

"Rest, little one." Lo's voice stroked her with comfort.

"I'm resting," she protested, letting her eyes drift shut as she listened to the sirens and shouts outside the safe bubble of the transport. The noise faded as they moved into the darkened areas of the city.

The memory of Chelle's sightless face came back to her. Maybe, not so easy. They'd been lucky and they'd had friends. That had made the difference.

"I hate to interrupt your beauty rest back there," said Knock. "But we have a long hike ahead of us. The roads to the port are shut down."

Samantha pushed up to look outside as the transport hummed to a stop in an alley behind a hotel. "The tunnel?"

Knock made an affirmative noise. "That's right. I followed you when you left with Rachel."

Lo tensed at Rachel's name. "It might not be safe."

Knock pushed open the door and stepped out then slid the back door open. "It's safe. I checked it myself."

Mercury pulled her against him and wrapped her around him as he climbed out of the transport. No one spoke as Knock led them through the service areas of the hotel and down into the tunnel. Samantha looked over Mercury's shoulder to see Captain Artane grinning back.

"Feels good," she said in a hushed voice. "Being back in the action. Didn't realize how much I missed it."

Samantha frowned. "I wish I had your enthusiasm, Captain. I'm afraid this isn't over. Not for me."

"Not for us." The Captain's grin stretched into something more serious. "You aren't alone Samantha." The grin popped back into place. "Even Pillar, that old coot, wants in on the action. Heard from him right after you left the ship. Seems he found something interesting on some symbol you asked him to look into."

"The surrogates." The word came out as nothing more than a breath, but Mercury heard.

He smoothed a hand along her spine and whispered back, "The Mothers."

CHAPTER THIRTY-SEVEN

The Gwendella
Earth Alliance Beta Sector
2210.186

Samantha wasn't sure how long she slept, but she woke feeling warm and safe and at peace. Knock had gotten them all safely back to the *Gwendella*. And they'd spent an uncomfortable forty-eight hours in the Captain's Closet before the *Gwendella* had been searched and cleared to leave the port. Carn and Hera had been there too. Despite the long stint in darkness and silence, they'd come out as exhausted as ever. Hopeful but exhausted.

She'd fallen into bed and to sleep the moment they'd arrived in Mercury and Lo's room. Lo's heat curled along her back and her cheek pressed against Mercury's broad chest. The steady rise and fall created a sense of intimacy she'd never expected to have. It spoke not of sex, but of the day-in, day-out constancy of love.

Mercury loved her.

He'd been willing to risk his life, Lo's life, to protect her. She'd known he had no lack of courage, but she hadn't understood the truth—that his willingness to risk came not from courage but from love. He'd loved his brothers then and now he loved her, too. She should have seen it earlier, but the miracle of it hadn't been able to penetrate the barrier she kept around her heart. Not until she'd met his eyes through that fence.

She traced her fingers over the ridges of his abdominal muscles, circled his belly button, delighted in the ripples of reaction.

He pressed a kiss to the top of her head as his hand stroked over her shoulder. "Welcome back, *courra*."

"Did I go somewhere?"

His hand tightened, then traced down to circle her wrist and bring it to his lips. "Don't ever leave me, Samantha." Worry and fear deepened his voice.

She reached up to frame his face. "I won't."

"Lo is here. You're in our cabin."

"I know. It's fine. I should never have tried to hide how I feel about you from the crew." Her voice shook. "How I feel about you both."

"Tell me how you feel, *courra*. Let me hear it."

"I love you."

He smiled, all dangerous teeth, and it filled her heart with happiness. He pressed his lips to hers and they took their time enjoying the simple pleasure of kisses.

When the kisses tapered away, Samantha traced his lips with her finger. "I'll love you even more if you tell me there's a shower system somewhere close."

His grin widened. "Built into the wall."

"Hallelujah," She whispered, trying not to wake Lo.

Mercury stretched beneath her and she realized he slept completely bare. She was nude too for that matter. She almost forgot how desperately she wanted to bathe. Almost.

"How did I get so lucky?" With a start she remembered the others. She looked around the room. "Carn and Hera?"

In a whisper of flowing movement, Mercury rose from the bunk and pulled her along with him. Lo sleepily edged into the warmth of the spot they'd vacated.

"The Captain gave them the quarters next to ours. They're fine." Mercury pressed a panel on the wall to reveal the shower. He urged her inside. "And I'm the fortunate one—to have a mate who will know how to properly adjust this temperature in this overly complex chamber."

"Don't tell me you were taking cold showers all the way from Haverlee to Roma."

His silence spoke for him.

"You should have said something."

"The cold showers proved...useful...at the time."

A laugh bubbled up and spilled over in frothy giggles. "Well, it isn't one of the great mysteries of life. You only have to say the temperature you want."

"I tried that, but it still gave only freezing cold spray."

"Probably that growly voice of yours."

Mercury silenced her with tiny kisses scattered over her face. His lips honed in on hers, licking, nipping, clinging.

Breathless, she stated the temperature they needed and a warm steamy spray soaked them. Mercury stroked the sudsy mixture over her curves. He left no centimeter of skin unattended. She returned the favor, endlessly fascinated by the strength and warmth of his body.

When the need their touches created grew too great, he turned her and placed her hands against the wall. One hand gripped her hip while he used a foot to encourage her to widen her stance. She complied, eager to take him inside.

His other hand stroked the length of her spine, pressing her shoulders forward even as he pulled her hips back. Her palms slipped down the wall. Her heart beat faster.

At the feel of his cock against her sex, she pressed her forehead to the smooth surface between her palms. She breathed deep and pushed back to take him.

He surged forward. Their earlier touches had readied her for him. He stroked deep, his cock filling and stretching her to her limits. Her moan seemed to urge him on. He stroked harder.

She felt wild and free. His fingers stroked along her belly then dipped down to press firmly against her needy clit.

Samantha screamed.

Mercury panted against her ear, blowing hot breath across her shoulder.

Her nipples puckered.

His hips slammed against her ass and his cock jerked inside her.

They panted together and kept each other from sliding to the floor in a puddle. Samantha let joy fill her heart—together they could accomplish anything.

Mercury wrapped his arms around the slick body of his mate and pulled her close. He should take her to the *Gwendella's* medic to ensure her health, but that would wait, for a short time. The shower spray had long since stopped and her skin would soon chill. He loved the way her body colored when they made love. The golden glow that spread across her skin had already started to fade when he tucked a length of soft cloth around her.

Her gaze caught on Lo and pink tinge bloomed on her cheeks. The shameless Dog sat nude, the evidence of how much he'd enjoyed watching them stood stiff as he dragged a leisurely hand up and down his length. Mercury knew she hadn't been aware when their loving had woken Lo. It had been inevitable. Their loving was rarely quiet and Mercury didn't mind sharing his beautiful mate with his pack brother. He took pride in her generous nature.

With an approving look from him she went to Lo, but it was concern, not passion, on her face.

"Lo." She crawled onto the bed and put her hands out palms up, waiting for him to lay his large hands in her small ones. When he complied she squeezed his fingers and pressed a chaste kiss to his lips.

Lo frowned and looked away as if he thought Samantha wouldn't share her body with him, but Mercury knew his mate better now.

Her hand slipped free and cupped Lo's cheek turning his face back to her. "I need to tell you, before I can...before we can..."

"Fuck," Lo finished for her. At her blushing nod, Lo turned a questioning look to him. "You need to help her with her vocabulary."

Mercury shrugged. "She gets me hard just fine."

"Good point," he agreed.

"Lo, please." Samantha made a little frustration noise. "I need to tell you about Rachel."

All the teasing leached out of Lo's face. "We found her by the wall. She told us where to find you and Hera."

"She helped me," said Samantha. "And I think she cares for you."

Lo spoke through a locked jaw. "She may not be an enemy to our people, but I can't forgive what she did to me." He covered Samantha's hand against his cheek. "You have taught me to give up my hatred, be content with that. I am."

Samantha pressed her forehead to Lo's. "Okay. I wouldn't have felt right not telling you."

"You told me." Lo lifted her chin and smiled. "Can we fuck

now?"

She laughed. "Yes."

Lo took her to her back in a flash of movement. Mercury leaned back against the wall and took his cock in his hand as he watched his pack brother bare Samantha's body. Lo licked at her pussy until her belly flushed a shining gold then crawled over her and sank his cock into her slick cunt.

Mercury moved his hand on his own cock, remembering the feel of being inside her. The pleasure on her face as she gasped for breath and tossed her head, overwhelmed with pleasure, made his balls tighten.

She turned her head and smiled at him. Only his shoulders touched the wall now. His hips thrust into his grip of their own will. Her eyes lowered to his cock and her pink tongue swiped across her lip. Her sated body came back to life. He could see it in the thrust of her hips and the way she threw her head back with a strangled groan.

Lo lost his rhythm and collapsed into her arms. She pulled him close, wrapping him in her warmth.

Mercury knew he'd chosen well for his pack. His courageous mate had freed them and helped them free Carn's mate. But more than that, she'd given them back their hope.

Samantha stroked Lo for a moment then pushed him up and sat-up alongside him. The flush of color still spread across her skin as she wrapped a length of the bed sheet around her. Lo tugged against her but stopped when she spoke.

"I have something else I have to tell you, but I'm not sure.."

Mercury moved closer and took one of her hands, twining his own around it. "You can tell us anything, *courra*."

"I know." She took a deep breath then released it slowly. "The medic," she began. "She seemed to think...." Mercury's heart suddenly beat a slow, grim march in his chest. Lo looked just as worried.

"She thought, maybe..." Samantha started again.

"Tell us, little Sam." Lo stroked a hand along her arm.

"Uh..." Samantha's gaze met Mercury's. Her eyes penetrating and unblinking. "I may be pregnant."

He stared at her, his brain frozen by her words. Could it be? Yes, of course. She'd given him everything. It was easy to believe she could somehow give him this one more impossible miracle. His lips tipped up and he suspected a smile would soon find its way onto his face. She carried his child. The happiness that gave him made him want to fuck her all over again.

When she saw his joy, she smiled then turned to Low and wrapped her hand around his jaw. "If I am pregnant..."

"The child is Mercury's," said Lo.

It was a reassurance, that his brother had followed their customs and taken what care he could to make sure Mercury would father his mate's child. But Mercury knew now that Samantha had committed to them, he didn't need to worry over such things.

"The next will be yours, brother." His words stopped Lo and left him speechless. His mate only smiled and nodded.

She met his gaze. "I love you." She turned back to Lo. "I love you both."

He stalked to the bunk and tangled his hand in his mate's hair as he kissed her. Taking her scent, the scent of his mate and his brother mingled together, into his lungs and his heart. As he released her, he ran an affectionate hand down his pack brother's back. Together they all tumbled down onto the bed, wrapped in each other's arms. Mercury thought he couldn't be happier to have his mate and his brother so close, so at peace.

When they'd been in the captain's closet, Samantha had explained that one of the resistance members had been sneaking out Dogs that had been declared dead in the arena. And the medics had implanted a sub-dermal data-slip in her arm. It would help the contact Haven, the base of the resistance. Jupiter and Senneca hadn't died that day in the arena. With Samantha's help they would find them, he was certain of it. She had changed everything for him and his pack. She would give him a child. The first of their kind to be born free. And she was well on her way to healing Lo's heart.

He rubbed his cheek against hers. "I love you, Samantha Devlin, for always."

A NOTE FROM THE AUTHOR

If you enjoyed reading *Stealing Mercury*, I'd love for you to help others enjoy it, too. You can help other readers find this book by recommending it to friends and readers' groups or by reviewing it online.

To be eligible for exclusive giveaways and get new release announcements, sign up for the "List" on my website: **www.charleeallden.com**.

Thank you for giving my books a try!

Charlee

ALSO AVAILABLE BY CHARLEE

Deadly Lover   *In the future, love can get you killed.*

Security contractor Lily Rowan is clawing her way back to normalcy after a training mission gone horrifically wrong left her physically and emotionally broken. She's returned to the city she grew up in, but not to hide from her nightmares, to face them. Living alongside the Ormney—genetically altered refugees who've settled in The Zone—is a daily reminder of the Ormney trainee who nearly took her life. Lily knew it would be tough, but she couldn't have known coming home would drop her straight into a madman's deadly game. Someone is drugging Ormney men and turning them into mindless killers, reenacting the attack Lily barely survived. To stop the killing spree and put her own demons behind her, Lily must overcome her fear and work with Jolaj, a refugee Law Keeper with dangerous secrets and hidden motives of his own.

Jolaj long ago dedicated his life to his people. As a Searcher he slipped into the black nothing of inter-dimensional space day after day, risking everything to find them a new home. As a Law Keeper he is once again tending to their future. But working with Lily could prove to be the most difficult task he's ever faced. Despite the Council's decree making relationships with the outsiders forbidden, he's finding it hard to keep the courageous Lily at a distance. With the fragile peace between their people on the line, Lily and Jolaj must stop the horrific crimes before their growing attraction makes them the killer's next targets.

ABOUT THE AUTHOR

Charlee Allden is a long time fan of love, adventure, and happily-ever-after. She writes sexy, intense, out-of-this-world romance and is a two time winner of the On the Far Side contest, sponsored by the FF&P chapter of Romance Writers of America®. She has also won the Golden Acorn contest and been a Reveal Your Inner Vixen contest finalist. She loves to hear from readers at **charleeallden@gmail.com**. You can also connect with her online at: **www.charleeallden.com** or find her on Facebook, Pinterest, or Twitter.

www.facebook.com/CharleeAlldenAuthor
www.pinterest.com/charleeallden/
@CharleeAllden

Made in the USA
Charleston, SC
25 April 2015